Praise for *Death Can't Take a Joke*

'*Where the Devil Can't Go* marked Anya Lipska out as a crime writer of bravura skills, and this latest book continues her upward trajectory. An edgy, visceral vision of modern London at the mercy of ambitious Eastern European criminals, *Death Can't Take a Joke* boasts complex protagonists, pungently realised locales and a keen social awareness'

BARRY FORSHAW, author of *Euro Noir*

'Welcome to a London you probably know nothing about and meet two detectives who might just be tough and smart enough to survive it. Hard-hitting, thought-provoking and deeply real, the Kiszka and Kershaw series has all the hallmarks of a classic in the making. Modern British crime fiction at its best'

EMLYN REES, author of *Hunted* and *Wanted*

Gripping, powerful, real and tremendously written – really taking the reader into the heart of places we haven't been before. Nothing new in the crime genre? Yes there is. There's Anya Lipska'

DAVID MARK, author of *Dark Winter*

'A fantastic mix of crime, grit, politics, suspense and sinister undercurrents with a unique sense of humour. This book has it all. Anya Lipska's first novel promised big things. Here, she more than builds on that. *Death Can't Take a Joke* is seriously good'

MARTYN WAITES, author of the Joe Donovan series

'Pacy and enthralling. Janusz is already one of the best protagonists in the business'

MALCOLM MACKAY, author of *The Necessary Death of Lewis Winter*

Praise for *Where the Devil Can't Go*

'A gripping reminder of how crime fiction reveals the world around us'

VAL MCDERMID

'Anya Lipska's remarkable novel has been accruing considerable praise … all of it justified'

The Good Book Guide

'Lipska's debut novel won't disappoint crime fiction fans … keeps the plot twists coming at every turn'

We Love This Book

'A frighteningly good debut'

CHRIS SIMMS, author of *The Edge* and *Hell's Fire*

'The moment I started reading this exciting thriller, I felt that thrill – the thrill of discovering a new favourite author'

MARK EDWARDS, author of *Catch Your Death*

'Lipska does for the East End what Rankin does for Edinburgh'

JAMES CRAIG, author of the Inspector Carlyle novels

'A most unusual and exciting thriller'

DAME JOAN BAKEWELL, broadcaster and author

'The story just flew off the page. An exciting new talent with a truly unique voice'

MARI HANNAH, author, the DCI Kate Daniels series

DEATH CAN'T TAKE A JOKE

By the same author

Where the Devil Can't Go

DEATH CAN'T TAKE A JOKE

ANYA LIPSKA

The Friday Project
An imprint of HarperCollins*Publishers*
77–85 Fulham Palace Road
Hammersmith, London W6 8JB
www.harpercollins.co.uk

First published in the UK by The Friday Project 2014

'On Death, without Exaggeration', from "The People on the Bridge",
1986. Used by permission of The Wislawa Szymborska Foundation.
Wisława Szymborska © The Wisława Szymborska Foundation,
www.szymborska.org.pl.

A catalogue record for this book is available from the British Library

ISBN 978-0-00-752440-2

Printed and bound in Great Britain by Clays Ltd, St Ives plc

MIX
Paper from
responsible sources
FSC® C007454

For my mother and father

DEATH CAN'T TAKE A JOKE

Prologue

If I don't hang on I will die. My fingers are curled into claws. So cold and numb they feel like they're frozen to the ledge. The blackness comes ... recedes again, but leaves only panic and confusion. Is this high, freezing place a mountaintop? I don't remember climbing it. But then I can't even recall my name right now above the wind's howl.

Memories flicker out of the darkness like fragments caught on celluloid, briefly illuminated. A door made of plastic. A man in orange overalls. The insolent swish of something heavy through the air. Ducking – too late.

I try to brace my legs, to keep from falling. But the tremors are so bad, they're useless. In a blinding surge of rage I vow: Somebody's going to die for this. *Then a great wind screams in my face and tears my fingers from their grip.*

And I realise the somebody is me.

One

Detective Constable Natalie Kershaw sat on the outdoor terrace of Starbucks in the lee of the Canary Wharf tower, treating herself to an overpriced and underpowered cappuccino. In her chalk stripe trousers and black wool jacket she could have passed for another of the City workers getting their early morning fix of caffeine.

Kershaw was celebrating the last day of her secondment to Docklands nick: the stint in financial crime would look good on her CV, but after three months navigating the murky channels of international money laundering, she was gagging to get back to some proper police work. And not just the routine stuff – the credit card frauds, street robberies and domestic violence that had dominated her career so far. *No.* In two days' time she'd finally become what she'd first set her sights on at the age of fourteen – a detective on Murder Squad.

Drinking the last of her coffee, she shivered. Despite the morning sun a chill hung in the air, and a light icing on her car windscreen that morning had signalled the first frost of autumn.

As she stood to go, something drew her gaze towards the glittering bulk of the tower less than twenty metres away.

Suddenly, she ducked: an instinctive reflex. The impression of something dark, flapping, the chequerboard windows of the tower flickering behind it like a reel of film. Then a colossal *whump*, followed by the sound of imploding glass and plastic. There was a split second of absolute silence before a woman at the next table started screaming, a thin high keening that bounced off the impassive facades of the high-rise office blocks surrounding the café.

Fuck! Kershaw took off running towards the site of the impact – a long dark limo parked nearby that had probably been waiting to pick someone up. There was a metre-wide crater in its roof and the windscreen lay shattered across the bonnet like imitation diamonds. She could hear an inanely cheery jingle still playing on the radio. The car was empty, the guy she presumed to be the driver standing just a few metres away, still holding the fag he'd left the car to smoke. His stricken gaze was fixed on the man-sized dent in the car roof – the spot where his head would have been moments earlier. Kershaw filed it away as a rare case of a cigarette extending someone's life.

Three or four metres beyond the limo, the falling man lay where he had come to rest, in a slowly spreading lake of his own blood. He'd fallen face down, his overcoat spread either side of him like the unfurled wings of an angel. By some quirk of physics or anatomy, the fall had twisted his head around by almost 180 degrees, so that his half-closed eyes appeared to be gazing up at the wall of glass and concrete, as if calculating how many floors he had fallen.

Two

Some eight hours later, Janusz Kiszka strode up the ramp from the tube station to the street, struggling to navigate the ill-mannered torrent of returning rush hour commuters. *Did no one in London say 'excuse me' any more?* he grumbled to himself, before recalling that his father, *God rest his soul,* used to make pretty much the same complaint – back in eighties Gdansk. A rueful grin crept across his jaw. He'd need to be on guard against turning into a grumpy old man now that he was approaching the wrong end of his forties.

Janusz was out here on the East End's northern fringe to meet one of his oldest friends, Jim Fulford, for an early evening jar, but he'd just picked up an apologetic message asking if they could delay their rendezvous. Which left him with a conundrum. *How the fuck was he supposed to kill a whole hour in Walthamstow?*

He stood irresolute at the crossroads on Hoe Street as people flowed around him. One woman in a yellow sari holding a tiny child by the hand stared openly as she passed. Even in this, one of the capital's motliest neighbourhoods, a man of his height and size wearing a shabby military greatcoat and smoking a cigar was an intriguing sight. Janusz caught a glimpse of one of those brown and white signs indicating a nearby attraction. *The William Morris Gallery*. Sighing, he threw down his cigar stub. An hour spent looking at Arts and Crafts furniture wasn't exactly top of his list of things to do but there weren't too many other options on offer.

Fifty minutes later, he was on his way to the pub where Jim and he had been meeting every couple of weeks for the last twenty years or so. The Rochester stood in a part of Walthamstow where fried chicken takeaways and Asian grocers had given way to the delicatessens and knick-knack shops beloved of the middle class. Estate agents called it the Village to distinguish it from the plebeian multiculturalism of Hoe Street – and to help justify the neighbourhood's inflated asking prices. It occurred to Janusz that history had come full circle. In the nineteenth century, the area had indeed been a pretty village settled initially by the genteel classes, before the advent of the railway and a building boom brought a surge of humbler folk from London's slums. He recalled with a grin that in one of Morris's diaries on display at the museum, the avowed socialist had bemoaned the arrival of the working classes, their mean houses lapping like a mucky tide around his own family's elegant mansion.

Janusz pushed open the door to the lounge bar of the Rochester – and experienced a sudden jolt of unfamiliarity. He scanned the bar: he was in the right pub alright, but the place had changed beyond recognition. Its patterned carpet and pool table were gone, replaced by bare floorboards, sofas in distressed leather, and tables and chairs that looked like rejects from a charity shop. The walls had been painted a dismal shade of green.

Mother of God, thought Janusz, *they've turned it into a fucking gastropub*.

He felt a surge of rage: sometimes it felt as if everything that had been a comforting fixture in his life for the twenty-five years or more he'd lived in London was doomed to change.

It came as a relief to see a familiar face, at least, behind the bar.

'Brendan,' he growled, in not-quite mock fury. 'What the fuck have you done with our boozer?'

Brendan chuckled but Janusz caught the way his gaze flickered round the bar, as a couple of people looked up, startled by the booming voice.

Janusz looked around, too, but didn't recognise any of the punters. The only other person at the bar was a young guy in a cardigan frowning into his laptop. His beard, which was carefully coiffed to a point, made him look like he'd just escaped from a Van Dyck painting. And when Janusz checked out his favourite spot by the fireplace, he found it taken by a well-dressed couple chatting softly over food served on what appeared to be kitchen chopping boards.

Lowering his voice, Janusz ordered two bottles of Tyskie. It was one minute to six and Jim was always on time.

'You'll be meeting Jimbo then?' asked Brendan, opening the fridge.

'Yeah,' said Janusz. 'He's the only guy I know you can order a beer for who'll turn up while it's still cold.'

'Ah, once a Marine always a Marine, as the man himself never tires of saying.'

'What does he make of his local's new look then?' said Janusz, a sly grin creeping across his face. He was picturing the expressions on the new punters' faces when all eighteen stone of his boisterous crew-cut mate came barrelling in.

Brendan popped the caps off the beers. 'He's not what you'd call entirely in sympathy with it,' he admitted in his Dublin lilt. 'Especially now he can't bring that dog of his in any more.'

Janusz winced. Jim owned a gym and fitness club off Hoe Street, and although his workout regime and armfuls of tattoos made him look like a member of some neo-Nazi cell, he was in reality the gentlest man Janusz had ever known. He was besotted with his wife Marika – who he'd first laid eyes on at a Polish wedding Janusz had taken him to a decade ago – but it was the way he fussed over his collie dog, Laika, that really gave the lie to his thuggish appearance.

Brendan named the new, eye-watering price for two bottles of beer and Janusz handed over a twenty.

Fifteen minutes later, Janusz sat frowning out of the window into the gathering dusk. Jim was unerringly punctual: he liked to say that in the Marines, being ten seconds late on operations could get your knob shot off. This would be followed by his trademark laugh, which resembled the joyous woof of a large but friendly dog. For all the joking, Janusz knew that Jim's experiences in the Falklands War had left worse scars than the shiny cicatrice that ran the length of his right arm from knuckles to armpit. Janusz had never once heard him speak of the conflict, but Marika had told him that Jim had been trapped below decks on HMS *Coventry* after it was struck by an Argentine torpedo.

Jim and Janusz had both been in their twenties when they first met while working on a building site, part of the Docklands development, back in the eighties. At the time, Janusz had his own troubles: he'd recently escaped life under Poland's communist regime – and a disastrous marriage. Although one hailed from Plaistow and the other from Gdansk, the two men quickly found they shared a black sense of humour and a healthy contempt for faceless authority.

Janusz ran a thoughtful finger down the mist of condensation on Jim's un-drunk bottle of Tyskie. Thinking about the past always made him melancholic. He pulled out his mobile phone and punched out a message.

Where the fuck are you? it read. *It's your round.*

Three

As last days at work go, this one had been seriously weird, thought DC Kershaw as she closed down her computer at Canary Wharf nick. It was gone 7 p.m. and she'd only just finished the paperwork on the roof jumper, which would make her late for her own leaving drinks.

That morning, the paramedics had reached the dead guy at the foot of the Canary Wharf tower around ten minutes after he hit the deck. It hadn't taken them long to confirm the stark staring obvious – that the guy with his head on the wrong way round wasn't going to make it.

Meanwhile, Kershaw had taken charge of diverting City workers around the scene. They were harmless rubber-neckers for the most part, interspersed with the occasional tosser who objected to some five-foot-two-inch blonde girl with a Cockney accent withdrawing his constitutional right to walk where he chose. To be really honest? She liked dealing with these ones the best.

Finally, the promised uniform had arrived from the nick.

'You took your time,' she said.

'Oh, was it urgent?' he replied, all innocence. 'I had a croissant on the way.'

She grinned: Nick Ferris was one of the good guys. Recent intake, with none of the 'who do you think you are, missy?' undercurrent she still sensed from some of the older uniformed cops.

'NOT that way, sir,' Kershaw told a master of the universe wearing a two-grand suit who was attempting a body swerve around her.

'Have the silly bankers been giving you grief?' Nick asked under his breath.

'Nah,' she said with a sigh of mock-disappointment. 'I haven't even had to get my stick out.'

He produced a reel of police tape and they started to cordon off the scene.

'What's the story here then?' Nick nodded towards the body, which the paramedics were in the process of shielding from view with a white pop-up tent. Kershaw shrugged. 'No idea. Maybe the market turned and he was left holding too many yen.'

In the tower reception, she'd found an upright fit-looking guy in his fifties with prematurely grey hair – unquestionably the head of security – rapping out instructions over his walkie-talkie. She flashed her warrant card and he introduced himself as Dougal Murray before ushering her through the metal security arch and straight into a lift.

'The highest floor where witnesses saw something go past is the 49th,' he told her in a no-nonsense Scots accent as they hummed skywards. 'There's only one level above that, so I've got my team questioning all the companies on 50 to establish whether they have anyone missing.'

'What about visitors?' Kershaw asked.

He unfolded a printout. 'All visitors sign in and out and are issued with a security pass,' he said. 'I've marked everyone who signed in to visit the 50th floor this morning.'

'That's brilliant,' Kershaw said, eyeing him with admiration. 'Are you ex-police by any chance?'

'RMP,' he said, sticking his chin out.

Military Police. Kershaw grinned. With a bit of luck she'd have the jumper identified and be back at the nick in time for elevenses.

Two hours later, it had begun to dawn on her that she'd be lucky to be back for afternoon tea. Nick the PC had searched the body but found no clues to his identity: no wallet, no Oystercard, nothing. She'd worked through the entire list of 50th floor office workers who'd swiped in that morning and found them all alive and breathing. And then she'd reached the end of the visitors list. That had produced one brief glimmer of hope – a guy who had apparently left after a 7 a.m. meeting but whom the system showed as still present in the building. But when Kershaw called him on his mobile, he'd discovered he was still wearing the pass round his neck. *Muppet*.

And there was another problem. She and Dougal had made a full tour of the 50th floor and found the windows, which weren't designed to be opened, sealed and intact. Above that there was only the roof, which was accessible via two flights of concrete stairs in the emergency stairwell. At the top, a push-bar fire door, of the kind you saw in cinemas, gave straight onto the exterior. Green and white letters spelt out the legend: 'ALARMED DOOR – FIRE EXIT ONLY'.

'You've checked the alarm was working?' Kershaw asked. Dougal nodded.

'Since it gives straight onto the roof I'd rather keep it locked,' he said. 'But health and safety won't allow it.' An arch of his eyebrow had told her what he thought of that.

As Kershaw stepped outside, a cold wind had whipped the hair from her face and stung her eyes.

They traversed the narrow walkway that skirted the building's iconic pyramid-shaped glass apex, stepping around the steel gantries used to haul window cleaners up and down the 700-foot length of the tower. Halfway along the east side they came to a stop and peered over the edge. At the foot of the yawning cliff of glass, they could see a white dot on the pavement below – the tent covering the body.

Kershaw buttoned her coat to the neck. Up here, the wind, barely noticeable at ground level, had a savage power. 'I don't get it,' she told Dougal, raising her voice above the wind's roar. 'There's no way to get out here without setting off the alarm.'

He shook his head.

She squinted down at the tent far below. 'Just my luck to get an unidentified suicide on my last day.'

'You're on the move then?'

'Yeah. I'm starting a new job up in Walthamstow. In Murder Squad.'

'Congratulations.'

'Thanks. But it looks like I'll be spending my first few days trying to find out who this guy is.' She worried at the nail on her little finger.

'Can you not just leave the case to Docklands police?' He pronounced it *poh-liss*.

'Yeah, I could,' she said, pulling a sheepish face. 'But I've got this thing. Once I start something I have to finish it.' From the set of her shoulders, Dougal could tell that the wee girl meant it.

Kershaw's dad used to tell her that she'd been that way ever since she was little. Not long after her mum died, he'd taken her fishing for the first time up at Walthamstow Reservoir. He said she'd taken to it right away, but the fish weren't biting that day. One by one the other anglers packed up, and as the sun faded he wanted to call it a day, too. But nine-year-old Natalie wouldn't leave. He'd tried everything, including the barefaced bribe of a visit to McDonalds. But she just kept saying: *Not till I've caught a fish*. By the time she bagged one – a respectable size tench – her dad was dozing on the bank and the moon had risen, spilling quicksilver across the water.

Descending in the lift with Dougal, Kershaw fell silent, puzzling over the mystery of the falling man. To gain access to the roof he must have disabled the alarm – or got someone to do it for him. But given that he'd fallen at about 9 a.m., when loads of people would have been at their desks, surely somebody must have noticed a strange man prowling around?

'I'm going to need to interview all your security staff,' she told Dougal.

He nodded. 'Including the ones who weren't on duty?'

'Especially the ones who weren't on duty. I think our chum might have got onto the roof during the night, when it was quiet.'

By the time Kershaw had left the tower, dusk had fallen, bringing a penetrating chill to the air. The body and its protective tent had gone and a two-man unit from the local council were using high-pressure hoses to clean blood from the impact site. The wet pavement shone in the reflected glow of a thousand brightly lit offices.

Back at Canary Wharf nick, the uniform skipper on front desk beckoned her over. 'I've got something for you,' he said. He held out a plastic evidence bag. 'PC Ferris found this in the gutter. It might have nothing to do with our friend, but he says it was just a few feet from the body.'

A silver coin winked through the polythene: about the same size as a 10p piece, but inset with a bronze roundel depicting a crowned eagle, wings spread wide. Squinting to read the inscription around the edge, one word jumped out at her. Kershaw was no linguist but she knew one thing. *Polska* meant Poland.

Four

At around 8 a.m. the morning after Jim had stood him up at the Rochester, Janusz Kiszka found himself back in Walthamstow, this time on the south side of Hoe Street. Reaching the end of a terrace of two-up two-downs, he spotted what he guessed to be his destination: just outside the ironwork gates of a cemetery, a low redbrick building in the Victorian municipal style. Checking on his phone that he had the right place, he went in and gave his name to the lady on reception.

As he stood waiting, the only thing that cut through the foggy hum that had enveloped his brain since he'd heard the news a couple of hours ago was the smell of the place – a century of dust and old paper mingled with a powerful disinfectant.

He barely acknowledged the uniformed cop awaiting him in the gloomy little anteroom at the end of the corridor. They exchanged a few words, then the cop led the way into a second, larger room. There, drawing back a blue sheet on a hospital-style gurney, he unveiled the face of Jim Fulford.

For a split second, Janusz didn't recognise him, so alien was this version of his friend. In total repose his face looked

... stern, an expression he couldn't remember ever seeing in the living Jim. But his moment of confusion – and irrational hope – didn't last. It might not be the friend he'd known for two decades, but there was no denying that this austere waxwork was his body. There was the thumbprint-sized dent in his left temple, souvenir of the time someone accidentally dropped a lump hammer off a scaffold tower. That had been a lifetime ago, on the Broadgate build – and yet Janusz could remember it as though it were yesterday.

A warning shout, Jim going down like a felled oak an arm's length away, blood streaming from his head. After coming round, he'd claimed he was absolutely fine, and wanted to get back to work. Janusz practically had to wrestle him into a cab, taking him to Whitechapel Hospital, where the medics diagnosed a severe concussion. Even twenty years later Jim was fond of saying, with his friendly bark of a laugh, that Janusz still owed him a monkey – five hundred quid – in lost earnings.

Janusz laid a tentative hand on his dead friend's chest, still covered by the blue sheet, and found it as cold and unyielding as a sack of flour. He thought of his mother then: her body had at least still felt warm when he'd kissed her goodbye. *Was that all life was then – a matter of temperature?*

He found himself out on the street again, with no memory of how he'd got there. His thoughts clashed and clattered like balls on a pool table, grief and disbelief battling rage at what had happened. How could it be that Jim had survived a decade working on building sites *and* an Argentinian torpedo, only to be stabbed to death on his own doorstep, apparently by a couple of junkies? It was *nieznosne* – unbearable.

People on their way to work averted their eyes as they passed the big man pounding the pavement, his jaw set and eyes narrowed in some blistering inner fury. *Mental health case: best avoided*, most of them concluded.

14

Ten minutes later, Janusz turned into Barclay Road, Jim and Marika's street. As he neared their neat, cream-painted terraced house, he slowed, and saw something that made his insides plummet. The low brick garden wall – a wall that Janusz and Jim had rebuilt with their own hands one hot, beer-fuelled summer's day – had all but disappeared beneath a drift of cellophane-wrapped bouquets that rustled in the breeze. Two tea lights in red perspex holders on top of the wall completed its transformation into a shrine.

As Janusz watched, a middle-aged woman approached, holding the hand of a little girl. She leaned down to whisper to the child, who, taking an awkward step forward, bent to add a bunch of yellow flowers to the pile.

He paused in the porch to take a couple of deep breaths, determined to master himself. Of course, Marika knew that the man who paramedics had rushed to hospital last night from this address could only be her husband, but as she hadn't been able to face identifying his body herself, she'd still be inhabiting that hazy hinterland of denial – a zone Janusz had barely left himself.

She opened the front door and searched his face, before sleepwalking into his arms. Holding her to his chest so tightly that her hot tears soaked through to his skin in an instant, he sent a grim-faced nod of greeting over her shoulder to Basia, her sister, who looked on from the kitchen doorway.

Finally, Marika drew her head back and looked up at him. 'Thank you, Janek, for going to him,' she said, her voice thick with tears. 'I will go to see him later, with Basia.'

The three of them sat around the kitchen table nursing un-drunk cups of tea, under the mournful gaze of Laika, who had not raced to greet Janusz today but instead lay silent in her basket, her long black-and-white nose resting on crossed paws.

'Basia and I, we had gone out to our Pilates class,' said Marika, 'and when we came back, about nine o'clock, the police were waiting outside.' Her voice was husky and almost toneless. 'They'd … taken him away to the hospital by then, but they say he was already dead.' Her eyes filled with tears again.

As Basia put an arm around her shoulder, murmuring words of comfort, Janusz realised that Marika was speaking in Polish, which he couldn't remember her doing since she'd married Jim. Now grief had stripped away the last ten years, throwing her back on her mother tongue.

After a moment, she pulled herself upright and used both hands to sweep the tears from her cheeks – a determined gesture.

'What did the cops say?' he asked. 'Did they question the neighbours straightaway? Right after the … after Jim was found?'

She nodded. 'Jason who lives two doors down heard a shout when he was putting out the rubbish bags.' She paused, took a steadying breath. 'It was starting to get dark, but he saw two men running away, through the garden gate.'

'Which way were they headed? Hoe Street? Or Lea Bridge Road?' Janusz was relieved to find himself slipping into private investigator mode.

'Hoe Street, I think he said.'

'What did they look like?'

'They both wore *hoodies* and *balaclavas*,' she said, dropping into English for these unfamiliar words. 'So all he could say was that one was tall – almost two metres – and slim, the other a little shorter.'

'Black? White?'

She gave a hopeless shrug. 'It was dark, and with the faces covered, he couldn't tell.'

Janusz hesitated. He needed to know exactly how Jim had died but he couldn't think of a sensitive way to frame the question. From Laika's basket came a tentative whine of distress.

Marika's swollen eyes met his and a look of understanding passed between them. 'The police said ...' her voice had fallen to a croak. 'They told me he had suffered several deep stab wounds ... in his stomach. One severed an artery ...' She tried to go on but then gave up. 'I'm sorry, Janek,' she said. 'Is it okay if I let Basia tell you the rest? I need to lie down.' She stood unsteadily, her chair grating harshly on the stone floor tiles.

Janusz jumped to his feet and went to her, his shovel-like hands encircling her slender forearms. At his touch, Marika's eyes filled with fresh tears.

'You know that he was an only child,' she said, grief roughening her voice. 'But he always said he didn't miss not having a brother – because he had you.'

She winced and Janusz realised that, without meaning to, he had tightened his grip on her arms.

'You rest, Marika,' he said, bending to lock his gaze on hers. 'But there's something I want you to know. Whatever it takes, I will find the *skurwysyny* who did this.'

They embraced then, three times on alternate cheeks in the Polish way. He stood watching her walk slowly down the hall, choosing her footing carefully, as though stepping through the debris of her shattered life. Laika rose to follow her, bushy tail down, claws tick-ticking on the wooden floor.

To avoid disturbing Marika – her bedroom lay right above the kitchen – Basia took Janusz into the front room and closed the door.

'There's no way he could have been saved,' she said, eyebrows steepled in sorrow. 'Marika doesn't know this, but the police told me those dirty *chuje* – excuse my language – they practically gutted him. He lost sixty per cent of his blood lying there on the garden path.'

17

Janusz blinked a few times, trying to dispel an image of his big strong mate lying helpless on the ground, his life ebbing away across the black and white tiles.

'They wouldn't let Marika near the house,' Basia went on. 'We went to my flat and I only brought her back here once …' her knuckles flew to her lips '… once everything was cleaned up.' Seeing her stricken face, Janusz remembered something. All those years ago, it had been Basia whom Jim had dated first, if only for a few weeks, before he'd become smitten with her older sister. Janusz had ensured, *naturalnie*, that Jim got plenty of ribbing down the building site for getting lucky with both sisters, but as far as he could recall, there had been no hard feelings between any of the trio when Jim and Marika became an item.

'On the phone, you said something about junkies?'

Basia tipped her head. 'It was something one of the policemen said, that maybe it was a robbery, to get money for *narkotyki*.'

Janusz frowned. The house was over a mile from the notorious council estates west of Hoe Street, bordering neighbouring Tottenham, that were home to Walthamstow's drug gangs. Would those scumbags really travel all the way up here to rob a random householder on the doorstep of his modest terraced house? Then he remembered Jim's text delaying their meeting.

'Do you know why he was running late for our pint at the Rochester?'

She nodded. 'Marika asked him to fix a leaking tap in the downstairs cloakroom, so he came back from work early to do it before going out again.'

'He didn't say anything about someone coming to the house to see him, before he came to meet me? Maybe that new deputy manager of his?'

The gym was doing so well that Jim had expanded six months earlier, taking on a young local guy to help manage it, although the last time they'd met, Jim had hinted that the new staff member wasn't proving a great success. *I'm not really cut out for bossing people about,* he'd confided to Janusz, his usually sunny face downcast.

'No,' said Basia. 'When we left here to go to Pilates, we were all joking around, Jim saying he couldn't wait to get rid of us so he could sit down and read the paper.' She lifted a shoulder in the peculiarly expressive way Polish women had. 'It was just a normal day.'

Janusz gazed out of the bay window that framed the tiny front garden and flower-strewn wall like a tableau. Through the half-closed slats of the blinds a young woman came into view, slowing to a halt in front of the wall. She stooped to lay something, and he saw her lips moving, as though in silent prayer. There was something about her that caught his attention. It wasn't just that, even half-obscured, she was strikingly beautiful; it was the powerful impression that the sadness on her face and in the slope of her shoulders seemed more profound – more *personal* – than might be expected from a neighbour or casual acquaintance of the dead man.

'Basia,' he growled in an undertone. 'Do you recognise that girl?'

Basia frowned out through the blinds, shook her head. Outside, the girl bent her head in a respectful gesture, crossed herself twice, and turned to leave.

Driven by some instinct he couldn't explain, Janusz leapt up from the sofa and, telling Basia that he'd phone to check on Marika later, let himself out of the front door. The girl had nestled a new bouquet among the other offerings, but her expensive-looking hand-tied bunch of cream calla lilies and vivid blue hyacinths stood out from the surrounding cellophane-sheafed blooms. After checking that there was no accompanying note or card, he scanned up and down the street. Empty. Crossing to the other side of the road, he was rewarded by the sight of the girl's slender figure a hundred metres away, walking towards the centre of Walthamstow.

Gradually, he closed the gap to around fifty metres. By a stroke of luck, a young guy carrying an architect's portfolio case had emerged from a garden gate ahead of him so that if the girl happened to glance behind she'd be unlikely to spot Janusz. From the glimpses he got he could see that, even allowing for the vertiginous heels, she was tall for a woman, her graceful stride reminiscent of a catwalk model's.

The girl passed the churchyard that marked the seventeenth-century heart of Walthamstow Village, where the breeze threw a handful of yellow leaves in her wake like confetti, but she didn't take the tiny passageway that led down to the tube as Janusz had half expected, heading instead for Hoe Street. Once she was enveloped by its pavement throng he was able to get closer, taking in details such as the discreetly expensive look of the bag slung over the girl's shoulder and the way her dark blonde hair shone like honey in the morning light.

Then a black Land Rover Discovery surged out of the stream of barely moving traffic with a throaty growl and came to a stop, two wheels up on the pavement, ahead of the girl. The driver, a youngish man with a number two crew cut, wearing a black leather jacket, jumped out and went over to her. When she shook her head and carried on, he walked alongside her, talking into her ear. A few seconds later, she tried to break away but he put a staying hand on her upper arm, a gesture at once intimate, yet controlling. She didn't shake it off, instead slowing to a halt. From the angle of his head it was clear the guy was cajoling her.

Janusz could make out a densely inked tattoo on the back of the guy's hand, which disappeared beneath the cuffs of his jacket, and emerged above the collar. *A snake*, he realised – its open jaws spread across his knuckles, the tip of its tail coiling up behind his ear. The girl's head was bent now, submissive. After a moment or two, she gave an almost imperceptible shrug, and allowed herself to be ushered to the car.

She climbed into the back seat where Janusz glimpsed the outline of another passenger – a man – before the Land Rover slid back into the traffic. He cursed softly: with no black cabs cruising for fares this far east, he had no way of following them. But twenty seconds later, just beyond a Polish *sklep* where Janusz sometimes bought rye bread flour, the Land Rover threw a sudden left turn that made its tyres shriek.

Janusz doubled his stride towards the turnoff. When he reached the corner it was just as he remembered: the road was a dead-end, and the big black car had pulled up not twenty metres away, its engine murmuring. He stopped, and pulling out his mobile, pretended to be taking a call. Through the rear window of the car, seated next to the girl, he could see a wide-shouldered, bullet-headed man. Judging by his angrily working profile and her bowed head, she was getting a tirade of abuse. Even from this distance the man gave off the unmistakable aura of power and menace. When he appeared to fall silent for a moment, the girl turned and said something. A swift blur of movement and the girl's head ricocheted off the side window. Janusz clenched his fists: *the fucker had hit her!* Only a conscious act of self-control stopped him sprinting to the car and dragging the *skurwiel* out to administer a lesson in the proper treatment of women. A half-second later, the kerbside door flew open and he pushed the girl out onto the pavement. The door slammed, the car

21

performed a screeching U-turn, mounting the opposite pavement in the process, and sped off back to Hoe Street.

Janusz could restrain himself no longer: he jogged over to where the girl half-sat, half-sprawled on the kerb, her long legs folded beneath her like a fawn. She looked up at him, a dazed look in her greenish eyes, before accepting his arm and getting to her feet. Her movements were calm and dignified, but he noticed how badly her hands were shaking as she attempted to button her coat.

He retrieved one of her high-heeled shoes from the gutter and, once he was sure she was steady on her feet, stepped back. The last thing she needed right now was a man crowding her personal space.

'Can I do anything?' he asked. 'I got the number plate – if you wanted to get the police involved, I mean?'

She touched the side of her head – the bastard had clearly hit her where the bruise wouldn't show – and met his eyes with a look that mixed resignation with wary gratitude.

'Thank you,' she said finally, her dry half-smile telling him that the police weren't really an option. 'It is kind of you. But really, is not a problem.' Her voice was attractively husky, with an Eastern European lilt – that much he was sure of – but not entirely Polish. If he had to lay money on it he'd say she hailed from further east, one of the countries bordering Russia, perhaps.

As she dusted the pavement grit from her palms his eyes lingered on her fine, long-boned fingers. Then he remembered why he had followed her in the first place: to find out her connection to Jim and why she would leave a bunch of expensive flowers in his memory. He was tempted for a moment to broach it with her there and then, but some instinct told him that a blunt enquiry would scare her off.

'Allow me to give you my card, all the same,' he said, proffering it with a little old-fashioned bow. It gave nothing away beyond his name and number and offered his only hope of future contact with the girl. 'In case you change your mind – or should ever find yourself in need of assistance.'

She took the card, the wariness in her eyes giving way to a cautious warmth.

'Thank you,' she said. 'A girl never knows when she might need a little assistance.' And pocketing it, she turned, as graceful as a ballet dancer, and started to walk away.

'May I know your name?' Janusz asked to her departing back.

For a moment he thought she wasn't going to answer, but then, without breaking step, she threw a single word over her shoulder.

'Varenka!'

Five

Natalie Kershaw woke with a jolt, her heart pounding, convinced she was falling from the top of the Canary Wharf tower. Then the dream was gone, as evanescent as the vapour made by breath in frosty air. Turning over, she threaded an arm across Ben's warm stomach and dozed, unconsciously synchronising her breathing with his. Ten minutes later, they both surfaced, woken by the muffled roar of a descending plane.

'Shouldn't you be getting up, Nat?' murmured Ben. 'First day of school and all that?'

Kershaw dug him in the ribs. 'Don't start pulling rank on me, just cos we're in the same nick now.'

'Am I sensing insubordination, Detective *Constable*?' said Ben, putting a hand on her hip and pulling her towards him. 'I hope this doesn't mean a return of your well-known issues with the chain of command.'

After a quick mental calculation of how long it would take her to get from Ben's place to Walthamstow, she added ten minutes to allow for traffic, then reached up to return his lazy kiss.

She and Ben had been together for almost two years now. They'd met while working at Canning Town CID but shortly afterwards their then-sergeant DS 'Streaky' Bacon had moved to Walthamstow, and encouraged Ben to apply for a sergeant post there in Divisional CID. Now that Kershaw was joining Streaky's team on Walthamstow Murder Squad, she and Ben would be working in the same nick again for the first time in ages, although not – luckily – in the same office.

The relationship had had its ups and downs, for sure, but despite her instinctive caution, Kershaw was pretty sure that Ben was a keeper. As a fellow detective, he knew the score, which meant that unlike her previous boyfriend, an estate agent, he never lost the plot if she had to stand him up for dinner or rolled in a bit pissed after drinking with the team. More to the point, he seemed to understand that for her, the Job wasn't, well, just a job. Okay, so she had, privately, felt somewhat irked when Ben had reached sergeant rank before her, but then he hadn't been hauled up in front of Professional Standards for 'flagrant disregard of the rulebook' like she had.

Ancient history, she told herself. *Today's a fresh start.*

She arrived at the nick a comfortable twelve minutes before the start of her shift. It had been three months since she'd heard she'd got the job, but when she told the receptionist that she was there to start work on Murder Squad, she felt her stomach perform a loop-the-loop.

Climbing the stairs, it hit her that she'd be thirty next year, and only now was her life panning out the way she'd imagined when she left uni. *Better late than never, girl,* she heard her dad saying. *Better late than never.* He'd been dead for three years, but so long as she could hear his voice in her head from time to time, it felt like he was still alongside her, somehow. Her mum was a much hazier memory but then Kershaw had been barely nine when she'd died, leaving Dad to bring her up single-handed.

She'd just reached the door marked Murder Squad when her mobile went off: *Ben.*

'I was about to tell you, before you went and distracted me this morning, that I got a call from the agents,' he said. 'We can move into the new flat end of next week.'

Christ, she thought. *That was quick.* Over the last few months, Ben had waged a quiet yet dogged campaign for them to move in together, and she'd finally caved in. A couple of weekends ago they'd found the perfect place, a cosy flat in Leytonstone with its own pocket-sized garden.

'Nat?'

'Yeah, that's fine,' she replied. 'Should give me plenty of time to box stuff up.' She hoped her voice didn't betray the sudden tightening she felt in her chest. *Wasn't this what she wanted?* Kershaw told herself. *To settle down, share her life with Ben?*

'You sure you're cool with this?' he asked. 'Moving in together, I mean. If it's too soon for you …'

The note of uncertainty in his voice prompted a rush of guilt. She tried to nail what it was, exactly, that was giving her the heebie jeebies. The prospect of giving up her independence after living on her own for the last two years? Partly, yes, but that wasn't the whole story. Was it because Ben was sometimes a bit, well, *too nice*? The thought had barely entered her head before she dismissed it, angry with herself.

'Of course I'm sure,' she reassured him. 'I was just … surprised that we were getting in so quickly.'

After hanging up, she gave herself a stern chat. *Too nice?! If you don't want to end up lying dead and undiscovered in some grimy flat being eaten by your own cats, Natalie Kershaw, you'd better waken your ideas up.*

She was pushing open the office door when there came a familiar voice in the corridor behind her.

'Ah! DC Kershaw!' It was her old boss Detective Sergeant Bacon. 'I see you've acquired a new hairstyle.'

'Yes ...' Suddenly self-conscious, her hand flew to her blonde hair, newly styled in an asymmetric cut, one side three inches shorter than the other.

Hitching up the trousers of his ancient suit, he squinted down at her hair.

'If I was you, I'd go back and ask for a refund,' he confided. 'Whoever cut it must've been three sheets to the wind.'

'Yeah, I'll do that, Sarge,' she grinned. He'd gained even more weight, and lost a bit more gingery hair from the top of his head, but he was still the same old Streaky.

'Anyway. Your arrival couldn't be more timely – we've got an old chum of yours in interview room 2.' Opening a door labelled *Remote Monitoring Room*, he winked at her. 'You can watch it all on the telly.'

After Streaky shut the door behind her, and Kershaw took in the hulking figure slouched in a chair on the video feed, she was properly gobsmacked.

What the fuck? The last time she'd laid eyes on Janusz Kiszka had been in Bart's hospital, after he'd got himself on the wrong end of a vendetta with a Polish drug gang. Since Kershaw's conduct in that case had earned her a disciplinary hearing, the sight of the big Pole's craggy mug, today of all days, was about as welcome as a cockroach in the cornflakes.

Hearing Streaky finish reading him the official caution, she forced herself to concentrate.

'According to the statement you gave my colleague yesterday,' said Streaky. 'You're aware that your friend James Fulford was stabbed to death on his doorstep at around 5.30 p.m. on Monday?'

Fuck! Kiszka was being questioned about a *murder*?

'Could you just refresh my memory as to your whereabouts at that time, Mr Kissa-ka?'

Kershaw grinned. Streaky knew perfectly well how to pronounce Kiszka's surname: he was mangling it deliberately to wind him up.

'The William Morris Gallery,' said Kiszka.

'Go to a lot of galleries, do you?'

He shrugged. 'I showed the other cop the text Jim sent me. He said he was going to be late for our meeting, so I had time to kill.'

Streaky paused, letting the word dangle in the air.

'The trouble is, Mr Kiss-aka, I had one of my most experienced officers take your photo down to this ... *furniture museum* – and there wasn't a single member of staff who remembers you.'

'It's the only photo I had to hand,' he hefted one shoulder. 'It isn't a very good likeness.'

Streaky opened the file in front of him and leafed through some papers.

'Of course, this isn't the first time you've been in a police interview room,' he went on, fixing his suspect with a deadpan stare. 'You were questioned in the course of another murder investigation a couple years back: one that involved drugs, shooting, and three dead bodies if memory serves.'

'I'm a private investigator – it's an occupation that sometimes requires me to deal with unsavoury characters,' said Kiszka, staring right back.

'I'll bet it does,' said Streaky, his voice heavy with irony. 'But you never really explained how someone who claims to make his living chasing bad debts and missing persons ends up in a Polish gangster's drug factory.'

'Does your file mention that if I hadn't been there the body count would have been even higher?' he growled.

Streaky dropped his gaze. *Advantage Kiszka*, thought Kershaw.

'Remind me how it was that you and James Fulford became friendly?'

28

'Like I told the other cop, we met on a building site back in the eighties.'

'And in all that time since then, you say you've just been drinking buddies, good mates, right?'

'Yeah, that's right,' he said, pulling a tin out from his pocket.

Kershaw wrinkled her nose, remembering the little stinky cigars he smoked.

'No smoking in here I'm afraid, Mr Kiss-aka,' said Streaky, pointing at a sign. 'So, you've never had any involvement in this gym he runs in Walthamstow?'

Kiszka shook his head.

'No business dealings of any kind with each other? No property deals, for instance?'

'No, nothing like that.'

Kershaw noticed he'd started tap-tapping his index finger on the cigar tin. A sign of impatience? Or a guilty conscience?

Streaky inserted the tip of his little finger into his ear. After rooting around for a few seconds, he examined the results of his excavation with a thoughtful expression.

'How old are you, Mr Kiss-aka? Fifty-something?'

'I'm forty-five,' he growled.

'Oh, sorry,' said Streaky, feigning surprise. 'Still, lots of people find the old memory banks start to let them down in their forties, don't they?'

'My memory is perfectly serviceable,' he drawled – but Kershaw could tell from the set of his jaw that he was struggling to control his temper. For all his apparent cool and his old-school way of talking, Kiszka could still make the air around him buzz with the possibility of violence.

Streaky took a document from the file in front of him and pushed it across the table.

'For the benefit of the tape, I have passed the interviewee a copy of the deeds held by the UK Land Registry for Jim's Gym, Walthamstow, dated the 11th of November 1992.'

Kiszka picked up the document.

'Would you care to confirm that that is your name on the first page, Mr Kiss-aka?'

As he examined it, the furrows on Kiszka's face deepened.

'We all have forgetful moments,' said Streaky. 'But I'm finding it hard to believe it slipped your mind that you're the *owner* of Jim's Gym.'

Kershaw gasped. *Game to Streaky!*

She held her breath as Kiszka opened his mouth to speak, then shut it again. He pushed the document back across the table.

'I want to call my solicitor.'

Six

'Just give me fifteen minutes with him, Sarge,' said Kershaw. 'We spent a lot of time together on that job so I know all his little tics and tells. I might get *something* useful out of him, even if it's not admissible.'

Kershaw was perched on the edge of Streaky's desk as she made her pitch for a chat with Kiszka, now installed in one of the holding cells downstairs. As the new girl on the squad, she was well aware she should be keeping her head down, restricting herself to 'getting to know you' chit-chat with the other DCs, gathering crucial first day intelligence like where the biros and the digestives were kept – but that might mean her missing the chance to get herself drafted onto the Fulford case.

As Streaky stared into the distance, apparently lost in a daydream, Kershaw waited, knowing that if she pushed him, he'd more than likely blow his top.

'Copernicus!' he said finally, slapping the surface of his desk.

'Sarge?'

'I've been trying to remember the name of Kiszka's cat,' he said. 'You mentioned it once – when you were investigating

31

the murder of that Polish girl he was mixed up in. Stuck in my mind. Not many people name their moggies after Renaissance astronomers.'

'Er?'

'Nicolaus Copernicus.' Streaky enunciated each syllable as though talking to a twelve-year-old. 'Polish. Established the principle of heliocentrism.' Peeling the foil back from a half-eaten pack of Rolos, he offered her one. 'Didn't they teach you anything at that comprehensive school of yours? Plaistow, wasn't it?'

'Poplar actually, Sarge,' she said, taking one. 'And I have heard of Copernicus. I'm just not quite sure what it has to do with Kiszka being a suspect.'

'It tells me, detective, that he's not your average villain,' said Streaky, through a mouthful of chocolate. 'Our Mr Kiszka fancies himself as a bit of an intellectual.'

Kershaw couldn't disagree with that. Kiszka had always struck her as a man bristling with contradictions. He might have a science degree and the tendency to talk like someone out of a Jane Austen novel, but she knew from experience he wouldn't hesitate to throw a punch – or break the law – in pursuit of an investigation.

'So if it was him who shivved his so-called mate – and he's top of my list at the moment,' Streaky went on, 'he might be tempted to play games with us.'

'And let something slip.'

'*Exactamundo*.'

She jumped to her feet. 'So I can have a chat with him?'

He turned his pale blue gaze on her. 'I hope you're not planning any of your old antics,' he said. 'Like restaging your famous impression of a one-woman crime-solving machine.'

'No, Sarge!' She felt her cheeks redden, aware of her new colleagues earwigging on the conversation. 'Nothing like that.'

He pointed the half-empty pack of Rolos at her. 'Don't make me regret bringing you here.'

'No, Sarge.'

'Alright, then,' he said. 'Take him a cuppa. And since you're putting the kettle on, mine's a builder's. Three sugars.'

Kershaw found Kiszka pacing up and down his cell wearing a thunderous expression. He looked huge in the tiny space, like Daddy Bear in Goldilocks' kitchen.

'I brought you a cup of tea,' she said brightly.

He glanced at the offering: 'I don't drink tea with milk in it,' he said, and threw himself down on the narrow bunk. He'd shown not a flicker of recognition or surprise on seeing her again.

'I'll have it then,' she said, settling herself at the foot of the bed and taking a sip. Close up he appeared pretty much unchanged – the same caveman good looks, maybe a bit thinner about the face. 'It must be getting on for two years since I saw you last.'

'Yeah, and it looks like the cops haven't got any more intelligent in that time,' he growled.

She had a sudden vision of their first meeting, a no-holds-barred stand-off which had ended with her – erroneously, as it later turned out – accusing him of murdering a girl, a Polish waitress found dead in a hotel room.

'Well, you've not been exactly helpful so far, have you?'

'I've told them everything I know, twice over! I showed them Jim's text, his wife has vouched for me – what the fuck else can I do?' He ran a hand through his dark brown hair, threaded with silver here and there, she noticed. 'I apologise for the bad language,' he added after a moment.

Kershaw didn't say so, but from the point of view of the investigation, the text simply put Kiszka in the right place at the right time for the murder.

'So why did you clam up when the Sarge showed you that mortgage deed?'

'No comment.'

She paused. 'Look, Janusz,' she said. 'I'm prepared to believe that you didn't kill your friend. And from what I know about you, you must be dying to see the scum who did kill him locked up.'

He shot her a look that said locking up wasn't what he had in mind.

'And the more time we spend fu... messing around following false trails, the less chance we have of finding the killers.' Actually, Kiszka was probably more than capable of killing someone in a murderous rage, Kershaw reflected, but the important thing right now was to gain his trust.

Janusz stared at her for a long moment, taking in the little heart-shaped face under the strangely lopsided hair, the steely set of her lips. His determination to find the *chuje* who had murdered Jim was as strong as ever but he had to admit it couldn't hurt to have the cops looking for them, too.

'Anything I say to you is off the record, agreed?'

'Absolutely.' This was true: although technically he was still under caution, the CPS took a seriously dim view of unrecorded unofficial chats, so nothing Kiszka told her could be used in court.

'Because I'm not making any further statements until I talk to my solicitor.'

'Understood.'

He exhaled. 'When I first met Jim, he wasn't in great shape. He'd had a ... breakdown, I suppose you'd call it – after fighting for his country.'

'Yeah, the Sarge mentioned he was a Falklands veteran.'

'A Royal Marine. He was no coward – they gave him a medal for bravery under fire.' He frowned at her, making sure she took the point. 'Anyway, by '92, he was just starting to get himself straightened out and he came up with the idea of starting a gymnasium – there wasn't anything like

34

that in Walthamstow back then. He found a spot he reckoned was perfect for it. A derelict space, under the railway ...?' He sketched a curved structure in mid-air.

'A railway arch?'

'Yes, a railway arch.'

'And you bought it for him?'

He snorted. 'No! He'd saved up for a deposit while working on the building sites – but he needed a loan to make up the rest and pay for the renovations, the machinery and so on.'

Kershaw paused, remembering that according to the system, Fulford had previous. 'But no one would lend him the money ... because of his criminal record? Assault, wasn't it?'

'The guy deserved it,' said Janusz. 'It was just after Jim had got out of military hospital – he'd had to have months of skin grafts – when some *imbecyl* buttonholed him at the bar. Told him that the men who'd fought the Falklands War were "Thatcher's stooges".'

Kershaw winced.

'The guy was lucky to get away with a broken jaw,' said Janusz. 'But the law didn't see it that way.'

Back then, he recalled, no one had heard of PTSD: in fact, the judge who sent Jim down for six months said he was making an example of him because his behaviour had been 'unfitting for a veteran of Her Majesty's forces'.

'So we had to make out the loan was for me. I signed all the paperwork, and the deeds were put in my name.'

'So why didn't you tell DS Bacon all this when he asked?'

'I'd completely forgotten! I haven't thought about it in twenty years.'

'Did anyone else know about the arrangement? His wife, for instance?'

'I don't know,' he shrugged. 'He might have told Marika when they got married, I suppose. He didn't keep any secrets from her, if that's what you mean.'

Kershaw's antennae twitched. At the mention of Jim's other half, Kiszka seemed suddenly defensive, like he was nursing a guilty conscience. Had he been having an affair with his best mate's wife?

In truth, the cause of Janusz's discomfiture lay somewhere else entirely. Remembering the sorrowful look on the face of the girl, Varenka, as she left flowers outside Jim's house he'd been struck by a sudden thought. *Had his mate and the mystery girl been lovers?* No way, he told himself, Jim wasn't the type.

He stood up to indicate their meeting was over, dwarfing Kershaw. 'It's been a pleasure to remake your acquaintance,' he said, bestowing his most charming *mittel* European smile on her. 'But now, perhaps you would be good enough to find out whether my solicitor has arrived.'

Back in the office, Kershaw had barely had ten minutes to commit the names of her fellow DCs to memory before Streaky called everyone together for a briefing.

'As you all know, we've pulled in James Fulford's Polish chum Janusz Kiszka for questioning,' Streaky told his audience: Kershaw, Ackroyd, three other DCs – two male, one female – and the Crime Scene Examiner. He brandished Kiszka's arrest mugshot. 'It turns out that Kiszka was the real owner of the gym Fulford ran. A fact uncovered due to the hard graft of DC Ackroyd who has spent two days wrestling with the jobsworths over at the Land Registry.'

All eyes turned to Adam Ackroyd – sitting next to Kershaw – who blinked rapidly and smiled. She had warmed to him when they were introduced – they were about the same age and had both done criminology at uni. But now she felt a little surge of competitiveness: at Canning Town CID she'd been the one getting the gold stars from Streaky.

'Mr Kiszka is currently enjoying our hospitality in the guest accommodation downstairs,' Streaky went on. 'But we're a long old way from nailing him for the murder, so let's go back to basics – what we know and what we can rule out. Adam?'

Ackroyd swivelled in his chair so everyone could hear him. 'The neighbour at number 159 saw two males in hoodies running from the scene at around 5.45 p.m. One was around six foot, slim build, and the other was an inch or two shorter and with a more muscular build. They were both wearing gloves and balaclavas, so no clue as to ethnicity.'

'Did the neighbour mention if either of them wore anything green?' the female DC asked.

'No, nothing like that,' said Ackroyd. 'Mind you, even the B-Street boys wouldn't be thick enough to wear the bandana while committing a murder.'

As a low chuckle ran round the team, Kershaw felt suddenly in the dark, hit by the realisation that she knew sod-all about her new patch.

Streaky must've caught her look. 'The B-Street gang are the local pond life,' he said. 'They were the soldiers for our local drug baron, Turkish bloke by the name of Arslan who recently got sent down for twenty years. The drugs boys raided one of his lock-ups and found 100 kilos of Afghan heroin cunningly disguised as china tea sets.'

'They still account for most of the area's drug dealing, street robbery, stabbings and so on,' the girl added. *Sophie.* Sophie Edgerton: that was her name, Kershaw suddenly remembered. 'And they wear green bandanas – it's, like, their gang colours.'

'Anyway, we've more or less ruled out a random doorstep mugging,' said Ackroyd. 'On the other side of Hoe Street, maybe. But it just doesn't happen in the Village.'

'And it feels too *specific*, anyway,' said Kershaw. Strictly speaking, as a newbie she should really shut up and listen, but she couldn't help herself.

'Explain yourself, Natalie,' said Streaky, although she knew he'd guessed where she was coming from.

'Well ... I don't know the area,' she said, 'but looking at the map, it seems to me if you're gonna do a quick and dirty mugging, you'd choose a house at the end of a road – so you're in and out fast? Instead they've risked going all the way up this great long road, Barclay Road.' She shrugged. 'If you ask me, this was a targeted killing. The perpetrators knew exactly who they were after.'

Streaky grunted his assent. 'Sophie, what about our mistaken identity theory?' he asked. 'Any drug dealers or other known villains living nearby?'

She shook her head: 'No, Sarge. It's a nice road, pretty much all owner-occupiers. The worst I could find on the database was a man with a ten-year-old conviction for insurance fraud.'

'Okay. Let's go back to Kiszka, who has freely admitted he was on his way to meet Fulford at the time of the murder,' said Streaky. 'My working hypothesis is this. There's a recession on, his private eye business is feeling the squeeze, but the gym – which he officially owns – is going great guns. He decides he wants a piece of it but his pal Fulford doesn't play ball.'

'But couldn't this Kiszka have sold the property out from under Fulford's feet, if he'd wanted to?' asked the other DC, the spoddy one whose name Kershaw had already forgotten.

'Fulford's an ex-Marine, did time for assault back in the eighties,' said Streaky. 'Maybe Kiszka decided that it would be less risky to off him in what looked like a random mugging, so he could take the place over, no questions asked.'

'Do we know what kind of weapon was used?' Kershaw asked the Crime Scene Examiner, an older guy called Tony.

'We're still waiting for the post-mortem report,' he said. 'But Dr King, the pathologist, reckons it was a long blade of some kind. He said the wounds were inflicted with great force – maximum prejudice – was the phrase he used, actually.'

Streaky gave a snort. 'Nathan King watches too many American crime shows. But it's true a nasty assault like that will often turn out to be a personal vendetta.'

The Sarge started divvying up who was in charge of what – co-ordinating evidence from CCTV cameras in the area, house-to-house enquiries, and an appeal for witnesses – but Kershaw was only half listening. As she picked at a ragged fingernail – she was on her umpteenth attempt to stop biting her nails – she tried to imagine Kiszka committing such a savage attack. Lashing out at someone in a rage, yes, killing them even, before the red mist cleared, very possibly. But planning and carrying out a cold-blooded execution? She couldn't quite see it.

She realised that Streaky was winding up the briefing – without giving her any action points.

'Sorry, Sarge, I know I'm playing catch up here,' she said. 'But Kiszka claims he was at some art gallery at the time of the murder? I assume none of the staff saw him there?'

'Over to DC Cargill,' said Streaky, indicating a guy in his late fifties, sitting off to the edge of the group. Red-faced and overweight, Cargill wore a brown pinstriped suit so out of date it could be one of Streaky's cast-offs. Kershaw wondered if he was even aware of the fashion crime he'd committed when he'd twinned it with grey shoes.

As Cargill leafed laboriously through his notebook, Ackroyd bent his head towards Kershaw's. 'We call Derek The Olympic Torch,' he murmured. Seeing Kershaw's incomprehension he added: 'He never goes out.'

Kershaw got it. Cargill was the old sweat of the squad, counting the days to retirement and keeping his workload to the absolute minimum.

'At approximately 1500 hours on Tuesday the 6th of November, I attended the William Morris Gallery in Lloyd Park,' Cargill intoned, 'and introduced myself to the female on the front desk. I duly established that she was the manager, name of Mrs Caroline Smalls.'

Kershaw saw a red flush starting to creep up Streaky's face from his chin, usually a reliable sign that he was about to spit the dummy.

'I showed her a picture of ... *Jay-nus* ... *Jah-nuzz* ...' After a couple of goes at pronouncing Kiszka's name, Cargill gave up. '... the suspect. I then proceeded to the first floor ...'

'For Christ's sake, Derek,' said Streaky, his entire face now a ketchup red. 'Get to the chuffing point!'

Cargill closed his notebook with some dignity. 'None of the staff saw him, Skipper.'

Kershaw jumped in. 'Kiszka did say that the photo he provided was way out of date, Sarge. I just wonder if it's worth going down there again with his arrest mugshot?'

Streaky didn't respond. He was still looking daggers at Cargill, who, apparently unconcerned, was now doodling on his copy of the *Express*.

'Because if we do charge Kiszka, it could come back to bite our arse in court,' Kershaw went on. 'We don't want his defence saying we didn't make best efforts to check out his alibi.'

Streaky tore his gaze from Cargill. 'Good thinking, DC Kershaw. Consider it your first action point.' He grinned, showing teeth as yellow as old piano keys. 'Welcome to Murder Squad.'

Seven

'So you're saying the cops charged *you* with Jim's murder?' Oskar said slowly, evidently struggling with the effort of processing this cataclysmic news.

'No, Oskar! I told you, they don't have any evidence,' said Janusz.

Janusz and his oldest mate were heading out to Essex in his battered white Transit van, where Oskar was landscaping the garden of some scrap metal millionaire.

'My solicitor said that the business with the mortgage deeds is a sideshow,' Janusz waved a hand. 'He says unless the cops find something really solid, like … a bloodstained knife in my apartment, they've got nothing to justify charging me.'

'And you haven't?' asked Oskar, a worried expression creasing his chubby face.

'Haven't what?'

'Got a bloodstained knife in your apartment?'

'Of course I fucking haven't, turniphead!'

'Calm down, Janek! I'm just trying to … establish the facts.'

'That doesn't mean they won't try to frame me for it, of course,' he growled. 'You know what the cops are like.'

Growing up in Soviet-era Poland had instilled in him a visceral distrust of the machinery of state that he'd never quite thrown off.

Seeing a traffic light some fifty metres ahead turn from green to amber, Oskar floored the accelerator. The engine responded with an ear-splitting whinny. A second or two later, realising they wouldn't make it across the junction in time, Oskar applied the brakes with equal ferocity, hurling both of them against their seat belts.

Janusz lit a cigar to steady his nerves. 'You need to get that fan belt fixed, *kolego*.'

'It just needs some WD40.' Oskar drummed his fingers on the wheel. 'You know, I still can't believe Jim's dead – God rest his soul.' The two men crossed themselves. 'Poor Marika! When is the funeral?'

'God only knows. She can't even plan it until they've done the post-mortem,' said Janusz.

Oskar mimed an elaborate shiver. 'I tell you something, Janek,' he said. 'If I die, don't you let those *kanibale* loose on me with their scalpels.' As the light changed to green, he pulled away. 'And don't forget what I told you – about putting a charged mobile in my coffin? They're always burying people who aren't actually dead.'

Janusz refrained from pointing out that a post-mortem might be the only sure-fire way of avoiding such a fate. He and Oskar had been best mates since they'd met on their first day of national service back in eighties Poland, but he'd learned one thing long ago: trying to have a logical discussion with him was like trying to herd chickens.

'Remember that time, years back, when Jim took us to see the doggies racing each other at Walthamstow? Oskar chuckled. '*Kurwa!* That was a good night.'

'I remember,' Janusz grinned. 'You got so legless that you kept trying to place a bet on the electric rabbit.'

'Bullshit! I don't remember that.'

'I swear. If Jim hadn't been watching your back, one of those bookies would have swung for you.'

They fell silent, smiling at their own memories.

'So, Janek. How are you going to track down the *skurwysyny* who murdered him?'

'That's why I wanted to see you,' said Janusz, tapping some cigar ash out of his window. 'Walthamstow is more your patch than mine so I thought you could do some sniffing around for me – find out if anyone knows this girl, Varenka, or the *chuj* who likes to use her as a punchbag.' He pointed his cigar at his mate 'But keep it discreet, okay, and don't mention Jim, obviously.'

'No problem!' said Oskar, his expression eager. 'I'll start asking around right away. We'll be like Cagney and Lacey!'

'Except they were girls, *idiota*,' said Janusz. 'Which reminds me, ladyboy – how is the "landscape gardening" going?'

'I'm making a mint, Janek,' Oskar declared, rubbing his fingers together. 'You should've come in with me when I gave you the chance.'

'So you're saying these people out in Essex pay you thousands of pounds to muck around with their gardens?' Janusz made no attempt to keep the incredulity from his voice.

'Why wouldn't they? I was in charge of building half the Olympic Park!' he said, striking his chest.

'Yeah, but construction isn't the same thing as landscaping,' said Janusz. 'You wouldn't know a begonia from a bramble patch!'

Oskar waved a dismissive hand. 'I get all the green stuff down B&Q,' he said. 'Anyway, I see my role as creating the architectural framework.'

Janusz grinned. 'Let me guess. They think they're getting Monty Don and they end up with paving as far as the eye can see?'

Oskar shrugged. 'Some people have no vision, Janek. I tell them, once the bushes and shit have grown up a bit, it'll look fine.'

The unmistakable tones of Homer Simpson singing 'Spider Pig' filled the van – Oskar's latest irritating ringtone.

'Hello, lady,' said Oskar into the phone. 'Yes, I'm on my way to your place right now.' He used his free hand to change gear, steering the van meanwhile with his knees. 'I didn't forget. A classical statue for the water feature.' Turning to Janusz, Oskar winked. 'You're going to love the one I picked out for you. See you soon.'

Throwing the mobile back into the tide of debris washed up on the dashboard, Oskar said: 'Once I drop this stuff off at Buckhurst Hill, we can head straight back to Walthamstow and start our investigation!'

Things didn't work out quite so simply. After they parked up on the broad gravel forecourt of a hacienda-style detached house, Janusz stayed in the van while Oskar unloaded and took the stuff round to the back garden. Even from this distance, he was able to ascertain from the pitch of the conversation that the lady of the house wasn't entirely happy.

After a good ten minutes, he heard Oskar crunching back across the gravel. A moment later he opened the driver's side door and started to push a large sculpture of some kind up onto the seat, with much huffing and puffing.

'Give me a hand, Janek!'

'Can't you put it in the back?'

'This is easier.'

'What the fuck is it meant to be anyway?' asked Janusz once they'd manhandled the thing up onto the bench seat.

'What does it look like?!' Oskar's tone was incredulous. 'It's a moo-eye, obviously.' Hauling his chunky frame into the front seat, he slammed the van door and threaded the seat belt around their passenger.

Janusz peered at its profile. He could see now that it was a giant head – a clumsy reproduction of one of the monumental Easter Island sculptures, cast in a pale grey resin intended to resemble stone.

'It's *moai*, donkey-brain.'

'Moo-eye – like I said!' Oskar started the van. 'She said she wanted something classical. How is a moo-eye not classical? They're hundreds of thousands of years old!' He shook his head. '*Now* she tells me she meant a naked lady.'

As they got closer to Walthamstow the traffic slowed and thickened. The sight of the huge, implacable stone face gazing out through the windscreen of a scruffy Transit van started to draw disbelieving stares from passers-by and appreciative blasts on the horn from fellow motorists.

Oskar lapped up the attention, returning the toots and scattering thumbs-ups left and right, while Janusz sat in silence, one hand spread across his face. The last straw came when Oskar wound down his window to receive a high five from a passing bus driver.

'Let me out, Oskar,' he growled. 'I can walk to the gym from here. And give me a call if you hear anything interesting.'

He found Jim's Gym open for business and packed with clients squeezing in a lunchtime workout. The faces were all male and for the most part either black, or Asian and bearded. The iron filings smell of sweat and testosterone filled the air like an unsettling background hum. Seeing Janusz, one of the older black guys, a regular called Wayne who sometimes came to the pub, set down the weights he'd been hefting and headed over. Wiping the sweat from his palms onto a towel, he offered his hand.

'Terrible news about Jim,' he said, eyes sorrowful, seeking Janusz's gaze. They shook hands and spoke briefly, before Janusz continued towards the little office at the rear, where he'd sometimes come to pick up Jim on the way to the boozer.

45

But as he reached for the door handle, he felt himself engulfed by a surge of grief so powerful he had to steady himself against the doorjamb. This had happened more than once since he'd identified Jim's body, every time it hit him – the dizzying realisation that he would never again see his mate's face, nor hear that big laugh.

Inside, he was confronted by the sight of the deputy manager, a young black guy called Andre, sprawled in Jim's chair, behind Jim's desk, chatting and laughing into a mobile phone. *Bad timing.* Two strides took Janusz across the room and before the guy could even get to his feet he found the phone slapped out of his hand and across the room.

'What the fuck, bruv?!'

'Show some respect,' said Janusz. 'Jim's not even buried yet. And who said you could take his desk?'

Andre jutted his chin out. 'And who's you to tell me I can't, old man?'

A grim smile tugged at the side of Janusz's mouth. 'Haven't you heard? I'm the new owner.' No need to tell the guy that he'd already instructed his solicitor to transfer ownership of the gym to Marika.

Andre opened his mouth to speak, then shut it again. Seating himself on the desk, facing the kid, Janusz lit a cigar. Smoking in here was probably against the law, but with a murder rap hanging over him he figured he could take the risk. 'I suppose you've had the cops down here already?'

'Yeah, they was in, asking all this and that,' said Andre, kissing his teeth.

Janusz suppressed an urgent desire to bitch-slap him. He raised his eyebrows. 'Ask about me, did they?'

'Yeah. Like did you and Jim ever have a fight, stuff like that.' He gave Janusz an assessing look. 'I told the feds, you might be big but if Jim wanted to he could've put you down –' he mimed a right hook and a left uppercut, '– *boof boof* … no contest.'

'You're right about that,' chuckled Janusz, leaning across him to tap ash into the wastepaper bin. 'Listen. Since it looks like we're going to be working together, I need to ask you some stuff.'

'Sure,' said Andre, although Janusz saw a guarded look come into his eyes.

'Did you ever see Jim with a woman, other than his wife, I mean?'

A broad grin spread across Andre's face, revealing what looked like – but almost certainly wasn't – a diamond, set in one of his incisors. 'You tellin' me Jimbo had a bit of poon on the sly?'

Janusz shrugged, non-committal. It hadn't escaped his attention that, on hearing the line of questioning, the guy had visibly relaxed. 'Did he ever mention a girl called Varenka? Tall, blonde, good-looking – speaks with an Eastern European accent? Maybe she's a member of the gym?'

'We don't get too many *ladeeez* in here,' said Andre. 'They might find themselves a bit too popular, if you get what I'm saying.' He pumped his arms and hips back and forth, miming rough sex, before creasing up at his own joke.

Janusz bent to grind his cigar out on the waste bin, so that Andre couldn't see the look in his eyes. By the time he'd straightened up, he was smiling. 'Do me a favour and have a discreet ask around, would you? You know, I'm going to need someone to manage this place once we've got the funeral out of the way.'

'Absolutely. I'll get straight on it.' Andre jumped to his feet, doing a passable impression of the young dynamic manager. 'And don't worry about things here – I'm all over it.'

Janusz's gaze swept the office. 'Where's Jim's laptop, by the way?'

Andre's gaze wavered. 'No idea, boss. All the gym records get kept on that old piece of junk,' he used his chin to indicate a scuffed PC in the corner. 'Like I told the feds, he took his laptop home most nights.'

Janusz knew that Marika had already checked at home and found no sign of it. Had this little punk grabbed the chance to get a free laptop? Or might there be something on the laptop to help solve the puzzle of Jim's murder, information someone wanted to conceal and had, perhaps, paid good money to get their hands on? Again, Janusz saw Varenka, long legs scissored across the pavement, after she'd been struck by the bullet-headed man. What did she – or her assailant – have to do with Jim?

Janusz opened his wallet and handed Andre his card, followed by two twenties. 'Send Marika a really nice bunch of flowers,' he said. 'With a message, offering sincere condolences from everyone at the gym.'

Eight

Kershaw began her second day on Murder Squad with a firm resolution: to make a real effort to get to know her fellow DCs. She was aware that elbowing her way onto the Fulford case probably hadn't been the most diplomatic way for a newbie to introduce herself. The police force was a bit like the Army: *okay*, bonding with your fellow detectives might not make the difference between life and death, but she'd learned the hard way that being Billy-no-mates could make a tough job a hundred times harder.

So she was making tea for everyone in the galley kitchen off the main corridor, when she felt a hand slip round her waist. She stomped backwards with her heel, a purely reflex action that brought a yelp of protest. Whipping round, she found Ben's chocolate-brown eyes screwed up in pain.

'Fuck! Sorry, Ben – but you really shouldn't have done that!'

He pulled a rueful grimace. 'I almost forgot I'm dating the woman who came top of her unarmed combat class.'

'Remember what we said? About trying to keep out of each other's way at work?' she said, turning back to the kettle.

'Yeah, 'course. I did make sure there was no one around before coming in,' he said, rubbing his foot.

Why was he always so goddamn reasonable?

'Well, it's not a very good start.' She was surprised at the vehemence in her own voice.

They'd agreed to keep their relationship quiet at work – neither of them fancied being the butt of banter or fresh meat for canteen gossip, but for Kershaw it went deeper than that. Ever since starting basic training, her strategy for survival in what was still largely a man's world had been to cultivate a 'one of the boys' persona, which, having spent her formative years hanging out with her dad and his mates, came easily to her. But the strategy had a downside: it meant never getting involved with a work colleague.

She had hoped that, with Ben working in a different part of the building, they'd barely see each other. But now, she felt as though the barriers she'd erected between her public and private lives were crumbling – and she didn't like the feeling one bit.

'What are you even doing on this floor, anyway?' she asked, glancing out through the half-open door.

'I had to see Streaky about something. Oh, and I wanted to ask if I could kip at yours tonight? I'm seeing Jamie Ryan for a drink later and I've got an early start at Woolwich Coroners Court – your place is closer than mine.'

That got her attention. 'Hannah Ryan's Dad? Has there been a development?'

It was over a year now since a paedophile picked up eleven-year-old Hannah Ryan, who'd been born with Down's Syndrome, during a trip to her local corner shop. He'd promised her a ride in a rowing boat at a nearby lakeside beauty spot called Hollow Ponds; instead, after sexually assaulting her, he tied a plastic bag round her neck and dumped her body in the lake. But Hannah survived. Ben, who'd been the investigating officer on the case, had shown Kershaw the casefile photo of Hannah before the attack – she could still see her trusting smile under a mop of curly red hair.

'*Nada.*' Ben shook his head. 'You'd think somewhere between the corner shop and Hollow Ponds *somebody* would have seen them.' He frowned at the floor. 'Officially, the case is still open, but after this long? You and I know it's dead as a doornail.'

Forensics had been unable to recover any DNA evidence, but one name kept coming up – Anthony Stride, a serial child sex offender who lived three streets away from the Ryans. When Hannah picked Stride out of a book of mugshots, a search warrant was granted and the police found evidence on his computer that he'd boasted about the attack under a pseudonym on a chat room used by abusers.

Kershaw remembered Ben's jubilation when he'd told her the news. But when the case came to court – disaster. The defence barrister put the DC who'd searched Stride's flat through the wringer, finally getting him to admit that he'd pulled up the search history on Stride's PC and clicked through to the chat room. The computer should have been bagged and sent straight to the Computer Crime Unit where specially trained officers would have preserved and cloned the data before investigating it further. The cock-up allowed Stride's barrister to plant the idea in the minds of jurors that the cops might have interfered with the crucial evidence. Next, cross-questioning Hannah via video link, he'd suggested that since Mr Stride and she were both regulars at the corner shop, she might have seen him there on a *previous* visit, thus sowing another seed of doubt. In his summing up, he had made much of the idea that, in the light of Hannah's learning diffi-culties, it would be 'all too understandable' for her to confuse Stride with her real attacker. The jury deliberations took seven hours, but they'd eventually returned a 'not guilty' verdict. When the judge revealed that Stride had already served time for offences against young girls, there had been gasps on the jury benches and two female jurors had openly wept.

Kershaw had never seen Ben so rocked. Although he hadn't been the Ryans' official FLO – family liaison officer – he'd spent a lot of time with them and grown particularly close to Hannah's Dad Jamie, a second-generation Irishman who ran the family haulage firm. Ben's distress at what he saw as his failure to nail Stride so alarmed her that she had even tried – unsuccessfully – to persuade him to put in for counselling. Recently, he'd seemed to be getting back to the old Ben, so finding out that he was still seeing Jamie Ryan socially made her uneasy: getting personally involved in a case was never a good idea. She decided to broach the subject with him when they were properly alone.

For now, she just touched his arm lightly, by way of apology for her bad temper. 'Of course you can stay. I'm on early turn tomorrow, so let yourself in. I'll see you in the morning.'

Ten minutes later, she was in mid-chat with fellow DC Sophie, who sat at the desk opposite hers, when Streaky swaggered over.

'Sorry to break up a good gossip, girls,' he said.

Sophie bridled. 'Actually, Sarge, I was just briefing Natalie on our most recent cases.'

'Swapping knitting patterns more like,' Streaky chuckled, pushing Kershaw's paperwork aside to clear space on the desk for his substantial backside.

As Sophie's face flamed red, Kershaw felt a mix of sympathy and amusement. She'd endured her fair share of Streaky's sexist banter in the past, before coming to realise that it was all just part of his act. He'd actually admitted to her once, at the end of a particularly long night in the

Drunken Monkey, that women made far better detectives than men; even if he'd gone on to spoil things by adding that their superior observational and deductive skills were down to them *'always being on the lookout for a husband'*.

'Sophie was briefing me on the local drug gangs, Sarge,' said Kershaw, shooting a supportive look her way. 'In case Jim Fulford's murder does turn out to have been a junkie mugging.'

'Not that you're going to have any time to spare for the Fulford case, DC Kershaw,' said Streaky, pointing a rolled-up printout at her. 'Docklands nick has just told me that you've taken it upon yourself to identify some mystery roof diver?'

'Ah, yes, I meant to talk to you about that, Sarge.'

'You do know we investigate *murders* here, don't you? Which if memory serves, tend to be defined as deliberate slayings at the hands of *a third party*?'

'Yes, Sarge, it's just that I was first on the scene, and since I did all the initial investigations, I thought it made sense for me to finish the job.' When she said it out loud like that, it struck her how *head-girlish* it sounded. And she had to admit that, now she had a murder case to get her teeth into, the mystery jumper could prove to be a major inconvenience.

Streaky unrolled the printout with a magisterial frown. 'Let me see … no identification of any kind on the body … no tattoos, birthmarks or unusual dentistry … no missing persons report fitting the description … number of people working in Canary Wharf tower 7,653 …' After shooting her a meaningful look, he turned to the second page. 'Oh, I do beg your pardon! If I implied that there were no clues to the identity of the deceased, I was wrong.'

By now, it was Sophie who was sneaking Kershaw the sympathetic looks.

'PC Percy Plod found a zloty in the gutter!' Streaky scooted the document onto Kershaw's desk. 'With a red-hot lead like that I should think you'll have the case solved by the end of your shift. It's a shame you'll have your hands full, because I was going to give you some more action points in the Fulford case.' Getting to his feet, he tucked an errant shirt tail back into his trousers, and strode off.

Nine

Janusz was kneading bread dough on his kitchen worktop when his mobile sounded.

'*Czesc*, Oskar,' he grunted, holding the phone to his ear with his thumb and index finger so as not to douse it in flour.

'Ask me what I found out about your friend with the Land Rover Discovery.'

'I haven't got time to play twenty questions,' said Janusz. 'I'm up to my elbows in sourdough.'

Oskar made kissing noises down the phone. 'You know, Janek, you'd make someone a lovely wife. I bet you're wearing a really cute apron, too.' Then, adopting a concerned voice: 'You do know that I'll always be there for you, don't you?'

'What?'

'When you finally decide to come out of the closet.'

Janusz held the phone away from his ear as Oskar roared with laughter. 'Actually, I'm cooking dinner for Kasia tonight, turniphead,' he said, one side of his mouth lifting in a private smile.

'Janek, Janek,' said Oskar. 'Are you *still* kidding yourself that she's going to leave that *dupek* Steve?'

Janusz leaned against the worktop and let Oskar carry on in this vein for a while. The worst of it was, he knew in his heart of hearts that his mate was probably right. The affair with Kasia had been going on for almost two years now yet she showed no sign of ending her marriage to her lazy, worthless husband.

'Spare me the relationship counselling, Oskar,' growled Janusz. 'Just tell me what you've got.'

'Keep your hair on, *kolego*, I was getting to that,' said Oskar. 'I dropped in on my mate, Marek, the one who owns a *Polski sklep* on Hoe Street? You should go there – he sells the best *wiejska* in London. And his *rolmopsy* …'

'Oskar!'

'Okay, okay. Anyway, it turns out that he knows the guy in the Discovery, the one you saw with that gorgeous bird!'

'What does he know about him?'

'He's Romanian, grew up there when that *kutas* Ceausescu ran the place. But he managed to get out and went to live in Poland after Solidarity got in – Marek says his mother was Polish.'

That made sense, thought Janusz. Poland had been the first country to throw off communist rule in 1989, making it a magnet for people escaping Soviet-backed regimes all over Eastern Europe.

'Does Marek know how the guy makes his money?'

'*Tak*. He has business interests in Poland, Ukraine, some of the other ex-Kommi states,' said Oskar. 'Marek just invested some cash with him actually – he says he's making a packet.'

'Shady business?' asked Janusz.

'No! He says it's all totally above board.'

Janusz just grunted. Some people didn't ask too many questions so long as the rate of return was attractive.

'Anyway, sisterfucker, listen to this,' said Oskar. 'Marek sees the Romanian going to some Turkish café opposite his shop in Hoe Street, twice a week, to drink coffee with the owner.'

Janusz had never had any dealings with London's Turks, who kept themselves pretty much to themselves, but during the recent riots they'd won his grudging admiration. While the cops had stood by, helpless and outnumbered, as lowlifes looted and torched his local shops, further north in Green Lanes the Turks had lined up to defend their businesses armed with hard stares and baseball bats. When the dust had settled, theirs were the only shopfronts that didn't require the attention of emergency glaziers.

'And the girl? Does she go along to these meetings?'

'Sometimes. But Marek says he's always there – four o'clock, Thursdays and Fridays, regular as clockwork.'

Marek sounded like a nosy bastard to Janusz. He checked his watch: it was Thursday and just after three. Plenty of time to get up there and back in time to cook dinner.

Janusz still had no idea of the precise nature of the relationship between the girl Varenka and the Romanian. She certainly wouldn't be the first girl to settle for an older, uglier lover in return for a luxurious life. But was he also her pimp? The scene Janusz had witnessed in Hoe Street, which had ended with the bastard assaulting her, suggested that was a strong possibility.

'Did you get the name of this Romanian?'

He heard Oskar fumbling with a bit of paper. 'Barbu Romescu.'

'You didn't let Marek know this was anything to do with Jim?'

'Of course not, Janek! I just dropped into the conversation that I'd seen this *seksowna* blonde girl getting into a fancy black 4X4 in Hoe Street. You know, man talk.'

'Not bad. Maybe you're not as bat-brained as you look.'

'I was thinking,' Oskar's voice became conspiratorial, tinged with suppressed excitement, 'I could park the van near the café, like I was doing deliveries, and when the Romanian comes out, tail him to his hideaway.'

Janusz grinned at the idea of Oskar and his old crock of a van with the squealing fan belt shadowing anyone undetected. 'I tell you what, *kolego*, here's the best thing you can do. Take Marek out for a drink. Drop into the conversation that you have a mate who's come into a pile of money and who is looking for investments paying a good return.'

Right after he'd hung up, the message waiting sign started flashing on his phone. It was a voicemail from Kasia.

'Janek, darling. Please don't hate me but I can't make it tonight. We have so many late bookings for extensions, I'm going to have to stay here and help out. I'm really sorry. I'll call again later and we can rebook? I love you, misiaczku.'

Janusz flung his phone down, sending up a dust cloud of flour, where it lay like an alien spacecraft crashed in a snowdrift. This wasn't the first time Kasia had stood him up lately. She was always protesting that he was the love of her life, but these days her burgeoning nail bar business and inconvenient husband left barely any time for him. When she'd left her job as a pole dancer, Janusz had hoped that she might move on from Steve, too, but on the subject of her marriage her position was unwavering: as a devout Catholic, she said, she couldn't countenance a divorce.

Staring at the sourdough, he contemplated binning it, but then resumed his kneading. It felt therapeutic, slamming the dough into the worktop. The cat, who was curled up on a kitchen chair cleaning himself, broke off from his ministrations to gaze up at Janusz.

'You probably won't see it this way, Copetka,' he told him, 'but when the vet took your nuts away, he saved you a world of trouble.'

Janusz arrived in Walthamstow ten minutes ahead of the Romanian's scheduled meeting time. He bought a half of lager in Hoe Street's last surviving pub and stationed himself in the window, almost directly opposite the Pasha Café, which had a sign advertising '*Cakes, Shakes and Shisha*'. And sure enough, even on this chilly day, there were two dark-skinned men seated at one of the pavement tables chatting and smoking shisha pipes beneath a plastic canopy. Janusz remembered reading somewhere that an hour spent smoking tobacco this way was the equivalent of getting through 100 cigarettes. *Lucky bastards*, he thought, cursing the smoking ban.

At two minutes to four, the black Discovery pulled up right outside the café and the bullet-headed man climbed out of the driver's seat – no chauffeur today. He bent to retrieve something from the rear seat, a manbag, from the look of it, then turned, giving Janusz a view of short-clipped hair, a muscled back under a well-cut jacket, before heading for the café entrance. Janusz was just thinking he'd have to wait till the guy came out again for a good look at his face when, at the threshold, he turned to aim his key fob at the 4X4. It took barely a second – but long enough for Janusz to take a mental snapshot. The thing that caught his attention was a curious scar running down the side of his face. Reaching from temple to jaw, it looked too wide to have been carved by a blade, and yet unusually regular for a burn.

Janusz took a slug of lager, aware of a pulse starting to thrum in his throat. He'd seen his type before. His bearing, the way he walked and held himself, revealed more accurately than any psychiatrist's report what kind of man he was: someone who saw other people as tools to achieve his ends – or as obstacles to be neutralised.

Around forty minutes later, Scarface re-emerged. Expressionless, he retrieved the plastic-wrapped parking ticket that a warden had left pinned under his wiper and dropped it into the gutter, before pulling out into the stream of traffic. Janusz decided that his disfigurement *was* a burn, despite its neat edges – the sort of thing that might be caused if someone had pressed a red-hot iron bar against the side of his face.

Janusz took his time finishing his drink and headed over to the café. Inside, it was surprisingly plush, kitted out with low, upholstered seating and Middle Eastern-style wall hangings. To the café's rear, a doorway hung with heavy dark red velvet curtains led to what he assumed was a private salon. The Christmas cake smell of fruit-flavoured shisha tobacco hung in the air. Opposite the long glass counter was a giant TV screen tuned to Al Jazeera, on which a female presenter in a headscarf was interviewing an Israeli diplomat. English subtitles revealed that the subject of the interview was the shelling of southern Israel by Hamas militants in Gaza; attacks returned – with sky-high inflation – by Israeli forces. Not for the first time, the shared guttural phonetics of the Arabic and Hebrew languages struck Janusz as deeply ironic.

A young man aged about eighteen or nineteen, wearing a Galatasaray shirt, appeared behind the counter through a tinkling bead curtain. He greeted Janusz across the counter: if he was surprised to find a big white Pole wearing a military greatcoat in a shisha café, he didn't show it.

Janusz pretended to be checking out the trays of sticky-looking pastries. There were squares of filo layered with green pistachio paste, nests of deep fried vermicelli, syrup-slicked dumpling balls … *Dupa blada!* You could get diabetes just looking at this stuff.

He made a random selection, then threw in: 'Is the boss around today?'

The kid paused, the serrated jaws of his steel tongs hovering over a pastry, and flashed Janusz a smile. 'I'm the boss,' he said, gesturing at a document on the wall behind him.

Yeah, thought Janusz, *and I'm the Dalai Llama.*

'That's too bad,' said Janusz. 'I might have some information that would work to his advantage.'

The guy shrugged regretfully, as though to say if Janusz refused to believe him, there was nothing he could do about it.

Janusz turned to watch the TV, which had now moved on to the situation in Syria, a conflict so savage it made the Hamas–Israel stand-off look like a game of pat-a-cake. A moment later, the velvet drapes guarding the private sanctum were parted by a tall, mournful-looking man with a moustache. After giving Janusz a tiny nod of acknowledgement, he stood beside him looking up at the TV.

'What is it you are selling, my friend?' he asked in a soft voice.

'I've just inherited a business, round the corner from here,' said Janusz, 'and I'm offering special rates to my fellow businessmen in Hoe Street.'

He turned to receive the box of pastries from the kid, passing a tenner across the counter.

'If it is a Polish supermarket,' said the man, 'I'm afraid we buy our supplies from Costco.' His gaze flicked back to the television, signalling an end to the conversation.

Janusz pocketed the change the kid gave him. 'No, nothing like that,' he said with a grin.

The man didn't move his gaze from the screen. 'What sort of business are we talking about then?'

Janusz held his silence until, finally, the man turned to look at him.

'I suppose you'd call it a fitness club,' he said. 'Used to be run by a good friend of mine. It's called Jim's Gym.'

The man blinked, once. Left a pause that was just a fraction of a second too long. 'I'm not familiar with it. But I'm afraid I am not a great exercise enthusiast.'

'Pity. But if you do change your mind, drop in any time,' said Janusz, holding out one of Jim's cards. 'We do a really competitive off-peak membership.' When the man made no move to take it, Janusz left it on the countertop.

It was almost dark when he emerged onto Hoe Street and the temperature had taken a nosedive, but after the warm sweet fug of the café he welcomed the clean chilly air. As he navigated his way through the rush-hour throng he reflected on what he'd just done. It had been a moment of impulse, an urge to heave a boulder into the lake, to see where the ripples might meet land. He had no idea whether the Turk who owned the Pasha Café would report back to his Romanian associate. Nor had he any clue to the nature of their dealings, or whether they were in some way connected to Jim's murder. All Janusz had was a powerful hunch: that the girl Varenka leaving flowers for Jim meant *something*. And he'd bet his apartment that the 'something' would lead him right back to Scarface.

Outside Walthamstow tube, he paused, and pulled out his phone: by the time he surfaced at Highbury it would be past office hours.

'*Czesc*, Wiktor! How's the weather in Swansea? ... Oh? Shame. Listen, have you had a chance to check that reg number I texted you? That's right, a black Land Rover Discovery ...'

His big face creased in a smile. '*Wspaniale*! Text me over the address, would you?'

Ten

Kershaw woke from sleep with a violent start, convinced there was an intruder in her flat. She held her breath, straining to hear what might have woken her. Then she heard the fridge door slam, hard enough to clank the bottles in the door against each other. *Ben.*

She threw herself back down and, putting a pillow over her head, waited for her heartbeat to subside. Just as she was starting to drift off, she heard the ringtone of Ben's mobile, muffled at first, like it was in his pocket, then getting louder as he retrieved it.

Fuck! Until now, having their own flats – hers at the wrong end of Canning Town, his in leafy Wanstead – meant that even though they spent most nights together, if she felt in need of a bit of space or a solid night's sleep, she could always escape. It struck her that in ten days' time, after they moved in together, that would no longer be an option.

Pulling on a dressing gown, she padded into the kitchen where she found Ben, bleary-eyed, a half-eaten kebab in front of him on the table, his mobile clamped to his ear. He looked up, and waved his free hand at the phone, his face telegraphing comic apology.

'Yeah, I know,' he said. 'Great to see you, too. Remember what I said, alright? Yeah, mate, definitely.'

She checked the clock – it was 2.30 a.m.

Ben hung up. 'Sorry, darlin',' he said, his words indistinct. 'That was Jamie, checking I got home.'

'Do you know what time it is?'

With the literalness of the very drunk, he squinted down at his phone. 'Two thirty-three,' he said.

'Did it slip your mind that I'm on earlies this week?' she asked. 'I've got to get up in three hours' time.'

'I've gotta get up early tomorrow, too,' said Ben, an aggrieved expression on his face.

Kershaw snapped. 'And if you want to get shit-faced on a school night, that's up to you! But you've got no right to come back here crashing around and waking me up!'

'Fine! If you don't want me here, I'll go!' Ben got to his feet, swaying. They stared at each other for a long and terrible moment.

'Don't be daft,' she said finally. 'I never said I wanted you to go.'

When the alarm started nagging her at half past five it was still dark outside, and properly chilly in the flat – she'd forgotten to reset the central heating timer. Kershaw hated being on early turn at this time of year – the cold she could tolerate, but the shortening of the days as autumn tumbled into winter stirred in her a near-primitive sense of dread.

She made a mug of tea and took it into the bedroom.

'Ben?' A muted groan came from under the duvet. 'You said to wake you before I leave.'

Ben pulled the duvet from his face and blinked a few times. 'Morning,' he croaked. Manoeuvring himself to a sitting position, he pulled a penitent face. 'I'm really sorry I woke you up last night. Twattish behaviour when you're on earlies, I know.'

Kershaw smiled. It was one of the things she loved about Ben: when he was in the wrong about something, he apologised quickly and with real class. It was a quality she had never really mastered.

'You're forgiven,' she said, handing him his tea.

'Are we good?' he asked, throwing her a look under his eyebrows.

'Yeah, we're good,' she told him. 'So, you never said, how was Jamie last night?'

'*Not* good.' A spasm of distress crossed his face. 'He's full of anger, still guilt-ridden for letting Hannah out of his sight – and drowning it all in beer and Jameson's. He says she's totally changed – despite the Downs she used to be a confident kid, always nagging him and Cath to let her do the things her friends were allowed to.'

Kershaw remembered that, agonisingly for Hannah's parents, it had been one of her first trips out alone to buy her favourite Cherry Coke that had thrown her into the path of Anthony Stride. 'I just can't imagine what they're going through, let alone her,' she said.

'Do you know the worst thing Jamie told me?'

She shook her head.

'Apparently, Hannah used to be a real daddy's girl, but since it happened, she hasn't let him near her. When she wakes up in the night, Cath's the only one she'll let comfort her.'

'Jesus Christ,' said Kershaw. She took a swig of his tea.

'I saw that … *bastard* in the street the other day,' said Ben.

She looked at him, alarmed by the sudden and unfamiliar ferocity in his voice. 'Really? You never mentioned it.'

'Didn't I?' he shrugged. 'When I think that he's free to stroll around while Hannah's too scared to leave the house, let alone go to school, or go out to play … It turns my stomach.'

'Do you think the Ryans need some professional help, like family therapy?'

'What they need is for that cunt Stride to step in front of a bus,' he said.

She couldn't remember hearing Ben use the c-word before: of the two of them she was by far the more prolific swearer. As her gaze scanned his face, she thought: *Maybe it's you who needs the therapist.*

'I know you got close to Jamie, to all of them,' she said, choosing her words carefully. 'I'd have done exactly the same, a case like that. But shouldn't you be thinking about handing over to family liaison by now?'

'What, now the case is dead in the water, it's time to dump the family and move on?'

Ben's voice sounded reasonable, but she saw that his top lip had thinned to a line – the only outward sign of anger he ever betrayed. *Tread carefully, my girl,* she heard her dad say.

'No, of course not. It's just … you know the score; if you go bush over a case like that' – she shrugged – 'you're gonna be less focused on catching the next evil scumbag – the one we *can* put away.'

Rocking his head back against the wall, he exhaled air through pursed lips, reminding Kershaw of the escape valve on a pressure cooker.

'I know, I know. You're right,' he said. 'I'm not even sure seeing me does him any good – I'm only gonna remind him of what happened, aren't I? I probably should back off a bit.'

'I think that's very sensible.'

He grinned, any trace of anger gone. 'Before you report for duty, Constable, stick me on a couple of bits of toast, would you?'

Kershaw managed to smile back, but an undercurrent of disquiet tugged at her still. She had no problem dealing with conflict – to her, it was part and parcel of a relationship

– but she got the feeling that Ben would sometimes simply *pretend* to roll over to avoid confrontation.

It came to her that maybe the misgivings she'd been having weren't exactly to do with Ben being too *nice*, but with his apparent difficulty in being *nasty*. She was no psycho-therapist, but she knew that would need to change when they lived together.

Eleven

The wooden shutter gave a single mournful squeak as it was pulled back from the wire grille.

'I present myself before the Holy Confession, for I have offended God,' murmured Janusz.

'Have I heard your confession before, my son?' asked the priest.

Janusz peered through the grille for a beat, before realising that Father Pietruski was winding him up.

'It's been –' a surreptitious count of his fingers '– a long time since my last confession.'

'I was thinking you must have run away with the gypsies,' said Pietruski, bone-dry. 'Or perhaps even gone home to honour your marriage vows to that wife of yours, not to mention your parental duties.'

Janusz shifted in his seat. Pietruski had been his priest for more than twenty years now, and it seemed he would always have this ability to make him feel like a wayward teenager.

'You know that Marta and I got divorced,' he said reasonably. The priest started to speak, but Janusz broke in. 'Yes, Father, I know the Church doesn't recognise divorce, but that's the reality in our hearts.'

Janusz had been just nineteen when he and Marta had wed. The ceremony took place in a fog of grief and *wodka*, just weeks after the death of his girlfriend Iza, and the marriage had proved to be a cataclysmic mistake. It had, however, produced one outcome for which he felt not a trace of regret. Years after they'd split up, during a single, ill-advised, night of reunion, they had created a child together.

Things had improved between Janusz and his ex-wife over the last year or so, and although he liked to think the thaw in their relations was due to his efforts to be a better father to their fourteen-year-old son Bobek, he half suspected that it had more to do with Marta's new boyfriend, six or seven years her junior, who she'd met at art evening classes. On the phone to Lublin, where she and the boy now lived, he had heard her laugh in a way she hadn't done for years – and was glad of her newfound happiness.

'As for Bobek, I'm a passably good father these days,' he continued. 'I flew over to see him only last month and we speak on the phone several times a week.'

'I see,' said the priest. 'So, aside from your personal decision to ignore the *unbreakable sacrament* of your marriage, are there any other sins you wish to report?'

Janusz thought for a moment. 'Coveting another man's wife,' he said, visualising Kasia, blonde hair tumbling over naked shoulders.

'Only coveting?'

'It's all I've had to make do with in the last few weeks.'

'Anything else?' Pietruski's tone had become even more acid.

Janusz hesitated. 'Murderous impulses,' he said, his voice a low rumble.

'Against whom?'

'Against the *skurwiele* who killed a friend of mine, Jim Fulford.'

That made Father Pietruski pause and squint through the grille. 'What a dreadful thing. I will pray for you – and your friend, God rest his soul.'

Both men crossed themselves. 'But you must leave it to the authorities to pursue the wrongdoers,' said the priest. 'You are not God: it is not given to you to look into a man's soul, to decide how to punish the guilty.'

Janusz's grunt was non-committal.

'We've spoken before about this anger of yours, my son. And how in the end these negative emotions can hurt only yourself.'

'Yes, Father,' said Janusz. But he was irritated by his confessor's recent tendency to couch things this way. He came here for the implacable wisdom of a 2000-year-old Church, not a serving of New Age psychobabble.

'Is that everything?' asked Pietruski.

Janusz opened his mouth, on the verge of admitting his plans to get inside Scarface's apartment later that day, before remembering that it wasn't the done thing to confess sins in advance. A wise man had once said: *Better to beg for forgiveness than ask for permission.*

'Yes, Father, that's it.'

Janusz lingered in St Stanislaus longer than was strictly necessary even to perform the elaborate menu of penances Father Pietruski had seen fit to give him. Wrapped in its cavernous quiet amid the smell of snuffed candles and incense, he allowed himself a few moments to grieve for Jim, but resisted the urge to pray for him. That might undermine his resolve. *Vengeance first, prayers later,* he told himself.

Finding out Barbu Romescu's address from Wiktor, his DVLA contact, had been a hundred quid well spent, but the next step – investigating his possible connection to Jim's murder – would be harder to pull off. Janusz had spent several hours on his laptop and printer the previous night in preparation for the afternoon's work, which he'd planned to coincide with the Romanian's second weekly meeting at the Turkish shisha café.

By the time he walked into Romescu's apartment block, twin needles of blue glass overlooking the old Millwall dock, not far from Canary Wharf, he'd completely immersed himself in his cover story.

Reaching inside his overalls, he pulled out a piece of paper and handed it to the skinny guy on reception, who, in a couple of years' time, might be old enough to start shaving.

'Tower Management. Leaking air-conditioning unit in apartment 117,' he said. How had he ever managed to do his job in the days before the internet, he wondered. Back then, even discovering the name of the management company would have taken hours of phone bashing, and as for photoshopping its logo into a fictional work docket? The idea would have been the stuff of science fiction.

'I'm really sorry.' The guy handed the document back to him with an uncertain shrug.

Don't tell me they've changed companies or something, thought Janusz.

'The concierge is off sick,' he went on. 'I'm just a temp from the agency, filling in.'

Alleluja!

Scowling, Janusz looked at his watch. 'Well, I've got four more jobs after this one so I haven't got time to muck around.'

'I'll see if the residents are at home.' The kid punched out a number on the phone.

With every passing second that the phone went unanswered, Janusz allowed himself to relax a little. He made a production of shifting his half-empty toolbox from one hand to the other, as though it weighed a ton.

Finally, the kid hung up. 'They're not in,' he admitted, gazing up at Janusz like a baby rabbit encountering a bear.

'Look, here's the drill,' sighed Janusz. 'You take me up to 117 and let me in, I do the job, you sign the docket afterwards to say it's done.'

The kid was already shaking his head. 'I can't. The agency told me I mustn't leave reception under any circumstances.'

Janusz checked his watch again and raised an eyebrow. 'Well, I'll leave you to explain that to the people in 117.' He started to walk away. 'Tell them to phone the office to rebook an engineer.'

He hadn't even reached the door when the kid called him back. 'What about if I give you the master key and you go up on your own?'

Janusz felt a pang of guilt at the kid's anxious expression. 'I don't know … I'd like to help you out, but strictly speaking, it's against company regulations.'

'Who would know, if neither of us says anything?'

Janusz took a moment to examine the toe of his workboot. 'Go on then,' he said, finally. 'But keep it to yourself, or we can both kiss goodbye to our jobs.'

Barbu Romescu's apartment was located on the 11th floor and his front door, like all the rest, was fitted with a state-of-the-art electronic lock. Janusz slipped the master card into the slot. A green light winked at him. As he pushed the door open, he grinned to himself. The first rule of security: humans were always the weakest link.

When he saw the apartment's open plan living area, Janusz gave a low whistle. Whatever the nature of Romescu's mysterious 'business interests', they apparently paid very handsome returns. Light coming through the floor-to-ceiling plate glass windows flooded the enormous room, bouncing off the highly polished wooden floor, some sort of golden-coloured hardwood. To his right stood a gleaming, minimalist kitchen.

He looked it over with an ex-builder's eye, noting the way in which the designer, not satisfied with hiding every appliance from view, had even eliminated door handles from the black acrylic units.

Testing how they worked – the merest touch on the surface caused it to swing open silently – Janusz chanced upon the fridge. He surveyed its contents with an expression of mystified disgust. Having worked alongside Romanians on building sites he knew they could put away pork, dumplings and a good feed of beer with as much gusto as any God-fearing Pole, yet all Romescu had in his fridge was vegan yoghurt, a tray of alfalfa sprouts, a carton of egg white and some goji juice.

Padding around the living area, Janusz had to admit that it wasn't half bad for a dodgy Romanian 'businessman'. The furniture looked expensive yet elegant, and the artworks on the walls were the kind you might find in an upmarket yoga studio. The largest, at around three metres across, was a rather good hyperrealist painting of a butterfly in flight, sunlight making its pale blue wings translucent.

A staircase with wooden treads that seemed to hang in mid-air took Janusz to an upper level, where a corridor lined with more works of art led to the master bedroom, which was almost as big as the living area. He raised an eyebrow at the twin beds before checking out the en-suite bathroom. To one side of the sink stood an electric razor and a black bottle of aftershave; to the other, half a dozen bottles of the lotions and potions that women set such store by. Did they belong to Varenka? And whether they belonged to her, or some other girl, where did she keep her clothes? Back in the bedroom, Janusz turned his attention to the room's longest wall, which looked to be panelled in a satin-smooth dark wood. But when he touched one of the panels, close by a seam, it opened smoothly, no doubt operated by the same hidden mechanism used in the kitchen. Inside he found a solid-looking safe with an old-style rotary dial – Romescu clearly preferred the certainty of old technology to the electronic versions on sale. Janusz rapped it with his knuckles: from the dull sound the steel made he calculated it to be at least eight mil thick. He knew of only two things that could break that open – a cutting torch, or a half-centimetre of Semtex.

Moving to a floor-to-ceiling panel at the end of the wall, he found it swung open at his touch to reveal some sort of darkened room.

Open Sesame! he muttered, stepping into the gloom. A light sprung to life, revealing a dressing room: stood to his left, a long rail in a recess packed with outfits, many shrouded in dry cleaner's plastic; to his right, a wall full of small, purpose-built drawers, each holding a pair of shoes. He flipped through the clothes on the rail: at one end, expensive looking suits and jackets – Romescu appeared to favour Hugo Boss, whoever he was – and at the other, a whole bunch of ladies' outfits. They were high-end but understated – the kind of thing Varenka had been wearing when he first saw her. At the room's far end stood a worktable with a fancy-looking sewing machine. He found it amusing, touching even, that a girl with such expensive clothes should prefer to do her own alterations.

Under the worktable stood a compact suitcase, its dimensions designed to meet the hold baggage restrictions that budget airlines enforced with Stalinist zeal. Janusz pulled it out and unzipped it. Empty. Turning it over he found the remains of one of those green and white sticky labels used to tell baggage handlers the destination airport. It bore the letters PCK, which struck him as vaguely familiar. As he replaced the suitcase under the worktable, he heard something – and froze. The soft clunk of the apartment's front door closing.

74

Kurwa mac! Was it Romescu, home early from his Walthamstow meeting? He had no illusions about how the Romanian would treat an intruder – whatever macrobiotic fucking diet he was on. There was no time to close the door, even if he could work out how to operate the mechanism from the inside. Moving as swiftly and smoothly as his bulky frame would allow, he slipped between a long black coat and a floor-length red dress, praying that they were long enough to hide his feet and legs. There was barely enough room for him at the rear of the recess: even with his back pressed right against the wall he could feel the sinister kiss of the laundry plastic against his face.

Keeping his breathing quiet and shallow, Janusz closed his eyes and focused every circuit of his brain on interpreting any sound coming from the living area. Relieved not to hear voices, he made out only a faint 'tap tap' sound. *High heels!* The sound of a lone woman crossing a wooden floor. But even as he surfed the wave of relief, the tapping grew closer, before disappearing altogether. *She must have reached the carpet of the bedroom.* Then, from only metres away, he heard her murmur something, a note of perplexity in her voice: she'd seen the open door to the dressing room. An unbearable pause, followed by a tiny current of air across his sweat-slicked forehead as she came in. He couldn't see anything, but he could smell her scent, a fresh lemony fragrance that summoned a memory of Varenka's drily humorous gaze.

He heard her tut softly to herself and then the sound of drawers opening and closing. The laundry plastic had adhered itself to his upper lip, filling him with an almost unbearable urge to pull it away. After what seemed like an age, he sensed her leaving the dressing room. He held his breath. The tap-tap of her heels signalled her reaching the living room, the sound receding, and then came the discreet clunk of the front door closing. He tore the hateful plastic from his face and took a couple of giant gulps of air. Parting the hanging clothes he saw a pair of shoes on the floor, the heel of one snapped in half. She'd obviously had a mishap and come back to change her shoes.

Turning sideways, he tried to slide out between the hanging clothes, but the red dress slithered free of its hanger and cascaded to the floor. He crouched, gathering up the slippery fabric in one fist, and was just getting to his feet when his gaze snagged on something. The wardrobe recess was lined with low-profile skirting board. Nothing unusual about that, except that close to the corner, a section maybe twenty centimetres long appeared to have been inserted as an afterthought. It was the kind of thing you might see in a cowboy conversion, but not in an upscale Docklands apartment.

Pulling out his penknife, he slipped the blade into one end of the suspicious section. It came out with ease. Behind it, set snugly in a space that had been roughly hacked out of the plaster, was a shallow, rectangular tin box. Elated at his find, Janusz took it into the bedroom, and sat on the bed to examine it properly. It was a child's pencil case, decorated with sugary illustrations of pink horses with flowing white manes and huge eyelashes, the kind of thing that little girls liked – until they moved on to boy bands. Inside, he found a few papers tied with a red velvet ribbon, a bundle of cash – ten bank-fresh hundred-dollar bills – and a child-sized ring, two intertwined hearts on a cheap-looking band of chrome, no doubt a childhood memento.

Untying the ribbon, he found a Ukrainian driving licence in the name of Varenka Kalina. He knew enough Ukrainian to glean that she had lived in Kharkov, the country's second largest city, and from her surname it was clear she belonged to the country's Polish-Catholic minority. From her date of birth she must be twenty-six now, but the Varenka captured in the photo was much younger and far less polished, wearing inexpertly applied eyeshadow and spidery fake lashes, her face framed with bottle-blonde hair. The licence recorded her occupation, no doubt euphemistically, as 'exotic dancer'.

Janusz remembered reading that Kharkov had been an important command centre for the Soviet military, which meant that its inhabitants had suffered worse than most in the dramatic economic meltdown that followed the collapse of communism. Normal society evaporated: there were frequent power cuts, the streets were piled head-high with rubbish, and thousands ended up destitute and homeless, *wodka* providing the only reliable currency – and the only way to dull the hunger and misery.

This was the world that Varenka had grown up in, Janusz realised, and if she came from a family without money or connections, prostitution would have been her only career option. He gazed at her photo: she'd been barely seventeen when it was taken and the world-weary expression she was aiming for couldn't quite conceal the spark of youthful hope in her eyes.

Another photograph, creased and faded by time, suggested happier days. The camera had captured two children as they peered into a rock pool, a broad white Baltic beach in the background. The older child, a sweet-faced boy aged eight or nine was using a stick to point something out to a fair-haired toddler with eyes like a china doll. The little girl had one chubby hand on her brother's forearm to steady herself, and a look of uncomplicated wonder on her face: an expression that Janusz could remember seeing on his son Bobek's face at the same age. The bond between the two children was as clear as the sun. So if the little girl was Varenka, as seemed likely, then where was her brother – and why had he not looked after his little sister, found some way to save her from becoming a whore?

The last item was a mystery: a bright pink book of matches bearing the name 'бар метелик'. 'бар' meant bar – and Varenka had clearly kept the matchbook for what was scrawled on the inside cover: '*GRA – Mr Churchill, London W1*'. He puzzled over it for a few seconds but could make no sense either of the acronym, or the name and hopelessly inadequate address. Why had she preserved this bar room scribble?

He started putting Varenka's stuff back in the tin, taking care to leave it the way he'd found it. The hidden driving licence, the thousand dollars and childhood snap – they felt like an escape pack, or a survival kit: the basics Varenka might need should she decide to leave Romescu. That wouldn't be as easy as it sounded. Not only did she live under the threat of violence, but since Ukraine wasn't in the EU, she was almost certainly here illegally. Janusz's suspicions were beginning to take shape: was Romescu involved in trafficking girls from the former Soviet Union? Was this the business he and his Turkish chum met to discuss? It certainly sounded feasible, but one big unanswered question remained: what in God's name could connect Jim to such a *straszny* business?

Checking his watch, Janusz decided he should probably make tracks – the last thing he needed was for the jittery kid on reception to lose his bottle and call the agency to report the engineer in room 117. At the door he paused, and heading back to the kitchen area, opened the fridge door and used his phone to photograph its contents. Without documentary evidence, Oskar would never believe him.

Twelve

While Janusz was rooting around in Romescu's apartment, just a couple of hundred yards away, in the Canary Wharf Tower, DC Kershaw was still interviewing what felt like a never-ending list of security guards.

She'd started the day full of optimism, convinced that even if the exercise failed to deliver the identity of her roof jumper, she'd at least be able to solve one mystery: how he got onto the roof without setting off the alarm in the first place. After drawing a blank with the last of the guards who'd been on duty that morning, she'd moved on to the night shift, pursuing her thesis that the guy might have gained access to the outside long before he jumped.

Two hours later, as the door closed on the last of them, she had to admit defeat. If any of the nine guys she interviewed – all of them solid, middle-aged types, and all but two of them ex-cops or ex-military – knew anything about the alarm being disabled at any stage then they were premier league liars. All she'd got out of three hours' worth of interviews was a jumpy caffeine high and a shitstorm of paperwork to type up when she got back to the nick.

As she drove north, she cursed her obsession with following things through. If she'd left it to the local nick to handle the case she could have spent the day working the Jim Fulford murder, doing real detective work. Reaching the outskirts of Walthamstow, she spotted a sign for the William Morris Gallery and remembered she still hadn't double-checked Janusz Kiszka's alibi. Minutes later, she was driving into the half-moon shaped driveway, the gravel growling under her tyres.

The gallery was located in Morris's old family home: a substantial Victorian mansion that put the scene of Kershaw's upbringing – a Canning Town council flat – to shame. At reception, she showed her warrant card to a lady whom she instantly categorised as a member of Walthamstow's recently arrived middle class, on account of her posh vowels and Boden-ish appliquéd top. Half an hour later, she was feeling a bit shamefaced at her narky assessment: Caroline couldn't have been more helpful, introducing her to every member of staff who'd been on duty at the time of the murder. Along the way she'd proved herself a mine of information about the various paintings, fabric designs and stained-glass panels that made up the great man's legacy. Kershaw made all the right noises, but she couldn't really see why he was such a big deal. It all looked a bit ... well, Laura Ashley, to her.

More to the point, after half an hour of questioning, the mugshot of Janusz Kiszka had drawn not a glimmer of recognition from any of the staff who'd been working there at the time of his claimed visit.

As she and Caroline descended the ornate staircase – a typical example of Arts and Crafts architecture, apparently – Kershaw wondered if she'd got it wrong. Whether, in fact, Kiszka *was* capable of premeditated murder, after all. Just because he'd turned out to be, more or less, one of the good guys the last time their paths had crossed, that didn't mean he was innocent this time around. Good and evil, black and white, everything nice and neat – of course she was inclined to see things that way: she was a cop. But she remembered Streaky telling her once how that kind of thinking could be a detective's worst enemy.

At the foot of the stairs, Kershaw thanked Caroline for her help. On the point of leaving, she decided she just had time to nip back to the gallery's café for a sneaky cuppa: it would give her a chance to tidy her notes up.

She sat in the glass conservatory overlooking the Morris family's huge landscaped garden, the bare branches of the trees stark against the pale winter sky, watching an old man in a waxed jacket raking dead leaves from the lawn. As she watched, he reached the footpath bordering the grass right beneath her, where he appeared to notice something on the ground. Bending down with some difficulty, he produced a plastic bag and started picking things up, the clockwork jerkiness of his movements betraying extreme irritation.

Kershaw bolted the rest of her tea, and dashing out through the garden door, flew down the steps.

'Excuse me, sir.' Up close, the gardener was an ancient guy with a brown, seamed face that suggested a lifetime working outdoors. 'Can I ask if you were working here on Monday?'

'Who's asking?' He stuck his chin out.

'I'm DC Kershaw, Walthamstow Murder Squad.' She wondered if she'd ever get over the thrill of saying that. 'I'm trying to find out if anyone saw this man here on that day.'

The guy put both hands on his thighs to lever himself up and squinted at Kiszka's mugshot. 'I couldn't tell you, I'm afraid my reading glasses are at home,' he said.

Bollocks.

'Because I saw you picking up cigarette butts, and this guy practically chain smokes cigars, so I thought …' She tailed off, realising how daft it sounded.

'You'd be surprised how many people there are who can't go half an hour without sucking on a nicotine tit,' said the old man. He was surprisingly well spoken, but she detected a bit of country burr running underneath. 'They always stand here, by the staircase where they think they can't be seen.' He shot her a cunning look. 'I catch quite a few of them though.'

'Good for you,' she said. 'So, this man I'm talking about is a big guy, dark hair, and he wears a longish coat, kind of military looking.'

The old gardener stared up at the sky for several seconds.

'Best pilots I ever saw!' he said suddenly.

What the fuck? Was the guy having a mini-stroke or something?

He sketched an arabesque in the air with one wrinkled hand. 'They'd already had practice fighting the Hun, you see.'

'I don't mean to be rude,' said Kershaw. 'But I haven't got the foggiest what you're talking about.'

'Polish fighter pilots, in the Battle of Britain. Don't they teach young people about the war these days?'

Her brain whirred and clicked. 'You did see him! But … how did you know he was Polish?'

'Because when I told him he couldn't drop his cigar butt here, he said *Koorr-vah Mahsch.*' He rolled the Polish round his mouth like a fine whiskey. 'Mother of a whore,' he added helpfully.

'Yeah, that sounds like him,' said Kershaw suppressing a grin.

'So I swore back at him in Polish.' He chuckled. 'To be fair, he was *very* apologetic, said he hadn't meant to curse, it had just slipped out.'

'What time do you finish?' asked Kershaw.

The old man looked at his watch. 'In about a quarter of an hour,' he said. 'Today's my half day – why do you ask?'

'Because I'd like to give you a lift home so you can look at this photo with your reading glasses on.'

'No need for a lift,' he said, pointing across the gardens to a row of terraced houses. 'I only live over there.'

Half an hour later, Edward Cotter had positively identified Janusz Kiszka and agreed to sign a statement confirming that their little encounter had taken place at 5.40 p.m., just before the end of his shift. Since that was minutes after James Fulford had been stabbed, a good mile from the museum, Kershaw reckoned that Kiszka had just got himself a concrete alibi.

Over a cup of tea, Edward told her that as a boy he had lived in a village in Sussex next to Chailey airfield, where a Polish fighter squadron had been based during the war. Gripped by the thrilling spectacle of their dogfights with Messerschmitts overhead, Edward and his chums would hang around outside the chain-link fence surrounding the airfield, grabbing every opportunity to chat to their heroes. His most treasured possession, framed and hung above his mantel-piece, was a twenty zloty note signed by half a dozen pilots from the squadron.

Seeing the Polish currency depressed Kershaw, reminding her of the unfinished business down at Canary Wharf. But right now, getting back to the nick and updating the Sarge on the latest development on Kiszka's alibi took priority.

Streaky was just finishing up a late lunch when she arrived in the office – a sausage roll by the look of the crumbs clinging to his chin and sprinkled over his beer gut. Kershaw delivered the news in as neutral a tone as possible: it was always a bit of a double-edged sword, eliminating a suspect.

'Of course, even if he wasn't actually at the scene, it's still possible he was behind the murder,' said Kershaw.

Streaky brushed the debris from his shirtfront into a cupped hand. 'Use your noddle, Detective,' he said. 'If Kiszka arranged a hit on his chum, he would have made damn sure he was miles away when it was going off, preferably having a nice cup of tea with that priest of his – what was his name? *Pietruski*.' After throwing the crumbs into his mouth, he dusted off his palms.

Kershaw marvelled at his powers of recall: it was years since Kiszka had been under investigation, but then the Sarge was famous for his ability to summon up the tiniest details from long-dead cases.

'Anyway,' he went on. 'I just put down the phone to his brief. He was calling to tell me that Kiszka's signed a document making over ownership of the gym and its assets to Marika Fulford, which rather puts the mockers on his supposed motive for the murder.'

'I'd love to have a crack at interviewing the wife, Sarge,' said Kershaw. 'Now the dust has settled, she might have remembered something that could give us a lead?'

Streaky folded his arms across his belly and gazed enquiringly at Kershaw. 'I'm confused, Detective. Haven't you got an anonymous suicide to identify at one of London's most famous high-rise landmarks?'

'I wanted to talk to you about that Sarge. I spent the whole day interviewing the security team down there and I'm drawing a total blank ...'

Raising a finger to silence her, Streaky screwed up his eyes. 'Listen. Can you hear that?'

'Sarge?'

'I thought I heard the distant strains of a violin. Spare me the sob story, Kershaw. The quicker you deliver a name for your roof diving chum, the sooner you can start doing the job I employed you for.'

'Right, Sarge.'

As Kershaw walked away, Streaky started whistling a tune. It took a couple of minutes before she realised what it was: the old Weather Girls song 'It's Raining Men'.

When she got back to her desk, Sophie Edgerton passed over a post-it note. 'The pathologist who did the PM on your Canary Wharf suicide called. He said to call him back on his mobile.'

Kershaw tapped out Nathan King's number with a distinct lack of enthusiasm. 'Hi, Dr King? It's DC Natalie Kershaw. Investigating officer on the Canary Wharf Tower fatality.'

As King gave Kershaw the lowdown, Sophie watched her colleague's expression travel through a series of emotions: from neutral professionalism, through bewilderment, culminating in outright incredulity. Finally, she spoke.

'You're fucking kidding!'

Thirteen

Janusz stood in the living room of his mansion flat looking out over Highbury Fields – the grass still silvered here and there by last night's frost – and savoured the smell of the *bigos* cooking in the kitchen. He didn't usually eat much at lunchtime, but he had some good-looking *zywiecka* he was keen to try and the sausage, pork rib, and sauerkraut stew would be good insulation against the unseasonably cold weather. Perhaps he also felt the need of comfort food to fortify him for the afternoon's sombre task: visiting a stone-mason to help Marika pick out a headstone for Jim.

It looked as though England was in for a series of proper winters, not as bitter as the ones he remembered from Poland, but enough to knock over the puny transport systems on a regular basis. Back home, childhood winters had meant blissful weeks of igloo building and skating on frozen rivers – he recalled his mate Osip losing the top of his ear to frost-bite one year. His thoughts drifted to Bobek: it would be good to have him over to stay again soon. In a couple of years he'd be more interested in girls and motorbikes than in his boring old man. *Christmas*, he decided. He'd ask Marta if the boy could spend a few days of his school holiday in London.

His entry phone buzzed. It was Oskar.

'I've been trying to reach you on your phone *and* email all morning, Janek,' he complained before he'd even got through the door.

'That fancy phone you made me buy ran out of juice again. And I haven't turned the laptop on yet.'

Oskar tutted. 'You need to stay connected, *kolego*, especially in your line of work.' He sniffed the air. '*Bigos*?'

'*Tak.*'

'Good. I haven't had lunch yet.'

'What was so urgent, anyway?'

'The Romanian!' said Oskar, beaming. 'He took the bait we laid for him!' He did a little jig of triumph, short legs pumping.

'The story you spun Marek about having a rich mate with money to invest?'

'Yeah! I told him you're a businessman who just inherited a pile of cash, and also dropped your fancy apartment in Highbury Fields into the conversation.' Going over to the bay window, Oskar looked out, shaking his head. 'You know, Janek, if you sold this place and moved further east, you could probably pocket half a million.'

It was a well-worn argument: Janusz had been lucky enough to buy the apartment for a bargain price from his landlord back in the eighties, and according to Oskar, any sane person would have cashed it in for a fat profit long ago.

'Put another record on, Oskar. What about the Romanian?'

'So Marek phoned me this morning and said the guy would like to invite you to a party he's throwing tonight for his investors.'

'You played it cool, like I told you?' asked Janusz.

'Of course!' said Oskar with a casual shrug. 'I said that you didn't really like parties – unless you counted the gay orgies.' He punched Janusz's shoulder. 'Only kidding! I told him you might be interested.'

'Where is this party, then?'

'If I give Marek the thumbs-up, someone will text you the details. So it might help if you worked out how to charge your phone, sisterfucker.' Oskar threw himself down on the sofa and beamed up at Janusz, transparently pleased with himself. 'I told you we'd make a good team. When will the *bigos* be ready?'

The unscheduled invite left Janusz with two problems. First, there was his promise to go and look at headstones with Marika. Second, he didn't have the first idea what a 'wealthy investor' might wear to a drinks party.

When he called Marika's place, it was her sister Basia who picked up the phone.

'*Czesc*, Basia. Listen, something's come up which means I won't be able to go to the masons with Marika this afternoon.'

'Oh, that's a shame,' she said. 'I know Marika was looking forward to seeing you.'

He felt a bolt of white-hot guilt in his guts.

'Is she around?' he asked. 'Maybe we can rearrange it for tomorrow.'

'She is sleeping now, I don't like to wake her,' said Basia. 'Shall I give her a message later?'

Janusz hesitated: he didn't want her to think he was cancelling for no good reason.

'Yes. Tell her it means the world to me, helping her to choose Jim's memorial stone ...' his throat closed up and he had to get a grip on himself before continuing. 'But there's something I need to do that can't be put off. It might even help me find Jim's killers.'

There was a shocked silence at the other end of the line. 'Really? You have found some evidence?'

'I really can't say,' he said. 'Just tell her that, will you?'

He heard Basia take a shaky breath. *'Tak.'* It was clear that she, too, was struggling with Jim's death.

Deciding what he should wear to fit the part he had to play at tonight's party was easier to fix: he phoned Kasia. She was glad of the chance to make up for standing him up the other night, and made him write down the outfit while he was still on the phone. Black jeans, a black crewneck cashmere sweater she'd bought for his birthday, and a black textured wool jacket she approved of that he'd had for years. After hanging up, he drew a sigh of relief: at least she didn't say he had to wear a suit.

The drinks party was taking place a stone's throw from Romescu's apartment, in another of the Millharbour high-rises. At reception, a beautiful black girl checked his name against the invite list and gave him a security pass that operated a private lift going to the 48th floor. The lift ascended at what he sensed was an incredible speed, although it made only the faintest of hums, stopping when it reached the highest level.

When the lift doors opened, a smartly dressed young guy with an Eastern European accent – who presumably worked for the Romanian – greeted him by name, which for tonight was Lukas Rozak. Janusz was ushered into a swanky bar area, where a crowd of thirty or forty men, mostly middle-aged, chatted in small groups.

Passing one such cluster, he saw at its heart a gorgeous girl wearing a revealing deep-pink evening gown. Her smile seemed genuine enough but when her gaze flickered across him he recognised the glazed look of a working girl. In their drab-coloured suits, the men resembled a swarm of locusts mobbing a flowering cherry.

Glancing around, Janusz saw that every group had been assigned its own hot girl, every one of them beautifully dressed and most of them toting the kind of breasts that kept silicon manufacturers in business.

At the heart of the throng, a close-cropped bullet head above a wide muscular back came into view.

'Mr Romescu?' said the flunky. 'May I introduce Mr Lukas Rozak?'

Romescu turned to shake Janusz's hand. 'A very great pleasure to meet you, Lukas – if I can call you that?' Without pausing to hear Janusz's reply, he went on: 'And of course you must call me Barbu.' He clapped Janusz on the shoulder – a gesture that, although appearing friendly enough, managed to telegraph who was in charge of this encounter. 'So you are the famous friend of Marek, yes?'

'A friend of a friend, actually.' Janusz smiled back, resisting the impulse to shake off Romescu's hand. 'But I have heard Marek is very impressed with the returns you're making for him.'

Romescu sketched a modest wave. 'There are lots of excellent business opportunities in the East, if you know where to find them.' He cocked his head on one side. 'I am guessing, Lukas, that you were brought up in Poland?'

'Yes, in Gdansk. I came here in the eighties.'

'In Romania we envied you Poles and your freedom to travel. Our "Little Father" liked to keep his people close.' A spasm of hatred twisted Romescu's face as he named Romania's Communist despot, Nikolai Ceausescu. 'I managed to get out, but I wouldn't have risked it if I'd had any family still alive.'

'There would have been reprisals?'

The Romanian nodded. 'My country is famous for two of its heads of state. But at least Vlad the Impaler didn't delude himself that he had the people's interests at heart.'

The exchange appeared to have exhausted Romescu's supply of emotion, for the folds of his face settled back into what Janusz deduced to be its usual cold expression. Only his eyes, which were a fierce yet chilly blue, seemed alive: they seemed never to rest, darting over Janusz's face, or over his shoulder – seeking out the next, potentially more profitable, encounter.

'Let's get you a drink,' he said, waving over one of the waiters doing the rounds of the crowd. Janusz asked for tonic water – he'd have killed for a beer but he couldn't risk it. If he should slip up and Romescu smelt a rat, he had a feeling it could seriously damage his health. He noticed that the Romanian ordered a soft drink, too, and remembered the unappetising contents of his fridge. The guy was a few years older than Janusz, late forties, maybe fifty, but the wide shoulders spoke of a regular workout regime and there was no hint of paunch under the soft material of his shirt.

'It's hard work staying in shape, when you get past forty,' sighed Janusz patting his stomach. 'I barely drink alcohol any more' – a vision of his beer and *bigos* lunch flashed before him – 'and I've given up red meat and processed carbs altogether. But it's a price I'm happy to pay, if it keeps me alive till I'm a hundred.'

'I am glad to hear you say it,' said Romescu, his rapacious gaze taking an inventory of Janusz's face. 'People don't understand that the body is a gift, something to be cherished and nurtured. And it can be snatched away from you –' he snapped his fingers, '– like that.'

Sensing he'd chanced upon some deeply held belief, Janusz let his gaze linger on the strange scar down the side of the older man's face, which he'd so far avoided looking at. 'Please tell me if it's none of my business, Barbu,' he said. 'But perhaps you speak from personal experience?'

Romescu gazed at him for a long moment, making Janusz wonder if he'd gone too far. Then he returned his hand to his shoulder. 'It's a long story, Lukas, and right now I've got to do my little speech, but maybe I'll bore you with it later on.'

As Romescu made his way to a raised area beside the bar, Janusz slipped to the very back of the crowd. The underling who had shown him in chimed softly on a glass with a spoon. 'The founder and chief executive of Triangle Investments, Barbu Romescu, asks his guests for a few moments of their time.'

'Gentlemen, ladies,' he began, his intent gaze raking the faces before him. 'I'm not a fan of long speeches, but I want to thank you all for coming this evening and to say just a few words about Triangle. Some of you became investors when I started the company six months ago, and I hope you approve of the returns we have delivered so far.' There was an approving murmur from parts of the crowd and one guy, clearly already well-oiled, raised his glass and cried *'Na zdrowie!'*, causing a ripple of laughter.

'What a coincidence, seeing you here.' A low-pitched voice speaking Polish in Janusz's ear sent a tingle up his neck. *Varenka.*

He turned and looked into her eyes, which held a look of satirical enquiry.

'Hello,' he said. 'I was rather hoping I'd run into you.' It was true, he realised, even if, having seen his real name on his business card, there was a risk she might betray him to Romescu.

She arched an eyebrow. 'Really? I thought you were here to make a million euros.'

Her dark blonde hair was captured in a loose knot to one side of her head tonight, Janusz noticed. 'Well, a million euros is always nice.' He tipped his head, never

92

taking his eyes off hers. 'Although, man cannot live by bread alone.'

'... but by every word that issues from the mouth of God?' she said, completing the quotation.

Janusz noted her amused yet deadpan expression. Was she saying she might be a whore, but she still knew her Bible?

Falling silent, they turned to watch Romescu speak.

'... from Poland all the way to the Balkans, we're getting in at the ground floor, buying into the rapid growth of the post-Soviet economies with an investment portfolio that includes commercial property, leisure and fitness, agriculture ...'

Yeah ... and trading women like livestock, thought Janusz.

He studied Varenka out of the corner of his eye. She stood with one hand to her throat, above a small, neat bust. Her expression was ambiguous, seeming to combine the vigilance of a caged wild animal watching its captor, with a sort of wary tolerance – affection, even. In profile, a tiny kink was visible just below the bridge of her nose – the result of a childhood accident? Or a blow from Romescu's fist? Whatever the cause, it added character to her otherwise flawless face.

'Do you think you will you invest?' she asked, under her breath.

'Would you advise me to?'

She held her bottom lip between her teeth momentarily, appearing to give it serious thought. 'Yes. Why not? Barbu always makes money, whatever business he goes into.'

'And what about you? Do you play a role in his business?'

'I would like to say that was true.' In her look he glimpsed the ghost of that youthful optimism which had shone out of her driving licence mugshot. 'I studied economics in night school at Kiev University – for a while.'

'I'm impressed. Why did you give it up?'

'Maybe I couldn't decide whether I was a Friedmanite or a Keynesian,' she joked. Holding her long hands out in front of her, she studied them dispassionately for a moment before going on. 'Truthfully? I could never really afford it. There were no government grants for students and I had ... family responsibilities. I had to work.'

Janusz was too much of a gentleman to press her on the form that work took.

'And you?' she asked. 'No doubt you went to university?'

'Yes, in Krakow.'

'Jagiellonski?' Her eyes widened.

He nodded. 'I read physics and chemistry. But I dropped out without finishing my degree.' He lifted one shoulder. 'It was the eighties, and I decided my duty lay out on the streets with my fellow Poles fighting the Commies.' His tone was self-deprecating, half-mocking the idealism of youth.

'You were a fool!' The vehemence of her words took him aback, but the next moment she touched his forearm in a gesture of apology. 'Please excuse my bad manners. But to throw away such an opportunity, to me that is like ... squandering water in the desert.'

Janusz hesitated, feeling the urge to fight his corner, to explain to her how his country's fight for freedom had come above all else – before deciding against it. She was too young truly to understand how communism had blighted lives, extinguished hope. Anyway, he was here to investigate Romescu's activities, not to debate political philosophy with a twenty-six-year-old.

'Would you like the opportunity to become more involved in Barbu's business?' he asked, playing the innocent, trying to get a handle on their relationship.

She sent him a look of mild reproach. 'I don't think that's very likely. I am here as his "plus one", and to improve the scenery for his guests – not for my proficiency in economics.' This was said in her usual tone of dry amusement and without apparent resentment. 'So far, I've spoken to two dentists, two Polish supermarket magnates, and a man who believes in UFOs. What about you? What do you do?'

'Oh, nothing exciting. Import and export, mostly,' he said. 'I'm here because I have money to invest from the sale of my mother's estate in Krakow and those sharks at the bank are only paying a couple of per cent.'

She turned to him, eyebrows arched in distress. 'I'm so sorry! Has your mama passed?'

'Yes, but it was a long time ago.'

'It doesn't matter how long ago,' Varenka's husky voice became passionate. 'Losing someone you love, it stays with you, here' – she pressed a fist to her breastbone – 'forever.'

The look on her face spoke of an inconsolable grief. *Had she been carer to a parent who'd become sick and later died?* Janusz wondered. Was that why she'd had to give up her studies? Or perhaps it was the older brother from the seaside photo who had died young? Whoever she had lost, it was apparent that she had never got over it. Sensing that he'd begun to win her confidence, Janusz was calculating how to press home his advantage when he heard the sound of clapping. Romescu had finished his speech.

Spreading his arms to acknowledge the applause, his searchlight gaze swept the room.

Janusz sensed Varenka freeze beside him and without turning her head she murmured, 'I have to go.' Before he could even reply, her half-naked back was gliding away from him through the crowd. Had Romescu registered the two of them? If so, he'd given no sign of it.

It was an hour or more before Romescu came looking for Janusz. He was outside, leaning on the parapet of the viewing deck, nursing his third tonic water of the evening and trying to pretend it was a cold Tyskie.

'Are you having a good evening, Lukas?' asked the Romanian.

'Most enjoyable,' said Janusz. 'And that's quite a view.'

They looked out over the rectilinear expanse of the old Millwall Dock far below, a once-mighty hub of world commerce trading timber and grain, its black waters empty now, reflecting the constellation of lights in the office and apartment blocks fringing its shores. Beyond it, the loop of Thames that curled around the Millennium Dome flowed steadily east, silver blue in the deepening winter dusk.

'I have an apartment not far from here,' said Romescu, pointing out the finger of glass where Janusz had done a little breaking and entering only yesterday.

He whistled appreciatively. 'Nice location. Did you buy it recently?'

'Two or three years back. Cost me a couple of million.'

Janusz always liked the bracing honesty with which immigrants talked about money: had Romescu been an Englishman he'd still have managed to get across what he paid for his place, but the information would have been conveyed with heavy hints and hedged about with false modesty.

Romescu gestured down at the dock. 'Maybe I'm sentimental, but I like to think I'm carrying on the tradition of international trade. Buying and selling real things, not spread betting against numbers on a computer screen.'

Janusz nodded. 'I couldn't agree more.' He swirled the ice in his tonic. 'So Barbu, I've got a pile of euros earning peanuts in a Polish bank account, which I *could* invest in a fancy Docklands apartment or two ...' As Romescu's gaze flickered towards him, he sensed his promotion up the league table of potential investors. 'On the other hand, who knows what will happen to the financial sector once the politicians stop handing the banks sackfuls of taxpayers' money. Maybe the UK isn't such a good bet any more.' Although he didn't believe the sentiment, he felt a stab of disloyalty at thus dismissing his adoptive home.

'And Germany, France, they're no better. Old economies, grinding away in the slow lane – like a granny on the motorway,' chuckled Romescu, mimicking an old codger hunched over a wheel. 'Young countries like Estonia, Lithuania, Poland, Ukraine ... that's where the new opportunities are.'

'I hear good things about Turkey as well,' said Janusz, remembering the spicy smell of fruit tobacco in the Pasha Café, venue for Romescu's mysterious meetings.

'Maybe, but it's too far east for me,' Romescu declared with a shrug.

Confirmation, as if it were needed, that the guy's dealings with the owner of the Pasha Café were the kind that had to be kept under wraps. Janusz was reaching the conclusion that this little soirée, the sales pitch, Triangle Investments, it was all just a front, a fiction designed to raise funds from unquestioning investors looking to make a quick buck. And he'd make a confident bet that their cash was destined for investment in the back room of the Pasha Café.

He leaned a little closer to his host. 'I hope you won't think me nosy, Barbu, but before I invest, I always like to know the man behind the business.'

Romescu hesitated for a microsecond, then threw his arms open. 'Go ahead! I have no secrets.'

'What did you do as a young man, back in Romania?'

'I trained as an aircraft engineer,' he said. 'That's how I got this,' he tapped the puckered scar that ran down the side of his face. 'I was testing a crappy old Tupelov when the turbine exploded. I call it my present from Brezhnev.'

Janusz laughed. 'And after you escaped? I think Marek said you ended up in Poland?'

'Yeah. Those union people of yours had just thrown out the Commies, and since my mother was Polish, I knew I'd get a passport.'

'And did you carry on working as an engineer?'

Romescu eyed him. 'For a while yes, but then I went to work for Zaleski Corporation – back when our head office was a portakabin on a derelict parking lot.'

'Really?' In Poland, Zaleski was a household name, an international conglomerate that had sprung up amid the ruins of the country's Soviet state industries. 'They're a pretty big player now, aren't they?'

'Yes,' said Romescu. 'I was a director there until ... very recently.' He hesitated, apparently torn between bigging himself up and an instinct for discretion. Vanity won. 'It's no exaggeration to say that it was me who got Orzelair off the ground. My knowledge of aircraft came in pretty useful.'

As Eastern Europe's first budget airline, Orzelair had been the motor that had powered Zaleski's expansion, and now boasted the region's most extensive network of routes.

'Impressive,' said Janusz, shooting him a look that conveyed the appropriate cocktail of admiration and envy. 'Your Zaleski shares must be worth a fortune by now.'

Romescu's lips sketched a tight smile – but it was a poor effort.

Twenty-odd years with the company and no share options? thought Janusz. *You got shafted,* kolego.

But Romescu had clearly tired of the twenty questions routine. Reaching inside his jacket, he extracted a business card bearing the Triangle logo and handed it to Janusz. 'If there's anything more you need to know before you make your decision, feel free to contact me – that's my personal mobile number and email.'

98

He put his arm around Janusz's shoulder and leant towards him, conspiratorial. 'Now we've got the business part over, it's time for my guests to have some fun.'

Janusz allowed himself to be led off the viewing deck back into the bar. Many of the men who'd been standing chatting in groups had now retreated to dimly-lit seating ranged around the walls, accompanied by one or more of the gorgeous girls. The drunk who'd made a fool of himself during Romescu's speech was sprawled on a low leather sofa. A girl perched on the arm was leaning over the drunken *dupek*, her long ash-blonde hair brushing his chest.

'See anyone you like the look of?' asked Romescu in a low suggestive voice. 'It's all on the house.' His head was so close that Janusz could smell the apple juice he'd been drinking. 'Or am I barking up the wrong tree?' He nodded towards one of the waiters, a tall, curly-haired youth who was leaning against the wall, bouncing an empty tray off his thigh. Romescu's warm sweet breath, the heat of his arm across Janusz's shoulders … Janusz had to fight down an overwhelming urge to grab him by both lapels and smash him against the plate glass window.

'I'd love to,' he said with a regretful grin, shooting the cuff of his jacket to check his watch. 'But I'm afraid I have to get back. I've got a call scheduled with a client on the West Coast.'

'Are you sure? "All work and no play …" as the English say.'

Seeing Janusz wasn't to be dissuaded, Romescu released him with a final comradely pat. 'But before you go, I'd like you to meet someone.' This was accompanied by an imperious, beckoning gesture over Janusz's shoulder.

Varenka appeared alongside Romescu, standing almost half a head taller than him.

'Lukas, may I introduce Varenka.'

Betraying no sign of recognition – nor surprise at the

99

unfamiliar name – Varenka offered Janusz the tips of her fingers and a polite smile.

'Pleased to meet you, Lukas.'

He made a tiny bow and, straightening, allowed his eyes to meet her amused gaze. Although the look they exchanged lasted less than a second, it was long enough to seal a pact: Janusz's real name, and the fact that they had already met on a kerbside in Walthamstow, would remain their secret.

'*Enchanté*,' he said.

The Romanian's stubby fingers encircled Varenka's slender wrist like a manacle. 'Not *too* enchanted, I hope,' he told Janusz. The tone was humorous enough but the message in those fierce blue eyes was clear as wodka.

Keep off the grass, it said.

Fourteen

It took all Janusz's reserves of self-control not to light up the moment he left the building's front entrance, but he thought it wise to continue playing the health freak until he'd put a bit of distance between himself and Romescu.

Reaching the end of the dockside walkway, he pulled out his tin of cigars, then threw a precautionary glance over his shoulder ... and saw the outline of a man in a leather jacket strolling some fifty metres behind him, looking out over the dock. Was there something a bit *too* casual about the guy's walk? Or was he just being paranoid? He cursed softly and pocketed his cigar tin. Checking his watch – it was just past ten – he quickened his pace as though there was somewhere he had to be. His intention wasn't so much to shake the guy off, but to discover whether he really was tailing him. He decided to head, not for the nearest tube, Canary Wharf, but to Mudchute, a little-used Docklands Light Railway stop further south on the Isle of Dogs. If the guy were still behind him then, he'd take it as confirmation he was being followed.

In the event, no such confirmation was needed. His phone,

set to vibrate, buzzed in his pocket, signalling the arrival of a text message. It read: *'You have company – Varenka.'*

Nosz, kurwa! She must have overheard Romescu sending leather jacket after him.

Ten minutes fast walking later, Janusz saw the turquoise DLR sign for Mudchute station. He reached the steelwork stairway up to the platform but instead of climbing it, ducked into the shadowy void behind the stairs, pressing himself back against the brickwork. Twenty seconds later, through the stairs' steel grating, he saw the man in the leather jacket ascending, taking the steps two at a time with an easy athleticism. Janusz couldn't see his face but his impression was one of a young man, thirty tops. As he heard him reach the top of the second flight, Janusz considered his options. Stay hidden and risk discovery? Or make a swift exit while he had the chance?

Deciding that an encounter with the guy could ruin an otherwise civilised evening, he slipped out of his hiding place and headed down East Ferry Road, towards the river. He was starting to regret the route he'd taken. After the bustle of nightlife around Canary Wharf, the outer reaches of the Isle of Dogs felt like another country. On his left lay the silent, darkened greenery of Millwall Park, to his right a council estate, now part-sold to city types judging by the mixed messages sent by the balconies: tubs of bay trees on some, discarded TV sets and drying clothes strung across others. The streets were abandoned: he'd only seen one person since leaving the dockside, an old lady walking her dog with an air of defiance.

Then Janusz heard a sound from behind him that sent a crackle across his scalp. *The sound of boots pounding the pavement.* He threw a quick glance over his shoulder, half hoping to find some skinny neighbourhood mugger. No such luck. Flashing through the pools of carbon light cast by the street-lamps he saw him. Close-cut hair, leather jacket – seventy metres away but gaining fast. The guy was clearly no longer content simply to follow him. Janusz broke into a sprint. Something about the man nagged at his memory. Then he remembered. It was Romescu's driver – the guy with the snake tattoo, who'd cajoled Varenka into the Discovery so his boss could thump her.

The guy must have realised his cover had been blown, but instead of giving up, had decided to chase down his prey. Janusz had a powerful premonition of what would happen if he let him catch up. A fight was one thing, but a guy like that would almost certainly be packing a blade – or even a gun.

By the time Janusz reached the end of the park, he was breathing hard, a stiletto of cramp jab-jabbing him in the side. Here, a curve in the road briefly hid him from his pursuer's view. He had two options – head for Island Gardens, the last DLR station this side of the river, or carry on south towards the Thames towpath. Deciding that Island Gardens would be deserted at this time of night, making it the perfect setting for a knifing, he ran on.

Two minutes later, he was jogging down the side of the old Rowing Club, a spot he'd got hammered in countless times with Oskar back in the day, when they'd been working the Docklands building sites. Its windows were darkened now. As the friendly riverine smell of the Thames rose to greet him he suddenly remembered something else. At the towpath he could go west or east, but there was a third option. The Greenwich foot tunnel. A quarter of a mile long, it connected the Isle of Dogs to Greenwich, emerging near the Cutty Sark, which would still be surrounded by gawping tourists even this late in the evening. *Safety.* And there was a good chance that his pursuer wouldn't even know of the tunnel's existence.

A small domed redbrick structure marked its northern end. Negotiating his way past a bike lock and a row of motorcycles parked outside, Janusz jogged into the entrance hall. He decided against taking the big wood-panelled Victorian lift down to the tunnel: if leather jacket were still close behind, the motor of the descending lift would act like a guiding klaxon. Descending the badly lit staircase took longer than he remembered, but felt a good deal easier on his aching lungs than running on the flat. By the time he reached the bottom he was still a bit breathless but his spirits were high. Even if his pursuer did stumble across the tunnel entrance Janusz had a good lead on him now. He reckoned he could cover the few hundred yards that stood between him and the Greenwich end of the tunnel in less than five minutes if he had to.

He paused, head cocked for the sound of feet clattering down the staircase. *Nothing.* He set off down the tunnel at a loping run. A near-perfect circular tube lined with white Victorian tiles, it was so narrow that three people couldn't walk comfortably abreast. The other end lay out of sight and without any distinguishing features to disturb the white tubular continuity Janusz had the curious sensation that he was running on the spot – that the tunnel would never end. After a few seconds, the combination of the fluorescent light overhead and the endless white of the tiles seemed to set up a low whine inside his head.

Then he got it. The whine wasn't coming from inside his head, but from the lift machinery behind him.

Time to put some distance between him and whoever would be emerging from that lift in half a minute. Janusz upped his pace. With his legs going like pistons, he assured himself he'd covered a good third of the tunnel's length. There was no way his pursuer could make up a deficit like that. The lift stopped with a clanking sound and he heard its rackety doors opening. Then another sound, quite unexpected in that confined space.

The angry insect roar of a two-stroke engine being gunned.

Kurwa mac! The fucker had stolen a motorbike! Sweat sprang from Janusz's pores. He forced himself to run faster, feeling the adrenaline open his blood vessels, powering oxygen into his bloodstream. *Thanks be to all the saints I stayed off the beer.* He considered discarding his heavy, flapping coat, before deciding it might lose him precious seconds.

The scream of the motorbike engine echoed around the tunnel, now getting so close that Janusz felt the skin between his shoulder blades itch, anticipating a blow from a fist or a knife.

He blinked the sweat out of his eyes, trying to make out how far he was from the tunnel end. And saw something, ten metres in front of him, which he'd completely forgotten about. A pair of waist-high parallel bars jutting out from either wall. They were offset so that pedestrians could easily pass through but to anyone on two wheels they might as well be a brick wall.

But Janusz could tell from the engine's undimmed roar that his pursuer wasn't slowing down. Then he realised why: the guy was so close and the tunnel so narrow that Janusz's coat flying out like a pair of wings prevented him from seeing the obstacle ahead.

Unable to risk slowing his own pace, all Janusz could do was to try to match his stride rate to the looming barrier. At the last moment he jinked to the right and made a grab for the second barrier. Then he was in the air, flying over it. The impact when his feet hit the ground the other side brought his jaws together so violently he heard the crack of a molar. Almost immediately came the screech of brakes and an explosive bang, metal on metal, rang out in the tunnel like a bomb blast, followed by the keening shriek a motor-cycle makes when it's locked on full throttle but its back wheel spins uselessly in the air.

Panting heavily, Janusz looked back down the tunnel. The impact had bent the bike in two, and left the mangled remains of its front wheel wrapped around the first barrier. Leather jacket had been catapulted over the second and lay spread-eagled on the concrete floor, one arm outstretched. Janusz could make out the tattooed head of the snake across his motionless knuckles: it looked as though it might be about to slither down his arm and escape the carnage.

The guy's left leg jerked once, like a broken marionette. The sight took Janusz right back to his university days, dissecting dead frogs: their limbs used to twitch like that when you applied electric current.

At the tunnel end, he entered the lift. Leaning heavily against the wall, he pulled out his mobile, tempted to text Romescu, to inform him that one of his employees had met with a workplace accident. Then the stern gaze of Father Pietruski swam before him. *Alright, alright,* he murmured. Once he reached street level he'd call 999 so someone could come and scrape the guy off the concrete.

Fifteen

The morning after receiving the surprise phone call from Dr King, the pathologist who'd done the PM on the Canary Wharf body, Kershaw found herself sitting in the marble-lined lobby of Court Two at the Old Bailey. Nathan King was appearing as an expert witness in a big murder case, so her best chance of a face-to-face chat would be to hang around and grab him between appearances.

'DC Kershaw?' a voice said.

She got to her feet, wondering, not the first time, what it was about her that seemed to say 'cop' so unmistakably. Dr King looked younger than he'd sounded on the phone, early thirties at most, with longish curly hair. Attractive, if a bit shambolic-looking.

'They might call me back in at any moment,' he said, pulling a file out of a rucksack as he sat down beside her, 'so forgive me if I race through this.' He flicked through his post-mortem report. 'Here we go,' he said, shuffling closer on the wooden bench to give her a better view. 'This is what I was telling you about on the phone.'

Kershaw squinted at the black and white photograph – the

image it captured looked like a jellyfish mottled with leopard skin spots – before turning an uncomprehending gaze on him.

He tapped the discs with his forefinger. 'These are gastric lesions. They're called Wischnewski spots.' He beamed at her. 'I've seen them in a lecture theatre but I never expected to see such a good set of them in the flesh.' He shook his head, marvelling at his good fortune.

Kershaw gazed at him, wondering what made anyone choose a career which involved plunging your hands into the entrails of dead strangers every day of your working life. The thought was swiftly followed by another: what must it be like *having sex* with someone you knew spent their days doing that?

She pushed the idea away. 'Right. And tell me again exactly what that means?'

'They're a strong indicator that our man was suffering from advanced hypothermia at the time of his death.'

'Which you get when you're exposed to extreme cold.'

'Yup.'

'So he might have been up on the roof for several hours, or maybe even spent the whole night there,' said Kershaw, pleased to find some concrete evidence for her thesis.

The doc turned down the corners of his mouth – he didn't buy the idea. 'The advanced hypothermia this suggests,' he said, tapping the photo, 'would almost certainly have rendered him semi-conscious at best.'

Kershaw felt her pulse flutter. 'So he wouldn't have been *able* to climb over the parapet – not on his own anyway?'

'That's right. And there's something else interesting.' He leafed through the file and angled it towards her, revealing a shot of the man's right hand, lying palm upward. 'See this?' He traced a darkened band of skin across the middle of his palm.

'It looks like … a burn.'

'Or a *freezer* burn.'

'You think somebody might have kept him in a freezer? And then *thrown* him over the parapet?' Kershaw could barely keep the excitement out of her voice.

'No.'

Her shoulders went down. 'So … What are you saying exactly?'

'There's no doubt in my mind that he died of severe head injuries sustained in the fall.'

'So can I ask why were you so keen to drag me into town when I could've been down at Canary Wharf finding out how he got onto the roof?' A bewigged barrister who was sitting nearby with his client shot Kershaw a disapproving look and she realised that she must have raised her voice. She softened her tone. 'Sorry, Dr King, but you did say on the phone that you thought it might *not* be suicide after all?'

'That's right,' he said. 'I don't think he fell from the roof.'

'But you just said …'

'That he was killed by a fall.' He waited until he had her full attention. 'A fall from an aircraft.'

Kershaw rocked back so far that she banged her head on the wooden bench back. 'Fuck!' she exclaimed – earning herself another dirty look and a headshake from the bloke in the silly wig. 'But if he fell out of a plane, surely he'd be much more badly messed up than if he fell off a tall building?'

King shook his head. 'Not necessarily. He had all the injuries I'd associate with a fall from height, including a shattered skull. But if he fell as the plane was coming in to land, then the height might not have made a significant difference.'

Kershaw tried to recall whether she'd heard the whine of a descending jet overhead just before the guy fell. She couldn't remember anything, but she knew that the human brain filtered out unimportant background info, sending it straight to 'trash'.

The doc was flipping to the back of his report. 'Canary Wharf tower is around 800 feet; a plane on its final approach into City airport might fly as low as 1500 feet.'

'What, and you're saying another 700 feet would be neither here nor there as regards the state of the body?' Kershaw's tone was politely incredulous.

'That's right,' said the doc. 'I've seen similar injuries in a window cleaner who fell twenty-five feet. Other people have survived falling ten storeys.'

Kershaw heard again the *whump* the guy had made when he landed on the limo.

'He did hit the roof of a car first ...'

'Yes. That would have made a big difference in helping to break his fall.'

'Although that probably isn't much consolation to him,' said Kershaw, biting her lip.

'Not in the final analysis, no,' said King, allowing himself a small grin.

She traced the outline of the discoloured band of skin across the dead man's palm. 'And this?'

'Ice burn, I'm guessing, possibly caused when he tried to hang onto some strut or other inside the wheel well, before he lost consciousness.'

Kershaw was only just beginning to digest this bombshell when the voice of an usher echoed around the lobby: 'Dr Nathan King to Court Two ... Dr King to Court Two.'

Getting to his feet, King reached for the file that lay on the bench next to Kershaw. 'Got to go, I'm afraid,' he said, shooting her an apologetic grin.

Instinctively, she grabbed one end of the file. 'So, he must have been in some unheated part of a plane,' she said, thinking aloud, 'and became hypothermic when it reached high altitude.'

'If the hypothesis is correct, yes,' said King, giving the file a polite tug. 'Look, I'm afraid I ...'

'But if he was in the baggage hold, how did he fall out?' she persisted.

The usher repeated his call, louder this time. Abandoning good manners, King wrenched the file from Kershaw's grip. 'I really have to go!' The last thing he said as he hurried away was: 'Do what I did – run a Google search on aeroplane stowaways.'

Taking the doc's advice, Kershaw had, by the end of the day, become an expert on the subject from the comfort of her office swivel chair. She was taken aback to discover that every year a handful of people, most of them from the world's poorest countries, crawled into the wheel wells of jet planes in a desperate search for a better life elsewhere. Some of them met their end almost immediately, getting mashed when the pilot retracted the landing gear. Others died from extended exposure to temperatures as low as minus sixty-five degrees Celsius combined with high altitude oxygen starvation. The handful who somehow survived the ordeal then risked plummeting to their death when the plane's undercarriage was lowered during its final descent, by which time they were usually semi-conscious at best – which was almost certainly what had happened to the Canary Wharf guy.

It was all fascinating stuff but it was hardly the kind of thing she'd joined Murder Squad for. Yawning, she looked up from her screen and let her gaze drift around the office. Her fellow DCs Sophie and Adam were on the phone talking to Jim Fulford's possible contacts: they looked motivated, purposeful. *That's what I should be doing,* she thought. When Sophie had finished her call, Kershaw leaned across the desk.

111

'Soph, have you got any idea where Streaky is?'

Sophie tapped her watch and raised a quizzical eyebrow. It was nearly six.

Kershaw grinned. 'Silly question?'

'Yep. He went to the Moon half an hour ago.'

So Streaky had already left for his daily visit to the Eagle and Child. Dubbed 'the Moon' due to its total lack of atmosphere, it had won his custom by virtue of a single impressive attribute: the beer was cheaper per fluid ounce than the mineral water.

Kershaw thought about leaving it to the morning to update him, then changed her mind. No, best to bosh this dead stowaway job right now so she could dive straight into the Fulford case first thing.

She found Streaky on a stool at the bar, a tabloid newspaper in one freckled hand, the other curled around a half-drunk pint of lager.

'Well, fuck me sideways! If it isn't Ms Marple,' he exclaimed. 'I thought you only patronised gastropubs these days. You do know they don't serve sun-dried tomato flavour crisps in this place?'

'I'll have to make do with cheese and onion then, Sarge,' she said, levering herself up onto an empty barstool. 'Can I get you a drink?'

He bugged his eyes at her. 'A woman buying a round? I've seen everything now.' He drained the remains of his pint in two throat-distending gulps and smacked the glass down. 'Mine's a pint of wifebeater.'

Catching the barman's attention, Kershaw ordered a Stella and a glass of Chilean Chenin for herself.

Folding up his paper, Streaky stabbed a finger at the front-page photo – an unremarkable-looking man in his fifties out shopping, beside the headline 'Monster of Worcester gets Day Release'. 'You weren't even born when this comedian came

112

to trial. He killed three little kids he was babysitting, then kebabbed them on some iron railings.'

'Christ on a bike! Was he deranged?'

'Nope, he just *"lost his temper"* when the baby wouldn't stop crying. This was back in the seventies – it was only about ten years after they abolished hanging.' Streaky's face became pensive. 'I remember having a right old ding-dong with my dad about the case. Brimming with youthful idealism, I was, telling him no matter how terrible the crime, nothing could justify judicial murder.'

'Really?' She tried to picture a youthful, freckled-faced Streaky, arguing earnestly for a child murderer's right to life – and failed.

He took a draught of his fresh pint and smacked his lips. 'I was talking a load of old bollocks, of course. Now, if they locked the bastards up and threw away the key, I could just about live with it, but how often does that happen? Those sandal-wearing dope smokers on the Parole Board always end up giving sick fuckers like him "another chance".'

Kershaw made all the right noises. Although part of her agreed with him, she was wondering how many innocent people would have got strung up during all those miscarriage of justice cases in the seventies.

She moved the conversation onto the Canary Wharf 'suicide', explaining the pathologist's theory that the mystery Pole fell to his death not from the tower, but from an aeroplane.

'It never ceases to amaze me – the lengths people will go to reach this sceptred isle,' said Streaky. Tearing open a packet of crisps he set it on the bar, inviting her to share them with a munificent gesture. 'Whereabouts do you reckon he got into the wheel well?'

'The only flight into City that fits with the time he fell comes out of some place in south-east Poland,' she said.

113

'Tiny little airport, out in the sticks, from what I could find out online.' She took a sip of her wine. 'Anyway, I wanted to ask you what's the drill now,' she said. 'Do you want me to call Canary Wharf nick or would you rather do it?'

'What's it got to do with them?' asked Streaky.

'Well … since he's definitely a Polish national, we've got no hope of identifying him, so surely it's down to them to bat it across to the Polish police?'

Streaky conveyed a stack of crisps to his mouth and crunched on them for a while. 'You say that two fellas dropped out of planes coming into Heathrow this year …' he said musingly. 'Flights from Europe, were they?'

'No,' she said. 'Africa, Angola … and somewhere else. Why do you ask?'

'Any of these wheel-well desperadoes ever fly in from *EU countries*?' he asked with an icy smile.

Kershaw shook her head. 'No, Sarge, but I don't see …'

'It just seems a bit of an *unusual* way to travel, given that Poles can come and go to the UK as they please.' Pausing to form the crisp packet deftly into a funnel shape, Streaky upended it into his mouth. 'I mean, I know Ryanair treat their passengers like cunts, but still, even they haven't started charging extra for oxygen yet.'

Kershaw shrugged. She didn't like the way this was going. 'Maybe he got over the border from …' Here her geography failed her. 'A non-EU country?'

He gave a judicious nod. 'Yes, that's certainly a possibility. In fact, I'd make it your main avenue of enquiry.'

'Me?'

'Yes, *detective*. You.' A warning flush began to spread up Streaky's cheeks. 'As you ought to know from the wildly expensive training you received, when a foreign national dies on UK soil it's up to *us* to conduct the enquiry. And if that requires the investigating officer to travel to Poland, or to chuffing *Timbuktu*, then that's what will happen. The only good news is it's all coming out of Docklands' budget and not mine!'

Kershaw felt her own face grow hot. 'But Sarge, I'm meant to be working on murder cases, not chasing round Europe identifying people who fall out of aeroplanes!'

'Maybe you should have thought about that before you volunteered to lighten the load of a nick that doesn't pay your fucking wages!'

'But it could take weeks!'

'So I suggest you get on the blower and find yourself a Polish interpreter pronto. Then you'll need to fill in a bunch of forms to send to the Polish police.'

Kershaw put her head in her hands. What had possessed her to be such a Girl Scout about this case? No one would have blinked an eye if she'd left the job to Canary Wharf nick.

'Another white wine?' asked Streaky, apparently unmoved by her misery.

'Yeah. Make it a large one.'

Sixteen

'So you really think the Romanian sent the tattooed guy after you to *kill you*?!'

'I said so, didn't I?' hissed Janusz. 'And keep your voice down.'

Oskar leant closer, his knife and fork clutched upright in chubby fists. 'Just imagine, *kolego*,' he said in a solemn whisper. 'Your Mama, *God rest her soul*, gives birth to you in Gdansk, and you might have breathed your dying breath in the *Greenwich foot tunnel*.' He crossed himself, then his expression brightened. 'All the same, I'd give 500 zloty to have been there – just to see you hurdling that barrier like Red Rum.' Chuckling, he impaled a couple of *pierogi* on his fork.

The two friends were having lunch in the *Polska Kuchnia*, a Polish café in Stratford that had sprung up a few years back to serve the legions of Poles working on the construction of the Olympics site and the redevelopment of the surrounding area.

The end of the building boom had brought a shift in the café's clientele, from burly workmen in stained overalls and steel-capped boots to well-groomed office- and shop-workers

116

from nearby Westfield shopping centre. For a few anxious weeks, Janusz and Oskar had feared that the arrival of this new, predominantly female clientele might result in an unwelcome refinement of the café's menu. Luckily the threat of salad had never materialised and the chef still favoured traditional Polish favourites like *kielbasa*, *pierogi*, and his speciality, pork stew served on a fried potato pancake the size of a saucepan lid.

'What I don't get with this Romescu guy,' whispered Oskar, glancing around him like someone given the word '*conspiratorial*' in a game of charades, 'is one minute you're some rich *dupek* he wants to milk for cash, then the next minute, he wants you dead.'

It was a conundrum that Janusz had given a good deal of thought since last night's little *dramat* in the tunnel. 'Now I think back, I reckon he must have been keeping an eye on me and Varenka the whole time he was giving that speech,' he said. Although Romescu had given no hint of it, there was probably very little that evaded that shark-like gaze.

'What, so he ordered you to be killed because you were muscling in on his girlfriend?'

Janusz took his time to answer, savouring a mouthful of *gulash*. Certainly, Romescu had made it clear in the little meeting he'd staged that Varenka was more than just another 'employee'. But Janusz had concluded that, however jealous he might be, the Romanian was unlikely to order a risky and impulsive killing over a girl – especially right at the moment he was expending so much money and effort on creating a respectable front.

'No, I think he knows I'm onto him,' he said. 'I was an *idiota*, stirring things up that day in the Turkish café. The Turk probably gave Romescu my description, told him I was a friend of Jim's.' He topped up their glasses with beer. 'Somewhere along the line last night he realised who I was.

117

The last thing he needs right now is someone sniffing round trying to nail him for a murder.'

Oskar tore a piece of rye bread in two. 'So how do you think him and Jim came across each other? Maybe Jim invested in this Triangle business?' His eyes lit up. 'I could try to find out, from Marek.'

Janusz pushed his plate away. 'No, I already asked Marika to check his credit card and bank statements. She says there are no outgoings she didn't already know about.' He remembered with a pang how she hadn't even asked why he wanted her to look. Her quiet trust in him was deeply touching, but it only added to the heavy feeling in his gut: the compulsion to deliver justice, for her and for Jim.

He pulled out the sheaf of articles he'd printed the previous night, the fruit of hours spent scouring the net for info on Romescu's history. Most of them came from the business pages of newspapers and charted Orzelair's rise from tiny provincial airline to Eastern Europe's biggest budget carrier.

'I've been doing some digging on Orzelair, to find out whether he really was such a big shot there as he claims.'

'So, was he bullshitting?' asked Oskar, before taking a deep gulp of his Tyskie.

'Quite the reverse,' said Janusz. 'They couldn't have set it up without him. When the Soviet Union started crumbling, Romescu went round the eastern bloc countries picking up second-hand Tupelovs. His experience as an engineer at Tarom – the Romanian state airline – meant he knew his planes. And how the system worked.'

Oskar rubbed his thumb and forefinger together.

'Exactly. So he sourced their first fleet of planes for peanuts. But that's not the most interesting thing I found out.'

Janusz retrieved the extraordinary story he'd stumbled across on about page fifteen of the search results. The aviation magazine in which it had originally appeared had long since closed down but, luckily for him, some aeroplane-addled anorak had taken the trouble to upload its contents to his blog. The piece was dated November 1996.

'Between 1947 and '96, twelve people stowed away in the wheel wells of aeroplanes,' said Janusz. 'Nowadays they're usually after a job in the West, but back then most of them were political refugees of some kind or other.'

'Nutters,' said Oskar.

'The odds aren't quite as bad as you'd think,' said Janusz. 'Six of them survived, including this one, in '89.' Turning to the second page of the article he showed Oskar a photograph. The blurred black and white shot showed a skinny young man propped up in a hospital bed, with one side of his head wrapped in a bandage. He wasn't smiling, but his right arm was extended stiffly towards the camera and he was giving the thumbs-up sign.

Oskar shook his head in disbelief. '"God looks after fools and children", eh?'

'God had nothing to do with it – this guy did his planning. He wore thermals from head to foot and picked a day when the weather was bad, which meant the plane flew at a lower altitude – 25,000 feet instead of 35,000 or more.' He paused. 'But then this guy wasn't your average Joe Stowaway.'

Setting the article aside, Janusz picked up his glass.

Oskar stared at his mate. 'Well, are you gonna tell me, prickteaser?!'

He took a drink of beer. 'He was an aircraft engineer – with Tarom.'

'*Nosz, Kurwa!*' Oskar struck the table with the flats of his hands.

Janusz nodded, then handed him the article.

'*Escape from Ceausescu's Romania:*' read Oskar from the caption beneath the picture. '*27-year-old aircraft engineer Barbu*

Romescu survived a two-hour flight from Bucharest to Warsaw hidden in the wheel well of a Tupolev Tu-154. On arrival, he was granted asylum by Poland's new democratically elected government.' He gave a low whistle. 'I tell you something, Janek. The guy might be a dirty murdering pimp, but you gotta admit he's got a fucking huge pair of *jaja* on him!'

Janusz grunted. 'Listen, Oskar. You need to keep all of this strictly to yourself, you understand? And I don't want you talking to Marek for a while – this guy is fucking dangerous.'

They were paying the bill when a red light started flashing on his mobile: it was a text message from the girl *detektyw.* It said she needed to see him 'urgently' to discuss some 'important information'. He cursed softly – he'd almost forgotten the absurd notion that he was still a suspect in Jim's murder. He started to punch out a message telling her to talk to his solicitor, before changing his mind. Having just paid the guy £700, he had no desire to inflate the bill further.

Seventeen

As Kershaw pressed the buzzer marked 'Kiszka' at the entrance to his swish mansion house apartment block, she remembered that the last time she'd been here, a couple of years back, she'd come perilously close to arresting him for a murder he didn't commit. There was a neat symmetry to the fact that this time she was here to tell him he was officially off the hook for the murder of Jim Fulford.

She should have known better than to expect gratitude from the big Pole, she reflected, not ten minutes later. Kiszka simply looked at her across his scarred, orange pine kitchen table, his craggy features unreadable. He was smoking one of his foul-smelling little cigars and although he'd had the good manners to open a window, the space had still filled with a throat-tickling blue haze. Ben had finally persuaded Kershaw to give up smoking around a year ago but now the fumes were triggering her old nicotine craving.

Fidgeting in her chair, she picked at the skin around a nail. 'Aren't you going to say anything?' She was half tempted to point out that he'd still be a suspect if she hadn't gone the extra mile to check his alibi.

'I wouldn't have been accused in the first place if your lot had done their job properly,' he said, sideswiping that line of argument. 'But maybe they were in too much of a hurry to charge someone – anyone – with Jim's murder.'

'Well, we'd have eliminated you a lot quicker if you'd told us you spoke to that gardener while you were at the museum.'

Janusz had to admit the girl had a point: the fact was he'd completely forgotten the little interchange over a dropped cigar butt. The sort of forgetfulness he would once have associated with advanced decrepitude was becoming a familiar occurrence.

He picked a flake of tobacco from his lip. 'How are you getting on with finding the real murderer?'

'We're pursuing all possible avenues of enquiry,' she said.

He remembered this tendency she had to lapse into officialese, a sinister echo of the doublespeak routinely employed by the enforcers of Poland's communist regime – when they weren't wielding the rubber truncheons, that is. Now it occurred to him that perhaps she did it when she was unsure of herself. Had the investigation hit a brick wall?

'If you can think of any of Jim's contacts we might have missed,' she went on, confirming his hunch, 'even if there's no obvious reason why they might want to harm him, it could make all the difference.'

He felt a pang of guilt. Should he tell her what he knew? About Varenka leaving flowers and his suspicion that her scar-faced boyfriend was behind the murder? *No.* He had not a jot of evidence against Romescu, and if the cops called his girlfriend in for questioning, it would only put him on his guard, while destroying all Janusz's efforts to gain her confidence. Better to pursue the investigation in his own fashion, at least for now.

'Nothing that comes immediately to mind,' he said.

But the way his gaze slid away from her made Kershaw's antennae twitch. It wouldn't be the first time he'd held out on her. Even more reason to get him to agree to her plan: it might give her the opportunity to suss out if he was hiding something significant.

'I'm as keen as you are to find the perpetrators,' she said. 'In fact, I wanted to ask you a favour – something that might help speed things along.'

'I'm confused,' he said. 'You put me in a cell and accuse me of murder, and now you're asking for a favour?' His deep voice rang with incredulous outrage.

Kershaw refrained from pointing out she hadn't even started work on the squad when Streaky had him pulled in. 'I have to go to Poland for a couple of days to try to identify someone who died here in London, and I need an interpreter.'

'And you expect me to expend valuable time finding an interpreter for you.'

She chanced a grin. 'Actually, no. I'm asking *you* to be my interpreter.'

Janusz stared at her, then chuckled: he had to admire the girl's nerve. 'And how exactly would dragging me off to Poland help you solve Jim's murder?'

'I'm off the case until I get this ID job out of the way. And finding a translator through the official channels could take weeks.'

'I can imagine,' he shrugged. 'But you can't be the only detective working on it.'

'No, of course not. But … I think I'm the only one who'll go the extra mile.'

The girl cocked her chin in that determined way she had which made her look like a pugnacious squirrel.

'Look,' he said. 'I can't just drop everything and head off to Poland. But if you give me a few days I can probably find you someone.'

Hearing the kindness in his tone, Kershaw felt a flare of disappointment. It said more clearly than anger would have done that he wasn't going to play ball.

Janusz stood to clear away their empty cups and saucers, feeling pain shoot through his thigh muscles – a reminder of last night's chase, and of his ebbing levels of fitness. He'd recently read a depressing fact: that after the age of thirty-five, the typical man loses a pound of muscle every year.

'How did this guy die, anyway?' he asked, carrying the dirty crockery over to the sink.

'He fell out of the wheel well of an aeroplane coming in to land at City Airport.'

Janusz was glad he had his back to the girl because it meant she couldn't see his expression but he couldn't stop the stack of china from rattling in his hands. He was seeing again the article he'd found on the internet, the picture of the young Romescu giving the thumbs-up from his hospital bed.

'A stowaway?' he asked, in as casual a tone as he could manage.

She shrugged. 'It looks that way, although God knows why, when Poland's in the EU.'

'Whereabouts in Poland did the plane fly in from?'

'Prez-ez-kof?' she tried, making an apologetic face. 'Near the border with Ukraine?'

'*Pshe-choh-kuff*,' he said, correcting her mangled pronunciation. Przeczokow was a smallish provincial city on the border with Ukraine. And he had a hunch that its IAATA-designated abbreviation, the one inscribed on your luggage tag if you were flying there, would be 'PCK' – just like the tag on Romescu's suitcase.

He lit another cigar. 'Orzelair flight?' he asked, blowing out a lazy plume of smoke.

Kershaw checked her notebook. 'Yes. How did you know?'

124

'I think I flew there once, years ago.'

Rather than speculate why Kiszka suddenly seemed interested, Kershaw focused on nailing the deal. 'You'd get paid the full police interpreter rate, plus all your expenses, of course.'

'Who would I have to interview?'

'Local cops, airport staff ... I dunno, maybe the local paper if it has one.'

'And I can go where I like – in my free time?'

'Of course.'

'I have to be back before Thursday, for Jim's funeral.'

'No problem, we'll only be there one night.'

Janusz ran a hand the size of a small shovel along his jaw. Since the fracas with Romescu's thug beneath the Thames, he'd been wondering how best to progress his investigation into Jim's murder. His priority was still to find out how his friend and the Romanian might be connected, but now his cover had been blown it was clear that any further direct contact with Romescu was out of the question. And although he sensed that Varenka might prove a useful conduit, he wanted a better handle on her boyfriend's activities before suggesting they meet. A quick trip to check out the Orzelair set-up at Przeczokow could deliver valuable intelligence on Romescu, with an added bonus – the cops would be picking up the tab.

He decided it was what the Americans called a no-brainer.

'Alright,' he sighed. 'When do we leave?'

Eighteen

Two days later, Janusz Kiszka and DC Natalie Kershaw were buckling up for the 10 a.m. Orzelair flight from City Airport to Przeczokow. An eccentric-looking couple, the big Pole in his ancient trench coat and the short blonde girl wearing the dark trouser suit and the serious expression, drew some curious glances from their fellow passengers.

Janusz was too preoccupied to notice. He'd been expecting to see Kasia the night before, on a rare evening off from the nail bar, but at the last minute she told him that she'd forgotten a promise to go out to dinner with her husband Steve. He'd lost his temper and slammed the phone down on her. Once he got back from Poland, he told himself, he was going to have it out with her once and for all. It didn't help his mood that he was expected to cram his big frame into an airline seat apparently designed for children and Japanese people. Still, at least the flight wasn't full, which meant that they had a row of three to themselves, him by the window and the girl taking the aisle seat.

When the drinks trolley came round he asked the stewardess

126

for a beer. To his irritation she hesitated, looking over at the girl detective as though to ask her permission.

'What was that about?' he growled once he'd got his drink and the trolley had moved on.

'No idea,' said Kershaw, but a moment later it dawned on her. 'They've clocked that I'm a cop.' She tried to keep from grinning. 'And they think you're ... my prisoner.'

'Oh, that's great,' he said. 'You'll probably need to come with me when I want to use the bathroom.'

Wearing a thunderous frown, he pulled a rolled-up wad of paperwork out of his coat and started reading.

Kershaw noticed that he twisted himself around towards her, his back set against the window. Maybe it was simply because the seat back was too narrow for his shoulders – but it also had the effect of preventing her from seeing the documents clutched in those big mitts.

She sipped her orange juice, her mind returning to the meeting in Kiszka's flat, and found herself unable to shake the uncomfortable feeling that his change of heart about the Poland trip had been suspiciously sudden. Maybe she was being paranoid: the Job did tend to make you question everyone's motives. She grinned to herself, remembering something her dad used to say. *Just because you're paranoid, it doesn't mean they're not out to get you.*

Janusz meanwhile, was immersing himself in a feature from *The Economist* on Zaleski Corporation – the industrial conglomerate that owned Orzelair – which he'd printed out just before leaving for the airport. Zaleski had been set up by a guy called Sebastian Fischer in 1990, after Poland's first democratic elections, and was lately being hailed one of Eastern Europe's great post-Soviet success stories.

The piece compared Poland to its former master, Russia, where the fall of communism had been followed by a rummage sale of state assets by the corrupt political class to their cronies in business: a rigged auction that had spawned hundreds of billionaires while leaving swathes of former Soviet citizens destitute.

By contrast, the article noted, Poland had been swift to reinstate the structures essential to civil society while taking a relatively cautious approach to the free market. Into this scenario had come Fischer, a young lawyer with a talent for predicting which Soviet-era businesses would flourish in the new Poland and for identifying emerging opportunities such as a soaring demand for cut-price flights.

A photograph showed a tall slim man in his forties who looked a little like a clean-shaven Steve Jobs. He wore evening dress and was dancing with a middle-aged woman in a lime-coloured gown. German Chancellor Angela Merkel. According to the picture caption, the event was some German-Polish trade beano. Reading on, Janusz discovered that in May that year Fischer had swung a highly lucrative deal, a joint venture between Orzelair and Lufthansa that gave the German carrier access to its extensive network of routes to emerging east European economies.

Janusz paused to drain the remains of his tiny can of beer, trying to puzzle it out. *Six months ago, Orzelair and parent company Zaleski Corp make a giant leap into the premier league of European businesses. Meanwhile, Romescu – the man who practically built the airline from scratch – exits stage left.* He recalled the sick look on his face when Janusz mentioned Zaleski shares. The article confirmed his hunch. The company's shares were 100 per cent owned by Fischer, his wife and other members of his family, so it appeared that Romescu had departed without so much as a gold-plated clock.

He crushed his empty beer can in one fist with a crunch that drew a wary look from two of the cabin staff standing by the galley kitchen. He attempted a placatory grin but the hasty way they looked away suggested the girl's guess was right: they thought he was a convict being escorted home!

Rolling up the sheaf of articles, he returned them to his coat pocket. They'd given him plenty of food for thought. Being director of an airline could certainly come in handy if Romescu were trafficking girls from non-EU countries to the West, assuming he'd found some way around border controls. Had Fischer got wind of his associate's criminal sideline and summarily kicked him out? But before he could pursue this train of thought, the girl detective piped up.

'So, Janusz, when did you come over to the UK?'

'1986.'

'Did you come over here to work?'

'Yes.'

'You had some kind of science degree, didn't you? Were you hoping to get a job in a lab or something?'

'I didn't finish my studies.'

'Really? How come?'

She clearly wasn't going to be put off. *Great*, he thought, *two hours being grilled by a cop*.

'Back then I thought it was more important to go out on the streets and fight the system.' He pulled a humourless grin. 'Then my girlfriend got killed because I took her to a demo. I turned into a drunk and married her best friend, which was a total disaster. So I ran away to England like a coward.'

He turned to look out of the window. But if he'd assumed he'd shut her up, he was wrong.

'Christ!' she exclaimed. 'This was when the Communists were in charge, right?'

He nodded wearily.

'I remember my dad telling me he used to watch it on the news every night, striking workers demonstrating at the gates of some shipyard?'

Her tough little face softened when she mentioned her

129

father, Janusz noticed, making her look a whole lot prettier. 'The Vladimir Lenin Shipyard in Gdansk,' he said. 'My hometown.'

'He was in the Communist Party, my dad.' Seeing Kiszka's aghast look she was swift to add: 'He worked on the docks in the sixties – loads of dockworkers were communists back then, apparently. But when the Russians invaded Czechoslovakia, he said that was it – he burnt his party card.'

Janusz just grunted. He'd heard it all before and it always made him feel the same way. Why did these armchair commies wait for Soviet tanks to crush the Prague Spring? Had they failed to notice the invasion of Hungary in '56? Not to mention Stalin's purges, or the well-publicised horrors of the Gulags?

'It must be nice for you,' she went on, 'now there are so many more Poles in London?'

'Not really. Back in the eighties I at least had rarity value. English people wanted to talk to me about Kieslowski and Polanski.' He puffed air through his lips – a dismissive sound. 'Now they just want to know if I do loft extensions.'

Christ on a bike! thought Kershaw. *What a grouchy bastard.*

Janusz stretched and yawned. 'So what's the story on this guy we're trying to identify, the one who fell out of the plane?'

'I wish I knew,' she said. 'Maybe he got over the Polish border, from Ukraine or Belarus?' She congratulated herself on doing her Google Maps homework the previous night. 'Then bribed someone at the airport to get on a plane to the UK?'

'Did he look like an economic migrant?'

'Not really, no.' Kershaw frowned. 'He was wearing a suit and a pretty expensive overcoat.'

Janusz wondered how many of the stowaways changed their minds when the temperature in the wheel well plunged and the air grew thin. If you started banging on the fuselage, would anyone even hear you above the noise of the engines?

'How old was he?'

'Forties, early fifties?' She shrugged. 'Perhaps he was a mental health case. You know, the type who thinks the TV is sending him messages? Maybe he thought the CIA was after him.'

'Or *Sluzba Bezpieczenstwa*.'

'Umm, you'll have to run that past me again.'

'The SB – the secret police from communist days. That would be the more likely delusion, for a Pole.' He pulled a savage grin. 'As far as we were concerned, the CIA were the good guys.'

She'd never thought about it before, but now it struck her how different the world might look, depending on the time and place you viewed it from.

When the aircraft began its descent, Janusz decided to visit the loo. Watching him walk up the aisle, Kershaw grinned to see one of the cabin attendants scuttle into the galley at his approach, drawing the dividing curtain behind her. As soon as Kershaw saw him turn the handle of the cubicle, she leaned across, dipping into his coat pocket. Retrieving the roll of paperwork he'd buried himself in earlier and with half an eye on the loo door, she leafed through the printouts ... *Stuff about Orzelair, and the group who owned it ... an article about wheel-well stowaways.*

Seeing the cubicle door open, she slipped the papers back into his pocket, a thoughtful look on her face. Either Janusz Kiszka had decided to become the world's most conscientious police translator, or he had an undisclosed interest of his own in Orzelair and the man who had fallen from one of its planes.

Twenty minutes later, they were clattering down the aeroplane steps, their breath solidifying in the bitterly cold air.

'Was that entirely necessary?' she asked, catching up with him on the apron.

'What?' he asked, all innocence.

'What you did to that cabin attendant.'

As he'd walked towards the plane entrance, Kershaw following behind him, Janusz had kept both hands together down in front of him as though wearing handcuffs under his coat sleeves. When he reached the cabin attendant doing the goodbyes at the door he'd pulled an axe murderer grin, then jerked his wrists apart.

'You totally freaked the poor girl out!' said Kershaw.

Despite her frown, a dimple in the girl detective's right cheek betrayed the effort she was making to keep a straight face. His gaze lingered on her for a long moment: he had to admit that, for a cop, she was remarkably easy on the eye.

Seeing her shift her overnight bag awkwardly from one hand to the other, Janusz insisted on taking it from her.

'Thanks,' she said, digging in her pocket for her gloves. 'But here's the deal. Could you try to remember that while you're here, you're representing the Metropolitan Police?'

He grunted in what she hoped was agreement, albeit grudging.

As they joined the passport queue, he turned to her. 'I meant to ask, what should I call you?' he asked. 'Detective Constable Kershaw?'

'Just call me Natalie,' she said.

'*Natalia*,' he said, his pronunciation transforming the name into something exotic and beautiful. 'I remember now. I shall call you Natalia.'

132

Nineteen

Przeczokow Airport was a brick and glass hangar reminiscent of one of the smaller branches of B&Q. The official on passport control barely glanced at their documents and less than a minute later they were passing through a corridor designated as custom control by the addition of a single low bench without having seen a single other member of staff.

Having arranged to meet a representative of airport management, Kershaw was irritated to find no one waiting for them in the arrivals hall. After they'd hung around for ten minutes or more, by which time their fellow passengers had all left the building, she sent Kiszka to approach a passing girl, whom she gathered must work here judging by her lack of a coat and bag. Kershaw could hear every word of their conversation but the mellifluous singsong of the language, interspersed with the occasional staccato '*tak, tak*' – like the pecking of a bird – was entirely alien to her. More used to travelling in the Med, where she understood so many words and phrases, her total ignorance of the language here gave her a feeling of powerlessness that she didn't like one bit.

When Kiszka returned, he was tapping one of his little cigars on its tin box. 'Angelika says the airport manager isn't here today but Orzelair has sent someone to meet us. We're to go to the main office in ten minutes' time.' He nodded towards a kiosk right behind her. 'Why don't you grab a drink, while I pop out for a smoke?'

Kershaw felt a wave of mild panic. 'How do I ask for a coffee?' she hissed at his departing back.

'Just say *kawa*, and flutter your eyelashes,' he threw over his shoulder.

When they were finally introduced to Mikal Janicki, the man from the airline, Kershaw was relieved to discover that he, at least, spoke perfect English with a slight American twang. Under his suit he wore a woven shirt without a tie, a casual look that matched his polite yet informal style.

The three of them sat at a round table as Angelika, the female assistant who Kiszka had buttonholed in arrivals, set a chrome pot of coffee and a plate of pastries down between them, before withdrawing to her own office.

'I must apologise for keeping you waiting,' said Janicki, pouring the coffee. 'I'm afraid our director of operations has gone down with the flu, so I had to drive down from Rszezow at short notice.'

'Please don't apologise,' said Kershaw. She pushed a clear plastic file containing images of the dead man across the table. Composited from post-mortem photographs, they showed him full face and profile, along with a shot of his suit and coat, arranged in such a way that you couldn't see the bloodstains. 'This is the man we are trying to identify. We have good reason to believe he stowed away in the wheel well of one of your jets.'

Janicki unfolded a pair of gold wire reading glasses and, setting them on his nose, studied the images one by one in silence for several moments, an intent frown creasing his brow. 'And this man carried no passport? No identification of any kind?'

'No, nothing at all,' said Kershaw.

'He doesn't look like the average stowaway, does he?' said Janicki. 'And I have to say that in all my fifteen years working for the airline, I've never heard of anyone stowing away on a Polish plane.' He took a sip of coffee. 'Once people make it to Poland, you see, there are far easier ways of reaching the UK.'

Kiszka, whose sole contribution so far had been to send Janicki a couple of his trademark glowering looks, chose this moment to pitch in. 'Maybe the guy was drunk, or maybe he just wasn't the sharpest tool in the box,' he said. 'Either way, he managed to get through your security systems and find his way into that wheel well.'

Kershaw shot him a look that said, *I'll ask the questions.* Kiszka obviously had issues with anyone in authority – not just the cops.

'Obviously, my priority is to identify this man and inform his family of his death,' she said. Janicki nodded, his expression solemn. 'I'm not remotely interested in your security systems – that's outside my remit – but I would like to get a handle on how he got into the plane, simply because it might give me some clue as to where he came from and what he was playing at.'

'Of course.' Janicki smiled. 'I've already arranged to take you airside to talk to our chief engineer – he will know better than anyone how and when we might have acquired a non-paying passenger.'

They emerged back onto the apron, and Janicki guided them along a walkway painted in yellow on the concrete. The twin-engined jet they'd flown in on stood silent and empty, the only plane to be seen. Janicki told them that it would complete another internal leg before returning ready for tomorrow morning's flight to City, the airport's only international route.

135

'I'm afraid there's no smoking at all airside,' he said to Kiszka, who was lifting a cigar to his lips. 'Too much kerosene around.'

A two-minute stroll later, Janicki opened the door to a portakabin sited at the far end of the terminal building. A thickset balding man in oil-stained orange overalls behind a battered eighties vintage desk, who'd clearly been expecting them, got to his feet. '*Dzien dobry, paniom,*' he said, followed by a glance down at his open hands, and a stream of Polish.

As Janicki and the man chuckled, Kershaw smiled, too, murmuring to Kiszka, 'What did he say?'

'He says he'd shake hands but we probably don't want to get our nice clothes covered in oil.'

After Janicki introduced the overalled man as Chief Engineer Mazurek, Kershaw handed over the pictures of the dead stowaway. Then she told Kiszka to ask him: 'Did you, or anyone on your team, see this man hanging around before the departure of the UK flight on November 6th?'

Mazurek examined them all before shaking his head slowly. '*Nie,*' he said finally, and pointing to the shot of the guy's clothes, reeled off something else. Kiszka turned to her: 'He says that anyone dressed like that hanging around airside would stand out like a sore thumb. But if he can keep the pictures, he will show them to everyone who was on shift that morning.'

Kershaw told him yes, he could keep them – she had a bunch more copies in her overnight bag.

After locking up the portakabin, Mazurek led them towards a corrugated structure about the size of a small house. They pushed their way through the flaps of plastic hanging down over the entrance and into the workshop. Inside, the air was filled with the volatile reek of engine oil. In one corner, a giant jet cowling strapped to some sort of hydraulic lifting device on wheels, cast a shadow over the long metal workbench in the middle of the room. There, a young man with fair hair clipped in a number two and safety glasses was drilling a hole into a curved piece of aluminium. So intent was he on his task that he didn't notice the visitors until Mazurek leant down to catch his eye, at which point he leapt backwards, tearing off his glasses. He gabbled something in Polish and his boss replied in reassuring tones, patting him on the shoulder.

'What's going on?' Kershaw asked Kiszka.

'The boy lost track of time,' said Kiszka. 'He's meant to be on his lunch break by now.'

Mazurek started a comprehensive rundown of the Orzelair maintenance operation at Przeczokow, pausing to allow Kiszka to translate it into English, which he did swiftly and fluently – although Kershaw noticed his eyes following the young technician as he donned a padded jacket and slipped out of the workshop.

After a few minutes hearing about the engineering set-up – as a small airport it was restricted solely to routine safety checks and minor maintenance jobs – Kershaw broke into the chief engineer's spiel with an apologetic smile. 'Sorry,' she said before turning to Kiszka. 'Can you ask him to tell me how and when a stowaway might gain access to the UK flight?'

Kiszka's question got a single word reply.

'*Niemozliwe*!'

Kiszka gave Kershaw a deadpan look. 'He says that's not possible.'

She turned her sweetest smile on the chunky engineer. 'In that case would you ask him if he can think of any other way a fifteen-stone Pole might fall out of one of his planes. Did he accidentally flush himself away, maybe, while using the toilet?'

As Kiszka relayed her words, trying to keep a straight face, Kershaw watched Mazurek's self-satisfied expression evaporate like kerosene fumes off hot tarmac.

Janicki cut in, all affable reason: 'If I may say something? Nothing like this has ever happened here before, so perhaps it's a bit difficult for Pan Mazurek to ... take it on board.' He turned to the grim-faced engineer and made what was clearly a conciliatory speech, at the end of which Mazurek gave a grudging nod.

'Pan Mazurek has agreed to suspend his ... understand-able scepticism,' said Janicki, 'and will take us through exactly what happens between an aircraft arriving and being turned around for next morning's departure.'

After half an hour stood staring at the underside of an aeroplane in sub-zero temperatures, Kershaw had lost all feeling in her hands and feet and developed a nasty crick in the neck, but on the upside, she could now claim a working knowledge of the architecture of the Airbus A318's wheel well. She'd discovered that it would be challenging but entirely possible for a reasonably fit, determined man to clamber up into the void, and that once in position, he stood little risk of being spotted when the captain conducted his last-minute visual check of the plane. In order to avoid the risk of detection by engineers running any final maintenance checks, the best moment to grab the ultimate budget seat would be about an hour before take-off: about 0630 hours in the case of the daily flight to the UK.

Kiszka appeared to have lapsed into semi-detached indif-ference since they'd left the workshop, restricting himself solely to translating her questions and Mazurek's answers.

She dropped back to chat to him as the group made its way back to the terminal building. 'You've gone very quiet.'

His response was a half-shrug half-grunt.

She breathed warm air onto her fingers through her gloves. 'You could have told me it would be this cold – I'd have worn my thermals!'

'You call this cold? You should come here in January.'

Entering the terminal was like slipping into a warm bath. After more coffee, Janicki and Angelika took them on a tour of the security protocols from check-in through to departure, which, in an airport the size of Przeczokow, took all of about four minutes. The only other person they saw was the guy who'd checked their passports earlier. He passed them with a polite nod, clearly on his way home going by the parka he now wore over his uniform and the large sandwich he was munching. After the feverish atmosphere of City Airport earlier that day, Kershaw found the airport's stillness – its shuttered café and silent departure gate – strangely unnerving.

'Is there anything else I can help with?' Janicki asked Kershaw as they returned to the check-in area.

'I think we've covered everything,' she said. 'As I said, I'm here primarily to look for clues to our stowaway's identity. How he got through your security cordon is really a matter for you.'

'And that seems destined to remain a mystery,' he said, looking unconcerned. 'Perhaps I can call for a taxi to take you into town, now that our business is completed?'

As they reached the top of the staircase, Janicki peeled off to answer his mobile and Kershaw turned to lean on the guardrail. Below her she could see Kiszka and Angelika, who'd fallen behind, approaching the foot of the stairs. They were walking slowly, and he had his head bent towards hers, speaking into her ear. Angelika had her eyes fixed on the deck, but she wasn't exactly knocking him back, either. *Kiszka must be, what – fifteen, twenty years older than her?* thought Kershaw. All the same, she had to concede that he had a whiff of danger about him that some girls would find irresistible.

Twenty

Janusz would have liked to spend the cab journey into town thinking over what he'd learnt and deciding on his next move but the girl detective – Natalia – wanted to chat.

'Their security systems looked alright to me,' she said, 'but there must be a hole in them somewhere, otherwise I don't see how our stowaway ended up in the belly of one of their planes.'

'Hmmm.' He had his own views on how that might have happened but he wasn't about to share them.

'Two rows of razor wire round the perimeter – and motion sensors. Unless he bribed his way onto the apron? Still, like this ...' she checked the airport man's business card, '... Janicki guy said, why waste your money, when there are easier ways to get the UK?'

'It's *Yan-its-ky*,' said Janusz.

'Sorry?'

'In Polish a "c" followed by a "k" is pronounced *"itsk"*.'

She stared at his craggy profile. 'Are you at all interested in our mystery stowaway?'

Janusz turned to her and grinned. 'If I say no, do I still get paid?'

They passed the end of the airport perimeter fence and plunged straight into a deep birch forest, a strangely claustrophobic vista of densely-planted pale trunks that stretched right to the edge of the road. It was twenty minutes before they emerged into more open country, a view broken only by farmhouses and the occasional industrial chimney. *A conveniently remote setting*, thought Janusz, *if you were using an airport for some nefarious activity like, say, human trafficking*.

The cab driver caught his eye in the mirror. 'You chose a bad time to visit Przeczokow, *prosze pana*,' he said, gesturing at the sky.

The girl turned those inquisitive blue eyes on Janusz.

'He says it's going to snow,' he told her.

'A lot?'

He shook his head. 'No more than half a metre.'

By the time they emerged from their hotel – an unremarkable budget chain affair on the edge of town – early that evening, the snow was falling steadily in flakes as big as a child's hand. Kershaw dived straight into the cab waiting at the kerb, but Janusz stood for a moment, absorbing the deep and pillowy silence snow always seemed to bring, feeling an echo of his childhood excitement at the first proper fall of winter.

They soon left behind the dreary post-war architecture of the Soviet era and entered the *stare miasto*, a labyrinth of medieval cobbled streets. A soft glow – almost certainly candlelight – spilled from the Gothic windows of several of the churches they passed.

'Is there some kind of religious festival on today?' asked Kershaw, frowning.

'It's probably just a saint's day.'

'Are there many of them?'

'One for every day of the year.' He grinned. 'I think yours is in July, Natalia.'

The cab dropped them beside the *Rynek*, the town's cobbled main square. As Janusz paid the driver, Kershaw gazed up at the imposing Hapsburgian merchants' houses, their steep roofs frosted white by the snow, and the turquoise coppered bell towers of the massive brick-built church that loomed over the wide sloping square.

'It's just like Prague!' she exclaimed after a moment.

'What did you expect? Mud huts?' asked Janusz. The girl's reaction wasn't uncommon, though. Sometimes it felt as though Poland's thousand-year history, its place as one of Europe's great powers, had been snuffed out when the country disappeared behind Stalin's Iron Curtain after the war. Poland might be a member of the EU now, but how long would it be before it was restored to the heart of Europe in people's consciousness?

They started looking for somewhere to eat, hugging the edge of the square where there was as yet only a thin covering of snow, but Janusz could see that the girl was struggling nonetheless.

'It's these boots,' she said with an apologetic grimace, pausing to show him an unridged sole.

He shook his head in mock exasperation, then offered her his arm, a gesture so old-fashioned, so *gallant*, that she almost expected him to click his heels.

Five minutes later, Janusz had dismissed every restaurant they had passed. 'Mother of God!' he grumbled. 'McDonald's, Starbucks ... a *sushi bar!*'

'That Italian looked okay,' said Kershaw, tottering along on her slippery soles, hanging off his arm.

'I don't come to my homeland to eat *pizza*,' he growled.

In a side turning off the square Janusz finally found what he was looking for: a traditional restaurant with a menu in Polish stuffed with his favourite dishes. A glowing log fire and timber-beamed ceiling made the interior feel as cosy as some *babcia*'s country parlour.

After their menus had been delivered by the softly spoken, middle-aged lady owner, Janusz asked Kershaw: 'So, what do you feel like eating?' For a moment, he couldn't understand why she was looking at him so blankly, before realising that he'd spoken in Polish. 'Sorry,' he said, scratching his ear. 'Let me tell you what they have. Okay. I'm going to start with the *kaszanka*. That's duck's blood sausage fried with buckwheat.'

Her almost-comical look of horror advised him to move on.

'Something lighter maybe? How about *zurek* – fermented wheat soup with boiled egg and some pork sausage? ... No?'

'I am usually quite an adventurous eater,' she said, trying not to sound defensive. 'But this stuff is a bit out of my comfort zone.'

After a few moments of negotiation Janusz had managed to persuade Natalia that smoked herring and potato pancakes followed by duck breast with sour cherry sauce didn't sound too daunting.

Once their starters had arrived, he said, 'You know, if you'd come to a town like this ten years ago, there would have been half a dozen restaurants like this on the main square – not all that fast food crap that's there now. Excuse my language.'

'These. Are. Amazing,' she said, eyes wide, pointing at the golden-brown potato cakes with her knife.

Her unselfconscious delight in the *placki ziemniaczane* made Janusz smile. So many young women were neurotic about eating these days, as though enjoying food were some kind of moral failing. He suddenly remembered one of Oskar's pet theories: that women whose idea of a meal was picking at a salad were, without exception, cold and uptight in the sack, while a love of food was a sure-fire indicator of a healthy appetite elsewhere. Watching Natalia tucking in, Janusz found himself wondering whether she'd bear out the theory.

'It is a shame there aren't more places like this still,' she said, putting her knife and fork together on her empty plate.

'But then, I suppose that's what people were fighting for when you threw out the Communist government, right?'

'I didn't spend my youth dodging rubber bullets for the right to drink weak American coffee,' he protested. 'I knew people who were jailed, who *died* fighting for democracy. Now all anyone seems to care about is flat screen televisions and shopping in IKEA.'

She shrugged. 'When people have the freedom to make choices, they don't always choose what you'd like them to.'

Janusz knew the girl had a point. Whenever he returned home he still half-hoped to find the traditional Poland he'd so loved when he was growing up – the Poland everyone had said they were fighting to reclaim from Soviet rule. Yet the irony was that communism – by uniting the country in opposition for nearly fifty years – had unwittingly helped to preserve its traditions and culture, its powerful sense of identity. And now that the battle for freedom was over, what did the younger generation want? For Poland to be just like every other European country.

'What do you make of the Orzelair set-up?' she asked, over their main courses.

He shot her a surreptitious glance but the expression in her grey-blue eyes appeared guileless.

'Nothing much.' He shrugged. 'They're the Ryanair of Eastern Europe, but with better customer service.' He made to top up her glass with the Hungarian Merlot they were drinking but she shook her head.

'You don't think they could be dodgy?'

'Dodgy how?'

'I'm not sure.' She met his gaze. 'Drug smuggling? People smuggling? We're right on the border with Ukraine here, aren't we? From what I've read, that's practically the developing world.'

He wondered how Varenka would take to her homeland being described this way – even if it was more or less true. In any event, he didn't like the turn the conversation was taking. He sneaked a look at his watch. Nearly 8.30 p.m. He needed to get going. But he had a nasty suspicion that the girl wouldn't believe him if he claimed to fancy an early night. And since the hotel was in the opposite direction to the airport, the elaborate masquerade of pretending to go to bed would only waste valuable time.

'Let's go and get a drink somewhere,' he said, signalling for the bill.

Just as he'd hoped, Natalia decided to use the bathroom before leaving.

As soon as she'd disappeared up the spiral staircase, he went over to the little desk where the lady proprietor was making out the bill. *Przepraszam pania bardzo*, could she please see the young lady safely into a cab, as regretfully he had to dash. Spying a rack of cigars in aluminium tubes he selected one – his favourite, a Romeo y Julieta – and handed her enough *zlotych* to cover everything. Then he left, using his hand to still the bell above the door on the way out.

It felt liberating to be striding across the creaking snow alone, taking great breaths of the chilly mentholated air, but by the time he hailed a passing taxi, he found himself struggling with a feeling of remorse. He was picturing the look on the girl's face when she discovered she'd been dumped.

Twenty-One

'You want go to the airport? You know there's no flight until the morning?' The cab driver was an elderly man, probably working to supplement a meagre pension.

'I'm meeting someone who works there,' said Janusz, knocking the snow off his boots against the sill of the car before climbing in. 'He works on the night flights.'

While chatting to Angelika, the director's assistant, during the airport tour, he'd discovered that the daily UK departure was not the only international flight after all; Przeczokow also operated 'cargo flights' involving three departures and arrivals a week. But when he'd started asking where they went and what cargo they brought back, she'd clammed up. Janusz had a powerful intuition that these flights lay at the heart of Barbu Romescu's real business interests. He might, as far as Orzelair's management were concerned, have left the company, but Janusz suspected Przeczokow remained his private fiefdom – the perfect backwoods spot to take delivery of a planeful of contraband 'cargo'– girls being trafficked into the UK sex trade. After landing at night they could be issued with faked or stolen passports, and transferred straight onto the morning flight to London. Janusz did a few sums, and calculated that if every girl paid a couple of thousand for the promise of a new life in the West, Romescu could be making £300,000 plus per flight – not even taking into account what the girls would be worth at the other end.

'*Tak,*' said the driver, easing the car away from the kerb. 'There was a bit of a fuss around here when they started up.'

'Really? When was that?'

'Oh, two or three years ago? Some people got up a petition to complain about the noise. Anyway, they must have changed the flight path because you don't often hear them any more.'

I'll bet they did, thought Janusz.

The driver picked up speed as they left town – the main road had already been cleared and gritted – and soon they were plunging into the birch forest. The view of white trees either side illuminated by the eerie snow-light, and the black road stretching ahead in the headlights, ruler-straight, was hypnotic.

'We haven't passed another car since we left Przeczokow,' observed Janusz.

'That's because this road only goes to the airport.' Chuckling, the old man offered Janusz a boiled sweet from a tin. 'Apparently the EU paid for it. More fool them, eh?'

After leaving the forest, a distant glow could be seen beyond the next rise in the road and a few minutes later the cab reached the airport perimeter fence. Beyond the wire, Janusz could see the floodlit tail of a plane sticking out from behind the terminal building. It was parked up in such a way that only its rear half was visible, but from its low-slung belly and blanked-out windows it looked like a freight plane. Using a cargo plane was no doubt part of the cover story, in case locals who saw a passenger airliner passing

147

overhead started asking awkward questions. Behind its sightless windows the plane probably had the standard array of passenger seating.

The cab pulled up at the empty drop-off zone and Janusz handed over a note.

The cab driver peered out at the darkened terminal through the falling snow. 'Are you going to wait for him out there, in the cold?' he asked in a worried voice.

'He'll be out soon,' said Janusz. And no sooner had he spoken than the air was split by a rising shriek: four jet engines accelerating for take-off.

As the cab pulled away, Janusz surveyed the airport car park opposite. Finding the white expanse unbroken but for a single vintage Polski Fiat, he gave a satisfied nod.

It had been a stressful day for nineteen-year-old aircraft technician Boguslaw Witorski, and he was looking forward to his dinner. When he worked late his mama would always leave a pot of stew – usually pork, sometimes beef – simmering on the stove for him, and a loaf of rye bread under a fresh tea towel. When he climbed into the driving seat, he was so focused on his first mouthful of stew that he couldn't work out at first what it was that felt wrong. Then it hit him: *the smell of cigar smoke*. Suddenly, a gravelly voice spoke his name from the rear seat.

'*Kurwa mac*!' he shouted, jumping so violently that his skull smacked against the roof of the Fiat.

'Don't turn around. And don't try to run away. I don't want to make a nasty mess of your Fiat.'

Boguslaw gasped as he felt something jab him through the seat back, just to the right of his spine. 'I haven't got any money!' he said. 'Take my bank card!' He went to pull the card from his back pocket, but the movement was rewarded with another warning prod.

'Keep still. I don't want your money, just some information.'

'Anything, *prosze pana*, I'll tell you everything I know, just don't shoot me!'

'Where's your boss?'

'He left an hour ago. These days he leaves me to turn the power off once the flight's left.'

'I bet he told you to make yourself scarce while the English cops were here, right?'

'Yes! But I forgot and went back to finish the job I was doing. After they left he was mad as a cut snake.'

With that gorilla Mazurek off the premises and the boy babbling like a mountain brook, Janusz allowed himself to relax a little.

'When does the plane fly back in?' he asked.

'5.30 tomorrow morning.'

Janusz frowned. If these so-called cargo flights were illegally trafficking women from the east, then arriving during daylight hours would surely be courting disaster, especially since by that time of the morning, the airport would be gearing up for the London flight.

'So how do you disembark the *laski*?' he asked.

'*Girls?*' The boy sounded mystified. 'What girls?'

Janusz could see the boy's frown reflected in the rear-view mirror. 'You're lying,' he growled. But even as he said it, he knew the boy wasn't smart enough – or brave enough – for that.

He paused, his brain racing. 'What *are* these flights bringing in then?'

'They don't bring anything in, *prosze pana*. They take stuff *out*.'

'Out where?'

'Someplace called Sukur – in Turkey.'

Turkey? Janusz sat in stunned silence, seeing again the

149

garish-coloured pastries and smelling the fruity shisha at the Pasha Café. A muffled mobile tone from the front seat broke into his thoughts.

'It's probably my mama,' said Boguslaw, sheepish. 'She worries if I'm not home on the dot.'

'Well, she'll have to fret for a while longer,' Janusz growled. 'And turn the engine on before our dicks get frostbite.'

The boy told him that, in the eighteen months he'd worked there, the pattern had remained more or less the same. A big freight truck would arrive a couple of hours before take-off and its two man crew would use the engineering department's forklift to transfer large wooden crates onto the plane via a loading ramp.

'So what's in the crates?' Janusz chafed his upper arms: he could hear the rattle of the Fiat's heater but the feeble warmth it produced didn't seem to reach the back seat.

'Pan Mazurek told me it was industrial fridges and freezers.' The boy glanced up at Janusz in the mirror, a look that said he didn't believe the story. 'But he never let me anywhere near the plane during loading. He said it was because of health and safety – I wasn't insured if they dropped a fridge on my head.'

'Do I look like a *kretyn*?' snorted Janusz. 'All this time watching this little scene, you never got a single clue as to what was really inside those crates?' When the boy didn't answer, Janusz delivered another incentivising jab in the back.

'*Dobrze*! *Dobrze*!' he said. 'There was one time when they dropped a crate. I was just coming back from the bogs and I got a glimpse of what was inside.'

Janusz grinned to himself: who needed a gun when an empty cigar tube did the job just as well?

'And?' he said.

'Brown metal boxes, maybe a metre and half long?'

Janusz frowned. 'Plain boxes?'

'I saw yellow numbers, letters, printed on one.' The boy shrugged. 'Not words, more like a code. It meant nothing to me.'

A distant bell chimed in Janusz's brain but right now he didn't have time to interrogate his ageing memory banks.

'What about the office – do they know what's going on?'

'The director, perhaps, but not Angelika – no way.'

As he mentioned the girl, his tone became resolute – maybe the boy did have some *jaja* after all, thought Janusz approvingly.

'She definitely thinks the cargo is fridges, because she's always joking with me.' Janusz saw a smile curl one side of the boy's mouth. 'She says my job is sending Polish ice cubes to Turkey.'

'Maybe as you say, the girl is as innocent as a lamb,' Janusz conceded, 'but all this cloak and dagger business over a few fridges – *you knew* something illegal was going on, didn't you?'

Boguslaw hung his head. 'I didn't want to get into trouble, *prosze pana*,' he said. 'There are hardly any jobs round here that pay a half-decent wage and my mama made me *promise* I wouldn't go to England to work.'

'Have you ever come across a Romanian called Romescu – visiting your boss maybe? Big scar down one side of his face?'

The boy shook his head in the mirror. '*Nie, pana.*'

Janusz grunted. Pulling a shot of the dead stowaway out of his pocket, he leaned forward to show the boy. 'What about this guy the English cops are trying to identify, the one who fell out of one of your planes?'

'I've never seen him before,' said the boy, frowning down at the picture.

Suddenly, Janusz's door flew open. A powerful hand

151

grabbed him roughly by the lapels of his coat and started to drag him through the open door. Janusz brought up both fists but before he could throw a punch he felt the icy kiss of a gun barrel jabbed against his throat. He unbunched his hands and as he was bundled through the doorway, he caught a glimpse of his assailant – a big man in a padded jacket wearing a dark green balaclava, the sort Janusz himself had been issued back when he'd started his national service.

The next thing he knew, the glittering white surface of the car park swung up crazily to meet him and he found himself lying face down, mouth and nostrils packed with snow. From that single glimpse of the man's eyes Janusz might not have recognised him, but the bulky outline and the faint smell of kerosene supplied the rest. *Mazurek*. Mama must have phoned the boss to ask where her baby boy had got to.

Janusz had a vivid premonition of the next frame of this *dramat*: he would be pinned down and shot through the back of the neck. *Executed.*

As he felt a boot land between his shoulder blades he knew he had only a split second. Tensing his upper body, and bracing his left arm against the snowy ground, he threw back his right arm and shoulder with all the force he could muster, a roar issuing from his throat. A moment of resistance, and then the weight disappeared from his back, accompanied by a grunt of surprise. Thrown onto his left foot, Mazurek staggered on the snow, his outstretched gun arm waving wildly as he tried to regain his balance. Janusz rolled his body and made a desperate grab for his leg. He couldn't get a proper grip, but he felt his scrabbling fingers close around the seam of his attacker's jeans, and tugged. There was barely any force behind the action – but it was enough. The off-balance Mazurek swayed like a tall ship in a high gale, and then, eyes wide at this unexpected turn of events, went down with a mighty *thwack*.

Janusz scrambled to his feet, looking for the gun, saw the black shape of it against the snow, centimetres from his assailant's outstretched hand. He'd have liked to boot it away but, deciding he couldn't reach it fast enough, kicked Mazurek in the nuts instead. He jack-knifed with an animal howl, making himself into a surprisingly small ball for such a big man, giving Janusz time to pick up the pistol.

The *chuj* didn't look like he'd be up and about anytime soon, Janusz decided, but just to be on the safe side he stooped to unlace Mazurek's trainers, keeping the gun pointed at his chest. Pulling them off by the heel, he heaved one, then the other into the snowy distance.

Locating the safety on the gun, he slid it to the 'on' position. His instinct had been right: Mazurek hadn't come to scare him off, but to kill him.

Leaning heavily on the roof of the car to catch his breath, he saw the boy staring out at the downed Mazurek, as if in a trance, and motioned to him to unwind his window.

'When your boss is feeling a bit better ...' he told the boy, in between breaths, 'give him a lift home. Remind him that I'm here with the London police, and if he wants to try any more shit, I'll have Interpol crawling all over this place by lunchtime. You hear me?'

The boy nodded, his eyes fixed on Janusz's right hand, which still held the gun. Janusz weighed it in his hand: a blunt nosed semi-automatic pistol, blue-black metal with a plastic grip – brand-new from the look of it. He hadn't held a gun since his military service and he'd forgotten the instant sense of power it bestowed.

He stowed it in his pocket. 'What's your name, kid?' he asked, his voice gruff but not unkind.

'Boguslaw, *pani*.'

'Well Slawek, here's a piece of advice. Buy your mama a

nice big bunch of flowers and tell her you've started looking on UK job websites. Sooner or later the *gowno* is gonna hit the fan at this place and everyone within 500 metres is going to get spattered.'

Pulling out his mobile, he punched in the number of the cab driver who'd brought him here. 'Who knows,' he winked at the boy. 'Maybe you can persuade the lovely Angelika to go with you.'

Twenty-Two

Since Kershaw had emerged from the restaurant bathroom to discover that Kiszka had given her the slip, she'd been spitting feathers. Despite sending him a number of increasingly forthright texts she'd received no reply. Now she lay on the bed in her hotel room watching ancient repeats of *Mr Bean* on the TV's one English language channel – a pastime that was doing little to assuage her fury. *Where the fuck was he? And what was he up to?*

Kershaw's room faced the street so she was able to jump up and look out the window when she heard cabs drawing up outside to deliver guests. The cab traffic slowed to a trickle as the evening progressed and by 11 p.m., the street lay empty and silent, so quiet that when she opened the window and leaned out she could actually hear the snow falling. Finally, just before midnight, there came the rumble of a diesel engine. Looking out, she saw Kiszka haul himself out of a cab, his movements as tentative as some old geezer. After the cab pulled away, he lingered at the kerb, looking up and down the empty street before turning towards the hotel. He looked like he was swearing to himself as he forced a path through the knee-deep snow, before finally disappearing out of view beneath the entrance porch.

When she heard his footsteps reach the corridor outside – his room was almost opposite hers – she opened her door, catching him just as he was getting out his key card. He whipped around, as though ready for a fight – and from the look of him, it wouldn't be the first one of the night. He had a trail of dried blood beneath one nostril, his greatcoat looked damp and stained like he'd been rolling around in the snow, and when she took a step closer she noticed a graze on his throat. The speech she'd been preparing for the last hour or more, about the professionalism and courtesy she expected from him while he was being paid by the Met, evaporated.

'What the fuck happened to you?'

'You should see the other guy,' he grunted, turning away to put his card in the lock.

'If you think you can fob me off like that, you can forget it,' she said.

'I went to a bar and got into a fight, okay?'

Kiszka was across the threshold of his room and clearly keen to shut the door on her. She planted her right foot inside the doorway and folded her arms.

'I'm not going anywhere till you tell me what's been going on,' she said, raising her chin at him. 'Were you with that girl from the airport?'

'And what if I was? It's none of your fucking business!' His eyes blazed down at her. 'You said my free time would be my own!'

'Yes, but I …'

'No! We're just here to work together. I'm not your boyfriend!'

He'd taken a step towards her during this exchange. They stood a hand's breadth apart, eyeballing each other. She felt

156

suddenly aware of the … *physicality* of him in a way she hadn't been before. Out of nowhere she was struck by the possibility that they might be about to kiss. The feeling lasted no more than a second before they both broke the gaze. From the way he was studying the wallpaper, she wondered if he'd had the same thought.

'I'm going to bed,' he growled. 'And unless you plan on joining me, I suggest we bid each other goodnight.'

After that little late-night contretemps, Kershaw had a lousy night's sleep and woke up feeling a vague sense of guilt, even though she'd nothing really to be ashamed of. She called Ben, feeling a surge of affection and relief when he answered.

'Hello,' he murmured, his voice still thickened by sleep.

'You should be up by now,' she scolded him. 'It's gone seven over there, isn't it?'

'I've still got five minutes.'

'Where were you last night? You weren't answering your mobile.'

'Oh … we had a few beers after work – sorry, I should've checked it. What's the weather like in the frozen East?'

'We've had loads of snow,' she said, separating the blinds with her free hand. 'Must be knee deep, at least. But they cleared the roads overnight and the flight's still on time – I checked.'

'Not like Blighty then, eh?'

Ben told her he'd already moved his gear into their new place in Leytonstone, and dealt with some of the more tedious chores like taking the meter readings, *bless him*. She planned to box up her first batch of stuff and take it over by the end of the week. By the time she hung up, Kershaw felt a lot better. Any last-minute qualms she'd had at the prospect of losing her independence, her silly worries about Ben, seemed to have disappeared. Now she felt a kind of

157

settled excitement, if that wasn't a contradiction, at the thought of setting up home with him.

One person she wasn't looking forward to seeing was Kiszka. But in the dining room where breakfast was served, he greeted her as though nothing untoward had happened. Then, over a plate of what looked – and smelt – horribly like pickled fish, he launched into a polite little speech.

'It was an unforgivable discourtesy to leave you like that in the restaurant last night. Please accept my apologies, Natalia.'

As was no doubt his intention, this pretty little speech made it difficult for her to reignite the dispute, to press him again on where he'd gone, without seeming churlish. Anyway, she thought, what was the point when they'd be on the flight home in four or five hours' time?

'Apology accepted,' she said instead. As she buttered a piece of croissant she was relieved to see that he'd spruced himself up a bit: still wearing the ever-present greatcoat – *natch* – but at least he'd shaved, and his face wasn't black and blue as she'd feared it might be, his only memento of last night's brawl a cut lip. She hadn't been looking forward to turning up to meet the Polish police accompanied by someone who looked more like a dangerous fugitive than a professional translator.

'So we're going to see the cops today, right?' he asked.

'Yeah. I'm not really expecting them to identify our stow-away. But you never know.' Then she checked her watch. 'Hey, we'd better get going – the cab's coming in five minutes. I've already paid the hotel bill.'

Kiszka seemed a bit alarmed at this, but she put it down to the fact that he still had a pile of pickled fish in front of him.

It was true that Janusz disliked having to rush his food, but doing justice to the rest of his *sledz* was the least of his

158

problems. No, what was uppermost in his mind was the prospect of walking into Przeczokow's police station with a loaded handgun in his pocket.

By midday, they were back at the airport, checking in for the UK flight. Once airside, Janusz made a beeline for the bar and ordered a large Zubr, one of the few Polish beers it was still hard to find in London. Natalia, who'd asked for an orange juice, looked a bit disapproving as he necked half the contents of the tall pilsner glass in one go, but what could she say, now he was off the clock? He closed his eyes and let the dopamine reward flood his synapses.

Mazurek's pistol had been an albatross around his neck ever since he'd separated the cursed thing from its owner. He'd slept with it under his pillow with the safety on – just in case the big thug was dumb enough to come after him – with some vague idea of sneaking out early in the morning to dump it in a litterbin. But he'd overslept. The next thing he knew, he was shaking hands with the chief of police in downtown Przeczokow, while packing a concealed weapon.

'What's the joke?' asked Natalia, her steely blue eyes surveying him over the lip of her glass.

'Oh, nothing,' he said, pressing the smile from his lips. He'd been picturing the look on the face of the unsuspecting plumber who would one day lift the lid of the cistern in the cop shop toilets to discover a semi automatic pistol nestling beside the ballcock. 'Do you fancy one of those pretzels?'

Just as they were about to head through passport control, Janusz spotted Angelika waving to them across the arrivals hall.

'*Dzien dobry*! I wanted to come and wish you both a very pleasant flight,' she said in Polish, a little out of breath.

Janusz eyed her flushed cheeks. 'That's very thoughtful of you.'

Kershaw gave the girl a polite nod of greeting. 'What's going on?' she muttered to Janusz.

'Angelika has come to bid us *bon voyage*.'

Suddenly, the girl put her arms around Janusz and kissed him three times on alternate cheeks in the Polish manner. Turning to Kershaw she hesitated, before offering her a handshake. Then, with a shy wave, she was gone.

'What was all that about?' Kershaw asked him, raising an eyebrow.

Janusz flashed a piratical grin. 'Didn't I tell you? Girls find me irresistible.'

In truth, he was a bit mystified, too. It had been a somewhat over-familiar embrace for a young girl to give an older man she barely knew and, joking aside, he didn't think for a moment that Angelika entertained any romantic thoughts about him. It occurred to him that the boy – her lovesick swain Boguslaw – might have reported some version of last night's events back to her. Perhaps she'd wanted to speak to him but had lost her nerve with the girl detective there, hanging on every word. Once he got home, perhaps he should call young Angelika for an off-the-record chat.

Twenty-Three

At a little after 7.30 the following morning, Kershaw was back in her East London comfort zone, attending a call at Whipps Cross Hospital accident and emergency department with a newbie uniform called Justin.

An ambulance had been called to a sixteen-year-old boy with gang-related stab wounds in Hoe Street in the early hours. He was out of danger, but when members of the rival gang started turning up in A&E, one of the nurses had called the nick. The uniform skipper wanted a detective down there, to see if the boy would lay a complaint, and as everyone in Divisional CID – Ben's department – was busy, Kershaw copped the job.

As soon as the police car pulled up outside A&E, blue lights and sirens blazing, the teenage gangsters melted away. The knifing victim was a soft-eyed boy called Jackson, who'd acquired a fearsome rack of stitches, like red barbed wire, from nipple to navel, but after ten minutes of one-sided and unproductive bedside chat, Kershaw gave up on him.

'Well, he was falling over himself to cooperate with the forces of law and order,' she said, slamming the passenger door.

'Yeah,' Justin started the engine. 'I *know* that kebab shop where he got stabbed – it's bang under a street lamp – but he can't even tell us if his attacker was black or white?'

'Yeah, funny that.'

'Isn't it just?'

Hearing the bitterness in his voice, Kershaw shot him a sideways look. It was one thing for her to play the battle-hardened cop after five years in the Job, but cynicism in a rookie like Justin was a bit ... depressing. At his age, she'd still been all starry-eyed about making a difference. Truth be told, there was a part of her that probably always would be. She was wondering whether to launch into a little speech about keeping the faith, when the radio fizzed into life.

'Control Room to Echo One, please attend a Sierra Delta 13 in the woods on the north-east side of Hollow Ponds.'

'An SD13?' asked Justin after Kershaw acknowledged the call.

'Do try and keep up, Justin,' she said. 'It's control room code for an unexpected death.'

'Awesome!' His acne-flecked cheeks flushed with excitement. 'Can we put the blues and twos on again?'

'Go on then,' she said, secretly pleased to see his world-weary cop routine give way to boyish enthusiasm.

It was easy to see why they'd been given the job. Hollow Ponds was less than two minutes drive from the hospital campus, just the other side of the main east-west route between the Green Man roundabout and the top of Lea Bridge Road. A couple of acres of scruffy woodland bounded on every side by busy roads, it was technically part of Epping Forest, but any first-time visitor who turned up expecting sylvan glades was in for a disappointment.

After pulling into the roadside car park, Justin and Kershaw crunched across the gravel to the log cabin café that overlooked the biggest of the man-made ponds the spot

162

was named after. Framed in the cabin's serving hatch, a big balding man was making tea from an urn.

'You must be Paul Jarrett?' asked Kershaw as they reached the hatch.

'That's me,' he said.

'Thanks for calling it in, sir. And the gentleman who discovered the body?'

The guy leaned his meaty forearms on the counter and nodded conspiratorially over their shoulder. 'He's over there.'

There was only one occupant at the outdoor picnic-style tables – which was hardly surprising given it was about two degrees above freezing. 'The chap in the Barbour jacket?'

A nod. 'It wasn't what you'd call *easy* to persuade him to stick around.' His husky voice sounded like it had been marinated in the smoke of about a million Benson & Hedges. *A Londoner, bred and buttered*, thought Kershaw.

'Oh, really?'

'Yeah. Said he had a "prior engagement".' Jarrett smiled, but his eyes didn't join the party. 'I gave him a cuppa and told him to sit tight where I could keep an eye on him till the Old Bill arrived.'

Kershaw sent Justin ahead with a reel of tape to secure the access points into the woodland to stop people tramping all over their scene, while she popped over for a heart to heart with Barbour man.

'So Mr …'

'Mr Green.'

Yeah right, thought Kershaw – the patently fake name simply confirming her suspicions.

'So, Mr uh, Green. Can I ask what you were doing in the woods back there at this time in the morning?' asked Kershaw, treating him to one of her most reasonable smiles.

'Simply taking a morning c-constitutional.' He stirred his tea in a doomed stab at nonchalance.

'Oh!' she said, as though something had just dawned on her. 'I didn't realise you had a dog with you.' She cast around as though hunting for the phantom pooch.

'No, I don't have a dog. I wasn't aware it was a legal requirement for a woodland walk.'

Bravo, thought Kershaw.

She eyed his Barbour – the real deal, not some Petticoat Lane knock off – and the posh-looking shirt beneath, one of those stripy jobs you only ever saw City boys wearing. 'Right. So other than the dead man, did you come across anyone else during your stroll?'

Green opened his mouth, closed it again. Then, 'I saw a couple of people, yes.'

Now she fixed him with a deadpan stare. 'Do you ever bring your *wife* on these early morning outings, Mr Green?'

He looked down at his wedding ring and then up at Kershaw. Although the air was cold enough to turn their breath to vapour, she noticed that his forehead was sheened with sweat.

'You know what?' she said with an elaborate shiver. 'It's freezing out here. Let's continue this interview at your house.'

Ten minutes later, she was ducking under the skein of blue and white tape Justin had strung across the footpath. Skirting the pond, she passed an armada of wooden rowboats, tied up and shrouded in blue tarpaulin, and suddenly remembered her dad bringing her here one baking hot summer day when she was about nine or ten. They'd taken one of the boats out and he'd taught her how to row. *Catch a crab*. That's what he'd called it when one of her oars hit the water at the wrong angle, making a splash.

By the time she reached the north shore, where Justin was waiting for her, a fine freezing drizzle was misting the air. For a so-called beauty spot, the view was pretty bleak: there was no grass underfoot, just compacted sand and gravel, presumably the spoil left from the dredging of the ponds a century or more ago. The khaki-coloured waters of the boating lake looked murky, sinister.

'He's just in here,' said Justin, indicating a narrow path through the trees.

'You checked his pulse, like I told you?'

'Yep. Long dead. I called the fire brigade to come and cut him down.'

'So what was the story with the witness at the caff?' asked Justin over his shoulder. 'Potential customer for us?'

'Nah,' said Kershaw. 'Just a member of the LGBT community looking for love in the undergrowth.'

Justin shivered theatrically. 'Bit flipping cold for that kind of thing.'

'Well, you're not a closet gay with a wife, two kids and a job at a merchant bank, are you?' said Kershaw. 'At least he called it in. He could have legged it and left it to some poor mum out with her kids to find the body.'

'Yeah, it's not a pretty sight, that's for sure.'

He was right about that.

The dead man hung from a blue nylon rope tied round one of the lower limbs of a tree in the middle of a clearing. Kershaw circled the hanging figure, treading carefully and scanning the leaf litter for anything out of place. Early middle-aged, white, heavily built, the man's hair was crew-cut. He wore jeans and a cheap-looking bomber jacket. His trainer-clad feet hanging in mid-air, no more than a foot from the ground.

It struck her that, unlike the hanged people you saw in films, the body wasn't twisting or swinging in the breeze, the rope creaking atmospherically. He just hung there, absolutely motionless, as though fixed to the ground by invisible steel hawsers, his utter stillness lending the scene an unambiguous finality.

Kershaw stepped closer. Beneath the tight-stretched noose was a deep ligature mark where the rope had cut into his neck. It was like the tideline on a beach: below it the skin appeared to be a normal colour, more or less; above it his face was a uniform, unnaturally deep red. The tip of a swollen tongue poked through his slightly parted lips, and there was a track of dried blood beneath one nostril. Standing on tiptoe to examine the skin around the rope she made out several bloody scratches above and below the shiny blue nylon.

She tried to picture the poor sap's last moments. He'd probably prepared the noose before climbing the tree, tying the rope just before jumping off. But it looked like the drop he'd given himself hadn't been long enough to break his neck cleanly. Finding himself slowly strangling, he'd scrabbled desperately at the rope, leaving those claw marks around the ligature line. She squatted to examine his right hand and nodded to herself. She'd lay a bet that the blood visible under the empurpled fingernails of his right hand would prove to be his own.

Going to view the body from the other side, she became aware of something nagging at the back of her mind, a feeling that his face looked vaguely familiar.

Before Kershaw had a chance to pursue the thought, she heard Justin say 'Morning, Sarge,' his voice respectful.

She turned to find Ben entering the clearing. It wouldn't have been apparent to anyone else, but she could see amusement dancing in his eyes. He'd crawled into her bed smelling of whiskey in the early hours, after some leaving do, and they hadn't really spoken that morning, unless you counted their sleepy fuck just before dawn.

'Morning, Natalie,' he said, raising an amused eyebrow as he awaited her response.

'Morning, *Skipper*,' she said, deliberately overdoing the deference.

'What have we got here then?'

He listened as she gave him the lowdown, barely glancing at the body. 'Suicide note?'

'I was just about to look.'

'Don't worry – I'll do it,' he said. 'It all looks pretty straightforward. Oh, and DS Bacon asked if you could head back to the nick.'

'We could hang around for a bit, if you like? Keep any rubberneckers at bay?'

'No need,' said Ben. 'I've got a couple more uniforms and the pathologist on their way.'

'Okay,' she said. 'Come on, Justin. I'll buy you a cuppa.'

With the case looking like a straight up and down suicide, she knew it was one for Divisional CID rather than Murder Squad. And Christ knew she could do without another unidentified suicide in her inbox. All the same, as she made her way back around the pond she couldn't help feeling slightly miffed at the way Ben had dismissed her from the scene.

Later that evening, Ben came by her place for a meal. He'd already moved his stuff into the new flat, only to discover that the cooker wasn't working.

'This looks a bit dry,' said Kershaw, bending to peer at the ready-made pizza she was heating up in the oven. 'I'm down to the last dregs of the freezer, so it's probably about a year past its sell-by date.' She reached a couple of plates down from the cupboard. 'Have you talked to the landlord about the cooker at the flat?'

'Yeah, he just texted me actually,' said Ben. 'He can get an electrician there tomorrow morning, but now we're going public with the Stride business, there's no way I'll make it.'

She screwed up her face at him. 'What Stride business?'

'You must have heard,' he said, applying the corkscrew to a bottle of red. 'It was all over the nick.'

She shook her head. 'I got stuck in court this afternoon – some credit card fraud from Canning Town come back to haunt me.'

'That guy who hanged himself up at Hollow Ponds?' Ben plucked the cork from the bottle with a pop. 'It only turned out to be Anthony Stride.'

She stared at him. 'You're fucking kidding.'

'Nope. Soon as I got a good look at him, I realised who it was.'

Kershaw saw again the face of the hanged man, dark with congested blood. *So that was why he had seemed familiar*. During his trial for the rape and attempted murder of Hannah Ryan, Anthony Stride's photograph had been regularly splattered across the *Walthamstow Guardian* and the national red tops.

'Christ! Any idea why he topped himself?'

'There was a neatly typed note, tucked in his jeans pocket, saying he could no longer live with *"the terrible things he'd done, all the pain he'd caused people"*.'

Kershaw frowned. 'A career paedophile discovering a conscience? That's a new one on me.'

Ben shrugged. 'Who gives a fuck. There's one less evil bastard on the planet tonight.'

She couldn't disagree with the sentiment, but felt a flicker of disquiet at the hardness in his voice.

'You must be relieved,' she said carefully.

He nodded. 'Yeah, it's a big weight off.' Sounding suddenly normal again.

After they sat down to eat, she asked: 'So how did the Ryans take the news?'

'I don't know. I've been trying to back off a bit.'

'Yeah, but you've known Hannah's dad a long time. Surely you're gonna give him a call?'

'I expect I'll see him at the press conference tomorrow. It's at 10 a.m. – which is why I can't get to the flat for the electrician. I don't suppose there's any chance you could make it over there instead?'

'Not tomorrow, sorry. I'm still on earlies. We'll have to move it.'

She only managed a few mouthfuls, before pushing her plate away.

'It's not that bad,' grinned Ben, nodding at her half-eaten pizza.

'I'm not especially hungry,' she said, topping up her wine glass.

'You're probably just excited about Saturday.'

'Saturday?'

He made a reproachful face. 'Moving into the flat?'

'Oh, sorry! Yeah, 'course I am.'

Get a grip, girlfriend, she told herself. *Everything is going to be just fine.*

Twenty-Four

Following a service at St Mary's Church in Walthamstow Village, James Fulford was buried in a plot at the City of London Cemetery, not far from the graves of his mother and father.

By Janusz's reckoning, there were sixty or more people crammed into the little terraced house in Barclay Road for the *stypa* – the post-funeral feast. Marika had been working flat out in preparation for the last two days and – with her sister Basia putting in late nights recently at her job in the City – Janusz was pleased that he'd been able to persuade her to let him help with the cooking. Now he and Marika stood side by side in the through living room surveying the spread with satisfaction. As well as the huge tureen of purple-red *barszcz* with *pierogi* that he'd made, there was an assortment of *kielbasa*, a huge *salatka*, potatoes with dill, the traditional *stypa* dish of buckwheat with honey and poppy seed dressing, and hot dumplings with mushroom sauce.

'Do you think I should have made English food as well?' asked Marika, fiddling with a stray lock of hair that had escaped her chignon. 'With so many of his English friends here?'

'*Nie, nie,*' he said, patting her arm. He nodded towards a

wiry man in an ill-fitting suit piling his plate with steaming dumplings, who had an anchor and the legend 'HMS *Coventry*' tattooed on the back of his weathered hand. 'Comfort food is the same in any language.'

'What if we run out?'

As Marika looked up at him anxiously, her reddened eyes standing out against the paper-white of her face, he felt a spasm of grief.

'I think I'll go and cut some more bread,' she said decisively. Laika the dog, a black ribbon of mourning tied to her collar, followed close at her heels. Janusz was on the point of going after her, when he felt a hand on his arm.

'Let her go,' said Oskar. 'She needs to keep busy.'

Janusz eyed his friend's face. His woebegone expression sat oddly with those chubby cheeks, the naturally mischievous eyes. 'You're probably right,' he said.

'All this. It makes you wonder, doesn't it?' Oskar gestured around him. 'How we might not have as much time as you think? I just called Gosia and fixed to go home in a couple of weeks, to see her and the girls. I should really put another few grand in the bank first but,' he said shrugging, 'it's only money, isn't it?'

'*Tak.*' Janusz looked around him – since they'd moved the furniture upstairs to make space for the guests, the living room looked strangely unfamiliar. 'Remember the last time we were here, only a few weeks ago? To watch the Poland-England game?' His face split in a smile. 'And Jim coming downstairs?'

'*Tak*!' Oskar shook his head admiringly. 'Wearing that footie strip Marika made for him!'

'England colours from the front, Polish colours from the back … because when he married Marika "*he didn't just marry a woman, he married a whole bastard country*".'

Grinning, the two men shook their heads, smiles slow to fade.

Before allowing himself a proper drink, Janusz did the rounds of Jim's closer friends, the ones who'd been in touch with him recently, exchanging reminiscences and sharing condolences. He was also probing discreetly, trying to find out whether they'd noticed any change in Jim's behaviour of late, and whether the names Romescu, Varenka, or Triangle rang any bells. He drew a total blank. When he touched on the motive behind the murder, they seemed depressingly willing to view it as a commonplace act of random violence – probably drug-related.

'It's why we left and went to Enfield,' one old Cockney guy told him. 'You're not safe here anymore, not even on your own doorstep.' The locals he spoke to had all, without exception, been on the sharp end of crime over the years – a mugging here, a couple of handbag thefts there, plus a clutch of burglaries and car break-ins. One lady had been car-jacked parking her car one night, someone else had a murder happen in the flat upstairs.

Stepping outside for a smoke, he bumped into Wayne, the regular from the gym. They stood in silence for a moment, looking down at the tea lights still burning atop the garden wall.

'You're a PI, right?' murmured Wayne. 'So I'm guessing you'll be looking for the lowlifes who killed Jim?' Janusz nodded – Wayne was completely trustworthy. 'Did you get anything out of that little punk Andre Terrell?' he went on.

'Why? Do you think he's involved somehow?' asked Janusz. From what he'd seen of Jim's deputy manager, he'd have said the kid was all front – strictly an armchair gangster.

'Nothing concrete.' He screwed his mouth to one side. 'But I think Jim regretted hiring him, you know?' Wayne dropped his h's like a Cockney but there was still a Caribbean sashay to his cadences.

'Did he say why?'

'Not in so many words – you know how the man was, he wouldn't badmouth anyone. But it was obvious they didn't get on. I seen that Terrell slam out of the office screaming and shouting more than one time.'

'I suppose the cops have been by to interview him?'

'Oh yeah.' They exchanged a dry look.

Later, clearing away some dirty plates, Janusz found Basia, washing up alone in the kitchen. Grabbing a tea towel he started to dry up the mountain of crockery on the draining board. She barely acknowledged him, just crashed another plate onto the pile, spraying him with soapy water. She seemed … *angry*, almost. He recalled that she and Jim had been lovers, albeit some ten years ago, and although he was no expert in the female psyche, he could imagine that today couldn't be easy for her, either. He was wondering what on earth he could say that might make her feel better, when Marika came in.

'Janek, I think we should do the toasts now everyone has eaten?'

The noise levels rose as numerous toasts to Jim were proposed in the Polish way, accompanied by industrial quantities of *krupnik*, after which Jim's old Navy chums sang a few sea shanties, assisted by Oskar's strident baritone. An hour later, it was all over, and Janusz was standing on the threshold, Marika by his side, the house empty and silent behind them.

He enveloped her in a bear hug. 'I haven't given up on finding who did this,' he said, his voice a hoarse whisper.

'I know, I know.' She patted his shoulder absently. 'There was something I had to tell you … *Tak*. The police called to say they found Jim's laptop.'

'Really? Do you know where?'

'I'm sorry, Janek, I don't remember.' She waved a helpless hand, lapsing back into the dazed, barely-seeing state of the recently bereaved.

He walked down the front path, eyes front, refusing to look down at those treacherous tiles that had been the last thing Jim had seen.

Oskar's van pulled up at the kerb and he wound down the window. 'Get in, Janek.'

'Are you in a fit state to drive?'

Oskar looked outraged. '*Nosz, kurwa*! I hardly drank anything! Anyway, I've had three really strong coffees.'

Janusz didn't have the strength to argue. 'Drop me off by Walthamstow tube then, *kolego*.'

'Uh-uh,' said Oskar, shaking his head. He waggled a bottle of Wyborowa. 'We've got an appointment.'

Which was how Janusz came to end the day scaling the two-metre-high railings of the City of London cemetery in the dark. As the taller of the two, he went first, covering the spikes with an old duvet Oskar used to protect garden ornaments, before using the van's roof rack to boost himself up and over.

The vast expanse of the cemetery, criss-crossed by pathways, receded into the silent darkness: Janusz hadn't noticed during the burial ceremony how huge the place was.

'How the fuck are we going to find him?' he hissed.

'What are you whispering for?' chuckled Oskar. 'You're not going to wake anyone up!' He pulled a scrap of paper from his pocket with a nonchalant flourish. 'I made a *mapa* after we buried him.'

As they started off down the nearest path, a marble angel kneeling atop of a catafalque sent Janusz a reproachful look. It pitched him back thirty years, to those late-night visits to his grandfather's grave on All Saints' Eve. He remembered how tightly he had clung to Mama's hand, eyes locked on the flame of his candle, knowing that if he should let his gaze flicker towards a candlelit grave, its inhabitant might suddenly sit up – grinning face crawling with worms, flesh hanging from the outstretched arms like seaweed. At least back then there had been the twinkling of a thousand candles and murmuring groups of people: here there was nothing but a silent dormitory of the dead.

He shivered. 'Are you sure about this? It's not as if Jim was Polish.'

'Tradition is tradition,' said Oskar staunchly. 'Anyway, he said it himself – being married to Marika made him an honorary Pole.'

When they reached Jim's grave, its freshly turned earth a darkened rectangle against the moonlit turf, they fell silent and crossed themselves. Janusz took the shot glass and held it out for Oskar to fill from the *wodka* bottle. He dropped to a crouch and carefully poured the contents onto the grave.

'*Na zdrowie, kolego,*' he murmured, hearing his voice break on the last word.

They each took a swig from the bottle, Janusz suppressing a grimace: having spent half his youth blind drunk on the stuff, he could no longer stand the taste.

A few minutes later they were clambering back over the railings, using the low branch of a tree for a leg-up. From behind him, Janusz heard Oskar say: 'You dropped something!'

It wasn't till they were in the van, safely back on the main road, that Oskar handed Janusz what had fallen out of his coat pocket. A USB stick.

He turned it over in his hands, frowning, unable to recall ever seeing it before, although the image it bore of an eagle with outstretched wings looked familiar. Then he remembered why.

It was the Orzelair logo.

Twenty-Five

When Kershaw returned his call the following morning Janusz cut straight to the point. 'I hear you found Jim Fulford's laptop.'

'You know I can't confirm something like that to someone outside the family.'

'It was Marika Fulford who told me,' he growled. 'I could get her to call you, but I'd really rather not disturb her the day after she buried her husband.'

Kershaw sighed: she didn't have much appetite for point-less protocol either. 'Okay. Strictly off the record, we have recovered his laptop.'

'Where did you find it?'

'Dawn raid on some toe-rag in Tottenham who trades stolen goods. I'm told his front room looked like the ware-house of PC World.'

And I bet I know who sold it to him, thought Janusz suddenly, seeing the flash of a fake diamond embedded in a tooth.

'The Computer Crime Unit have had it for three days but they only just told us it was Jim's,' she went on. 'All the files had been deleted, of course.'

'But they were still there on the hard drive?'

'Yep. They got them all back.'

'If you'd let me have a look, I might be able to spot something.' He kept his voice casual, as if he'd be doing her a favour.

Kershaw hesitated. When she'd returned from Poland, Streaky had magnanimously allowed her back on the Fulford case, and had just assigned her and Sophie the task of wading through the recovered files. But without any suspect currently in the frame, or any idea what they were looking for, it looked like it would take until Christmas. As Jim's best mate, Kiszka would undeniably have a better nose for anything out of the ordinary; on the other hand, after that stunt he'd pulled in Poland, going AWOL on her, she still felt disinclined to trust him.

'I don't think so,' she said.

The rasp of a lighter came down the phone followed by an exhaled breath.

'What if I told you I could identify your stowaway?'

Kershaw felt her pulse rate jump. 'Really,' she drawled, deadpan.

'Yes, really.'

By the end of the day, the pair of them were installed in a conference room on the third floor at the nick, eyeing each other across a round table. After cloning the drive to secure the evidence, the computer crime boys had sent the laptop back for review and Streaky had approved Kershaw's request to get Kiszka's help in searching the files.

The only sound in the chilly, windowless room was the pathetic whirr of a tiny fan heater. They must look like a couple of gunslingers in a spaghetti western preparing for a shootout, thought Kershaw, but instead of a gun she had the laptop, and he had a USB stick.

A couple of seconds passed before Janusz pushed the nugget of plastic towards her, as though making the opening gambit in a game of chess.

Kershaw plugged it into the computer.

She stroked the trackpad, flipping through the PDF. 'All I can see on here is some old annual report for Orzelair. I don't see ...'

'Keep going. There's a bunch of photos, near the back.'

'Oh, yeah. *"Orzelair's new Berlin office* ... um ... *Meet the directors ..."'*

She bent to peer at the screen. *'Christ on a bike!'*

'I told you.'

'That's him, isn't it?' Eyes wide, she spun the laptop round and jabbed at a head and shoulders shot of a middle-aged man. 'That's the stowaway!'

Janusz lifted one shoulder in assent.

'Where did you get this?'

'That's not part of the deal, Natalia.' He had no intention of telling her what he'd worked out – that Angelika must have slipped the stick into his coat pocket during that farewell embrace at the airport. When he'd shown her one of the composite photos of the dead stowaway during their tour of airport security the previous day, she'd shaken her head – but he'd caught a flicker of recognition in her eyes.

'Anatol Woj-tek,' read Kershaw from the caption, pronouncing the 'W' and 'J' in his surname in the English way.

'It's *Voy-tek.'*

'Okay, whatever,' she said, dragging her chair around the table so they could both comfortably view the screen. 'But what does it say?'

'It says *"Pan Wojtek will be doing a charity skydive over London ..."'*

She gave him a hard stare.

'Okay, okay. It says *"Anatol Wojtek is one of Orzelair's longest serving employees, becoming head of security in 2009".*

Then it goes on about *"global challenges ... threat of terrorism ... new technology ..."* corporate hot air. That's all.'

'So how come that guy from Orzelair – Janicki? – didn't recognise the company's *head of security*?!'

Janusz drew himself upright and adopted a stuffy, lawyerly tone: 'I'm sure you will appreciate how difficult it would have been for Pan Janicki to match his memory of a living breathing colleague, whom he saw only rarely, with an artificially constructed post-mortem image of a cadaver ...'

'Why would he lie about it? Wouldn't he *care* about the guy's family?'

'I guess having your head of security drop out of one of your planes over Canary Wharf could be a bit embarrassing? Especially now the company's playing in the big boys' league with their Lufthansa deal.'

'But what the fuck was this Wojtek doing in the wheel well, anyway? He sure as hell wasn't an economic migrant.'

Kiszka felt a twinge of discomfort at hearing profanity from such pretty lips. 'Maybe he was a crazy person.' He fidgeted with his tin of cigars. *Or maybe he was trying to get to the bottom of what Romescu and his gang were up to at Przeczokow Airport, and got killed for his trouble.*

'Is there anything you want to tell me?' She scanned his face. 'Anything at all? Do I need to remind you that you were an employee of the Met on our Poland trip? If you're hiding anything you could be charged with obstructing a police investigation.'

He gave her a long, level stare that said, clearer than any words, that they both knew she was talking a load of horseshit.

Kershaw glared back at him. The fact that the 'stowaway' had turned out to be a senior employee only added to the general air of ... *whiffiness* she'd smelt around the Orzelair set-up. This Wojtek character couldn't have been murdered, could he? Even if he had, there was very little chance of her getting to the bottom of it all. And she had to admit that the prospect of spending the next God-knew-how-long flying back and forth to Poland to represent the London end of a murder investigation filled her with gloom.

Janusz nodded at the laptop. 'I've supplied my half of the bargain, now it's your turn. I want to run a search of Jim's files for a few names.'

She waited, fingers hovering over the keyboard.

'They wouldn't be potential suspects that it slipped your mind to mention, would they?' she enquired in a voice you could etch glass with.

He was ready for that one. 'No, they're just names I overheard at Jim's funeral that I didn't recognise.' He opened his hands. 'I'm clutching at straws here.'

That makes two of us, she thought. Twelve days into the investigation of Jim Fulford's murder and the team was no closer to unearthing a feasible motive than it had been on day one, which was probably why Streaky had agreed to let Kiszka have supervised access to his dead friend's computer files.

'Barbu Romescu and Varenka Kalina,' he said.

'You're going to have to spell those for me.'

Ten minutes later, having searched Jim's documents, emails and even his internet search history, they'd drawn a total blank.

Kershaw felt deflated: Kiszka really had just been clutching at straws. 'Is there anything else we can look for?' she asked.

He rested his jaw in one of those giant mitts.

'Have you run a search for Jim's deputy manager, Andre Terrell?' It was as well to leave no stone unturned: Terrell might know what connected his boss to Romescu.

'Not personally, but I know one of my colleagues has already been through Jim's email traffic.'

180

One corner of his mouth twitched upwards. 'Jim wasn't a big fan of email. Try looking in documents.'

Not surprisingly, Jim's deputy was name-checked in hundreds of the recovered documents, most of which were routine stuff about payroll, health and safety training, insurance and the like. But twenty minutes into the search, Kershaw found something. A letter addressed to Andre Terrell from his boss.

'Listen to this,' she said. '"*After issuing three formal warnings for misdemeanours ranging from persistent poor timekeeping to failure to upkeep membership records, I regret that I have no choice but to dismiss you from your position with one month's notice.*"'

Janusz peered at the screen. 'Look at the date.'

'It's the day before Jim's murder.' Kershaw's voice was flat, matter-of-fact, but her face had grown pale with excitement. 'Did Jim tell you that he was sacking this guy?'

He shook his head. 'No, nor even Marika, or she'd have mentioned it. The only other person who would need to know was the payroll lady, but she only came in once a month and he probably hadn't got round to telling her.'

Janusz recalled how shifty Terrell had been when he'd questioned him about the laptop: now it seemed his suspicion that the boy was behind its disappearance had been well grounded.

'So Terrell gets the sack,' said Kershaw, thinking out loud. 'But when his boss gets killed, he sees a chance to keep his job.'

'Right. And he steals the laptop because it's the only record of his dismissal.'

Kershaw turned a look on him that was unnerving in its intensity.

'Or because it's evidence of a motive for murder.'

Twenty-Six

It was just before six the following morning and the receptionist at Whipps Cross A&E was looking forward to clocking
off when the automatic doors opened to admit a large,
angry-looking man in a long coat. Even though her desk
was behind a security screen, her eyes went to the panic
button: the night shift brought all manner of lowlifes and
psychos through the door.

When the man gave her the name of someone who'd
been admitted in the early hours she let herself relax a little.
Foreign accent aside, he was nicely spoken, his manners a
vast improvement on the average customer, even if his hands
were bunched so tight on the counter that the knucklebones
were visible through the skin.

'I can't find anyone of that name on the system,' she said,
peering at the screen.

'Could you check again, please?' asked Janusz, struggling
to keep his voice calm. 'It's O-S-K-A-R – with a "k".'

Finally, the computer system gave up the information that
Oskar had been brought in by ambulance just after midnight
the previous night.

'He's on Billingham Ward, over in the main building,' said the receptionist.

'*Dzięki Bogu*!'

The thanks that Janusz sent God couldn't have been more heartfelt.

The message from the hospital had woken him at five, so Oskar must have been conscious then, in order to tell them who to call, but ever since that moment he had lived with the crushing sense of fear that he'd find his mate in the intensive care unit – or worse. The fact that he was on a regular ward had to be good news, didn't it?

The sight of Oskar laid out in a hospital bed brought him little consolation, however. He lay quite still, his twinkling eyes closed, and the chubby features above the neck brace sagged, as if they belonged to an old, sad stranger.

'How are you doing, *chłopie*?' murmured Janusz, his voice cracking as he took in the fresh bruising around both eye sockets, the lip darkened and split like an overripe plum.

A nurse came in carrying a plastic bag of clear fluid. 'So you're Oskar's brother?' she asked as she replaced the near-empty one hanging on the bedside drip stand.

'Yes, that's right.'

'Great, I can get you to sign a consent form.' Checking the numbers on the monitor above her patient's head she turned to Janusz. 'So, apart from the obvious contusions, he's got badly bruised kidneys and a wrist fracture.' She nodded to his right arm, which was encased in a temporary splint. 'He's had a very bad bump on the head, but the CT scan didn't find any nasties, so that's the biggest worry out of the way. He has regained consciousness but be aware he's under sedation.'

Janusz just nodded, grateful for her dry cheerfulness. Gently, he pulled up the neck of his mate's absurdly jaunty multicoloured hospital gown to cover more of his naked chest. As he did so, Oskar's swollen eyes opened just a crack.

183

'Janek. Don't tell Gosia.' His voice was hoarse but the words were crystal clear.

'Good to hear your voice, *broski.*'

'Don't tell Gosia,' he repeated with more urgency.

'*Tak, tak,*' Janusz soothed. 'If you hurry up and get better, I won't need to tell her.' He glanced over his shoulder: the nurse was talking to someone just outside the drawn bed curtains. 'Who did this, Oskar?' he asked in a fierce whisper.

His mate's eyes drifted shut again.

'Oskar. Who was it?'

The eyes opened lazily, semi-focusing on Janusz. He frowned.

'One of them ...'

'Yes?'

'Tattoo.'

'What sort of tattoo?'

Oskar's eyelids slid over his pupils.

'*Oskar!*'

His eyes stayed closed but lifting his left hand a few centimetres he made a vague gesture towards Janusz's forearm.

'*Waz.*'

A snake? Kurwa mac! The snake tattoo. Romescu's thug, the one who'd chased him in the tunnel. Janusz felt guilt and fury wrestle it out across his face. Guilt won. *Congratulations*, he thought bitterly. *Investigating Jim's death nearly got another friend of yours killed.*

'What did the *skurwysyny* want?'

'Where you live ... and why you're so interested in Romescu ...'

'You should have just told them,' said Janusz, his voice hoarse with anguish.

Oskar half-opened his eyes and lifted one shoulder. 'I said' – the ghost of a mischievous expression crossed his ruined face – 'that you have a thing for Romanian guys.'

The nurse stuck her head back in. 'Can I get you to sign those consent forms on your way out?'

Janusz knew a dismissal when he heard one. He stood and patted Oskar on the arm. 'Get some sleep, *kolego*.'

At the nurses' station Janusz signed a bunch of forms, explaining away the difference in surnames by saying they had different fathers.

'Where was he found?' he asked.

'Not far from here. Do you know Hollow Ponds, where the boating lake is? He managed to crawl to the roadside and a car stopped for him. I expect the police will want to question him.'

Janusz wondered what story Oskar would spin them.

'It was a particularly nasty assault,' her gaze scanned Janusz's face. 'I didn't like to say in front of him, but he has rope marks on his wrists and … what look like cigarette burns. I thought you should know.' Somewhat taken aback at the look in his eyes, she wondered whether her instinct had been right. 'We have support services in the hospital, if you want to talk to someone?'

Janusz pulled a mirthless smile. 'Oh, I want to talk to someone alright.'

He exploded through the doors of A&E in a blind fury, every molecule of his being harnessed to a single impulse: revenge. He scrolled through the address book on his phone – *Osip, Mirek, Gregor, Tomek* – men who knew and loved Oskar and who could handle themselves. They'd jump at the chance to administer retribution to Romescu and his tattooed thug with the business end of a baseball bat.

But as he was punching out the first number, Janusz hesitated. Forcing himself to think things through, he reached a reluctant conclusion: however tempting the idea of cracking open a few *gangsterskie* skulls, it was a self-indulgent fantasy. The likeliest outcome of such an encounter would be him

185

and his mates getting riddled with bullets – and the idea of seeing anybody else suffer on his account was unthinkable.

Nie! There were better ways to punish Romescu. First, put him behind bars for Jim's murder. Second, bust up his smuggling ring, an enterprise evidently so valuable to him that it merited the risk of eliminating Orzelair's head of security. It was clear to Janusz that Wojtek had got too close to the truth, and his bizarre death, with its echo of the young Romescu's escape to the West, had the Romanian's fingerprints all over it. The guy clearly had one sick sense of humour.

Ten minutes after leaving the hospital, Janusz reached the boating lake at Hollow Ponds, where Oskar had been found the previous night. At the log cabin café he ordered a cup of tea from the balding Cockney manning the counter.

'Do you mind if I ...' Janusz held up the cigar. Even though they were out in the open, English people could be paranoid about smoking.

'Nah, it's a free country, or so they keep telling us ... Milk and sugar?'

'No thanks, just black.'

The guy handed him his tea in a massive china mug. 'Polish?' he asked. Janusz nodded. 'What do you think of Szczesny, then?'

It struck Janusz that the handful of his countrymen who played in the Premier League had done more to promote a grasp of Polish pronunciation than the million or so who'd come here to find work in the last ten years.

'I think he's got the makings of a great goalkeeper,' he tapped some ash onto the gravel. 'But at his age it's hard to be sure.'

'Did you see the save he made in the UEFA qualifiers? The boy's got a cool head, I'll say that for him.'

'Yeah! 59th minute!'

They shook their heads in shared admiration. The guy put

186

a Tunnocks wafer in front of Janusz. 'On the house,' he said, resting his forearms on the counter. 'I hear he said he wants to stay at Arsenal his whole career – you won't hear many English players saying that. Do you think he means it?'

Janusz shrugged. 'Maybe. Loyalty's important to Poles.' Fighting down a sudden image of Oskar undergoing torture rather than grass him up, he turned to scan the café. There were half a dozen people at the picnic-style tables and a row of cars visible in the car park beyond. 'You're quite busy already – what time do you open?'

'6 a.m., on the dot, rain or shine – usually rain. I close at dusk.'

Janusz met the man's gaze. 'My mate got beaten up near here, late last night.'

'Mugging?'

'I think it might have been … personal. They gave him a proper working over – he's going to be in hospital for a while.'

The guy winced as though he'd sucked on a slice of lemon. 'Nasty. Was he dipping his wick where he shouldn't be?'

'Something like that,' conceded Janusz with a man-to-man grin. 'The jealous boyfriend drives a black 4X4 – a Land Rover Discovery? I don't suppose you noticed one in the car park anytime yesterday?'

The guy shrugged apologetically. 'We had a really busy day, it being sunny and all, so I can't say I noticed.'

Janusz left a card with the guy, in case any of his customers mentioned seeing anything, and drank off the rest of his tea, trying not to grimace. In all the time he'd lived here there was one mystery he'd never solved: why the English took their coffee weak as dishwater and their tea strong enough to stain furniture.

He pocketed his uneaten Tunnocks wafer. 'Thanks for the biscuit,' he said.

Twenty-Seven

Around the time Janusz left Hollow Ponds, Kershaw and Ben were driving into work under a sky as grey and implacable as the side of a battleship.

'I hope we're not going to get snow,' she said, peering through the windscreen. 'I don't fancy taking the car out fully loaded if the roads are slippery.'

A 'man with a van' had already moved Ben's furniture and belongings to their new place in Leytonstone, but she wasn't taking her stuff over till later that day.

'Are you sure you can get all your stuff in here?' asked Ben, looking in the back of the Ka.

'Yeah. I haven't got any furniture, and anyway, it's bigger than it looks.'

Kershaw realised with a stab of nostalgia that she had spent her last night in her little flat – although whether it was at the thought of leaving Canning Town, where she'd grown up and lived for most of her adult life, or at no longer having a place of her own, she couldn't say.

Ben used his sleeve to clear a viewing hole in the steamed-up windscreen. 'Why don't I cook us a really special dinner tomorrow, to celebrate getting into the flat? I'm sick to death of takeaway.'

'Me too,' said Kershaw. 'I suppose it is time I put your alleged cooking abilities to the test.'

Ben sent her a stern look. 'I'll have you know that my rendition of Jamie Oliver's spaghetti marinara has been known to make grown men weep.'

'Too much chilli?'

'Ha. Ha.'

'And Sunday morning we're going to IKEA, right?'

'Yep. Just like a couple of sad old marrieds.'

Kershaw felt a flutter of excited anticipation. Not only was she a detective working her first murder case – the dream she'd had since she was a teenager – she was setting up home with the man she loved. For the first time ever, she had a clear view of the future unfolding in front of her – and the view looked pretty good.

'How did the press conference go yesterday?' she asked, as they waited for a space in the oncoming traffic at the Green Man roundabout.

'Fine,' he said. 'Jamie and his missus were pretty shaky, but I suppose that was inevitable – Stride topping himself has dragged it all up again.' He stared out of the window – they were just passing the boating lake at Hollow Ponds. 'Still, it's the kind of closure they wouldn't have got any other way, not even if we'd managed to put the fucker in jail.'

An image of Stride, the one that had been in all the papers during the trial, flashed up in her mind's eye. 'Did anyone find his specs near the scene?'

Ben leaned forward to wipe the windscreen again. 'I don't recall. Why?'

'I think that's why I didn't recognise him, up at Hollow Ponds.' It had been nagging at the back of her mind ever since she'd seen the body hanging in the clearing. 'All the pictures I'd seen of him in the paper, he was always wearing glasses. Narrow frames, sixties style, remember?'

'Yeah, it does ring a vague bell.'

'Come on, Ben, you interviewed him – you must remember!'

He pulled a self-mocking face: 'You know me and face recognition skills.'

'So, the uniforms didn't find anything when they searched the woods?' The indicator tick-tocked as she turned left onto Church Lane to take the shortcut through the Village.

'Nope – not unless you count half a dozen used condoms and a syringe or two.'

Her fingers tapped on the steering wheel. 'It would be seriously weird though, wouldn't it? Going into a wood – at night – to kill himself, without wearing his glasses?'

Ben leant back in his seat. 'Especially when he knew he'd have to tie knots in that rope.'

Kershaw flicked a look at him, saw his troubled expression. 'Look, chances are he left the specs at home 'cos he was in a state,' she said. 'But if some dog walker stumbles on them, hands them in … Well, it's gonna look like we dropped a bollock.'

Ben nodded slowly. 'You're right. As soon as I get in I'll collar whoever attended Stride's flat, find out if they logged any glasses.'

Kershaw's first task of the morning was to update Detective Sergeant Bacon on the developments on her Polish stowaway.

'Maybe the guy was a headcase,' said Streaky with a shrug – apparently sharing Janusz Kiszka's conclusion as to why Orzelair's head of security would hitch a lift in the wheel well of one of the airline's own planes.

'I'm not sure that's the correct terminology for an emotionally disturbed person these days, Sarge.'

190

He nodded, as though conceding the point. 'Nutjob?' he offered.

Kershaw raised an eyebrow. If any of the brass overheard the way Streaky talked, he was going to land in big trouble one of these days – however stellar his clear-up rate.

'Anyway,' he said, cleaning his nails with a paperclip, 'the Polish cops are dealing with the death message, right? So let's see what the family says. If I was you, I'd be hoping that your Wojtek turns out to be a plane-spotting paranoid schizophrenic with a lifelong compulsion for inserting himself into small spaces. Then you can get that file off your desk and back where it belongs – in Docklands nick.'

He picked up a document from his desk – the letter retrieved from Jim Fulford's hard drive dismissing his deputy manager. 'This, on the other hand, is a rather promising lead, Detective.' She felt her face flush – praise from Streaky was rare. 'Is the fence prepared to identify Andre Terrell as the one who sold him Fulford's laptop?'

'Apparently, Sarge, yes. In exchange for us putting in a good word with the judge.'

'It's heartening to see one of our customers suddenly so keen on our good opinion when they're about to face a man in a horsehair wig,' said Streaky. 'Right, so, Terrell had a five-star motive to off his boss. Now we need to prove that he had the opportunity. He gave us an alibi when we first questioned him, didn't he?'

'Yes, Sarge,' said Kershaw. 'A mate of his came in and made a statement saying they were playing squash at the leisure centre about the time when Fulford was getting knifed.'

'Calcott?'

She nodded.

'There's a CCTV camera on the main entrance, if memory serves,' said Streaky. 'Put in a request for the footage

– assuming the beancounters haven't switched it off to save cash, that is.'

He plucked a straggly hair from one nostril and studied it.

'And I think we'd better invite young Mr Terrell in for another chat.'

Twenty-Eight

By the time Janusz reached Millharbour, a low sun had broken through the cloud and was glinting off the wind-ruffled surface like knives floating on the dark water.

He stationed himself behind a large steel 'sculpture' just north of Romescu's apartment block and unwrapped the biscuit the café guy had given him: it might be his only sustenance for many hours. The spot gave him a good view of anyone emerging from the block's only entrance, whether they chose the pedestrian walkway down the side of the dock or cut west to the pickup point on Millharbour where he'd seen car valets delivering residents' motors. With a black cab rank less than twenty seconds walk away, he reckoned he had all the options covered.

His target wasn't the tattooed thug who'd beaten and tortured Oskar, nor even his boss, Romescu. It was Varenka Kalina.

Janusz remained convinced that Varenka was Romescu's Achilles heel. She might have been promoted from his stable of hookers to become his 'girlfriend', aka his exclusive property, but her body language around him, her hidden 'escape kit', the fact she endured his blows, all spoke of servitude rather than a relationship of equals. Despite the lack of a smoking gun on Jim's laptop, he was surer than ever that Varenka's visit to Jim's house to lay flowers meant that she knew Romescu was implicated in the murder. She probably knew about his smuggling activities, too. In other words, enough dirt to put him away for a very long time. The challenge would be persuading her to share.

The initial stage of his plan was simple: shadow the pair of them until he saw a chance to get Varenka on her own. After that, he'd just have to busk it.

Just after 9 a.m., he saw the boxy outline of the black Discovery nosing its way into the pick-up point. Switching his gaze to the block's front door, he saw Romescu emerge, alone, pulling a carry-on suitcase. He climbed into the back seat and the car accelerated away.

Janusz was delighted to have Romescu out of the way – and apparently heading out of the country – but it left him with a dilemma. Should he simply turn up on Varenka's doorstep and risk scaring her off? He was still weighing it up when, not five minutes after Romescu's exit, he saw the girl herself step through the block's revolving door. Outside, she paused to button up her hussar-style red coat, then strode off down the dock, in the direction of South Quay DLR station.

He slipped down a passageway between two high-rises to Millharbour, a road running parallel to the dockside walkway. She couldn't really be heading anywhere except South Quay DLR, but when he passed another passageway and saw a sliver of red flash past, he gave a little nod of satisfaction.

Five minutes later, on reaching the end of the glass and concrete cliff formed by the dockside skyscrapers, he ducked behind a parked van. Its windows framed the stairway up to the DLR platform, which a moment later, was ascended by Varenka's red-clad figure. Once she'd reached the top he followed, taking the stairs two at a time. At the ticket gate he paused, clocking a CCTV monitor that showed her tall slender figure walking to the other end of the platform.

They boarded the same train, Janusz leaving three carriages between them. Half a dozen stops later, at Bank, he saw her disembark. Within a few minutes they were both riding a westbound Central line tube train heading for the West End.

He followed her off the train at Bond Street, keeping her in view ahead of him on the up escalator, only to get stuck behind a German tourist fumbling for his Oystercard at the barrier. As the guy gave up on his pockets and started rooting in his manbag, Janusz threw a look around for any uniforms, and vaulted a barrier, drawing shocked looks from his fellow travellers. No sign of her in the thronged ticket hall. Faced with a choice of exits, he had to take a gamble. He jogged up the escalator to emerge on the south side of Oxford Street into a heaving sea of shoppers.

Kurwa. He scoured the crowd for her, lapped by the babbling tide of humanity, feeling the slither of panic in his gut that a crush always triggered. But she'd disappeared.

He was on the verge of admitting defeat when he spotted something. A red-coated figure exiting the underpass on the north side of the street, heading in the direction of Selfridges. As he crossed the road, keeping her in view, he realised she was probably on one of those marathon shopping trips women were so keen on. *Jesus Maria!* The irony of the situation was not lost on him: he'd spent two years ducking Kasia's repeated attempts to drag him on her clothes-buying expeditions, only to face God-only-knew how many hours watching a woman he barely knew go shopping.

Just as he'd resolved to bump into her 'by accident', she made a sharp turn off the street, up an alleyway. He followed at a safe distance, keeping two or three clusters of ambling tourists between him and his target.

Suddenly, she stopped to look in a shop window, throwing a casual glance back behind her. He slipped behind a rack of postcards outside a newsagent. If she had spotted him, she gave no sign of it.

Varenka took a right onto Wigmore Street, then left onto Welbeck. The streets here were long and ruler-straight, allowing Janusz to keep her in view from a safe distance.

Where was she going? There were no shops around here – just terrace after terrace of early Georgian houses, largely converted into offices and private clinics of one kind or another. Harley Street was just a couple of streets east. Moments later, she disappeared into a building a block long, its clean lines suggestive of twenties or thirties architecture.

Janusz stopped to light a cigar. After allowing five minutes in case she came straight back out, he headed for the entrance. Outside, the word 'AMBULANCE' was painted in the road, and next to the door a brass plate read: 'Princess Louise Hospital'. Janusz raised an eyebrow. The Princess Louise wasn't some lunch-hour Botox clinic; it was London's private hospital of choice for major celebs, minor royalty and foreign billionaires.

He ground out his cigar in the ambulance bay, buttoned his coat and ventured inside.

'Can I help you, sir?' asked the pretty Indian girl on reception.

'My wife and I have just moved to the area – we have a place on Regents Park,' Janusz said, making a self-deprecating wave northward, 'and she asked me to drop in and find out what … *procedures* you carry out here.' He hoped that his vagueness might be taken for discretion.

'I see,' said the girl, lowering her voice. 'Would it be something of a feminine nature, perhaps?'

He grimaced good-naturedly. 'I'm not entirely sure, to be frank with you. Is that your main … *area*, as it were?'

'Well, we cover all sorts of specialisms here, sir. Perhaps I could give you a brochure, then your wife can look at it at her leisure?'

Thanking the girl, Janusz accepted the cream-coloured brochure with the waxy finish that she held out.

He found a corner café with a view of the hospital entrance and after ordering a black coffee, started to leaf through the brochure. The Princess Louise appeared to leave no profit opportunity unturned: food allergy testing, acupuncture, and breast enlargement were on offer alongside kidney dialysis, cancer treatment and psychiatry. Its contents left him none the wiser as to the purpose of Varenka's visit. She might simply have been visiting someone – and even if she had come for treatment of some kind, her medical issues were hardly likely to help him nail Romescu.

Three coffees later, Janusz decided that she must have left the Princess Louise by another exit. Had she had simply used the hospital as a ruse to shake off anyone who might be following her? He was sure that she hadn't spotted him, but perhaps Romescu was in the habit of keeping tabs on her when he was out of the country. Straightforward proprietorial jealousy? Or was he worried that she might be about to fly the coop?

In any event, letting the girl give him the slip meant he'd wasted half a day. He was just wondering what his next move should be when the 'message waiting light' on his phone started winking.

Foreboding rushed in on him. Was it the hospital calling with bad news about Oskar? But as he played the voice message, his frown evaporated, to be replaced by a slow grin of triumph.

'I hope you don't mind me contacting you' – a woman's voice, low-pitched, familiar: *Varenka* – 'but my boyfriend had to go to Poland on business, leaving me with a spare ticket for the Royal Opera House tonight. Will you come?'

Twenty-Nine

'You do not have to say anything but it may harm your defence if you do not mention when questioned something which you later rely on in Court ...'

As DC Natalie Kershaw read him his rights, Andre Terrell sprawled in his chair, arms crossed and legs wide open, crotch aimed straight at her – body language that semaphored his lack of concern, spiked with contempt at the 'feds' for imposing on his valuable time.

'And anything you do say may be given in evidence,' she concluded. 'Andre, do you understand what being interviewed under caution means?'

'Yeah. It means I don't have to say nothing,' he scoffed, 'and if I want a brief you've gotta give me one.' His salacious grin told her the double entendre was intentional.

She gave him her brightest smile. 'Right! I almost forgot, it's not exactly the first time you've been in a police interview room, is it?'

For an answer, Terrell kissed his teeth and directed a blank stare at the wall over her shoulder.

'You've always been a bit of a tea leaf haven't you, Andre?'

she said, peering at his rap sheet. 'Stealing a mobile off a schoolmate … shoplifting at JD Sports … taking a car without the owner's consent …'

'All that was when I was a kid,' he muttered.

Kershaw sent him a pitying smile. 'Exactly. You're twenty years old now, you've not been in trouble for a couple of years *and* you've landed a good job. So here's the thing – why did you risk it all by stealing your boss's laptop? Didn't he pay you enough?'

'I didn't steal nothing.' He yawned operatically, giving her a flash of diamond-studded incisor.

'I'm afraid we have a statement from Courtney Carisford, giving us chapter and verse on how you sold him Jim Fulford's laptop in the Five Kings pub, the Wednesday before last.'

'He's lying!'

'He says he gave you fifty quid for it.'

Terrell opened his mouth to speak, and for a joyful split second Kershaw thought he was actually going to take the bait and complain that Carisford had only paid him thirty quid, but instead he gave a little shake of his head. 'It's my word against his – reasonable doubt, innit?'

Kershaw knew this wasn't just wishful thinking on Terrell's part – inner city juries were notoriously reluctant to convict their peers if there was even a molecule of doubt. She shuffled the paperwork in front of her, as if struggling for her next move. In her peripheral vision, she sensed something in his body language, an infinitesimal relaxation.

'What I'm wondering,' she said, 'is whether Jim Fulford got the chance to give you the sack *before* he got knifed to death? Or did you just happen to see the letter on the screen of his laptop?'

Hoicking himself up in his chair, Terrell gaped at her. She had his full attention now.

'What letter?' His voice had gone up half an octave.

'Are you saying you have no knowledge of the letter giving you notice from your position as deputy manager at the gym?'

Kershaw could see his eyes flickering around, no doubt trying to reassure himself that he had deleted all the files from the computer. From the way he folded his arms with a return to his former bravado, he'd clearly decided he was safe. 'There ain't no such letter.'

'Would you say you're good with computers, Andre?'

'Yeah, course. I'm young aren't I?' *Not like you*, his grin said.

'I'm hopeless, to be honest.' She pulled a self-deprecating smile. 'For instance, I always thought if you deleted a file, then emptied the trash – *ping!* – that would be it gone forever.' She shook her head, marvelling at her own stupidity.

He stared at her, uncertainty clouding his eyes.

'So you can imagine how embarrassed I was when our computer forensics guy explained it to me. You know,' she said, flapping a hand in a pantomime of female ditsyness, 'how the files are actually still there in the background, until the space they occupy on the hard drive gets overwritten by new data?'

Fear froze Terrell's face.

Bingo, thought Kershaw. Retrieving the printout of the letter from her file, she pushed it across the desk, spinning it around for him. He craned his head to read it, apparently unwilling to pick it up.

'I think the court would be very interested to hear that Jim Fulford wrote a letter sacking you the day before he was murdered, don't you?'

Kershaw noticed that Terrell's knee had started to jig up and down.

'Yeah but … the person who stole the laptop, they could have deleted everything without knowing what was on it, couldn't they?'

'That's true. Except it was the *only file* that had been opened and individually deleted, before the whole laptop was wiped. If it was a random theft, then why the focus on that one letter?'

His knee was jigging in double time now.

'Look Andre, it seems to me you've got two options. Start telling the truth now and you've got a good chance of walking away with a fine and a probation order for theft. If you carry on telling lies … well, I know what I'd think if I was on a jury, I'd think the laptop theft wasn't about making a few bob, it was about hiding the fact you'd been sacked. Hiding your motive for Jim Fulford's murder.'

'I didn't kill him! I already told the fed … the police, I was playing squash at the leisure centre when it happened!'

She leaned back in her chair, shaking her head. 'If I was you Andre, and I was facing a life sentence for murder, I'd think very carefully before relying on the uncorroborated alibi of a mate. What if he gets cold feet, or you have a falling out?'

Judging by his wavering gaze, this was a scenario that Terrell found all too credible. 'I didn't have nothing to do with it, you know?' he said.

Kershaw picked up the note of desperation in his voice. 'All the more reason to tell the truth. If you volunteer an honest statement now, in your first interview, it will show the court that you're a straight-up kind of person.'

Twenty minutes later, Kershaw had the whole story. Terrell had got his marching orders the day before Jim's murder, but when the cops had called with the news he'd seen a chance to rewrite history and keep his job, at least for the time being. He'd pinched the laptop and after his ham-fisted attempt to delete its contents sold it to Carisford, the neighbourhood fence. He gambled – correctly, as it happened – that Jim hadn't got round to telling the lady who did the payroll about his dismissal.

Kershaw did wonder, briefly, whether *technically* the interview had been conducted within the mind-numbing requirements of the Police and Criminal Evidence Act guidelines, considering what had turned up in her inbox earlier that afternoon. The Calcott Leisure Centre had turned out to be surprisingly on the ball when it came to storage and retrieval of its CCTV footage, and the images they'd sent over of Andre and his friend leaving through the turnstiles around ten minutes after Jim was murdered had been crystal clear.

As she was ushering Terrell out through reception, he turned to her. 'Listen. If I give you some information, will you tell the judge I helped out?'

She suppressed a grin at his expression: the wannabe gangsta act had disappeared, leaving behind a jumpy kid who was probably wondering how to break it to his mum he was in trouble with the cops again.

She shrugged, non-committal. 'Depends how useful it is, Andre.'

'The word on the street is that the murder, it was pussy-related ... to do with a lady, I mean.'

'Is that so?' Kershaw said.

'For real! You know that big Polish bruvva he was friends with? *Yah-nuz*?'

'Yan-oosh,' she corrected, automatically.

'Yeah, whatever.' Narrowing his eyes, he gave a nod. 'Well, he reckoned Jim was seeing someone on the side.'

'Go on.' Kershaw's tone was cool but could feel her heart start to thump.

'An Eastern European lady – a tall, blonde stunner.'

'And did this vision of loveliness have a name?'

'It sounded Russian, something beginning with V ...' Terrell screwed one eye almost shut. 'Verruca ...?'

Two minutes later, Kershaw was making her way up the stairs to the office when she bumped into Ben coming down.

'What's up, Nat?' he asked, an amused yet quizzical look in his dark eyes.

She realised she must have been scowling. 'Oh, nothing. I just found out that bastard Kiszka has been holding out on me.' It hadn't taken her long to work out that Terrell's stab at the name of the mystery blonde was actually 'Varenka' – one of the names that Kiszka had asked her to look for on Jim's laptop.

'Anything important?'

'I don't know yet, but I'm gonna find out.'

'If I was him, I'd be properly scared,' he said, miming a terrified shiver.

'Very funny. Anyway, I've gotta go, some of us have got murders to solve.'

'By the way,' he said. 'I spoke to Carl, the PC who checked out Stride's flat? His specs *were* there, thank goodness. He must've just rushed out without them.'

'Oh, that's good,' she said. 'You know what Streaky says about loose ends ...'

'... they have a nasty habit of tripping people up.'

Thirty

From the instructions Varenka gave Janusz over the phone, it was clear that she didn't want Romescu finding out about their evening at the opera. They were to arrive separately; his ticket would be waiting at the box office; and he shouldn't join her until just before curtain up. Janusz made no comment on the cloak-and-dagger flavour of their rendezvous, but took it as further evidence that, rightly or wrongly, she expected to be followed. He hoped it was also a sign that she was starting to see him as a potential ally, someone to turn to should she decide to escape her gangster boyfriend.

Janusz had never actually been inside the Royal Opera House, unless you counted the stint he did there back in the nineties when the place was a building site undergoing a top to bottom renovation. He was impressed by the *fin de siècle* grandeur of the foyer and main staircase but nothing could prepare him for what lay the other side of the nondescript door marked Box 7 up on the third level.

As he entered the box, the first thing that hit him was the noise. The moans, squeaks and clatter of the orchestra tuning up, combined with the rustle and hum of the audience, bubbled out of the auditorium like steam off a cauldron. As he gazed out at the vast blood-red space intersected by the curved cream-coloured ribs of the balconies, he felt for a moment as though he were inside the belly of some colossal beast.

Varenka turned to him. 'You came,' she said.

Janusz sat beside her, taking in at a glance the long lithe body, the silvery-green shift that finished just above her honey-coloured knees – a ribbon of the same material woven through her hair, which she wore in a loose chignon.

Ale laska! He'd almost forgotten what an extraordinary-looking girl she was. If he ended up having to take her to bed in order to get to the bottom of Jim's murder, well, he'd suffered worse hardships.

They'd barely exchanged 'hellos' before a shushing sound swept the packed auditorium and, after a few last-minute coughs and snuffles, the orchestra struck up the dramatic opening chords of Dvorak's *Rusalka*.

Janusz knew the opera, which told the story of a doomed love affair between a prince and the beautiful water nymph of the title, having seen it in Warsaw as a young man, but when the curtain rose he was mystified. Rusalka had been relocated from her usual setting of lakeside forest glade to a *kitsch* modern-day bedsit, and she and her sister nymphs had become under-dressed girls lounging on red plastic sofas. He squinted at the stage in confusion before the awful truth dawned on him: this was an *art-house* production.

To his relief, Janusz discovered that by closing his eyes he could still lose himself in the transporting beauty of the music. Ten minutes later, hearing the opening bars of the 'Song to the Moon', Rusalka's poignant plea to be transformed into a human so that she could join her lover, he opened his eyes and glanced sideways at Varenka's profile. She was leaning forward in her seat, lips slightly parted, gaze riveted on the spotlit figure of the soprano, looking for all the world as if her own future depended on the water nymph's wish being granted.

When the curtain fell for the interval, he turned to her. 'Shall we get a drink?'

Crushed into a corner of the busy bar they stood toe to toe in enforced proximity.

'*Na zdrowie*,' he said, raising his glass of champagne.

'*Na zdrowie*,' she murmured, taking a decorous sip of her drink.

'What do you make of it?'

'It is *przepiekna*,' she said, eyes wide.

'Exquisite? Really?' he raised an eyebrow. 'Even the panto-mime cat?' The agent of Rusalka's metamorphosis from water nymph to woman was a giant black cat that had clawed off her fishy tail before raping her, prompting uncomfortable titters from the audience.

'Well, perhaps that was an experiment too far,' she allowed, a faint blush climbing into her cheeks.

'Where was the supernatural element, the spirit world of nymphs and sprites? How can a garish … *bedsit* replace that?'

'Bedsit?' She looked at him under her brows. 'You surely know it is a brothel?'

It was his turn to feel foolish. '*Kurwa*! So the director turned the wood nymphs into whores?!'

She raised an eyebrow. 'I think sex worker is a nicer word, no?'

Janusz gave a little bow. 'You are right, it's a discourteous expression.' He sometimes forgot where and when this poised, intelligent girl had been raised and that she had no doubt been selling her body to men all her adult life. 'But I still don't see the point of changing the setting.'

'I think the director is using the sex business as a modern real-life parallel, to frame Rusalka's dilemma.' Varenka peered at the bubbles in her champagne. 'She can leave the world of the wood nymph, just as she can leave the world of prostitution, but in reality, she can leave neither. When she becomes human she loses the power of speech, which means she will never truly be accepted.' She shrugged. 'It's the same for a sex worker. Whatever she does to transform herself, to the world she will always be a girl who sold her body for money.'

It was a brutal yet honest summation of the life of a prostitute, thought Janusz. There probably wasn't a culture in the world that didn't view the stain of whoredom as indelible, and a girl from a Catholic background – even a liberated one – would have had that way of thinking seared into her soul from infancy.

'So where does the Prince fit in? Does she love him, or does he just offer a way out of her predicament?' asked Janusz.

'I think a girl can truly love the person who rescues her from a terrible place, but perhaps she discovers later that she has exchanged one prison for another.'

On the face of it, they were still discussing the opera, but Janusz could tell from the sadness around Varenka's eyes and the feeling in her voice that the scenario she described was, to her, a daily reality.

'Escape is not impossible, you know,' he said, bending his head to seek her gaze. 'In this country there are ways for girls in that kind of trouble to seek refuge.'

Varenka let her eyes rest on his, and he held his breath, sensing that she was on the verge of accepting his implicit offer of help. But just then the bell signalling the end of the interval rang, shattering the moment.

Depositing her glass on a nearby ledge, she smiled up at him. 'We will have to wait and see what happens to Rusalka in the end, no?'

She hadn't exactly spoken openly about her situation but neither had she taken fright at the turn the conversation had taken. Janusz decided he'd ask her to go for a drink afterwards. With more time to talk, and some alcohol inside her, she might be persuaded to unburden herself.

Back in their box watching the second half, Janusz found himself more sympathetic to the director's vision: portraying Rusalka as a sexual plaything unable to escape her destiny did bring a fresh poignancy to her plight. When the Prince, inevitably, abandoned his mute lover for being insufficiently human, Rusalka stabbed herself to death.

The stage lights dimmed for a scene change. Janusz knew that the remorseful Prince had still to seek out his lover's undead spirit but, much as he wanted to see the disloyal *chuj* get his comeuppance, he had other plans. Carefully pushing back his chair, he got to his feet. When Varenka shot him a quizzical look he made an apologetic face and opened his hand, spreading thumb and fingers. *Five minutes.*

Making his way down the wide red staircase back to ground level, he found the emergency exit he'd clocked on the way in. Pressing down the push bar he slipped out, inserting his cigar tin at the foot of the door to stop it closing. Outside in the cold night air he found himself in a narrow alleyway leading to a side street off of Covent Garden Piazza. He worked his way around the edge of the square, keeping himself concealed behind groups of evening promenaders.

Barely two minutes later, he found what he was looking for. Silhouetted against the spotlit stucco façade of the opera house, the outline of a familiar figure: Romescu's driver. It was too dark to make out his snake tattoo, even if it hadn't been encased in the gleaming white plaster cast that emerged from the sleeve of his jacket, covering his knuckles – a souvenir, Janusz guessed, of his 'accident' in the Greenwich foot tunnel. He leaned against an ornate lamp post, smoke curling idly from his cigarette, keeping a casual but practised eye on the Opera House entrance. So Varenka's precautions hadn't been the result of an overactive imagination: Romescu *was* keeping tabs on her.

Nosz, Kurwa! Janusz had been banking on taking her somewhere after the performance, to continue the work of gaining her trust – but the presence of snake-boy exploded that idea. They couldn't leave the Opera House together now. Could he persuade her to slip out through the fire exit? After a few moments' thought, he dismissed the idea as too risky. If she were to be seen with another man – let alone an enemy of Romescu … Janusz still held himself culpable for the death of his girlfriend Iza nearly thirty years ago, and he wasn't about to risk another girl's life, not even for the sake of dear old Jim.

Turning a reluctant back on the lights of the Opera House, he headed north for Holborn tube, punching out a text message as he walked. *A thousand apologies, but I had to leave*, it said. *I can't explain now, but I will be in touch soon – I promise.*

Thirty-One

'Is all this lot just for dinner, or are we stocking an aquarium?'

After seeing the list of fish and crustaceans Ben needed for his famous spaghetti marinara, Kershaw ditched her plan to pop into Tesco Express and drove up to the Waitrose at South Woodford, where the local yummy mummies did their shopping. She knew it wouldn't be cheap but was still shocked to discover at the checkout that she'd spent almost twenty quid on a single meal – not including the cava. Wasn't living together supposed to *save* money?

Relax, she told herself. *It's not every day you move in with the guy you aim to spend the rest of your life with.*

The crisp new resident's parking permit in her windscreen meant she could park practically in front of their new place, in the tree-lined Bushwood area of Leytonstone – which was just as well, given the bulging black bags and boxes pressed up against the windows of her Ford Ka. Turning her shiny new key in the front door lock brought a surge of excitement, but inside the corniced hallway she stopped short. An image of her dad, in paint-spattered blue overalls, flashed into her mind, as clear as if he was standing beside her. She was remembering her first flat, where he had helped her to cover up the headache-inducing lime green wallpaper – a task that had taken five coats of magnolia emulsion. He'd died less than a year later. Throat cancer. *That'll teach me for smoking sixty a day when I was young and foolish,* he'd croaked, dry and mischievous right to the end.

Then the image of him was gone, the bittersweet emotions it had resurrected giving way to a panicky feeling that she might never sense him alongside her like this ever again. She took a steadying breath. *Come on, Nat,* she murmured. *This won't get the baby bathed.* He couldn't really be gone, she reassured herself, not so long as the daft things he used to say lived on.

In the front room she could see the trouble Ben had taken to make the place welcoming. As well as setting up the TV and set-top box – *funny that* – he'd scattered his old leather sofa with cushions and rolled out the rug with the a bright blue abstract swirl that they'd picked up on their first trip to IKEA together. On the fireplace mantelpiece was a bunch of yellow hothouse roses beside an envelope with 'Natalie' written on it in Ben's looping handwriting. Inside was a splotchy painting of a picturesque house covered with bougainvillea, sunshine dappling its stone walls. She smiled at the message inside: 'Looking forward to our new life together – love, Ben.'

The kitchen was more of a work in progress. A quick check of the cupboards unearthed the saucepans they'd need to make dinner, but she couldn't find a single cooking implement, nor any cutlery or glasses to lay the table.

She returned to the bedroom where she'd seen a stack of yet-to-be-unpacked boxes on Ben's side of the bed. The trouble was, the idea of marking up boxes to make it easy to retrieve things hadn't occurred to Ben – *bless him*. With a good-natured sigh, she started to check the boxes' contents.

DVDs and sci-fi novels in one … cycling gear, a camera and workout kit in another … but no sign of any kitchenware. As she stopped to pick up a book she'd dropped, she spotted a black bag shoved under the bed. It looked like it was full of clothes, but remembering how she'd used her jumpers as packing material to protect breakables, she reached under to drag it out. Inside she found nothing but balled-up T-shirts and jeans. Then, as she started shoving it all back inside, her fingers touched something unexpected. It was a small jiffy bag, sealed with grey duct tape. *What was that doing there?* Guessing that Ben had probably scooped it up accidentally with a pile of clothes, she set it on his bedside table.

Moving to the window, she stood for a moment with her arms folded, gazing out at the garden. It looked wintry and denuded, the only patch of green a shabby-looking conifer in a pot on the tiny terrace. She imagined the two of them out there in the summer, drinking cold wine, the smell of lamb sizzling on the barbecue. But she couldn't suppress the feeling welling up in her chest: the sensation she sometimes got at a crime scene when something didn't quite fit. It was a bit like listening to an orchestra in which one instrument was being played in the wrong key.

Her gaze was dragged inexorably back to the bedside table, to the jiffy bag – which sat there, seeming to mock her with its sheer ordinariness. She stood, irresolute, biting her thumbnail. *What was a relationship without trust?* she chided herself. But other questions, unbidden, bubbled to the surface of her mind. *What was inside? Why wasn't it in the boxes with his other things?*

It was no good. Two steps and the package was in her hand. Something irregular and frail inside. It felt like … She could feel the patter of her pulse, hear the blood whooshing in her ears. She tore the duct tape off. Pulled out the contents.

A pair of glasses, in a clear plastic evidence bag. She dropped it on the bed like it was on fire. Looked at the ceiling for one, two, three seconds. Looked back at what lay on the bed. There was no deleting the image or undoing what she had found. Narrow, retro-style frames – Anthony Stride's glasses – the ones she remembered staring out of the news reports on the Hannah Ryan case.

She only just made it to the kitchen sink. After throwing up her afternoon coffee, she rested her head on the cool stainless steel for what seemed like an age. Then she took a big drink of cold water from the tap and returned to the bedroom. Forcing herself into professional mode, she picked up the evidence bag by one corner and peered at the contents. The lenses of the glasses were dusty and there was a fragment of dead leaf caught in one of the hinges. On the surface of the right lens was a smear of what looked like dried blood.

Kershaw sat back on the bed. There was only one possible conclusion: Ben had come across Stride's glasses up at Hollow Ponds but had failed to turn them in as evidence. If he'd simply forgotten to sign them in, they'd be in a drawer at work, not at home, hidden at the bottom of a bag of clothes. There could be no justification or explanation for taking evidence out of the nick. *Why would he hide his discovery?* Racking her brains she dredged up her brief but thorough search of the clearing where Stride hanged himself: she was stone cold certain there were no glasses in the immediate vicinity of the body. So where had Ben found them? And more to the point, *why the fuck* would he cover up his find?

The answer pinged into her brain. *Because the glasses weren't close enough to the scene for Stride to have dropped them while he was hanging himself.* Ben had found them some distance away, and realised they presented a totally different scenario. That Stride had been taken to Hollow Ponds against his will, and anticipating his fate, had put up a desperate fight: a struggle

214

in which he'd lost his glasses, possibly accounting for the blood on the lens.

A scenario that turned Anthony Stride's death from the suicide of a repentant paedophile to a cold-blooded murder.

Kershaw imagined the scene. It would take two people, one to scale the tree and throw down the noose to the one keeping hold of Stride, who was probably gagged, his hands tied.

Then what? The noose goes over his head. He's hauled up by the rope, the one on the ground holding him aloft while the rope is tied off to the branch. He starts to strangle. She remembered the scratch marks under Stride's jaw around the noose, how she'd assumed he must have changed his mind. In fact, he'd have started scrabbling at the rope the second the killers freed his hands. They must have stood there, watching. You'd have to wait, just in case. She imagined two executioners, sombre-faced in the gloom. Got a flash of Ben's face, lips thinned to a savage line. *No!*

She shook her head violently to rid herself of the image. Okay, she reasoned to herself, so Ben had covered up Stride's killing – probably to protect Hannah Ryan and her family from a headline-hitting murder case, and maybe because he thought the guy had got his just desserts. But Ben, a cold-blooded murderer? *No fucking way.*

It was little consolation. The fact remained that the man she loved had covered up a murder, breaking every promise he had signed up to when he became a police officer. What was worse, he had broken the bond of trust between them, even telling her the barefaced lie that the missing glasses had been found at Stride's place. And by hiding them in their flat he had risked not just his career – but hers, too. This wasn't ignoring some bureaucratic directive or fudging a technicality: stealing evidence and obstructing an investigation was breaking the law.

Replacing the glasses in the jiffy bag, she wandered into the front room. Standing there, arms wrapped around herself, her mind fumbled for some way of her and Ben getting through this. Her gaze snagged on the roses, the card on the mantelpiece: they struck her now like artefacts of some long lost, innocent age. She felt hot tears track down her face.

She couldn't stay here, she decided, couldn't face seeing Ben. She'd write him a letter, then she'd go home – back to Canning Town.

Thirty-Two

Seeing Oskar's hospital bed shrouded by curtains gave Janusz a bit of a scare, but when he pulled them aside he found his mate propped up on his pillows, playing cards with an old man wearing a faded tartan dressing gown.

'Close the curtain!' hissed Oskar.

'Why?' asked Janusz, twitching it across behind him.

'The nurses say we aren't allowed to play for money. I tell you, Janek, it's like living under communism in here.' This with a mournful shake of his head. 'Give me a break, Harry!' he groaned as the old man laid down three aces. 'You're slaying me today!'

After Harry had pocketed his pile of coins and shuffled off, Janusz peered into Oskar's face. The bruises were ripening into a banana yellow and one eye was still swollen shut, but he was relieved to see the spark back in his mate's other eye.

'How are you feeling, *kolego*?'

'Fine, fine.' Oskar waved a pudgy hand. 'I've told the doctors I need to get out of here soon – I've got a job to price up in Redbridge.' He leaned towards Janusz and waggled his eyebrows. 'Did you bring the Zubrowka?'

With a quick look over his shoulder, Janusz slipped him a small hip flask.

Oskar shook it disparagingly. 'That wouldn't keep a *babcia* warm on her way to church!'

'I'm not going to be held responsible for getting you drunk, Oskar.'

'Bison grass is *medicinal*, Janek – it builds your strength up.' He took a swig. 'I thought you were supposed to know about science and shit.'

Janusz grinned. 'Since you're obviously feeling better, maybe you can tell me now exactly what happened?'

'It's all a bit of a blur, to tell you the truth.'

'What I can't work out is, how did Romescu's *gangsterzy* track you down? Do you think it was that shopkeeper – Marek?'

Oskar half-shrugged, half-shook his head, took another nip of *wodka*.

Janusz narrowed his eyes. He'd seen that look before. He was suddenly reminded of an incident back in that shit-hole of an army camp where they did their national service. He'd caught Oskar skinning some rat-like carcass in the boot room and, after lengthy questioning, discovered that he'd been secretly trapping squirrels and trading them for cigarettes with the quartermaster. The squirrels had been served to visiting Party members and top brass in the officers' mess under the description 'woodland rabbit', allowing the quartermaster to sell some of the pork and chicken usually reserved for the high-ups on the black market. As a patriot, he'd of course ensured that the rest reached the protein-starved conscripts. Janusz remembered pointing out quite forcefully to Oskar that if his little scam were uncovered, he'd probably be accused of assisting a CIA-backed plot to poison loyal comrades, and get thrown in prison – or shot.

Now he said: 'Don't treat me like a *dupek*, Oskar. What is it that you're not telling me?'

'Nothing!'

'*Oskar!*'

'Calm down, Janek, you'll have a stroke if you're not careful.' He chuckled. 'Still, at least you'd be in the right place for it.'

Janusz gave him a hard stare.

'*Dobrze*! Okay! So I did a bit of freelance detective work into the Romanian guy.'

Janusz took a swig of Zubrowka. He had a feeling he was going to need it. 'Go on,' he said.

'I went and parked opposite that Turkish café in Walthamstow, Friday afternoon. I remembered Marek saying that was one of the days he goes there.'

'And did he turn up?'

Oskar levered himself up on his pillows, grimacing as the weight shifted onto his plastered arm. 'No, but he sent his driver – the one with all the tattoos? He had a rucksack with him.'

Cash collection – or delivery, thought Janusz. 'Did the rucksack look any different between when he went in and when he came out?'

Oskar screwed his eyes half shut. 'It looked bulkier when he came out.'

Collection.

'So you followed him?'

'*Tak*, in the van.' He tapped the side of his nose. 'And I made sure I was super *dyskretny*.'

Janusz pictured Oskar's beaten-up van with the squealing fan belt 'discreetly' tailing Romescu's Discovery around the East End.

'Then what?'

'When we got to the A406, he suddenly took off, and I lost him.'

'Until he turned up at your flat later on.'

Oskar turned an astonished gaze on him. 'How did you know?!'

'He took your licence plate, *kolego*,' growled Janusz, 'and used it to get your address.'

Later that night, Oskar had answered the doorbell to find a man wearing a balaclava on the doorstep.

'He coshed me over the head. *Whack!* After that, I don't remember a thing, not till I woke up in here and saw your ugly mug leering down at me.'

'Nothing about what happened up at Hollow Ponds, the woods?' Janusz felt his jaw clench. 'You told me they ... hurt you, to find out why I'm investigating Romescu.'

'Did I say that?' Oskar looked blank. 'It's all gone now. *Pfouff!*'

'What did you tell the cops?'

'That I got mugged taking a walk in the woods,' said Oskar. 'They didn't seem all that interested. They probably thought I was some Eastern European gangster.' He looked quite pleased with this idea.

'A lonely old *pedzio* looking for a blowjob, more like,' said Janusz, grinning.

'Well, you'd know more about that than me,' said Oskar.

The curtain rattled aside to reveal a nurse with a business-like air.

'Hello, sweetheart,' said Oskar, reverting to English. 'No Susie today?'

'Susie has taken a holiday,' said the nurse, checking the overhead monitor. 'I am Jadwiga.'

'You're Polish?' asked Oskar, his eyes following her brisk movements.

She nodded. 'I'm afraid visiting time is over,' she told Janusz.

'Okay, *prosze pani*,' he said, getting to his feet. Then he remembered something. 'Oskar. Back home, do you remember seeing brown metal boxes with yellow lettering on them?'

The answer his mate gave him made him feel like a total *idiota. Of course.*

As Janusz had bid Oskar goodbye the nurse had started sniffing suspiciously at the air – bison grass being a highly aromatic herb. By the time he'd reached the doors of the ward he could hear his mate's voice raised in plaintive protest.

'You can't confiscate that – it's private property!'

Waiting for a bus to take him back to Walthamstow tube, Janusz turned on his mobile and found a text message waiting for him. Paul Jarrett, the guy at the Hollow Ponds café, wanted to talk to him. *Nothing urgent*, it said.

Less than ten minutes later, the boating lake came into view. The place was heaving: it might only be eight or nine degrees out, but it was a Sunday, the sky was a milky blue and people were clearly making the most of what could be the last bit of decent weather before winter closed its icy fist. At the café, Jarrett was serving a queue of people, but when he spotted Janusz he nodded and held up two fingers. *Two minutes.*

A few minutes later, a teenage girl appeared behind the counter, and Jarrett came over to Janusz's table carrying two mugs of tea.

'Brrrr! Brass monkeys, ain't it?' he said. 'Still, this probably feels like the Caribbean compared to where you come from.'

Janusz grinned in rueful agreement: he'd given up explaining that at least in Poland the summer brought many months of reliably warm and sunny weather, something which he found himself missing the longer he lived on this rain-lashed island buffeted by Atlantic weather systems.

'Thanks for the tea.' He lit a cigar, inhaled. 'So, did you hear something, about the night my mate got mugged?'

'Nah, it's not that,' said Jarrett. 'I'm probably just wasting your time. But I recall you said something about a black 4X4?'

Janusz nodded, smothering a grimace at the alien taste of milk in his tea.

'Yeah well, it's probably nothing, like I say, but one of the rangers was in for a cuppa the other day, and he was saying they're going to replace some of the logs around the car park.' He gestured towards the gravelled rectangle, with its rough cordon of tree trunks, clearly laid long ago to prevent vehicles parking in the scrub and woodland beyond. 'He says he was driving back from the pub the other night when he just happens to glance in here. He sees a motor with its lights off, creeping out of the wood there, through that gap. Before he can do anything, the car pulls onto the road and tears off in the opposite direction.'

'And he reckons it was a Discovery, right?'

Jarrett nodded. 'Yeah. Which is why I thought you might be interested.'

'But this wasn't Friday night, when my mate got beaten up?'

''Fraid not.' Then Jarrett struck his forehead with the flat of his hand in frustration. 'I can't remember now if he said it was Tuesday or Wednesday. Mind you, it'd be easy enough to find out.'

'You could call him?'

'Nah, sorry, I haven't got his number – but he said it was the night before that guy was found?' He lowered his voice. 'You know, the dirty fucking nonce who hanged himself in the woods?'

Frowning, Janusz shook his head.

'Are you serious? It was all over the papers. Stride his name was – interfered with a little handicapped girl a while back and got off scot-free.' Jarrett looked over at the cabin.

The rush of customers had subsided and the young girl leaned on the counter, chatting on her mobile phone. He shook his head. 'If anybody laid a finger on my Deena, I'd …' The muscles worked in his jaw. 'And I'm not a violent man.'

Five minutes later, Janusz took a stroll over to the gap Jarrett had indicated in the car park's perimeter. Finding a set of tyre tracks through the undergrowth, he followed the trail ten metres or so into the scrub. The tracks ended behind a tangle of elder and bramble bush extensive enough to keep even a sizeable car out of sight of the road.

Thirty-Three

Back in her old flat, Kershaw endured the worst night of her life since her dad had died, the thoughts churning in her head like washing on an endless rinse cycle.

To end up doing what he'd done, to cross the line so dramatically, Ben had clearly become *obsessed* with Anthony Stride during the time he'd spent with the Ryan family. How had she missed the signs? Could she have done more to pull him back from the brink, maybe even prevented it from happening? More importantly, *what the fuck* was she going to do now? Finally, towards dawn, she slept fitfully for an hour or so.

She awoke filled with a powerful sense of resolve: she had to do *something* to try to fix this unholy mess.

There were five missed calls and a bunch of texts waiting on her phone: all from Ben. The note she'd left him at the flat had made it clear she knew everything and that she'd taken the glasses 'for safekeeping': she couldn't risk him panicking, making things worse by getting rid of them.

After taking a hot shower, she primed herself with a strong coffee and called him back.

'Natalie, thank God! I've been going out of my mind!'

At the sound of his voice, she fought down a clamour of emotions. 'It's not been a great time for me, either.'

They fell silent, both aware that they were speaking over an open phone line.

'Just what the fuck did you think you were doing, Ben?'

'I … I don't know. It just happened. I'm sorry.'

She couldn't detect any real regret in his voice.

'You don't get it, do you?' she said. 'What you did, it puts my career on the line – not just yours!'

'What do you mean? You weren't involved.'

'We were moving in together! After that, everything that *you* do has consequences for *both of us*. Especially given the job that we do.'

'You surely don't care about … what happened to that guy?' said Ben. 'You thought the same as me – good riddance.'

'I care about *the law!*'

'*The law* screwed up when it let him off!'

This wasn't going as Kershaw had planned. She tried for a reasonable tone. 'Look, what's happened has happened. What's important now is that you do the right thing.'

'Which is?'

'Go to your DI, tell him what happened, say you forgot to hand the … item in, whatever …'

'No way!'

'Ben! You have to.'

A longer pause. She could picture his stubborn expression on the other end.

'You're not going to hand them in, are you?'

'No. What would it achieve?'

Kershaw ignored the question. It was like they were speaking different languages.

'I can't brush this under the carpet, Ben. This is really serious. I need to talk to someone, get some advice.' She let it sink in. 'I'm going to talk to Streaky. Unless *you* want to?'

'No. You do whatever you think you have to.'

His voice was cold and the call ended without any glimmer of reconciliation.

Without allowing herself to pause and think about what she was about to do, she pulled up Streaky's number and pressed dial.

For perhaps the first time ever, he actually answered his mobile.

'Sarge, it's Kershaw. Look, I'm not working today but I really need to see you.'

'I've been expecting this,' he said.

'Sorry?'

'The day when you realised you could no longer repress your feelings for a devilishly attractive senior detective of mature years.'

He agreed to meet her in Leytonstone, at a pub where they would be highly unlikely to run into anyone from the nick. While he was up at the bar ordering drinks, she got a sudden bout of cold feet. *What the fuck was she doing?* If she grassed up Ben, wouldn't Streaky be duty bound to report him? Was she really ready to take responsibility for ending Ben's career?

She drank half her glass of red wine in a single draught. Streaky sipped his pint, waiting for her to speak.

'Thanks for seeing me, Sarge. I didn't know what else to do. You're the only person I can talk to.' Her words came out in a gabble.

'Calm down, woman,' he said, not unkindly. 'There's nothing so bad it can't be sorted out.'

'I'm not so sure about that.'

As she told the story, Streaky's face remained impassive, the only visible reaction a fractional raising of his gingery eyebrows at her mention of the blood on Stride's glasses.

'I realise that you might have to report this,' she said, her face tense with misery. 'And the last thing in the world I want to do is drop Ben in it, but the only alternative I could see was for me to resign – leave the Job. And I'm not sure I could bear to do that.'

Putting it into words crystallised what she felt for the first time. She had no idea whether she and Ben had a future, but she knew one thing sure as Christmas: she couldn't cover up for him, pretend nothing had happened, and continue to work as someone whose entire purpose was to uphold the law. That kind of hypocrisy would turn her stomach.

Streaky brushed some crumbs from the table. 'So you think our friend Stride was offed by vigilantes?'

She nodded.

'The post-mortem is on Tuesday, if memory serves. If you're right, then the pathologist should find some evidence of a struggle – bruising, contusions, whatever.'

'Yeah, but it's not a Home Office PM, is it? He might easily put it down to Stride blundering into trees in the dark, especially since we presented it as a Cat 2 death.'

'Fair point,' said Streaky, wiping foam from his upper lip. 'A bog-standard PM won't necessarily pick up on the little clues.'

She scanned his face, trying to work out what he was thinking. 'It's not like I'm shedding any tears for Stride, Sarge, but if we let murdering scumbags start to dish out justice, then we might as well close the nick, issue everyone with an Uzi, and fuck off home. Don't you think?'

'Eloquently put,' he said. 'Do you have the article with you?'

Filing the jiffy bag inside his jacket, Streaky dug out his mobile and a packet of fags, before stepping out into the street. After he'd gone, Kershaw started feeling panicky again, desperate to know what was going on. What was he doing? Destroying the evidence? Phoning Divisional Standards? It struck her that he might be sending someone to arrest Ben *right now*.

Well, what did you expect, she asked herself, *for Streaky to wave a magic wand and make everything alright?*

Five minutes later, he came back in, sat down, and opened a packet of crisps, as though nothing had happened. She didn't know what to think: was the jiffy bag still there in his inside pocket, or had he got rid of it?

'What's going to happen to Ben, Sarge?'

'You let me worry about that.'

'But what am I supposed to do?'

'You stay away from loverboy – and don't discuss this with *anybody*, especially over a mobile phone.'

He sluiced the last of his pint down his throat and, setting the empty glass back on the table, sent her a meaningful look. She looked back at him, uncomprehending.

'Look lively, detective: it's your round.'

As Kershaw drove back to Canning Town, she savaged her nails, her mind whirring with questions. Streaky had played his cards very close to his chest. Was he just being circumspect, given the seriousness of what she'd told him? Or was there something else going on? He had pretty trenchant views on the death penalty, after all. Where would it leave her if he simply pretended none of this had happened? With just two options, she realised, both of them seriously unattractive: keep *schtum*, or take the matter higher, which would mean dropping Ben *and* Streaky in it.

Then she remembered something Streaky himself had said after a Hackney cop reported a colleague who liked beating up suspects in the back of the van.

You know what happens to whistleblowers in the end, don't you? he'd said. *They end up having their whistles inserted where the sun don't shine.*

Thirty-Four

Janusz pocketed the SIM card from his mobile phone and slotted in the new one he'd just bought from an Asian newsagent on Lea Bridge Road.

Jim's murder was more than two weeks old and he still felt like he was getting nowhere. Finding out that Romescu's Discovery had been parked at Hollow Ponds the night some paedophile hanged himself only confused matters – after racking his brains for a possible connection, Janusz had more or less dismissed it as a weird coincidence. The woodland was the closest thing the area had to a wilderness, and its proximity to the drugs, gangs and other assorted villainy of the East End inevitably made it a magnet for those whose business was best conducted in private.

Snapping shut the cover of his phone he dialled Varenka's number, ready to hang up if somebody else answered. Without anything else to go on, it was time to take a risk and apply some gentle pressure, see if she would confide in him, reveal something that might provide the missing link between Romescu and Jim. She hadn't answered Janusz's text after their evening at the opera, and it occurred to him that her boyfriend might be monitoring her calls – hence the precaution of a new SIM card, to ensure he'd show up as an unknown number.

'Varenka speaking.'

'Can you talk? If not, just say it's the wrong number.'

A pause and then she said, 'It's okay, please wait a moment.' He heard her steps as she took the phone somewhere … quieter? Safer?

'I need to see you,' he said. If she thought his urgency was romantically motivated, so be it; with one friend dead and another in hospital, disappointing a pretty girl came pretty low on his list on concerns.

She hesitated for a beat. 'I could say I need to go shopping? But I will probably have company.'

An hour later, Janusz was riding an escalator into the glassy maw of Stratford Westfield, a recently built temple to the god of shopping that, given his intense dislike of crowds, he'd so far managed to avoid. It occurred to him that Varenka wasn't the only one who needed to keep a low profile: the nail bar where Kasia worked was only five minutes away, and although he suspected that their relationship was entering its terminal stages, the prospect of her spotting him with another woman was nonetheless an unattractive one.

He found Varenka leafing through a book in the gardening section of Foyles – a rendezvous she'd probably chosen because the store lay in one of the quieter reaches of the mall, and its cookery and gardening section was tucked away at the rear, safe from the gaze of passers-by.

She was dressed more casually than he'd seen her so far, in flat pumps, a pair of artfully ripped jeans and a soft black jumper under her red coat. Her face looked younger and more vulnerable than it had under the evening makeup she'd worn for Romescu's soiree and the opera.

Janusz took up position where he'd get advance warning of anyone coming into their section of the store and picked up a book on bread making.

'Do you have company?' he asked.

'Yes. But he decided to wait in the car park, playing games on his phone.'

The tattooed driver.

She shot Janusz an amused look. 'Even if he decides to come after me, it would never occur to him to look in a bookshop.'

Nodding down at the book in her hands, he raised an eyebrow. 'Are you a keen gardener?'

She looked at the page, open at a picture of a wildflower meadow, and her expression grew wistful. 'I've never had a garden,' she said. 'But when I was tiny I remember staying with my *babcia* and *dziadek* – they had a smallholding, up near the Bialystok Forest? I spent hours in that garden, picking flowers I wasn't supposed to, pottering about with a mini watering can. A couple of times, they even took us to the seaside.'

He smiled at the echo of childish excitement in her voice, recalling the photograph of little Varenka and her brother beside the rock pool, the look of uncomplicated happiness on her face. Most people, as they grew up, experienced many kinds of happiness, he reflected, but the pure, unconscious joy of a small child? That could never be recaptured.

'Wouldn't your mama and tata let you stay there, with your grandparents?'

'I never knew my father. And my mother … she said she couldn't bear to be parted from me.' She looked at the floor. 'The truth was she liked having me around to fetch and carry for her, run to buy *wodka* after she got money from one of the truck drivers.'

231

Confirmation that her home was one in which the family business was prostitution.

Closing the book, she stroked its cover once, before replacing it on the shelf. 'One winter, when the power was cut off, she wanted to put my schoolbooks in the stove – this was after we lost the apartment and were living in a shack by the truck stop. When I tried to stop her, she gave me a beating that broke two ribs.'

Janusz couldn't detect a trace of self-pity in her expression, only the clear-eyed realism of the survivor. Recalling her outburst when he'd admitted abandoning his studies to join Poland's anti-communist protests, he felt a hot wave of shame. Given the realities of her life at the same age, it was no wonder she'd been angry.

'So how did you get out of … Ukraine?' He only just avoided naming her home town, which he knew only from her hidden driving licence, at the apartment.

'I was working as a dancer in a club in Kharkov. Barbu was in the city on business and he came in one night with a group of men. After that, he came back on his own every night for the rest of his trip.' She shook her head, a half smile on her face. 'The same show five nights in a row!'

'And it was he who took you out of there, out of Kharkov?'

'Yes. And my life changed –' she clicked her fingers '– like that.'

Janusz fell silent, pondering his next move, aware that bad-mouthing Romescu was a strategy that could backfire.

'You must feel you owe him a great debt.'

She lifted one shoulder. 'Of course.'

'But life with him … I'm guessing it's not what you hoped for?'

'I used to tell myself he wasn't a bad man. But now, when innocent people get hurt …' Her voice trailed off and she shot a look over her shoulder towards the store entrance.

He wanted to ask her outright if she meant Jim, if that was why she'd come to be leaving flowers for his dead friend, but to do so would mean revealing his hand. *Patience*, he told himself.

'What kind of things?'

She scanned his face and for a wild moment he thought she was going to tell him. Then she gave a tiny shake of the head.

'Listen, Varenka,' he took her hand. 'I will help you to leave him, if that's what you want.'

As he said the words, Janusz felt a total heel – the scenario playing out here was as old as the Bible. A young woman without resources or family, utterly reliant on a violent man, desperate to leave, whose only hope was to find a new protector. Many would condemn her for that – but they were people who couldn't comprehend how limited are the options of the powerless.

She looked down at their linked hands. 'You are very kind. But what can I do? If I leave him then I must go back to Ukraine. I don't think I could bear that.'

He ran a hand across his jaw – racking his brains for how he might help her to find her feet. Living as an illegal, beneath the radar of the authorities, was easy when you had a rich boyfriend, but if you had to find work and a place to stay with limited resources and lacking an NI number, life became far more precarious. It was one reason why girls who'd been trafficked found it so hard to escape their pimps, however abusive.

'Would you allow me to lend you some money, so you can find somewhere to stay?'

Slipping her hand out of his, she lifted her chin. 'Thank you, but I have enough money. If I leave – *when* I leave – I will not accept money from a man ever again.'

Her phone chirped. After a brief conversation in Ukrainian, she hung up.

'He's saying we have to go,' she bit her lip. 'Would you follow me back to the car? Just in case he saw me talking to you?'

'Of course. But listen, I understand you don't want money, but I am going to work out a way for you to leave, I promise.'

'I believe you,' she said simply.

Hanging back a good thirty metres – Varenka's red coat making it easy to keep her in view as she passed through the idling throng – Janusz replayed their encounter. She had seemed less assured, more anxious than he'd seen her before. Was it his fault? Had Romescu somehow found out she'd been in touch with him? Whatever the reason, he had to think of a way of getting her to safety – and not just for her sake. Once she'd escaped Romescu's control, he was convinced she'd feel able to confide why Jim had been killed.

At the multi-storey car park, he took the service stairs up to the third floor where she'd said the Discovery was parked, and walked parallel with her, keeping two aisles, four rows of parked cars between them. Coming to a halt behind a wide concrete pillar, he saw snake-boy, still wearing his plaster cast, emerge from the driver's side and go round the car to open the rear passenger door for her. His body language was anything but chivalrous, however, signalling instead his dominance and a lazy contempt. He slammed the door on her with unnecessary force, the sound bouncing off the concrete ceiling like a bomb going off.

Thirty-Five

Kershaw was struggling to navigate the catastrophic shitstorm that had engulfed her life since she'd stumbled on Stride's glasses. Her normal impulse in a crisis would be to go out on the piss with one of her mates, have a good cry on a friendly shoulder, but what was the point? She couldn't reveal what Ben had done, explain why they hadn't moved in together as planned. She'd taken two days off work, arranged in order to give herself time to get settled in the new place; instead, she'd spent the time watching old movies and getting slaughtered on red wine, alone. The second night she'd ended up scrabbling drunkenly through the boxes she'd labelled for the move in search of a half-finished bottle of Baileys.

Now it was Tuesday morning, and the moment she'd been dreading: going back to work. It would be bad enough seeing Streaky and not being able to say anything about the secret they shared, but there was another, even worse prospect: what the fuck would she do if she bumped into Ben?

He hadn't called again, which probably meant that Streaky had been in touch, told him to keep his head down. What could she take from that? Was it a simple act of loyalty by the Sarge, to warn his protégé in advance that he would have to report his concealment of evidence up the chain of command? *Maybe.* But deep down, she couldn't shake the feeling that there might be something more sinister, some old-school-style cover-up going on.

Streaky was nowhere to be seen when she arrived at work, although the evidence sitting on his desk – an unopened Greggs bag transparent with grease – suggested he'd been unexpectedly called upstairs. On his return, half an hour later, he called the team together round his desk for a briefing – and dropped his bombshell.

'You'll all be aware of the sudden, if widely unmourned, death of Anthony Stride, convicted paedophile, late of this parish.'

Fuck! Kershaw tried to ignore the speculative looks ricocheting between her colleagues, making a supreme effort to keep her gaze fixed on the Sarge and her expression one of detached curiosity.

'It appeared to be a nice simple case of suicide, with Mr Stride hanging himself from "yon lonely oak" following a sudden attack of conscience. But there has been a development.' Kershaw held her breath. 'This morning, a member of the public handed in a pair of spectacles which they found in the undergrowth up at Hollow Ponds. Anthony Stride's spectacles.'

There were murmurs of surprise, and all eyes flickered towards Kershaw as people remembered that she'd been first on scene and wondered, understandably enough, whether she'd dropped a bollock. But all she felt was a great rolling wave of relief: relief that Streaky had made things right by engineering the retrieval of the evidence – and without revealing Ben's crime.

'This public-spirited citizen even took the trouble to mark the spot where he found the evidence,' Streaky went on, 'which was more than a hundred yards from Stride's body.' That brought a sharp little gasp from Kershaw's fellow DC, Sophie, sitting in front of her.

A memory of Ben turning up at the scene that day flashed into Kershaw's mind, something about his manner and the way he'd seemed keen to get rid of her. She was gripped by a sudden and searing knowledge. At that moment, Ben had *already found* the glasses, had them tucked in his pocket, and even as he joked with her, had already decided not to hand them in.

'Of course,' Streaky was saying, 'it's possible that Stride simply dropped his specs and failed to pick them up, but initial examination has revealed damage to one of the arms and possible traces of blood. Furthermore, they were found on the edge of the car park, close to some tyre tracks, suggesting they may have fallen off while he was being dragged from a vehicle.'

Pausing to extract what looked like a steak and onion slice from the grease-stained paper bag on his desk, he frowned at it, as though a valuable clue might be concealed beneath its pallid crust. 'The upshot is that the case has been promoted to a Category 1 death and has just plummeted from a great height into Murder Squad's inbox.'

'Are the press being told, Sarge – that the initial search of the area didn't find his glasses?' The question came from Ackroyd.

'They'll have to be, at some stage,' sighed Streaky. 'And of course they'll make a meal of it – which will no doubt result in above average levels of impatience from our masters upstairs. So I want everyone working on this for the foreseeable. Except for DC Kershaw.' All eyes swivelled back to her. 'Natalie, after you've briefed the team on your initial assessment of the Stride scene, I'll need you 100 per cent focused on the Jim Fulford case – it's been sixteen days now and we still haven't got a single decent lead. Go back to basics, see if we've missed anything.'

'And now,' he announced, raising the steak slice to his lips. 'I'm going to have my breakfast.'

Reviewing the evidence in the Fulford case kept Kershaw busy all day, with scant opportunity to catch Streaky on his own. At five o'clock, she saw him pick his jacket up off the back of his chair and disappear. Two minutes later, she shrugged on her own coat and, with a general wave goodbye, headed down the stairs. She caught up with him halfway across the car park.

'Ah, DC Kershaw,' he said. 'Good day at the office?'

'I've had better. So, Sarge … How did you pull that off? He didn't slow his pace. 'Pull what off?'

'Come on, Sarge!' Her voice was low but urgent. 'Where does this leave Ben? This is my life – our lives – we're talking about here. You can't leave me hanging like that!'

He appeared to relent. 'Walk with me as far as the boozer then. And pay attention – I'm only going to say this once.'

Leaving the car park, they took a right turn towards Hoe Street.

'You came to me with a situation that threatened the proper upholding of law and order. I have dealt with it in such a way that the investigations that *should have* taken place *will now* take place. Beyond that, the less you know about it, the better.'

'Thank you, Sarge.' She knew what a big deal it was for him to have stuck his neck out, to put things right the way he had. If anyone upstairs ever found out, it would mean instant dismissal, the end of a twenty-odd-year career, and probably goodbye to his pension, too. For all his macho posturing, Streaky's loyalty to his troops was legendary. 'So … what about Ben?'

Streaky's face became grim. 'DS Crowther is taking an extended period of sick leave during which he will be conducting a thorough examination of his attitude to policing in general and the disinterested enforcement of the law in particular.'

Kershaw pictured for a moment the colossal bollocking Streaky must have given his protégé, in the light of Ben's spectacular fuck-up – especially since the Sarge had played a big part in getting him the job in Divisional CID.

'Will people believe the cover story, that he's off sick?'

'I don't see why not.' Streaky turned innocent blue eyes on her. 'He's provided a sick note saying he's got a suspected slipped disc. And by the time he comes back, the furore over Stride's glasses, the search, it will all have blown over.'

She chewed at a fingernail. 'What about me and him?' she said in a low voice.

'I'm afraid I can't help you with that one, not being a qualified relationship counsellor.' He came to a halt – they were now at the doorstep of the pub – and met her gaze. 'Look, Natalie, I've known Ben for a long old time now and I'm sure of one thing: he's one of the good guys. He got over-involved in the Ryan case, happens to the best of us. He saw an opportunity to save the family any further grief – and took it. Moment of madness, he called it.'

Just as Kershaw had suspected: Ben had been protecting the Ryans. An honourable motive, at least.

He stood there scanning her face. 'I'm sure you two'll get over it.' Then, hiking up his trousers, he pushed open the door to the bar, releasing a gust of beery warmth and low-pitched chatter.

'Just one more thing, Sarge.' He looked back at her, one eyebrow raised. 'How did you work the business with the glasses?'

'Eh?'

'The guy you had recover them – he must be someone you'd trust with your life.'

Streaky's lips twitched as he tried to resist the temptation to tell her – and failed.

'The public-spirited gent who stumbled across the specs, you mean? Here's a funny thing: he used to be in the Royal Artillery back in the day – just like me. Small world, isn't it?'

Kershaw watched him disappear into the bar, a wry smile on her face.

Thirty-Six

As Kershaw walked back towards the car park, she pulled up Ben's number on her mobile. Her thumb hovered over the button, an inner voice telling her that they needed to talk about what had happened, whether there was any way around or over it, or whether, for her, his 'moment of madness' as he was now calling it, was a deal-breaker. Half a minute passed before she pocketed the phone, number undialled. She just couldn't face seeing him yet: the feeling of betrayal was still too raw. Maybe in a couple of days' time.

Halfway through the doorway of Tesco Express, where she was planning to replenish her supplies of cheap red wine, Kershaw came to a halt abrupt enough to cause the man behind to bump into her. Why spend yet another evening getting pissed in her empty flat, torturing herself over the Ben situation, she asked herself, when she could be focusing on the Jim Fulford murder? Her review of the painfully sparse evidence in the case had confirmed Streaky's assessment: they had hit a brick wall. She knew that with every passing day, the chances of finding who killed Fulford, and why, were slipping away.

The only unexplored lead was Andre Terrell's claim that, according to Janusz Kiszka, Jim Fulford had been seeing some gorgeous Eastern European girl, the mysterious Varenka Kalina. The time had come, she decided, to have another crack at the double-dealing Pole.

Half an hour later, Kiszka was buzzing her into his apartment.

'Can you explain something to me?' she asked, on the offensive the moment she got through his front door. 'Why would you share significant information about Jim Fulford's private life with Andre Terrell, but withhold it from the detectives investigating his murder?'

'What information?'

'The fact that he had an East European girlfriend.'

'I didn't tell him that. He's a lying little scumbag.'

'So he pulled the name Varenka out of the air, did he? And by another staggering coincidence, wasn't Varenka Kalina one of the names you had me search for on Jim's laptop?'

'Yes, but I didn't know, and I *still* don't know that they were having an affair.'

'But you knew that they knew each other.'

'No! I'm not sure they ever even met!'

They stood there, either side of his kitchen table, eyeballing each other.

'You look terrible,' he said, peering into her face. 'Sit down, I'm making you something to eat.'

She sunk onto a kitchen chair, feeling suddenly and alarmingly bone-weak, her sleepless nights and diet of red wine and toast catching up with her. 'A biscuit wouldn't go amiss, if you've got one,' she admitted.

'You're getting chicken and wild mushroom soup,' he said over his shoulder from the stove.

As Kershaw took her first mouthfuls of soup – steaming and woodily autumnal – she told herself she was skating on

242

thin ice. Having a cosy meal with a potential witness in a murder case without getting permission from the Sarge was the kind of thing that had got her in trouble with Divisional Standards a couple of years back. But given the events of the last few days, the rules and regs felt like some foreign country she'd visited long ago.

'So, what's the story with this Varenka woman?' she asked.

Scanning the girl's serious little face as she tucked into the soup, Janusz felt a stirring of remorse. Maybe he had nothing to lose, sharing some of what he knew.

He sawed a couple of slabs of sourdough off the still-warm loaf. 'I saw her leaving flowers outside Jim's house, after the murder.'

'And assumed that she must have known him?'

He tipped his head – *perhaps.*

Kershaw made a sceptical face. 'Couldn't she simply have read about it in the local paper?'

'It's unlikely. She lives in Canary Wharf, and …' He paused, visualising the beautifully groomed Varenka walking down Hoe Street, a hummingbird in a crowd of pigeons. 'She just didn't belong there.'

'So you think she could be a suspect in the murder?'

'I think it's more likely that her boyfriend is involved. Do you like the sourdough?'

'It's awesome,' she said, taking another slice from the board he held out. 'Is it home-made?'

'Of course,' he shrugged. 'If you want decent sourdough in this country you have to make it yourself.'

'So who's the boyfriend?'

Janusz hesitated, but only for a moment. 'Barbu Romescu. A Romanian "businessman"' – the quotes were audible – 'I think one of his activities is bringing in girls from Ukraine to work in the sex trade. I think she was one of the girls he trafficked, before she got promoted to girlfriend status.' *No*

need to tell her about the smuggling, and the nature of the contra-
band – it would only complicate matters.

'Could Jim have been one of her ... customers?'

'Not in a million years,' he growled.

'Have you asked her? Whether she met Jim through her job as a sex worker?'

He stared at her. 'That's not the kind of question a man can put to a lady.'

Christ Almighty, thought Kershaw, this guy would never cease to amaze her.

She made a sceptical face. 'So what could your friend Jim have to do with a Romanian gangster?'

'I don't know. I've been trying to ... befriend the girl, to try to find out.'

Something in his manner made her ask: 'Good looking, is she?'

'I haven't noticed,' he said, flashing her a grin said that yes, she was.

Kershaw pursed her lips. 'And you think she would grass this Romescu up?'

Janusz paused, finishing a mouthful of bread, sensing the first stirrings of a plan that could get Varenka to safety.

'She might, but not while she's living with him.'

Pushing her bowl to one side she said: 'That was delicious.' Chin propped on one hand, she drummed her fingers on her cheekbone. 'It's not enough to bring him in for questioning, and I'm guessing that interviewing the girl might put her in danger?'

A sombre nod from Kiszka.

He stood to clear the plates, declining her offer of help with a graceful incline of his head. After setting a coffee pot on the stove, he turned, and leaned his back against the worktop, folding his arms. He reminded Kershaw of a colossal statue she'd seen once, on a school trip to the British Museum. *Zeus, was it? Or one of the Roman emperors?*

'Look,' he said. 'She wants to leave Romescu and I think once she's somewhere safe, she can be persuaded to talk. Can the cops arrange for her to get some kind of asylum status, in return for her giving evidence – so she doesn't get sent back to Ukraine?'

Kershaw pulled a doubtful grimace; she could already hear Streaky's response: *If she gives us some rock-solid evidence that might actually solve a crime, I'll have a word with those muppets at the Home Office – not a moment before.*

'I can ask,' she said, 'but to be honest, without a bit more to go on, I don't hold out much hope.'

He grunted: from the cops' perspective, he could see that the link between Jim and Romescu was tenuous, to say the least. Returning to the seat opposite her, he ran a thumbnail along his unshaven jaw, making the bristles rasp.

'There's something else – although I doubt if it is any help at all,' he said. 'You know that suicide up at Hollow Ponds a week or so back? Do the cops think there was anything suspicious about it?' He went on to give her the edited version: how Romescu's 4X4 was parked in the undergrowth the night that Stride died, but reassigning Oskar's beating to 'a friend of a friend'.

'I should think it's just coincidence,' Kershaw shrugged. 'But I'll tell the team investigating Stride's death, just in case.'

It took all her training and then some not to react to Kiszka's revelation. She couldn't get her head round it. The execution of Stride had vigilantism written all over it, which would be a pointless and risky exercise for an organised criminal to carry out. Why would a Romanian gangster kill some lowlife paedophile – or a local gym owner, come to that? And what possible connection could there be between the two victims?

The way they left it, Kiszka would continue to work on Varenka while Kershaw promised to see whether it might be possible to cut a deal to keep her in the country, in return for information connecting Barbu Romescu to serious crimes committed on UK soil.

As Kershaw drove back to Canning Town, something dawned on her. She might be feeling more confused than ever about the murders of James Fulford and Anthony Stride, but the time spent in Kiszka's company had left her calmer and more centred than she'd felt for days.

Thirty-Seven

Kershaw was starting lates the following day so she was less than impressed when the doorbell woke her just after 8 a.m. Rolling over in bed, she ignored it, but after a second, longer ring she rolled, cursing, out of bed and stumbled to the entryphone beside the front door.

It was Ben.

'Nat, I really need to see you.'

He spoke in a low voice but the underlying note of desperation brought the storm of emotions she'd been suppressing rushing in on her. She hesitated for no more than a second or two before buzzing him in, hastily dragging on a pair of jeans and a jumper, and using her fingers as a comb to untangle her bedhair.

At the sight of his face, drawn and pale, and those troubled brown eyes it was all Kershaw could do not to put her arms around him, to try to make it better. *If only it were that easy*, she thought. Instead, she accepted the bouquet that he proffered with an awkward gesture, and he followed her into the kitchen.

She made tea in her best bone china mugs, the ones

nearest the top of the box of crockery she'd brought back from their new place.

'Teabags, I'm afraid,' she said. 'Can't find the teapot.' They sat face to face across the kitchen table to drink it, avoiding each other's gaze.

'Look, Nat, I've been thinking about what you said on the phone. And I know now that you were right.' He thumbed his forehead with both hands. 'What I did – hiding those glasses, risking getting you in trouble – that was me acting like I was still on my own instead of being part of a couple. I'm really sorry.'

She met his eyes. 'Just tell me one thing. What went through your mind when you saw me at the scene, with Stride's body hanging there behind me, knowing that you had his bloodstained glasses in your pocket?' She didn't try to suppress the undertow of anger in her voice.

'I …' He raised a despairing hand, then let it drop. 'I suppose at that stage I was still thinking that I might hand them in.'

She noted that he didn't deny seeing the dried blood – the thing with the potential to transform an everyday suicide into something more sinister. 'And at what stage did you decide you were going to play God with a suspicious death, exactly?' She'd fallen into the tone she used when challenging a recalcitrant suspect, but she couldn't help herself.

Ben stared at the ceiling, his face a picture of misery. 'There wasn't really any one moment. I suppose I kept thinking I could still change my mind and send them down to forensics … but I kept putting it off. Then it got too late to back out.'

'What were you thinking?!' She pressed her hands hard against her temples. 'Risking your career; lying to me, the person you were about to move in with!'

'I know. That was unforgivable.' Ben raised his eyes to hers. 'I know that trust is really, really important to you.'

'And all this to save the Ryans a couple of weeks' unwanted media attention?' His gaze flickered away momentarily, the kind of telltale sign she looked out for in a suspect. 'You told Streaky that was why you did it, didn't you?' Then it dawned on her. 'Oh my God. You thought *Jamie Ryan* killed Stride, didn't you? In revenge for what he did to Hannah?'

Ben let out a ragged sigh, like he'd been holding his breath. 'Yes. It's practically all he's talked about since the trial fell apart – the thought of watching Stride die.'

'So you weren't just covering up some random vigilante killing – you were protecting someone you knew to be a prime suspect in the murder.'

'You've got to believe me, Nat, I wasn't thinking straight.' He raked a hand through hair that looked like it hadn't been washed in days. 'I haven't been thinking straight for ages. Not since the trial collapsed.'

'All this because …'

'Because it was my fault that Stride got off in the first place.' Bitterness surfacing in his voice.

'Some dozy DC couldn't resist checking Stride's search history on his computer – and that's your fault? How do you work that out?'

'I should have been at the flat when they did that search. I got held up, arrived late. If I'd been there earlier I wouldn't have let anyone touch that bastard computer.'

'Sometimes you have to rely on your team. It wasn't you who made the cock-up.'

'It happened on my watch.' He gave a single shake of his head.

'I can understand you feeling that, but you know the score, Ben. Shit happens, we have to get over it and move on – that's the Job.'

'I know, I know. Which is exactly what I was trying to do when I practically trod on those bastard glasses.'

'Why didn't you talk to me instead of bottling it all up? It makes me feel like I don't even know you.' At the look of misery on his face, Kershaw couldn't suppress a rush of sympathy. 'Look, you probably haven't heard, but Jamie Ryan has a cast-iron alibi. He was away on business the night Stride died.'

His head snapped up. 'Are you sure?'

'Yep. He was at some hauliers' conference in the Midlands – Sophie checked it out.'

Ben grimaced. 'So I've risked everything for someone who didn't even need protecting.' His voice was flat.

They sat there for a long moment, neither speaking nor pretending to drink their cooling tea. Ben was the first to break the silence.

'I'm not going to ask you to forgive me, Natalie. If you can't see a way past what I did, I totally understand. But if you do give me another chance, I honestly think we could have a great life together.'

She looked into his eyes, wishing she could believe him, trying to resurrect the vision she'd had of their future.

'I don't know, Ben. I just don't know.'

After he was gone, she washed up their mugs in the kitchen sink, watching the odd tear plink into the soapy water. After drying them, she hesitated, unsure whether to put them back in their packing box or into the kitchen cupboard. In the end, she left them on the draining board, finding herself incapable of even this simple decision.

Thirty-Eight

Around the time that Ben and Kershaw were having their heart-to-heart, Janusz was on his way to Café Krakowia in Islington on a mercy mission. Oskar had been texting him several times a day, complaining about the food in hospital, and finally Janusz had promised to bring him a slab of Pani Markowitz's famous baked cheesecake. Run by a grumpy old Pole and his Jewish wife, the Krakowia had been around forever, long before he'd moved into the area, and as he strolled down the side street where it was located, he sent up his usual fervent prayer that it would still be open.

It was. The paint might be peeling and the glass front door's sixties spiderweb design long past its sell-by date, but the café's position on the ground floor of a fine Georgian terrace made it a serious piece of real estate, so Janusz could only guess that some arcane restrictive covenant saved the place from conversion into another multi-million-pound abode for an investment banker.

The doorbell jangled its old-fashioned peal and Janusz scanned the café, wondering afresh how it survived – only one of the gleamingly clean Formica tables was occupied, by

251

an impoverished-looking man nursing a cup of tea. But in the chilled cabinet, alongside the egg mayo and slices of pallid ham, he found what he'd come for: the legendary cheesecake, its filling a rich, claggy yellow studded with dried fruits.

After scoring a kilo of the stuff, he was back on the street when his phone rang. The display showed the name *Varenka*.

He was on the point of greeting her when he heard an unexpected voice.

'Kiszka? It's Barbu Romescu. Triangle Investments.'

Janusz nearly dropped his box of cake. Not only had Romescu discovered his real name, but the fact that he'd used his girlfriend's phone suggested that he suspected, at the very least, that the two of them had been in touch – and wanted Janusz to know it. Or maybe the girl had been in on it all along, had never had any intention of betraying her boyfriend over Jim's murder. Then a much worse explanation occurred to him – that Romescu might have done the girl some serious harm.

'We need to meet up.' Romescu sounded relaxed, almost friendly. 'I'll be at the Pasha Café in Walthamstow at one.'

'I'd love to,' said Janusz, 'but I'm having my hair trimmed this afternoon.'

'Perhaps I should come to your apartment, instead?' Superficially, Romescu's tone was still affable enough, but it had acquired an underpinning of tungsten steel.

Janusz paused, considering his options, before deciding he didn't have any. Anyway, so long as he watched his back, a face to face with Romescu could prove illuminating.

'Where is this Pasha Café, anyway?' he asked.

'Don't treat me like a *kretyn*, Kiszka.' And with that, Romescu hung up.

Janusz took the comment as confirmation of something he'd long suspected: that it had been his first visit to the Pasha Café, his reckless outburst about Jim's murder, which had alerted Romescu to his investigation. The Turk who owned the place had clearly informed his business associate, so when a big Pole fitting Janusz's description had waltzed into the investor soiree wearing his best jacket a couple of days later, it wouldn't have taken long for the Romanian to put two and two together.

At ten past one, Janusz – uncharacteristically and deliberately unpunctual – walked off Hoe Street and into his second café of the day. The mustachioed Turkish owner gave him a mournful nod from behind the counter. 'Mr Romescu is waiting for you,' he said. 'Please go through to the salon.' He waved a hand towards the doorway hung with thick red plush curtains.

Noting the solid-looking closed door behind the drapes, Janusz decided that his life expectancy might be enhanced by staying in the café. Here there were witnesses at least: two of the tables were occupied by middle-aged Turkish guys watching Al Jazeera on the giant overhead screen, coffee and pastries in front of them. He chose a table near the window, taking a seat facing back into the café.

When Romescu emerged a few minutes later, all eyes flickered towards him and then slid away. He was an unsettling presence, his fierce gaze and scarred face incongruous against the beautifully-cut shirt and jacket, the shiny, expensive looking brogues on his feet. As he sat down opposite Janusz, the owner set down a tray bearing two tiny glasses and a silver teapot from which rose a sweet yet bracing aroma.

'Mint tea?' asked Romescu. 'Or do you want something stronger?'

'This is fine,' said Janusz.

Romescu spread a napkin across his lap, a curiously fastidious gesture given he was only drinking tea. 'How do I know you're not wearing a wire?' he said, fixing his piercing stare on Janusz. 'I hear you work as a translator for the English cops, when you're not playing at the private eye business.'

So Romescu had learned of Janusz's eventful visit to Przeczokow Airport with the girl detective, which was no doubt how he'd discovered his real name: one of his stooges there could easily have accessed the flight passenger list.

After checking that no one was watching, Janusz parted his coat a few inches. Romescu reached across the table and ran a swift outspread hand from his chest down to his belly. Janusz suppressed a shiver of disgust: even after Romescu withdrew his hand, he could still feel the trail the questing fingers had left on his skin, nerve endings jangling in its wake.

Romescu gave a curt nod – he was satisfied. 'What exactly are you doing digging around in my private business, Kiszka?' His voice, although still reasonable-sounding, was as cold and sharp as a glacier's edge.

Janusz took a sip of his tea, shrugged. 'I made a pile of money selling properties in Krakow, and I'm looking to invest it in the right project. Like I told you at your drinks do, I like to do my research on the people I invest in.'

Romescu's searching gaze became incredulous. 'Really! And what did your "research" tell you?'

'That your Triangle Investments set-up has an asset you've been keeping under your hat. Something with the potential to deliver serious returns – not the ten or fifteen per cent you give your Polish shopkeepers.'

'And what is that?'

'A highly discreet, super-fast delivery route to the East, avoiding the risk and inconvenience of border crossings and customs checks.'

Romescu reached for the teapot to top up their glasses. 'And what merchandise do you imagine I am exporting in this way?' He sounded complacent, amused even, apparently confident that the cloak of secrecy around the cargo flying out of Przeczokow was intact.

Janusz lifted his eyes to look over Romescu's head. Face creasing with irritation, he twisted round in his seat to follow Janusz's gaze. The TV screen behind them showed a group of Middle Eastern combatants bouncing around in the back of a moving truck. They wore *keffiyeh* twinned with ill-assorted camouflage gear, and each cradled an assault rifle. The strapline at the bottom of the screen said '*SYRIA: Jihadist fighters well armed despite international sanctions, say analysts.*'

A muscle jumped in Romescu's face as he stirred his tea.

Janusz nodded to the mustachioed Turk, sitting behind the counter, apparently intent on his newspaper. 'Your friend here supplies the customers; you source and deliver the *materiel*. London, Poland, Turkey.' Sketching the route on the table, he shot Romescu an appreciative grin. 'A *triangle*, right?'

That night in the snowy airport car park at Przeczokow, the young mechanic Slawek had told him that the freight planes were bound for Sukur, in southern Turkey, which had turned out to be a tiny airfield close to the Syrian border. But the only clue to the cargo they carried had been the boy's brief glimpse of brown metal boxes with yellow lettering – a description that had rung a distant yet elusive bell. It had been Oskar who'd supplied the answer. Back during their national service, boxes fitting that description were found on the shelves of the camp's armoury. The smallest ones, the size of a family Bible, held ammunition; grenades and mortars came in larger square ones; and the long rectangular ones carried Polish-made AK-47s and carbines.

'I don't know what you are talking about, Kiszka.'

'I suppose we Poles should be grateful that the Soviets left us something useful after fifty years of shit,' Janusz chuckled. 'All those armament factories making rifles and carbines, they're probably the only bit of Communist industry still standing, right?'

It was no secret that Poland's thriving arms industry supplied weapons, perfectly legally, to conflicts all over the world, but Syria was another matter: selling arms to either side of the country's vicious fratricidal conflict was forbidden by international law.

'Look, I'm a realist,' Janusz opened his hands. 'One stroke of a bureaucrat's pen and arms dealing goes from crime to valued export activity. I always say guns are like water – they find their own level.' He half-meant it – to him, Romescu's gun smuggling offered leverage, pure and simple, and the only hope he had of pressuring the guy into revealing why Jim had died.

Romescu shot the cuff of his jacket to check his watch.

'I think you started your export sideline when you were still an Orzelair director – and saw no reason to stop it after they ditched you.' Janusz shrugged. 'After all, Przeczokow airport was your own little fiefdom by then. Your first "cargo" was girls, right? Till things kicked off in Syria and sent the market price of an AK-47 through the roof.'

Romescu rearranged the napkin on his lap, looking unperturbed. 'There isn't a shred of evidence for what you're suggesting.'

Janusz suspected he was speaking the truth. If customs officials paid a surprise visit to inspect the cargo being loaded onto the night flights now, they'd find nothing but industrial fridges, or whatever goods were listed on the flight manifest.

'You do like to take risks though, don't you?' Janusz grinned, trying to provok. him. 'There was a good chance the cops would come sniffing around Przeczokow after Wojtek dropped out of a plane, but you gambled that the airline would choose to bury the scandal rather than identify their own head of security.'

A flicker of arrogant amusement crossed Romescu's face: a look that said he was used to dealing with fucking idiots. And Janusz suddenly understood. The little regional airline that had, in the space of a few hectic years, become a powerful multinational ... a business that had started out buying ex-Soviet state assets at knockdown prices ... Romescu edged out of the company he helped to create.

'Sebastian Fischer knew about the flights from the start, didn't he?' said Janusz. *Of course! An outfit like Zaleski built on ex-state assets would be bound to have an arms manufacturer in its portfolio.* 'But gun running must have lost its appeal – after he swung the Lufthansa deal and started going to dinner dances with Angela Merkel.' Janusz shook his head. 'Killing Wojtek was a warning, wasn't it? Leave you alone, or you'd take the whole company down with you.'

'I don't understand what you think you stand to gain from all this, Kiszka.' Romescu's cold blue eyes narrowed in confusion. 'We both know you're not an investor, so why the interest in what you claim are my ... business activities? If you're looking for a payoff, money to shut up and go away, then just say so.'

Now we're getting somewhere, thought Janusz. Putting the operation on ice was clearly hurting Romescu in the pocket.

'That's generous of you,' he said. 'But what I really want is some information.' Deciding he had nothing to lose, he levelled his gaze on Romescu. 'I want to know why James Fulford was killed.'

'I'm afraid I can't help you with that.' His answer came too fast, as though he'd been expecting the question.

'I think you can,' growled Janusz.

Romescu held Janusz's eyes without blinking. 'You are mistaken.' Then he leaned forward, adopting a reasonable tone. 'Look, I'm prepared to make an *ex-gratia* payment, so you can go back to investigating philandering husbands … let's say 25,000 sterling?'

Janusz didn't bother pointing out that he never worked for jealous spouses, having discovered long ago that he was allergic to the sight of crying women – let alone crying men.

'You could even give the money to your friend's widow,' said Romescu, 'if you were feeling charitable.'

Struggling to tamp down the rage building in his gut, Janusz felt his fists bunch – the fucker was more or less admitting he'd had Jim killed. 'The only thing she wants is to know that the cowardly *skurwysyny* who butchered her husband are rotting in a prison cell.' He leaned forward, eyeballing Romescu. 'And I am going to make sure her wish is fulfilled.'

Romescu's eyes were like two chips of Arctic ice. 'If you seriously think I'm going to sit around like a fucking whore with my legs spread waiting for you to fuck me then you don't know who you are dealing with.' He jabbed a finger at the long shiny scar on the side of his face. 'I got this from two and a half hours spent in the belly of a jet at 30,000 feet. It was minus 40. When I came to, my face was frozen to the fuselage – the paramedics had to cut me off it.' He shook his head. 'If you think you can scare me then you are an even bigger fucking *chuj* than I thought.'

Janusz could see flecks of spit at the corners of Romescu's mouth. 'At least you got to wear thermals,' he shot back. 'Not like poor old Wojtek.'

Romescu picked up the napkin from his lap and patted his lips, before getting to his feet. He gave a single imperious jerk of his chin through the café window, and then, putting both hands on the back of his chair, bent down to bring his face level with Janusz's.

'I made you a very generous offer in good faith, Kiszka,' he murmured. 'I am giving you one last chance to take the

258

cash and get your nose out of my business.'

Janusz made a regretful face.

'You just made the biggest fucking mistake of your life,' Romescu spat.

'Really?' Janusz frowned. 'I think the biggest mistake of my life was backing Chelsea for the league last season.'

But if he thought he'd had the last word, he was wrong.

'You know what I found out today? It's only two hours' drive from Przeczokow to Lublin.' Romescu's eyes were alive with malice. 'My men could be inside your flat – and your ex-wife – before dinnertime.'

Janusz froze for a beat, his brain scrabbling to catch up. Then he lunged across the table, going for Romescu's throat, images flashing before his eyes. *That gorilla Mazurek hurting Marta … Bobek's terrified face.* Then something hit him square in the chest, hurling him back with such force that the impact broke the seat back.

Romescu straightened his jacket and smiled. 'I'll get them to film it and send you the video.'

Then he was off out of the door.

A big Turkish guy – still holding the baseball bat he'd used on Janusz – stepped in front of him. Clutching his ribs, Janusz whipped round to see the black Discovery drawing up at the kerb, and Romescu climbing into the front passenger seat. There was a different driver at the wheel this time, older looking than the tattooed guy. And the outline of someone in the back seat.

Varenka. Their eyes met through the window. Her lower lip was split and he could make out a fresh bruise around her left eye socket. But it was her expression that transfixed him – she was rigid with fear.

Thirty-Nine

Barely half a mile from the Pasha Café, in the Murder Squad office, Kershaw had spent the morning trying, without much joy, to pin Streaky down for a chat.

The news about Stride's 'suicide' becoming a murder investigation had been splashed on LBC's 8 a.m. news bulletin and was now running as the lead story across TV and radio news. Since the original case against Stride had collapsed through a police cock-up, it wasn't exactly a surprise that the angle reporters were taking was further Met incompetence in failing to find the 'bloodstained glasses', as they were calling them.

Kershaw had arrived in the office to find the team running around like blue-arsed flies digging up info for the media department, and the Sarge in back-to-back meetings with the brass. The only upside was that, so far, the press didn't seem to be naming Ben as the officer in charge of the 'botched search' at Hollow Ponds.

'Rolling news,' sighed Streaky, when he finally granted her a five-minute audience. 'Biggest waste of police time since PACE. And in a couple of weeks' time, all those scrotes in the media will be running headlines asking why we haven't made any progress finding Stride's killers.' Kershaw made a sympathetic face.

'So you reckon this girl Vạrenka knows something about the Fulford murder, and a promise of asylum might oil the wheels?'

'It's a long shot, Sarge, but at the moment we've got sod-all else to go on.'

'You didn't turn up anything new, when you reviewed the witness statements, the door-to-door enquiries?' A head-shake. 'And his contacts – none of them have dredged up a possible motive?'

'No, Sarge. In fact, I'm getting a bit tired of hearing how much everyone loved Jim Fulford.'

'Yeah.' Streaky scratched his belly. 'When looking for a murder motive, give me a drug-dealing scumbag over a pillar of the community any day of the week. So you're going to question Marika Fulford again today, right?'

'Yes,' she glanced at her watch. 'Oops, I'd better get going. Not that I'm holding out much hope of anything new.'

'She wasn't a lot of help when I interviewed her, the day after the murder,' said Streaky. 'But she's buried him now. Puts you in a different frame of mind. She might surprise you.'

'I'll do my best, Sarge.'

'Make sure you do. It's been, what, seventeen days? Another week and I reckon the case will be as dead as the proverbial parrot.'

The phone on his desk bleeped.

'DS Bacon. Yes, I'll hold.' Streaky cupped a hand over the mouthpiece and rolled his eyes. 'It's Barrington,' he told her, naming the Assistant Chief Constable.

Kershaw raised her eyebrows: the Stride story must be making waves if it warranted a call from The Dream Factory – as the Sarge invariably called Scotland Yard.

'Listen,' he said, under his breath. 'If you can get Varenka on her own, see what she's got, we'll talk again about approaching the Home Office.'

Kershaw grinned her thanks and was turning to go when he pointed a stern finger at her. 'And if you're planning on going to that Romanian gangster's gaff to doorstep her? *Take a fucking uniform.* None of your girl scout heroics.'

On her way to get her coat, she spotted Adam Ackroyd at the water cooler.

'Hey, Adam. Nightmare day, huh?'

'Yup. Getting our arses kicked from all sides.'

He smiled but didn't sustain eye contact, she noticed. Were her workmates blaming her for the failed search of Hollow Ponds and the media fallout they'd been left to wrestle with? She was still the office newbie and the last thing she needed was to be the focus of any team resentment. An image of Ben slipped into her mind, and she asked herself again, *How could he have done it?* Then she pushed all thought of him away. With their relationship still in this horrible limbo, work was the best therapy.

'Listen, Adam, I just wanted to let you know. The night before we found Stride? One of my contacts says a car was seen driving out of the bushes up at Hollow Ponds.'

'I didn't know you had a CHIS, Natalie,' said Ackroyd, his grin allaying her paranoia somewhat. 'I hope you had it properly authorised.' These days, you had to get a stack of permissions before signing up a Covert Human Intelligence Source, aka an informer.

'He's not really a CHIS,' she said. 'It's Jim Fulford's best mate, Janusz Kiszka.'

'The Polish PI who we had in the frame early on?'

'Yeah. Anyway, according to him, one of the Forest Rangers was driving past late that night and saw a black Land Rover Discovery creeping out of the woodland. You might want to send someone down there to talk to the guy who runs the café? Apparently, he knows the name of the Ranger.'

The moment Janusz got out of the Pasha Café he called Marta – but her mobile kept going through to voicemail. So he phoned Bobek's school, and got hold of the headmistress, who he'd met once at a parents' evening. She told him the best news ever – the school was closed and Bobek was away on holiday. He remembered then – Marta had mentioned that she and the new boyfriend were taking the boy on a skiing trip.

As he hung up, he reflected that Romescu had probably just been winding him up – if he was really going to do something, why would he give advance warning? But one thing continued to gnaw at Janusz's gut: Romescu had found out somehow that Marta and Bobek lived in Lublin. When Marta called back he'd have to tell her to move out, find somewhere safe to stay, at least for a while.

When Janusz finally arrived at the hospital he found Oskar's bed stripped and his bedside table cleared, a sight that triggered a fresh flare of panic. The only nurse in sight was at the far end of the ward helping an elderly man back into bed.

Then he nearly jumped out of his skin as a hand fell on his shoulder.

'*Kurwa mac*!' he burst out.

'You'd better not let Jadwiga hear you,' said Oskar, shaking his head. 'She says that every time somebody curses, the baby Jesus sheds a tear.'

Janusz grunted. 'What are you doing up and dressed, anyway?'

'I'm getting out of here.'

'Are the medics okay with that?'

263

'Fuck the medics! If I don't go and price that patio job in Redbridge some guy called Paddy is gonna come along and steal it from under my nose.'

Twenty minutes later, after Oskar had signed a form saying he was discharging himself against medical advice, he was climbing into the Transit van, which one of his labourers had delivered to the hospital car park earlier that day.

Janusz lagged behind, glancing around the car park, on the lookout for anyone who seemed out of place. After slamming the passenger door, he turned to his mate. 'Listen Oskar, I'll go with you to price this job because I want to watch your back, but after that, I'm deadly serious – I want you to come and stay with me for a few days. Romescu's quite capable of going after anyone close to me.'

Oskar didn't appear to be paying any attention – he was concentrating on trying to tune the radio with his left, unplastered, hand. '*Dupa blada*, Janek, stop fussing and make yourself useful. Find LBC for me – I haven't heard the news in days.'

Janusz dashed an exasperated hand over his scalp. 'For fuck's sake, Oskar! Romescu knows where you live – he could be sending his goons after you right now! Do you *want* to get all fucked up again?'

He regretted the words the moment they were out of his mouth. Oskar frowned at the radio, fallen uncharacteristically silent.

As Janusz tried to imagine the ordeal those bastards had put his mate through, he remembered with a jolt an experience back home, at the peak of the Solidarity uprising. He'd just turned seventeen when the *milicja* caught him daubing anti-Communist graffiti on a railway bridge. After dragging him off to the cells they'd spent the whole night working him over. The bruises had faded within a few weeks but the memory of his own powerlessness, the deep sense of shame and humiliation, had left scars as indelible as the rings within the trunk of a tree.

'I'm sorry, Oskar. I just feel so bad about … what happened to you because of me. I'm probably being paranoid but I'd still feel a whole lot better if you moved into my apartment for now.'

Oskar drummed his fingers on the steering wheel. 'So I'd be coming to stay with you to make you feel less jumpy?'

'Yes.'

He heaved a theatrical sigh. 'Alright then. On one condition.'

'Name it.'

Oskar started the van up. 'You promise to wear your pinny when you give me a blowjob.'

As they left the car park, Janusz checked his messages to see if the girl detective had returned his call. Nothing. He'd been trying to reach her, gripped by a steadily growing conviction, triggered by the sight of Varenka's terrified face, that her life was in danger.

Oskar took a corner at speed, hurling Janusz against his door, the impact bringing a stab of pain from his bruised ribs so fierce it made his eyes water. 'Are you sure you're safe to drive?' he asked, eyeing the cast on Oskar's right arm.

'Don't be such an old woman, Janek! I've got another arm, haven't I?' Oskar nodded towards the dashboard onto which someone appeared to have upended a wastepaper basket. 'And look that address up in the A-Z will you? Piotr forgot to bring the satnav.'

After a few moments mining the strata of envelopes, drinks cans and sweet wrappers, Janusz retrieved the piece of paper his mate was after. On it, in Oskar's barely legible scrawl was written: *Mrs Martin, 11 Park Rd.*

Janusz flicked through the index of the A-Z, squinting to read the tiny type. 'There are two Park Roads in Redbridge – one in E11 and one in E12. What's the postcode, donkey-brain?'

Oskar hesitated for a split second before replying 'E11.'

His tone sounded unambiguous enough, but after knowing him for nearly thirty years, Janusz could tell his mate didn't have a clue.

On the garden wall outside the Fulford house, tea lights still flickered in their red perspex holders, but most of the floral tributes, long wilted, had been cleared away.

Marika ushered Kershaw into the tiny front room. Bending swiftly to pick up a pillow on the floor beside the settee, she caught Kershaw's inquiring look. 'I've been sleeping down here since ...' She looked around the room with a slight frown, as though she'd mislaid something. 'I'm thinking of putting the house on the market,' she said, waving her hand in a vague gesture. 'Basia – my sister – thinks it would be good for me to move. We might buy a little house together, on the coast somewhere.'

As they sat drinking tea, Kershaw ran through her list of questions. Was there anyone who might have wished Jim harm? Had he ever taken drugs? Fallen out with anyone at the gym? Had an affair? Marika gave each question careful thought – but answered them all in the negative. Between note taking, Kershaw studied the older woman discreetly. Her face was chalk white, the features blurred, like an image printed on a tea towel faded by countless washes.

'I'm sorry, Marika. I know you've been asked these questions several times already.'

'I am happy to answer them,' she said in her not-quite-perfect English, 'if it means that you are still trying to find out who took my Jim away from me. When the police stop coming, when the journalists stop telephoning, this will be much harder. It will mean people have started to forget him.'

Kershaw was reminded of the first few weeks after her dad died. The cascade of cards and phone calls from his old

266

friends, the funeral, had all given that early period of grieving an almost festive feel – and a sense of unreality. The worst part had come in the weeks and months afterwards: waking every day to face a gaping void – the inescapable and unbearable finality of his irrevocable absence.

She tipped her head towards the front garden. 'Your friend Mr Kiszka thinks it was strange that this Ukrainian girl, Varenka Kalina, should leave flowers when she didn't know Jim.'

'Yes, he told me he was following it up. She is connected to a Romanian gangster, I think?'

'Barbu Romescu. Can you think of any connection at all Jim might have had to either of them? Had he ever been to Romania, or Ukraine, or made investments in those countries?' Both enquiries were met with a shake of the head.

Kershaw hesitated for a moment. 'Look, I don't know if Mr Kiszka told you, but the girl may have been, at least until recently …'

'… a prostitute. Yes, Janek told me. I think he wanted to ask me if Jim had ever paid for sex but couldn't bring himself to.' The eyes of the two women met in a moment of humorous understanding. 'I have thought about it a lot since he mentioned this girl. I looked through all Jim's bank and credit card statements again to see if there was anything strange about his spending.'

'And?' Asked Kershaw.

'*Zero*. Sorry – nothing.' She shrugged. 'It was funny. I didn't know whether I wanted to find something – because it might help explain why he was killed – or whether I wouldn't be able to bear it.'

Kershaw's gaze fell on a framed photograph of Jim on the mantelpiece. He was sitting at an outdoor café, somewhere hot judging by the sunlit vines tumbling down the whitewashed wall behind him, peering through his specs at what appeared to be a Spanish language newspaper on the table in front of him. She nodded towards the photo. 'Did Jim speak Spanish?'

'Not really,' said Marika with a rueful smile. 'He picked up a little bit in the Falklands when he had to guard some Argentine prisoners, and every time we took a holiday in Spain he tried to speak it, but he never really got beyond ordering a beer and *"hasta la vista"*.'

Kershaw looked again at the photograph. Something about it had set up a distant hum at the back of her mind, but she couldn't for the life of her work out why.

As they said goodbye at the door, Marika suddenly said: 'I nearly forgot, would you please pass my sincere thanks on to Sergeant Bacon? I haven't had a chance to write to everyone yet, but please tell him I was very touched by the beautiful wreath he sent to Jim's funeral.'

Kershaw smiled and said she would, like it was the most normal thing on earth for an Investigating Officer to send flowers to a murder victim's spouse. But inside she was thinking: *Streaky a closet sentimentalist! Who knew?*

Forty

While Janusz and Oskar were on the way to the second Park Road, in E12 – the first address having turned out to be the home of an elderly Asian lady who clearly thought they'd come to rob her – a news report came on the radio that made Janusz's brain race. Apparently, the cops were now treating the death of Anthony Stride, the dirty *chuj* who'd abused the little Downs Syndrome girl, as murder.

The girl detective finally returned his call just as they were arriving back in Walthamstow. 'Where are you?' he asked, bellowing to be heard over the van's diesel growl.

'I've just left Marika Fulford's,' said Kershaw. 'Why?'

'Good. Do you know the Rochester – the gastropub at the end of Jim's road? I'll meet you there in ten minutes.'

Before she had time to protest, he'd gone.

The pub was half empty at the fag-end of the lunchtime rush.

'Where's the fire then?' she asked, taking a sip of her coffee – much as she'd have liked a drink, she was still on duty.

Janusz chose to ignore her sarcastic tone. 'I heard the news on the radio – that your lot have decided that the paedophile found hanged in the woods was murdered?'

'Well, we're still investigating the circum—'

'Spare me the official version.' His voice was curt. 'Was he or wasn't he?'

'We won't know till the second post-mortem, but between you and me, I'd say everything points that way.'

It only served to make the puzzle even more bafflingly impenetrable, thought Janusz, staring into his pint. Romescu's 4X4 had been parked in the undergrowth at Hollow Ponds the night Stride was killed, the same woods where, just three days earlier, his thugs had taken Oskar to be beaten and tortured. If, as looked likely, the Romanian was behind Stride's execution, what – if anything – could that have to do with Jim's murder? What could connect a lowlife like Stride to a man like Jim Fulford? A tiny bell-like voice in his head supplied one perfectly feasible link. He mentally batted it away, furious at himself for even thinking it.

The girl detective was eyeing him uncertainly. *Of course!* The same thought must have occurred to her.

He set his pint glass on the table with exaggerated care. 'There's no way that Jim would ever harm a child.' His tone declared that line of enquiry closed. Forever.

'Anyway,' he said. 'The reason I needed to talk to you is that I saw the girl, Varenka, today.' He pulled a mirthless grin. 'It seems she's been careless enough to walk into Romescu's fists again. I'm guessing he's found out that she's been talking to me, and that means her life is in peril.'

A frown line furrowed kershaw's forehead. 'I've got permission to have a chat with her, if she'll speak to me, but I wasn't planning on doing it today.'

'If you don't, you might be pulling another murder victim out of the undergrowth tomorrow.'

She caught her top lip between her teeth. Then, with a decisive gesture, pulled out her notepad. 'Give me Romescu's address, I'll try to get down there this afternoon.'

He was just reading it out from his phone when he remembered Oskar's mix-up over addresses earlier that day. And stopped in mid-sentence.

'What is it?' she asked, eyes searching his.

'Stride lived in Walthamstow, right?'

She gave a half-nod, half-shrug, as if to say, *So what?*

'What was his address?' he said.

'You know I can't divulge that.'

'Fuck that, Natalia.' He leaned across the table, his eyes boring into hers. 'This is important.'

She gazed back at him, noticing the crow's feet around his eyes for the first time. He was what, forty-five? But the wrinkles only softened his craggy features, making him more attractive.

'I don't know it,' she said finally, 'but I can find out easily enough.'

Letting herself out of the pub's front door, she dialled a number. Janusz watched through the window as she put the phone to her ear and turned away from him. As she rejoined him, moments later, the look on her face told Janusz that she'd discovered something.

'Stride lived at 157 Berkeley Rd, E17,' she said, her voice troubled.

'And Jim and Marika's place?' *As if he didn't know*.

'157 *Barclay* Rd, E17,' she said. 'Unless you see them written down, they sound identical.'

Kershaw suddenly realised what it was that had been niggling away at the back of her brain since she saw the holiday snap of Jim reading a Spanish newspaper. 'Jim wore glasses for reading, didn't he?'

'So?'

She flicked back through her notes of the interview with Marika. 'When Marika and her sister left him at home that day he said he was looking forward to reading his paper.'

'So when he answered the door to his killers, he was probably still wearing his spectacles,' Janusz's voice had dropped to a hoarse whisper.

Kershaw pictured Stride's spectacles through the clear plastic of the evidence bag – the narrow rectangular lenses not unlike Jim's reading glasses. 'The killers thought they had the right address, and at night a crew-cut middle-aged guy in glasses could easily have passed for Anthony Stride.'

Janusz jumped to his feet, knocking his empty pint glass off the table. As it rolled around on the wooden boards, the room darkened before his eyes. Jim had died because some numbskulled *kutas* carried out a hit at the wrong house? It was like some bad cosmic joke. To be killed over a girl, or money, that would have been bad enough, but to die for nothing? It made his friend's death meaningless, somehow.

He rounded on the girl: 'The cops knew the addresses! Why didn't you put two and two together?'

She shrugged awkwardly. 'There was nothing to link the two cases, and anyway, we've only just started treating Stride's death as a murder.'

The rage left Janusz as suddenly as it had arrived, his strength seeming to drain away with it. He lowered himself back into his seat like an old man, wrestling with a sudden, terrible thought. How would Marika take the news?

Kershaw's brain was whirring and chiming like a faulty cuckoo clock. Two murders barely a week apart, at addresses that sounded identical unless you saw them written down … it was beyond coincidence. Jim Fulford's murder had clearly been a case of mistaken identity. The person with the most obvious motive for killing Stride was Jamie Ryan, who had a solid alibi for the night Stride died. But now it occurred to her that maybe he'd taken out a contract on Stride with local gangster Romescu? Then after the thugs screwed up and killed the wrong man, they might have been sent to finish the job by faking Stride's suicide – a ruse to prevent police linking the murders.

They both sat for several minutes, lost in their own thoughts, until Janusz broke the silence.

'Listen,' he said. 'Before you do anything else, please go and see Varenka, before Romescu does something terrible to her? She knows something about Jim's murder, I'm sure of it. Another woman might be able to persuade her that there's a way out of her situation.'

Kershaw hesitated. She could really do with getting back to the nick. But Kiszka's hunches had a nasty habit of turning out to be right and she didn't want the death of this girl on her conscience any more than he did. And there was another compelling reason to do a bit more digging: if she were able to deliver a breakthrough, get something from the girl that nailed Romescu, it would wipe away any lingering stain on her reputation from the cock-up over the Stride scene.

She left Janusz hunched in his coat, staring into the fire-place, so preoccupied with his thoughts that he didn't even return her goodbye.

Forty-One

The mirror glass apartment blocks that ringed Millwall Dock looked soulless and unwelcoming under a leaden sky, Kershaw thought, although she knew that a luxury flat here could easily knock you back a couple of million. As she neared Barbu Romescu's high-rise – its gleaming twin towers like two glassy fingers raised to the world – she slowed her pace, feeling a twinge of conscience. She was remembering her promise to the Sarge to bring back-up in case she should run into Romescu himself. There wouldn't have been a hope in hell of getting a uniform allocated at such short notice, of course, but she knew that line of argument would cut no ice with Streaky.

She hovered by the dockside and gazed over the wind-ruffled waters, shoulders hunched against the horizontal wind. The indecisive weather echoed her mood, the skies a solid grey one minute, the sun breaking through the clouds the next, surprisingly bright for a November afternoon. She knew that going to the flat alone could be risky, but she trusted Kiszka's instincts when he said the girl was in imminent danger.

A couple of minutes later, she'd come up with a plan. Stepping into the foyer of the apartment block, her ears still

274

stinging from the cold, she showed the guy on reception her warrant card. After a brief chat, he picked up the phone and dialled a number.

'Hello, it's reception here. I have a delivery for Mr Romescu?' Kershaw gave him an encouraging smile across the desk. 'Is he there to sign for it?' She held her breath. Meeting her eyes, the guy shook his head. *Result!* The girl was alone. 'Oh, right ...' he said, 'I'll check if that's okay.' A nod from Kershaw. 'Yes, that will be fine. It's on the way up.'

'Thanks for that,' she told him, scribbling her mobile number on a scrap of paper. 'Okay, you know what this Romescu guy looks like, yes? So if he turns up, you call me straight away.'

As the lift swished her up to the eleventh floor Kershaw reflected that, as a risk avoidance plan, it wasn't exactly bulletproof, but in the real world, there were times when you had to ditch the health and safety rulebook. And as for Streaky, she reckoned that if she went back to the nick with a solid lead on the Fulford and Stride murders he'd probably never even ask whether she'd taken a minder.

The first thing that struck her about the girl who answered the door at flat 117 was how tall she was: even allowing for the spiky high heels, she must be knocking on for six foot. She was perhaps a couple of years younger than Kershaw, with legs to die for, although there was no makeup outside a circus that could entirely disguise her blackening eye and split lower lip – both injuries only a few hours old from the look of them.

'Are you alone?' Kershaw asked in a low voice.

The girl shot a half-look over her shoulder, but the gesture appeared to have been no more than a reflex because the next moment she nodded.

Only then did Kershaw flash her warrant card. 'Detective Constable Natalie Kershaw,' she said. 'We need to talk.'

'What is this about, please?' she asked, alarm blooming in her eyes. Her voice was husky, with an Eastern European lilt.

'I really need to come in to explain properly,' said Kershaw. 'Unless you'd feel safer coming to the police station?' She was maintaining eye contact, working the sympathetic but firm approach to the max, aware that the door could get slammed in her face at any moment. If you looked past her injuries, the girl was pretty enough, Kershaw decided – if not as gorgeous as Kiszka had made out.

Varenka twiddled a lock of hair, still damp at the ends from the shower. Then, with a sideways dip of her head: 'Please, come in.'

They sat either side of the granite-topped breakfast bar. From her position, Kershaw could see right across the vast living room and through the plate glass to the great curve of the Thames cradling the Isle of Dogs, mouse grey and sluggish in the lowering half-light.

'I would make you some coffee but … I'm afraid that I have run out of milk,' said Varenka. 'Unless you would like it black?'

Kershaw declined the half-hearted offer. She noticed a little cairn of blue beads lying on the granite beside a mobile phone – it looked like the girl had been saying her rosary.

'Can I speak frankly with you, Varenka?' she asked. 'Just in case you are worrying that we might be disturbed, I've arranged to be alerted if Mr Romescu returns.'

'It is okay,' said Varenka with a little shrug, 'I'm not expecting him back.'

'Oh, right. Is he out for the day or has he gone back to Poland?'

'Poland … yes, a business trip. He isn't back until tomorrow.'

Kershaw allowed herself to relax a little. 'Okay, good. I'd like to ask you about a murder that happened on Monday,

6th of November, in Walthamstow. A man called Jim Fulford?'

The girl showed no reaction.

'Are you familiar with the name?' Scanning her face, Kershaw wondered which way she'd jump. If she was going to deny even having heard of Fulford, it probably meant she'd decided to back Romescu.

'Oh yes, that was such a terrible thing. I read about it in the *Metro*.' She lifted one shoulder, a self-deprecating gesture. 'I took a bouquet' – she pronounced it *boo-ku-ette* – 'to leave outside his house. This is the English tradition, yes?'

'Kind of,' said Kershaw, although now she thought about it, she couldn't remember seeing any roadside shrines back when she was a kid. 'Do you often do that? Buy flowers for a murder victim you didn't know?' Just a glint of steel under the words, enough for the girl to know she wasn't going to be fobbed off.

Varenka spread her long fingers on the granite, frowning down at the nails. They were perfectly manicured and polished, but for the nail extension on her thumb, which Kershaw noticed was ripped clean off. 'I don't know why, really. Perhaps because I heard he was married to a Polish lady. I am from Ukraine but my blood, my family, is Polish.'

'What about a man called Anthony Stride? The child abuser found hanged in the woods at Hollow Ponds? Did you read about him in the paper, too?'

Varenka shook her head, twisting a ring she wore on her little finger – her only piece of jewellery.

'You see, Varenka, we have good reason to believe that Barbu Romescu was involved in the deaths of both these men,' said Kershaw. Bit of stretch, really, given that the evidence was thinner than a size zero model, but she sensed she was going to need a tin opener to get this girl to talk. 'And I think you know something about his involvement in

277

at least one of the murders. That was the real reason you left flowers at Jim Fulford's house, wasn't it? I'm sure you did feel sorry for his wife – but I think what made it so unbearable was the knowledge that it was your boyfriend who had him killed.'

Varenka had become very still, but from her distracted expression Kershaw could see that her brain was working overtime.

Kershaw looked out through the huge window at seagulls wheeling lazily above the dock. Her dad used to say that when they ventured this far inland it meant a storm was brewing out at sea. Leaning across the worktop, she adopted a new voice, one that was soft but deadly serious.

'I have to make you aware that failure to pass any information you have relating to these murders on to the police would mean you being charged with a very serious offence.'

That seemed to do the job – the girl's eyes darted around wildly.

'Maybe he talked to you about it?' Kershaw turned up the dial now, her eyes never leaving Varenka's face. 'Or perhaps you overheard him on the phone, giving someone the order to kill Stride? Does the name Jamie Ryan mean anything to you?'

Something changed in Varenka's eyes, as though she'd reached a decision of some kind.

'You cannot imagine how much Barbu has done for me,' she said, the threat of tears thickening her voice.

'I'm sure you must feel you owe him a lot,' said Kershaw. 'But he hasn't always been kind to you, has he?' She let her gaze linger on Varenka's bruised eye, the busted lip. 'In my experience, once a man starts to hit a woman, they very rarely stop.'

Kershaw heard a faint 'thump' from upstairs. For a wild moment, she wondered if Romescu was up there – had been

278

here all along – but Varenka showed no reaction. Outside the sky had filled with rolling purple clouds and wind whistled across the plate glass.

'If you make a statement and agree to testify against him, we can protect you,' Kershaw went on. 'And get you permission to remain in the UK, if that's what you want.'

Varenka stared at the worktop, twisting that ring of hers round and round. Kershaw squinted at it. Two interlocking hearts on a cheap-looking chrome band, the kind of thing a little girl might buy with her pocket money – an eccentric choice for such a well-groomed woman.

When Varenka finally raised her eyes to meet Kershaw's, they were full of sorrow. 'It is true,' she said. 'I heard Barbu on the phone, a few weeks ago.' She paused, her voice dropping to a whisper. 'He was telling someone to get rid of this Anthony Stride.' She pronounced the '*th*' in 'Anthony' phonetically.

Yes! Kershaw felt the hairs prickle upright on her forearms.

'Okay, that's good,' she said, keeping her tone neutral. 'Was an address mentioned? Did it sound like he was ordering a contract killing?'

'Yes. I know that he sometimes killed people. Or better to say, paid other men to kill them for him.'

'Which other people did he have killed?'

She shook her head. 'I don't know the names, he kept them from me.'

Kershaw noted that she was speaking of Romescu in the past tense. A good sign, she thought, suggesting that Varenka had well and truly moved on from any misplaced loyalty to – or more likely fear of – her 'boyfriend'.

'Did you hear him say anything later, about the killer making a mistake? Did he mention Jim Fulford's name at all?'

Varenka took a deep breath, gave a little shake of her head. 'I don't want to say any more. I don't feel safe, not

279

until you have him locked up.'

Time to back off a bit.

To lighten the mood, Kershaw nodded at the ring on Varenka's little finger. 'My mum gave me a ring just like that when I was little – does it have sentimental value?'

'Yes.' Just for a moment, the look Kershaw caught in those greeny-gold eyes was no longer sorrowful, but as cool and unreadable as the eyes of a puma. 'I keep it because of a promise I made to someone, a long time ago.'

At the Rochester, Janusz was halfway through his second pint of beer. After some deliberation, he'd decided against calling on Marika, telling her the latest on Jim's murder, at least until the cops had confirmed the mistaken identity theory. The girl detective, Natalia, had promised to call him as soon as she had anything solid. If anyone could get the truth out of Varenka, she could.

He recalled his clandestine visit to Romescu's apartment, having to hide in the closet, and his discovery of Varenka's 'escape kit' – the school pencil case with the keepsakes and the roll of dollars. He wondered whether she'd ever tried to get away from Romescu, only to discover perhaps, that her boyfriend had her followed round the clock. Or perhaps, as she had hinted at the opera, she believed she could never truly escape, that it was impossible for a working girl to transform herself and leave that kind of life behind. It can hardly have been the life she had dreamt of as a child, the little girl by the rock pool with the china doll eyes.

He was reaching out for his pint. And then it hit him.

'I totally understand how anxious you must feel, with him still at liberty,' Kershaw was telling Varenka. 'We'll intercept him at the airport tomorrow and bring him in. Right now, though, I think we should find you somewhere safe to stay.'

'It is okay, there is a friend I can stay with tonight. I'll call her now.'

Picking up her phone, Varenka got up from the breakfast bar.

Kershaw sensed a shift in her mood since she had agreed to testify against Romescu. There was a new decisiveness in her body language and something else – a hint of suppressed excitement. Perhaps it was simply relief now that she'd made the decision to talk.

Then Kershaw's phone rang, making her jump. Was it the guy on reception, warning her that someone was on his way up?

She whipped it out of her pocket. Relieved to see it was only Janusz Kiszka, she pressed *'Ignore'*.

Janusz had no idea whether the connection he had made was pure coincidence – or something real and deadly serious. Either way, he wasn't taking any chances. And when Natalia failed to answer her phone it sent him into a lather of fear. It had been he who had sent her to Romescu's flat, and the idea that he might have sent her into danger ... he couldn't bear to think of it.

'I need a cab to Canary Wharf straightaway,' he told the guy behind the bar. 'Tell them there's fifty quid in it if they're here in less than five.'

He raced outside to wait for it and pulled his phone out again. She hadn't phoned back or replied to his text. He paced up and down the pavement raking a hand through his hair. Then stopped in his tracks, realizing that he had to do something he wouldn't have imagined possible until this moment.

Thirty seconds later a flat, official-sounding voice answered his phone call and he heard himself saying: 'Put me through to Sergeant Bacon – it's an emergency.'

In Millharbour, a single beam of sunlight had escaped the bank of purple cloud, flooding the living room of the apartment with a lurid light. Varenka paced the shiny floor, talking into her phone, occasionally glancing across at Kershaw.

Kershaw was finding it hard to think above the murmuring Polish, underscored by the 'tap tap' of high heels across the mirrored wood. But she was aware of an uneasy feeling stirring in her gut. She'd expected Varenka to demand more reassurances about being granted residency before agreeing to turn witness against Romescu. Her gaze fell on the girl's shoes. Ivory-coloured suede, the flash of red soles. *Louboutins*. Probably cost more than she earned in a week.

Suddenly, hail raked the windows like a burst of automatic gunfire, jangling her nerves. *Was she missing something here?*

'Could I use your loo?' She needed to be somewhere quiet for a minute, to think things over.

'Of course,' said Varenka. 'I will show you where it is.'

She clattered up the staircase, each stair a slab of shiny honey-coloured wood that appeared to float in mid air, Kershaw following. On the upper level, a gloomy corridor lined with artworks led to two doorways at the far end. As they got closer, Kershaw could see that one of the doors stood slightly ajar. Varenka pulled it to, before opening the bathroom door. Then shooting Kershaw a smile, she clack-clacked back down the corridor.

Locking the bathroom door behind her, Kershaw could feel her pulse thrumming in her throat. She stared at her reflection in the mirror over the sink, the discreet purr of the extractor fan the only sound in the windowless room.

She couldn't put her finger on it, but *something* just didn't feel right.

Opening the bathroom door as quietly as she could,

Kershaw paused on the threshold. She could hear Varenka on the phone downstairs, the musical glissading of the Polish sounding oddly like Welsh at this distance. She covered the three or four metres to the door Varenka had closed on tiptoe – even in flats it was difficult to cross the polished hardwood without making a sound.

As her hand closed around the door handle, she hesitated, imagining what Streaky might have to say about her embarking on an unauthorised search without having the faintest idea of what she expected to find. She suspected he might use the phrase *'women's intuition'* – and most definitely *not* in a positive way.

Heart bumping alarmingly against her chest wall, she turned the door handle, grimacing at the faint grating of the mechanism, and pushed the door open just far enough to slip inside. She left the door a couple of centimetres ajar so that she would hear if Varenka set foot on the staircase.

She scanned the room quickly. In her heightened state, her brain seemed to capture images like the shutter on an old-school camera. *Click.* To the left, set into a wall of wood, a safe – its door hanging open. *Click.* Ahead, on the bed, a half-packed suitcase. Two neatly folded men's shirts visible on top. *Click.* A door set into the wall next to the bed – probably to an en-suite bathroom. And waist high on the door's shiny white surface, the clear outline of a bloody palm print.

The important thing was to keep calm.

She had a searing memory of a safety briefing at the nick only that week – instructing detectives to carry their Airwaves radios at all times. And a pin-sharp picture of hers, sitting in the desk drawer. Creeping out of the room, she closed the door carefully behind her and paused to listen. All was silent down below. She headed down the corridor at a normal pace, as though innocently returning from the bathroom.

She'd almost reached the top of the staircase when

283

Varenka stepped out from an alcove that Kershaw hadn't noticed on her way up.

Her hand flew to her chest. 'You scared me!' she said.

As Kershaw had predicted when she first laid eyes on her, Varenka did indeed stand nearly six feet tall even without her high heels. Her eyes were the colour of wet seaweed and they looked as cold and empty as those of a long-dead creature at the bottom of an underground sea.

As Varenka's arm shot out in a blur, Kershaw ducked into a crouch, step one of a self-defence move drummed into her during training.

The next thing she knew, she was lying on the deck, feeling badly winded. She studied the polished floor next to her cheek, wondering if it was walnut. Her nan used to have a walnut dressing table the exact same colour that she'd been very proud of. She felt her eyelids starting to drift shut. The last thing she saw, forming a silvery 'V' against the wood half a metre away, were the open blades of a pair of dress-making scissors.

Forty-Two

By the time Janusz arrived at Millharbour, it was nearly dark, the clouded sky turned the colour of ink, an icy rain sheeting across the dock.

The minicab was still moving when he jumped out, flinging some notes on the seat, and ran at full tilt onto the dockside. He could see that the entrance to Romescu's apartment block had been cordoned off with police tape, with a uniformed cop standing guard at the revolving door. *Praise be to Mary, Mother of God,* he said in a fervent whisper, crossing himself. But the wave of relief evaporated when he realised that the tape, the cop, were confirmation that a crime had taken place.

'Listen,' he panted, as he reached the cop. 'I need to go up, I was the one who called it in.'

Taking in Janusz's dishevelled appearance with a single dry glance, the cop redirected his gaze past him, towards the dock. 'I'm afraid no one's allowed in at the moment, sir, not even the residents.'

'Call Sergeant Bacon, tell him Kiszka is here.'

'Sergeant *who*?'

Kurwa! Of course: the quickest way to get back-up to the apartment would have been to mobilise the local cops. This guy's folded arms and impassive expression told Janusz that he was wasting his time. So he shrugged, backed off a few metres and pulled out his phone, as though to make a call. Out of the corner of his eye, he was taking in the block's other door, next to the revolving one, the one he'd used on his last visit, when he'd been impersonating an aircon engineer. Would it still be open now?

The second the cop's attention drifted elsewhere, Janusz ducked under the tape and pushed at the door. It swung inward. *Brawo!* Ignoring the shout of outrage at his back, he sprinted for the lift, praying there would be one waiting. There was. Through its closing doors he caught a glimpse of the cop's angry face as he crashed through the lobby. *Too slow, my friend.*

On the eleventh floor, he'd almost reached Romescu's apartment when another cop bowled round the corner and shoulder-charged him, shoving him up against the wall. Then, over the cop's burly shoulder, a welcome sight: the ginger-haired Sergeant Bacon, his gut busting out of a shabby brown suit.

Streaky's face wore a thunderous expression. He came right up close, his nose almost touching Janusz's. 'Are you behind this fucking fiasco, Kiszka?'

'Natalia – is she okay?'

'Well, that depends,' said Streaky, his voice tense with sarcastic fury.

'On what?'

'On whether you can be okay after having a pair of six-inch scissors stuck in your gut.'

Mother of God! Janusz slumped back against the wall.

'Did you put her up to this? Charging in here, on her own, like the Lone fucking Ranger?'

'On her own?' He tried to blink away an image of the girl detective on the deck, bleeding and helpless … *just like Jim*. What an *imbecyl* he had been, not to realise earlier the situation she'd be walking into. When they'd parted, he'd been too caught up in his own emotions, grappling with the discovery that Jim's murder had been something as banal as an address cock-up.

Straightening up, he met Streaky's ice-pick stare. 'It was me who told her that the girl was in danger, earlier today,' he said. 'What happened … it's my responsibility.'

Streaky eyed his face, his expression relenting a little. 'I wouldn't go that far,' he said. 'In my experience, DC Kershaw does whatever the fuck she likes.'

'Is she …?' Janusz couldn't complete the question.

'She's in hospital, having surgery right now. I'll let you know as soon as I know.' Streaky hitched up his trousers. 'Meanwhile, you can make yourself useful.'

Sunk in a miserable daze, Janusz followed him down the corridor. After donning white paper boilersuits and shoe covers they entered the apartment, which was abuzz with activity. In the kitchen they passed a girl in a protective suit dusting the surface of the breakfast bar, and at the top of the stairs a man in the same get-up was taking photographs of a dark and sticky-looking pool of blood.

Janusz shot Streaky a questioning look. Wordlessly, his expression telegraphed back: Yes, the blood is Kershaw's.

In the master bedroom, the concealed door to the walk-in wardrobe stood ajar. Streaky nodded him in first. 'Watch where you put your feet.'

Inside the long narrow room, the first thing to hit him was the citrusy perfume that Varenka wore, followed by a stronger, ferrous undernote. At the far end, under the clothes rail, lay its source: Barbu Romescu, sprawled face down in a blood-soaked heap of his own suits. His face was in profile,

287

the left eye open wide, his expression one of almost comic puzzlement. The cause of his demise was clear: in the side of his neck, a jagged, gaping wound so savage that Janusz could make out the curve of a cervical vertebra.

'For the record, can you confirm this is Barbu Romescu?' asked Streaky, at his shoulder.

'Yes, it's him.' Janusz stared at the scar on the side of Romescu's face, the legacy of his daring escape from Communist Romania. In death, it looked paler, less prominent.

Clutched in Romescu's outstretched right hand was a white shirt, pristine and still on its hanger. 'He was packing, she comes up behind him ...' Streaky raised a clenched fist high, brought it down with great force. 'Goodnight, Vienna.'

'Varenka.' It was more statement than question.

Streaky nodded. 'It certainly looks that way. There's a bloodstained dress in the linen bin in the en-suite and blood all over the shower. I reckon Kershaw arrived not long after it happened.'

Janusz dragged a hand through his hair. 'Then what?'

'After attacking Kershaw, she legged it. The receptionist saw her saunter out of the lift, cool as you like, pulling a suitcase. The car valet says there was a black 4X4 waiting for her, engine running.'

'Let me guess: the driver wore a plaster cast and had a snake's head tattooed on the back of his hand,' said Janusz, with a grim smile.

'That's right. You know him?'

'Only by sight.'

Janusz was picturing the way that snake tattoo had coaxed Varenka into the Discovery on Hoe Street that first day, after she'd left the flowers at Jim's house. How could he have missed the signals? In hindsight, the way the guy had bent his head to hers, her responding body language, had about it the unmistakable air of two people stepping the quadrille of early courtship.

'The safe was completely cleared out, of course.' Streaky shot him a dry look. 'The pair of them must have decided they were owed some severance pay.'

'They probably had it planned for a while,' said Janusz. 'And thanks to me, Natalia turned up just as they were about to do a runner.'

Streaky scanned Janusz's face for a moment. 'Well, now's your chance to make up for it,' he said. 'Go wait in the lobby. I'll be down in ten minutes – and you can tell me what the fuck's been going on.'

Half an hour later, the two men were sitting in a bar overlooking the dock where the beer cost a shade under £6 a pint.

Streaky squinted at Janusz over his glass. 'I get how you and Natalie arrived at the mistaken identity theory – your pal getting killed because his address sounded the same as Stride's – but what made you suddenly decide Varenka Kalina was behind the murders?'

'It was a photograph I found – in the hiding place I showed you in the closet.'

Streaky raised a meaningful eyebrow. 'Ah yes, while pursuing your other career as a bogus aircon engineer and burglar.'

Janusz ignored the wind-up. 'I was trying to find out how Jim was linked to Romescu, something – *anything* – to explain why he'd been killed.'

'Why did you think there was a connection in the first place?'

'I saw Varenka leave a bunch of flowers at his house the day after he died, and came to the conclusion that she was atoning for her boyfriend's sins.'

As Streaky emitted a snort, Janusz made a gesture that acknowledged he'd been an idiot. It seemed so obvious now that Varenka's impulse had been born of guilt, not for anything Romescu had done, but for her own terrible mistake in having Jim killed instead of Stride. He'd jumped too easily to the conclusion that Romescu was behind the killing, a conviction that had only got stronger with the discovery of his arms smuggling operation and the ruthless way he'd had Orzelair's head of security eliminated.

'So, this photo?' asked Streaky, breaking into his reflections.

Janusz nodded. 'It was an old holiday snap of two children – a toddler, who I assumed to be Varenka, and an older boy. But the little girl had quite distinctive eyes, almond-shaped, nothing like Varenka's. So I realised that Varenka must have been the one taking the picture – and the girl in the shot was her little sister.'

'Go on.' Streaky's ruddy face was creased with perplexity.

'Then I thought about the little girl's eyes again, and it hit me. Varenka's sister had Downs Syndrome.'

Streaky's face cleared, his eyes widening. 'Like Hannah Ryan, the girl Stride raped.'

Janusz nodded.

'So Varenka reads about Stride escaping punishment after abusing a little Downs girl, and has him killed because Hannah Ryan reminds her of her sister?' Streaky prepared to take a slug of beer. 'It's all a bit *extreme*, isn't it?'

Janusz recalled the sordid details that Varenka had let slip regarding her childhood and teenage years. 'Varenka's mother was a truck stop prostitute with a *wodka* habit. She and the children lived in a shack, if you can call it living, in a place called Kharkov.'

'Shithole?' asked Streaky.

'After the end of Soviet rule, the Ukrainian economy

imploded. People's jobs, pensions, it all disappeared overnight. Kharkov was notorious – the kind of place where people would literally trade their children, mothers – Christ, even their *grandmothers* – for alcohol.'

'Fuck me,' said Streaky. 'Sounds worse than Third World.'

Janusz took a slug of his pint. 'Imagine trying to look after a little disabled girl in a place like that, when the mother is out selling herself, and probably Varenka, too.'

Streaky tapped the side of his pint glass, thinking it over. 'So some dirty nonce abuses her little sister. And years later, she takes revenge on Stride.'

Janusz tipped his head sideways. 'It's just a theory.'

Streaky leaned both elbows on the table. 'You think she got her new boyfriend, tattoo boy, to carry out the hit on Jim Fulford with a mate, right?'

'Yes.'

Streaky shook his head slowly. 'I'm not so sure. In my experience, revenge killings are nearly always carried out in person.'

'You think she was there?' Janusz frowned. Marika's neighbour had described of one of the balaclava-clad attackers as tall and slim. Had her height, athletic build and small breasts enabled Varenka to pass for a young man?

'Yeah, and I don't mean as a hanger-on – I think there's a good chance she wielded the knife.'

Janusz sat back in his chair. *Yes.* There had always been a certain steeliness about her, and now that he was viewing her through a different prism – the right one this time – it was all too easy to imagine her committing an act of ruthless brutality.

'When they got the target right, the second time around, she must have helped tattoo boy string up Stride.' A wistful note entered Streaky's voice. 'They did a pretty good job making it look like suicide, too. For a while, at least.'

Recalling the sight of Varenka's bruised and scared face through the back window of the Discovery, Janusz realised something. 'That's why Romescu gave her such a beating yesterday! Because he heard on the news that Stride's death was being treated as murder.'

'He guessed she was behind it, you mean?'

Janusz nodded slowly, remembering how he'd met her, sprawled across the pavement after Romescu threw her out of his car – the day after Jim was stabbed. 'Maybe he suspected that she was involved in Jim's death, too.'

'So when he was trying to buy you off, he was trying to protect her as much as himself.'

Streaky's phone, lying next to his pint, vibrated. He snatched it up. 'Yes, this is DS Bacon … Yes, I am DC Kershaw's superior officer.' His eyes flicked across to Janusz. 'Uh huh … I understand.'

Mother of God! What was going on? Janusz felt like grabbing the phone out of his hand.

Finally, he hung up.

'Well?!'

'She was in surgery for two hours. Internal repairs. They say she's still a very sick woman, and a lot depends on how she does overnight.'

Forty-Three

The next morning, Janusz made his way up the ramp from Walthamstow tube station, barely aware of the stream of people rushing either side of him on their way to work. Red-eyed and dishevelled after a sleepless night worrying about Natalia, he was desperate for news, but Streaky still hadn't called to say how she was doing or if she was even alive.

As he emerged onto the street, it struck him that he'd always associated this journey with the happy prospect of a beer with Jim – a fortnightly fixture in his life for the last twenty-odd years that would now never be repeated. Today he faced a different encounter – and one he was dreading. Although the cops weren't ready to go public with who killed Jim and why, he'd told Sergeant Bacon in no uncertain terms that Marika had a right to know straight away. To the man's credit, he hadn't come over all official or attempted to talk Janusz out of it.

As he reached the church at the heart of the old village, Janusz saw her again in his mind's eye, stepping through the confetti of falling leaves – the striking mystery woman who'd just left flowers outside Jim's house. Searching for a way to describe her demeanour, the word he settled on was *carefree*. Having assuaged her graphene-thin conscience with a floral tribute and a Hail Mary, Varenka had apparently felt cleansed of guilt.

He reckoned he'd got it pretty much worked out now. Varenka's determination to visit retribution on Anthony Stride was an understandable impulse, but not an easy one to enact – unless your boyfriend happened to be a murderous gangster. So it must have come as a disappointment when Romescu had turned down her demand to have Stride eliminated. Having just launched a dummy investment company to raise funds for arms buying, he was hardly likely to risk it all for some personal vendetta of his girlfriend's.

A darkly comic notion struck Janusz: maybe even gangsters got nagged by their girlfriends, not for the usual domestic misdemeanours like leaving their dirty socks on the floor, but for refusing to kill people to order.

In any event, Varenka hadn't let Romescu's rebuff derail her plan: she had simply recruited his driver instead.

Janusz chose his words carefully as he laid out for Marika the sordid tale of how her husband had come to die – but her reaction wasn't what he'd expected.

'Thank God!' said Marika, hands flying to her face. Laika, who was lying across her mistress's feet, gazed up at her enquiringly.

Seeing the look of confusion on Janusz's face, Marika hastened to explain. 'The not knowing, that was the truly unbearable part. I was beginning to fear that perhaps I would never know – and then what? The idea of living in this limbo forever ...'

'Well, now we know who killed him, even if she picked completely the wrong person,' growled Janusz.

Marika gazed out of the bay window at the row of tea lights in red perspex holders sitting on the garden wall. 'I know this will sound strange, Janek, but somehow it makes me feel a little better, to find out that all that … *hatred* wasn't meant for my Jim.' Her voice broke as she said his name, and Janusz reached over to pat her, his big hand feeling rough and clumsy against her slender forearm. 'It's as though he was just … an innocent bystander.'

'I'm glad you feel that way.' He frowned into his coffee cup. 'But I should have worked it out a hell of a lot sooner. If I had, there might have been a chance of making her pay for what she's done.' He didn't think there was a hope in hell now of seeing Varenka caught and charged with murder.

What a fool she had made of him. He'd assumed he was the one in control of their relationship, and yet all along she'd been playing him, like an angler plays an especially dimwitted and myopic carp. Her masterstroke had been to warn him, after he left the Triangle party, that he was being followed: a simple yet brilliant move that had swept away any lingering distrust of her he might have had. After that, it had never crossed his mind that his tattooed pursuer had been sent, not by Romescu, but by her.

Marika dried her eyes on a handkerchief and took a sip of coffee. 'I'm just relieved that she didn't kill you, too – once she realised you were getting close to the truth.'

'I got lucky,' he said. 'When I saw the guy with the snake tattoo outside the Opera House, I thought Romescu was keeping her under surveillance. But of course, Varenka set the whole thing up.'

'She invited you there so that her new boyfriend could follow you home and …?'

'And get rid of me. Yes,' said Janusz.

'Holy Mary, Mother of God,' said Marika, crossing herself.

Janusz snorted. 'To think, I left that night in order to protect *her*!'

'Because you knew that the Romanian gangster beat her?'

'Yeah. I'm like a knight on a white charger. Except the fair maiden in the tower was actually a murdering—'

'Now you listen to me, Janusz Piotr Kiszka!' Shocked at her tone, his head snapped up to meet her determined gaze. 'I won't have you talk in this way. You seem to think that there is something *wrong* with wanting to help a woman in trouble.'

'Well, there is, if it stops me seeing things clearly.'

'So because one woman in trouble turns out to be a monster, better to be cynical about all of them?' She shook her head, but her tone became gentler. 'We need more men to look out for women like you do, Janek, not fewer.'

He inclined his head a fraction. 'I still should have worked it out more quickly.'

Marika breathed an impatient sigh. 'You must see that if you hadn't spotted her leaving those flowers and sensed something odd about it, I should *never* have found out who killed my Jim. You can't give my husband back to me, Janek, but you have given me back my life.'

When they'd finished their coffee they went into the front garden. Standing side by side on the patch of lawn no bigger than a hearthrug that Jim had always kept so neatly mown and edged, they looked down at the fragile flames of the tea lights guttering in their holders.

Half-kneeling, Marika picked up the nearest one and, raising it to her lips, blew out the flame. Then she picked up the next one. When they had all been extinguished, Janusz helped her to her feet. They stood there looking at the wall, hands loosely linked.

'He will always be here with us,' said Marika, her tone that of someone making a simple statement of fact.

Janusz only nodded, unable to trust his voice.

'*It can't take a joke, find a star, make a bridge …*' Although Marika had spoken in a murmur, he recognised the words instantly. They came from a famous poem about Death and how, ultimately, it was impotent – incapable of erasing the magnificence of a human life.

Squeezing her hand, he supplied the poem's closing line: '*As far as you've come, can't be undone.*'

Forty-Four

'Your boyfriend's here, dear, if you feel up to a visitor.'

Opening one eye, Kershaw saw Lovely Irish Nurse, as she'd dubbed her, the one who'd stroked her head when she'd been in such an agitated state after coming round from the operation. *Had that been yesterday? No, the day before.* In here, time had become an irrelevance. The thing that consumed and governed every waking thought, the only force you respected – and dreaded – was *pain*. At first, it had come in great racking waves so fierce that she'd wanted to throw herself out of bed, desperate to knock herself unconscious. She could still feel it, like a hot spiked band around her abdomen, but the white-hot screech of it had muted to a background drone.

Boyfriend? Kershaw thought for a moment, before realising she must mean Ben.

'Yeah, okay.'

With the nurse's help she levered herself up onto her pillows, wincing as she felt the stitches pull, but noticing that the manoeuvre was noticeably easier than when she'd attempted it the first time.

Ben's Bournville-dark eyes above his absurdly large bouquet were still gorgeous, although the skin around them was cross-hatched with anxiety.

'Hello, Nat,' he said, perching on the edge of the visitor's armchair.

'Hi,' she managed a smile. 'They're pretty.'

The nurse lifted the flowers from his hands. 'Let me put them in a vase.'

They made small talk for a bit about the gossip at the nick, the number of cards and flowers she had, her Auntie Carol's visit, before falling silent.

'You gave me a terrible scare there, Nat.'

'Yeah, sorry about that. It wasn't intentional.'

'No, 'course not. But when they told me you might not make it, just before you went into surgery ...' He stared up at the ceiling, blinking, and blew out a controlled but ragged breath. 'I ... I couldn't imagine what my future would be without you. I literally couldn't see it.'

'Ben ...'

'Hear me out. It's made me realise how much you mean to me, Nat. And I figured something else out. After what happened, me staying in the Job, it would just make the situation even more difficult for you. So I've decided, I'm packing it in.'

Her head jerked up. 'What? You can't do that. You just made Sergeant!'

'I don't deserve it. I let everyone down – and not just you.'

Their eyes met. *Streaky.* Without whom Ben would never have been promoted, and who had risked career suicide to cover for him and put right his monumental screw-up.

'In all honesty, Nat? I don't think I have it in my blood like you do. It's a job to me,' he shrugged. 'I can find another job. I can't get – I don't *want* to get – another girlfriend.'

Kershaw felt a wave of tiredness break over her. 'It's a lot to take on board ...'

'I know, and I don't want you fretting about anything right now. You need to concentrate on getting better. We'll talk about it when you come out, yeah?'

'Yeah.'

After Ben left, Kershaw felt herself drifting back to sleep, a vivid image playing on her retina: the scrap of back garden at the new flat, the lawn dappled with sunshine, and Ben leaning over a smoking barbecue, busy with the tongs. Her last conscious thought before sleep engulfed her: was it just a morphine-fuelled fantasy or a plausible picture of her future?

Forty-Five

'What time are you coming home, Janek?'

'I told you this morning, Oskar. I've got to go and see that guy in Barking, the one whose factory keeps getting burgled.'

Even though he was no longer in any danger, Oskar had taken up Janusz's offer to stay at his Highbury apartment, saying that after sharing a maisonette with four other blokes for the last year he could do with a holiday. But Janusz was finding the experience far from restful.

'Well, what do you expect me to eat for my dinner?' Oskar sighed down the phone. 'You know, while you sit on your *dupe* having meetings and drinking latte, some of us have been up since 7 a.m. doing man's work.'

'There's some *pierogi* in the fridge,' said Janusz.

'I had them for breakfast,' said Oskar. 'And if you ask my opinion? You put in a tiny bit too much pepper.'

'I didn't ask your opinion,' growled Janusz, shifting the phone to his other ear. 'And remember what I said about cleaning your work tools in the sink ...'

'Oh, I nearly forgot,' said Oskar, ignoring his comment. 'Sergeant Backgammon called on the landline ...'

'You mean Sergeant Bacon?'

'*Tak. Fantastyczne* name for a cop!' Oskar chuckled. 'He asked you to call him at the office.'

'*Dobrze*,' said Janusz. 'I'll see you about half seven then.'

'Haven't you forgotten something?' Oskar's voice was plaintive.

'What?'

'Aren't you going to tell me you love me?'

'Fuck off, Oskar.' But a smile tugged at one corner of Janusz's mouth.

DS Bacon didn't want to talk on the phone so Janusz agreed to drop by the nick on his way to Barking.

Now they sat across a table in the same interview room where the Sergeant had questioned him about Jim's murder, what felt like 300 years ago.

DS Bacon caught his look. 'Sorry we're in here, but we're having a visitation of IT types – they're crawling all over the offices upstairs.'

Janusz took the paper cup of tea the Sergeant handed him. 'How's Natalia?' he asked. It had been three days since the medics had declared her out of serious danger but he knew that, with such a deep wound, infection was a constant risk.

'Yeah, she's fine. Bending everyone's ear about when she's allowed to come back to work.'

Janusz raised an amused eyebrow. 'She's not going to be in any trouble, is she, for going to Romescu's place on her own?'

Streaky shook his head. 'In the ordinary run of things she'd probably be due some time on the naughty step, but in this case I'd say there are "extenuating circumstances".'

'Because it was only due to her initiative that you were able to identify a murderer?' asked Janusz.

'The Metropolitan Police *reward initiative*?! Wash your mouth out!' Streaky chuckled. 'No. Let's just say that since the Stride debacle, the brass have been gagging for a "good news" story. And *"Brave girl cop stabbed confronting murder suspect"* has a better ring to it than *"Brave girl cop disciplined on numbskull health and safety charge"*.'

Janusz gave a grunt, remembering a recent story in the newspaper about a cop who'd dived into an icy pond to save a drowning child. In the England he'd arrived in twenty-five years ago they'd have given him a medal; these days the guy's actions had earned him a reprimand for failing to conduct a proper risk assessment. The world had gone crazy.

'Anyway.' Streaky took a document from a file and pushed it across the table. 'I wanted to let you know that your hunch was right.'

Janusz frowned at the unfamiliar words and letters. 'Sorry, I don't really read Ukrainian.'

'It's a report from the Kharkov police.' He pointed out the date, 11th November 1998. 'They've confirmed that the person you know as Varenka Kalina had a little sister, name of Anna. She was born with what they called a "chromosomal deficiency".'

'Downs Syndrome.'

Streaky nodded. 'Varenka's mother was a prostitute, as you said, and one day when Mummy was out cold on vodka, Anna was raped and beaten by one of the clients. She died in hospital a few weeks later. She was eight years old.'

'God rest her soul,' muttered Janusz.

'The bastard got off with manslaughter, and his tariff is almost up. They're letting him out in a couple of weeks.'

Janusz imagined Varenka's reaction to the news of his impending release, how it must have brought the horror of her little sister's murder come flooding back. 'She couldn't take revenge on *him*, so she executed another paedophile in his place.'

Streaky made a gesture indicating that he shared that conclusion.

Not for the first time, Janusz reflected on the long shadow cast by Stalin's fifty-year domination of Eastern Europe, and the chaos that had convulsed the region when communism fell. It was no wonder, really, that such desperation, such suffering, had spawned some twisted and ruthless progeny.

Then he remembered something the Sergeant had said. 'Why did you say the person I *"know as Varenka Kalina"*? Is it an alias?'

'Well, it's a name she's entitled to use on her passport,' said the Sergeant with a strange half-smile. 'But it's not the one she was christened with.'

Seeing Janusz's complete incomprehension, he handed him another document from the file. 'Birth certificate,' he said, and indicated one of the boxes.

Janusz squinted down at it. The Ukrainian alphabet shared enough characters with the Russian Cyrillic he'd been forced to learn at school to allow him to read the surname *Kalina*. But although the Christian name started with the letter 'V', rendered in Cyrillic as 'B', it wasn't *Varenka*. The name it spelled out was *Valentyn*.

Janusz stared at the Sergeant. 'Varenka was born a *boy*?!'

He nodded, evidently enjoying himself. 'Yep.'

Janusz realised his jaw was hanging open. 'It must be a mistake – she was so beautiful and … ladylike.' His mind whirred, flicking through a mental album of images of Varenka. Yes, she was tall for a woman, and her hands weren't exactly dainty, but she was a million miles from the 'truck driver in drag' image that the phrase 'sex change' summoned up in his mind.

Streaky shrugged. 'Appa ently, as long as you take the right hormones in early puberty, you never develop facial hair, an Adam's apple, or the rugged good looks you and I enjoy.'

'But she had breasts …' Janusz stopped, realising what a dumb comment that was in the era of implants you could literally buy off the shelf. As for the hormones, in post-Soviet Ukraine there wasn't anything that couldn't be obtained with hard currency.

In fact, the more he thought about it, the more it fell into place. Even without the height and her husky voice, there had always been something indefinably *different* about Varenka – the sense that she possessed some mystery no man could unravel.

'Did she still have …?' Janusz waved vaguely below the waist.

'I was going to ask you that,' deadpanned the Sergeant.

'*Kurwa mac*!' he protested, squirming in his chair. 'I never laid a finger on her!'

'I'll believe you,' grinned Streaky. 'Anyway, our boy Romescu obviously had more exotic tastes than you. That place in Kharkov where she danced must have been a tranny club.'

Janusz chewed his thumb, remembering Varenka's mysterious trip to the private hospital. Then the letters *GRA* and the name *Churchill* scrawled inside the pink matchbook from the bar where she'd worked jumped out at him.

'*Gender Re-Assignment*,' he said out loud.

'Come again?'

'I think she was still undergoing her sex change treatment at the Princess Louise Hospital – a private place in the West End – and I'll bet you a tenner that the specialist there is called Churchill.'

Then the night at the opera came flooding back, the story of the water nymph Rusalka who underwent a traumatic metamorphosis so that she could join her human lover. When Varenka had spoken so feelingly that night about the difficulty of transforming oneself, he'd assumed she'd meant escaping a life of prostitution: now it was clear she'd meant something far more fundamental.

As the Sergeant scribbled a note in the file, Janusz went on: 'That's why she didn't leave Romescu earlier. It wasn't because she was scared of him; she was just waiting till he'd funded her transformation.'

'What I don't get,' said Streaky, frowning, 'is if he fell for her when she was a geezer, then why would he fancy her after ...' he made a sawing motion across his lap.

Both men avoided the other's gaze, crossing their legs in unison.

'How should I know?' growled Janusz. 'He was bisexual? He was in love with her, with or without a dick?' He waved a hand. 'Nothing surprises me about what people get up to these days.'

As they headed downstairs in the lift, Janusz was lost in his own thoughts. He was still struggling to absorb the alarming truth about Varenka, a girl he had flirted with and, with whom, given the right mood and moment, he might have taken things a lot further.

By the time the door of the police station closed behind him, he had made one unshakeable resolution: *Oskar must never know.*

Forty-Six

Standing at the bar of the Rochester, Janusz asked for two bottles of Tyskie, the order he'd placed several hundred times over the years meeting Jim here, before correcting himself.

He carried the drinks over to the table by the window where Kershaw sat, looking out into the thickening dusk. It was almost a fortnight since she'd been stabbed and when he got her text suggesting they meet, he hadn't been entirely sure what to expect.

'Cheers,' she said, taking the large glass of white wine he handed her. 'I'm not really supposed to be drinking yet, but you know what? I've decided life's too short.'

'*Na zdrowie*,' Janusz toasted her, and took a swig of beer. 'What harm can a couple of glasses of wine do? Doctors are a bunch of old women.'

He saw a tremor of pain cross her face as she set her glass down on the table.

'So, they say you will make a full recovery, right?'

'Yeah. I got lucky,' she grinned. 'According to my surgeon, if you have to lose an organ then the spleen is the one to go for. Apparently it's a bit of an optional extra – like alloy wheels or a sun roof.'

It was the sort of tongue-in-cheek bravado that Janusz had come across many times in the company of men – a bit of bluster intended not exactly to deny fear, but to cut it down to a manageable size.

After a pause she said: 'I wanted to see you as soon as I got out, to thank you.'

'Thank me?!' Janusz raised his eyebrows. 'For sending you to interrogate a cross-dressing psychopath?'

'If you hadn't called the nick when you did and insisted on talking to Streaky – to the Sergeant – they say I probably would have bled to death in that apartment.'

The note of bewilderment in her voice told Janusz she was still coming to terms with this momentous idea. He tried to recall when he'd first been confronted with the reality of his own mortality. Probably at the demo where Iza had died, slipping lifeless from his disbelieving fingers – so nineteen years old, a good deal younger than Natalia, but then he had lived in interesting times.

'If I had only realised what was going on earlier,' he said, 'I would never have asked you to go and talk to her.'

'Well, you didn't exactly have all the facts, did you?' she said, staring into her wine, seeing an image of Ben pocketing Stride's glasses. 'I hear the person you spoke to when you called the nick took quite a bit of convincing.' Recalling Adam Ackroyd's account of the call, she shook her head at him in mock reproach. 'I'm told you used swearwords he never even knew existed.'

'Ten years on English building sites,' said Janusz modestly, before clearing his throat. 'There's something I wanted to tell you, too – about that guy who fell out of the Orzelair plane?'

'Oh yes?' said Kershaw.

He told her what he'd discovered during their trip to Poland – omitting certain unnecessary details like the handgun he'd dumped in the lavatory cistern at the police station – laying out Romescu's smuggling operation, and what had really happened to Orzelair's head of security.

Folding her arms, she skewered him with a stare. 'You're telling me that Anatol *Voy-tek* was investigating the goings-on at … *P-shay-joke-off* Airport?

'Not bad,' he nodded, acknowledging her attempt at the correct pronunciation. 'Yeah, Prczeczokow.'

'Whatever. And he got bopped on the head and stuffed in the wheel well by that big ugly mechanic?'

'Mazurek. Yes, almost certainly.'

'Because Wojtek was trying to close down Romescu's arms-smuggling malarkey?'

He lifted one shoulder, bracing himself. She hadn't raised her voice but he could tell from the set of her jaw that she wasn't happy.

'I knew you were keeping something from me in Poland!'

'I wasn't a hundred per cent sure of my facts …'

'I was in charge of the fucking investigation, not you! It's up to me to make those decisions.'

Janusz winced: even after all this time living in the UK it still pained him to hear a girl curse. 'After my … discussion with Mazurek I knew Romescu would cover his tracks. You wouldn't be able to prove anything.'

Kershaw made a noise of angry disbelief.

'Okay … and it's true that I wanted you here in London, looking for Jim's killer. Not haring around Poland on a wild goose chase.'

Glaring at him, she drained the rest of her wine.

'You have to understand something,' he said. 'When I was growing up, an informer' – he uttered the word as though ejecting something disagreeable from his mouth – 'was a traitor, pure and simple. No ... *decent* person would dream of talking to the cops. I guess it's a tough habit to shake.'

She fell silent for a moment, before nodding at his half-empty beer bottle: 'Another one of those?' and rose to go the bar, rebuffing his attempts to buy the round.

As she waited for the drinks, Kershaw brooded over the way that Kiszka had kept her in the dark, before it struck her that Ben, her supposed boyfriend, had done exactly the same. There were further uncomfortable parallels – both Ben and Kiszka had tried to alter the course of justice by covering up evidence of a suspicious death. There was one big fat glaring distinction, though. Kiszka wasn't a police officer.

Back at the table, she set down the drinks and lowered herself carefully into her chair, her fragility an unwelcome glimpse of the old lady she would one day become.

'Well, at least you told me in the end,' she said. 'I'll have a chat with the detective we met in Poland. Now Romescu's dead, maybe someone at the airport can be persuaded to spill the beans on Mazurek.' She paused, picturing the body spreadeagled on the pavement in the shadow of Canary Wharf tower, the pool of blood beside his head like a crimson speech bubble. 'There's no way he could have got a big geezer like Wojtek into that plane without some help.'

Looking at Janusz over the rim of her wineglass, she cocked her head: 'What made you change your mind about telling me, anyway?'

He stared past her blonde head out into the street. The sky was already dark and a mist had come down, spinning whorls of gauzy light around the streetlamps. 'I realised that Wojtek's wife, his family, they have a right to know what happened to him. You might not nail Mazurek, but at least they won't have to wake up every day for the rest of their lives wondering how he ended up in the wheel well of that plane.'

'You realise it will mean going back to Poland, to make a statement?'

He gave an assenting half-shrug, then grinned: 'I'll take you back to that restaurant in the old town if you like. The one where you ate all the potato cakes.'

'Okay, as long as you don't do a runner this time.' She tried for a stern look but her smile muscles weren't playing ball.

Their eyes met, and they both held the gaze for a long beat, acknowledging that the trip would be no hardship.

'Natalia,' his voice deepened, becoming serious. 'You've been through a shattering experience. Don't ask too much of yourself. And don't expect your life to return to ... how it was before. That's all.'

'Believe me, I don't,' she said. 'In fact, I'm thinking about joining SCO19.' Seeing his uncomprehending look, she translated: 'Firearms unit.' She downed the rest of her wine. 'Nothing evens the score with the bad guys like a Heckler & Koch.'

Eyeing her set little face, features blurred by alcohol, he wanted to say more, tempted to share his own hard-won knowledge that drink was, at best, a temporary respite from troubles, at worst, a new and bottomless well of misery. But he knew there was no point.

She picked up her coat, manoeuvring her arms into the sleeves as though moving underwater, deflecting his attempt to help her with a single shake of the head.

'So what are you up to tonight? Hot date?' he asked, joshing her.

'Yeah, kind of.'

'Blind date, maybe?'

'You could call it that.'

It would be the first time Kershaw had seen Ben since getting out of hospital – back in the real world. Maybe the only chance of salvaging their relationship would be to find some way of starting from scratch. But she wasn't holding out much hope.

Janusz watched through the window as she walked out of view, feeling suddenly and unaccountably despondent at the thought of not seeing her, at least until the Poland trip. What was it about the girl that got to him?

A phrase his *Babcia* used to say rang out in his head: she was *'like a stone in his shoe'*.

Epilogue

Around ten days later, Janusz was in the *Polski sklep* on Highbury Corner, stocking up on dill cucumbers and rye flour, when his phone rang.

Seeing *'Number Unavailable'* on the screen he almost pressed *'Ignore'* – he'd been suffering an onslaught of calls lately from Indian guys calling themselves 'Josh' and 'Barry', imploring him to switch energy providers. But something told him to take the call.

'Hello, Janusz.' A voice familiar in its honeyed huskiness, the grumble of traffic in the background.

Kurwa mac! He stood stock-still in the middle of the aisle.

'I called because I wanted to say sorry, for all the trouble I caused you ... and your friends.'

'Trouble?!' His voice incredulous at the scale of her understatement.

'Yes. And I wanted you to know that I honestly liked you – *still* like you. It wasn't just ... business, you know?'

The hint of flirtatiousness in Varenka's voice enraged him, but it occurred to him that if he could keep her talking, maybe the cops could use the signal to find out where she'd been calling from. No sooner had the thought occurred to him than there came a sound in the background, a distant squealing caused by some sort of metallic friction. A train? *Nie.* But something naggingly familiar.

'How is the girl policeman?' she asked.

'She'll live,' he said. 'But she'll never be the same again.'

Varenka sighed. 'Believe me, that was the last thing I wanted to happen. But she was snooping around ... and I had to leave.'

'And now you and your new boyfriend are having a nice time spending Romescu's money.'

A pause.

'I am single again, actually,' she said. He could almost see her drily amused expression across the ether.

So the tattooed driver had been dumped – or disposed of – having performed his function as her getaway driver.

'It's quite a skill you have, your ability to use people,' he said, finding himself unable to say her name. 'You get Romescu to bring you over from Ukraine, then, once he's paid your hospital bills, outlived his usefulness, you murder him and move on.'

'All my life, people – or should I say – men, have used *me*,' she said, bitterness curdling her voice. 'From when I was twelve years old. Can you even imagine what that is like? Your mama probably bought you a bunny rabbit for your twelfth birthday. Mine demonstrated how to use a condom on a client.'

'Lots of people have terrible childhoods. They don't all turn into knife-wielding maniacs,' growled Janusz.

'What would you know about it? With your nice middle-class upbringing, your university education, your wife and son. People like me? We do whatever we have to do to survive.'

The words *'wife and son'* jumped out at Janusz. How did she know about Marta and Bobek? Just as Romescu had ...

Was it Varenka who'd done the digging to discover their address?

He heard the high-pitched noise in the background again, and this time it clicked: it was the sound of *a tram*, metal wheels squealing as it rounded a bend in the track. He felt like someone had tipped a glass of ice water down his back. *Was she in Poland? In Lublin? Mother of God! Don't let this* psychol *be anywhere near Marta and the boy!*

'I didn't protect the one who needed my protection the most.' She spoke precisely, meaningfully. 'I have to spend the rest of my life paying for that.'

Was she taunting him, saying he should be in Poland to protect Bobek?

'Does everyone else have to pay for your failure, whether they're innocent or guilty?' he asked, desperation roughening his voice.

She breathed a heartfelt sigh of the sort an actress might learn at the Hollywood school of heartfelt sighs.

'I've got to go,' she said suddenly. Her voice had quickened, as though with suppressed excitement. 'I've just seen the person I'm meeting.'

'Who's that then?' asked Janusz, dreading her reply.

'An old friend who's getting out of prison today.'

Realising where she was, he felt the tension flood out of his body.

'Goodbye, Janusz,' she said. 'I have a feeling you don't know it, but you are the luckiest man alive.'

As he hung up he realised that about that, at least, she was right.

Glossary

After the release of my debut novel, *Where the Devil Can't Go*, several readers said they'd appreciate a bit of assistance with the unfamiliar Polish words. So, here goes …

The Polish alphabet contains many characters unknown in English – such as 'Ł', which makes a 'w' sound, and combinations like 'sz', which sound like 'sh' – as well as a host of special accents. For simplicity's sake, I have anglicised the characters and dispensed with all accent marks throughout – for which, apologies to Polish speakers. Many of the Polish words scattered throughout the text – such as *dramat, kolego, kanibale* – were chosen on the basis of their comprehensibility. I hope that the remainder can be understood by their context.

Below is a brief but by no means comprehensive guide to the Polish in the novel, including pronunciation, a few general pointers to language, and a handy guide to Polish swearing.

Czesc (chesh) – '*Hi*'. Similar to the Italian *Ciao*. '*cz*' gives a slightly harder 'ch' sound than the 'sh' of '*sc*'

Janusz (Yan-ush) – 'J' is always a 'y' sound; 'sz' is 'sh'

Kasia (Kash-ah) – 'Si' is another 'sh' sound

Wodka (vod-ka) – 'W' is always pronounced 'v'

Zurek (zhur-ek) – 'Z' is often (but not always!) pronounced with a soft 'j' sound as in this, *zurek*, a kind of soup

Pan/Pani (pronounced phonetically) – The polite forms of address, which also double up as Mr and Mrs. (NB Like many other Polish words, *pan/pani* take many alternative endings: *panie, paniom, panu* … If you notice a change in a word ending it is (I hope) not a typo, but a reflection of the number and gender of the persons being addressed, and of the person doing the addressing.)

Ale laska! (a-lay-laska) – What a chick!

Babcia (bab-cha) – Granny

Chlopie (hwo-pee-ay) – Mate

Dobrze (dob-zha) – Okay

Dziadek (dzhia-dek) – Grandpa

Dzien dobry (zhin dobry) – Good day

Dziekuje (zhin koo-ya) – Thank you

Na zdrowie (nazh-drovia) – Cheers

Przepraszam (prruh-shuh-prasham) – Sorry/excuse me (polite form)

Prosze (pro-sheh) – Please

Sklep (sklep) – Shop

Stare miasto (star-ah mi-as-to) – Old Town

Straszny (straj-ny) – Dirty, sleazy

Tak – Yes

Wspaniale (vsp-an-ya-we) – Splendid

Poles love diminutives, and *'ek'* is one of the most common, giving something akin to Johnny, Billy, etc. So Janusz becomes Janek (*Yan-ek*), and Boguslaw, Slawek (*Swah-vek*). Another common diminutive uses the *'sia'* (*sha*) or *'zia'* ending, making Barbara Basia, and Magda Madzia. A variety of endings like *'cku'* or *'czek'* can be added to the end of words and names as an endearment. When Kasia calls Janusz *misiaczku* in a message, she's in diminutive endearment overdrive: *mis* means bear; *misiaczku* means '(my) little teddy bear'.

Swearwords, insults, and exclamations
In ascending order of offensive magnitude …

Dupa blada! – Pale arse! (An exclamation that defies translation)

Dupe (dupa) – Literally, 'arse', but actually means idiot, fool, twat

Dzieki Bogu! (zhee-ky Bog-u) – Thank God!

Gowno (goov-no) – Shit

Jaja (yah-yah) – Balls

Kutas (koo-tas) – Prick

Kurwa (Koor-vah), and its stronger forms: *Nosz, kurwa (Nosh, koorvah), Kurwa mac (koorvah mash)* – Literally, 'whore', or 'your mother is a whore', but used as an all-purpose exclamation like 'fuck' or 'shit'. Anyone who has overheard Polish workmen chatting will know that *kurwa* is used less as a swearword, more as a conversational condiment …

Pedzio (ped-zhio) – Derogatory term for a gay man

Skurwysyn (skoor-vis-in) – Literally, 'son of a whore' or 'son of a bitch'

Skurwiel (skoor-veel) – Fuckhead

Chuj (Hoo-ey) – literally, 'prick', but the closest Anglo Saxon equivalent to this, the worst possible term of abuse, would be 'cunt'.

Acknowledgements

This book is a product of many hands and brains – not to mention drinks.

It wouldn't have happened but for my ever-supportive husband Tomasz, who, thanks to his upbringing in communist Poland and experiences as an émigré Pole, provide such a rich vein of ideas – as well as being a fact-checking resource conveniently located in my own home …

I am also very grateful to the Polish Cultural Institute, especially its head of literature, Magda Raczynska, for her professionalism, kind advice and enthusiastic support of my work. Then there's Asia, aka fellow writer A. M. Bakalar, who corrected the Polish, gave me some excellent swearwords, and stopped me from making an embarrassing hash of the glossary. (Any errors are mine.) Thanks also go to The Wisława Szymborska Foundation, who gave permission for use of the extract from Szymborska's poem 'On Death, Without Exaggeration', which inspired the book's title.

I'd like to thank pathologist Olaf Biedrzycki, who takes the most bizarre questions about post-mortem procedures and the fragility of the human body in his stride. I finally got to make full use of aviation anorak Tom Bristey's specialist subject. And once again, I couldn't have created DC Kershaw's world without the patient help of Detective Sergeant Paula James, who as well as trying to ensure I get the details right, is also a splendid drinking buddy. Any departures from proper procedure are down to me and come under the heading of artistic license ...

The close friends who've supported me, spread the word, and put up with my endless obsessing are too numerous to list, but I must thank my dear friend Selina O'Grady and her finely tuned crime fiction antennae, for all the early reads and incisive comments.

I continue to be overawed by the generous reception and huge encouragement the crime writing and reviewing community has given my work. The list of writers to whom I owe thanks (aka drinks) would fill a medium-sized pub, but I'm especially grateful for the support of Joan Bakewell, Stav Sherez, Malcolm McKay, Emlyn Rees, James Craig, Mari Hannah, Mark Edwards, C A James, and my chum and fellow coffee addict Denise Danks.

As ever, Ivan and Caitriona at my agency Mulcahy Associates have been tireless cheerleaders; as has my pal, the brilliant publicist Jamie-Lee Nardone.

A heartfelt thank you goes to Rachel, and everyone at The Friday Project, who have been so refreshingly uncorporate to work with, and especially to my publisher Scott Pack, who manages to maintain a Zen-like tolerance towards perhaps the most headstrong mare in his stable of authors.

Finally, a colossal thank you to Val McDermid, who made my year ... scratch that, my *decade*, by including me on her legendary New Blood Panel at Harrogate Crime Festival. When I was wrestling with the half-formed idea of creating a Polish private eye in London, I could never have dreamt that my all-time crime-writing heroine would one day read and enjoy my work.

www.anyalipska.com
Connect with Anya on Twitter @AnyaLipska